WHERE THE FOREST MEETS THE RIVER

ALSO BY

SHANNON BOWRING

The Road to Dalton

Shannon Bowring

WHERE THE FOREST MEETS THE RIVER

A DALTON NOVEL

Europa
editions

Europa Editions
27 Union Square West, Suite 302
New York NY 10003
www.europaeditions.com
info@europaeditions.com

Library of Congress Cataloging in Publication Data is available
ISBN 979-8-88966-043-9

Bowring, Shannon
Where the Forest Meets the River

Cover design and illustration by Ginevra Rapisardi

Prepress by Grafica Punto Print – Rome

Printed in Canada

CONTENTS

This one is for The Fella.

MAY

"The road was new to me,
as roads always are, going back."
—SARAH ORNE JEWETT,
The Country of the Pointed Firs and Other Stories

RETURNING

The way home gets longer each time he returns, the miles dragging out in an unbroken chain of forest, field, sky, forest, field, sky . . . Greg can't shake the feeling he's fallen into an episode of *The Twilight Zone*, doomed to drive the same blank stretch of Route 11 for eternity. He can practically hear Rod Serling's voice as he eases his mother's old Chevy around another blind corner. *And here, on this road to nowhere, we have a young man devoted to nothing but distance; distance between himself and the Northern Maine town he left behind . . .*

Greg rolls down the window to let the warm spring breeze punch him in the face. Good. He cranks the volume on the tape deck to hear Linda Perry wailing about her disappointment in the world. Better.

In the trunk and backseat, stuffed in boxes, is his life as a college freshman: term papers, textbooks, ticket stubs from the Orono Movie House (*Pulp Fiction, Dolores Claiborne*). There's the geometric-print comforter his mother bought him ("Isn't it cool, sweetie?") and piles of laundry. Razors, half-empty shampoo bottles, flip-flops for the communal showers. Somehow he ended up with his roommate's Black Bears sweatshirt, the one David wore so often first semester Greg mocked him for being a walking UMaine billboard.

A green sign appears on the shoulder of the road to tell Greg he's got forty-two miles to go. Imagining what waits for him ahead in Dalton, he wishes it were forty-two thousand.

Lame enough his sister is marrying the Potato King in a

couple weeks, but why did she have to force Greg into being their best man? He and Sarah have barely talked since he left for college last fall—hell, they barely talked before that, when he was still at home and she was living in a one-bedroom apartment over the Store 'N More.

"Why doesn't Ian have *his* brother do it?" Greg asked when she cornered him beside their parents' fake Christmas tree the last time he was up north.

"Charlie's unreliable. And you'll look better in a suit."

"Seriously?"

"No, not seriously. But at least you'll fit into one now. *Greggie*. You skinny little stud." Then she poked at his flat stomach, laughing as he tried to squirm away.

All through high school, he had been The Fat Kid, and then the summer before college, Greg had a late-to-the-party growth spurt. Shot up two inches and could practically *feel* his metabolism running on high, vibrating through his veins. Suddenly in possession of more energy than he ever dreamed possible, he stopped bingeing junk food and took up running instead, hitting the deserted streets of Dalton on early summer mornings before the sun was all the way awake. By the time he left for college, he'd lost thirty-six pounds. "It's just such a miracle," his mother said, which he guessed was meant to be a compliment but felt more like a slap to the face. As if only divine intervention could have saved him from a lifetime of stretchy pants and hardened arteries.

When he looks in the mirror these days, Greg can now admit he isn't terrible-looking—thanks to his diet and daily jogs, the weight has stayed off, the acne has cleared up, and his thick brown hair behaves without any of that nasty product David uses. At school, girls flirted with him, asked him to parties and late-night study sessions, even though he almost always declined.

But the truth is, he's just as self-conscious now as he was when he was fat. The few times he accepted invitations to frat houses or dorm rooms, he couldn't do much more than choke down stale beer, laugh nervously, and spout off unasked-for facts about how many inches bamboo can grow in a day (thirty-five) and how many pencils could be created from the wood of an average-sized tree (about 170,000). In those moments of attempted socialization, Greg always felt like he was flubbing the lines of a character he didn't understand in a play he'd never pay to see, let alone one he would expect other people to suffer through.

The pavement and the forest unspool before him, unchanging, while the Cranberries play on the mixed tape. Rod Serling really would love this . . . *And here we see our queer nineteen-year-old as he drives toward the town he left behind; driving closer, but getting, somehow, further and further away* . . .

He's got to get off this damn road.

His first stop in Dalton is Trudy Haskell's house. He pulls into the driveway, tooting his horn several times just to get her agitated. Not that that's difficult. Looking up from where she's watering her allium patch, Trudy scowls. "Dammit, Gregory," she shouts. "You scared away my birds."

He parks the car and strides across the lawn, inhaling the heady scent of lilac and viburnum, taking in the sight of new growth and soon-to-blossom flowers. "Garden looks good," he says as he hands Trudy a small, unwrapped box.

"What the hell is this? You shouldn't be spending money on an old lady."

"I didn't. You won't be officially old for a few more years."

"For Chrissake."

She sets down her watering can and lifts the lid on the box, her eyes shifting from cold iron to partially molten silver. "A four-leaf clover," she says. "I'll be damned. You know, all these years in the garden, and I only ever found one. Then I got distracted and couldn't find the sonofabitch again."

"Try not to lose this one." Greg lifts the delicate pane of pressed glass from the box and holds it up so the sun hits the clover from behind, illuminating all the tiny veins. "I spent hours lying on the quad with a magnifying glass, looking for this guy."

"Did you really?"

"God, no. Found it by accident outside my dorm."

"Little shit."

She leads him on a tour around the garden, pointing out the remaining yellow tulips, the buds on the peonies. "Getting pretty overrun here," says Greg, crouching down to rip a handful of weeds from the ground.

"You'll have your work cut out for you this season. Hope you're up for it."

Greg's stomach clenches. Throughout high school, most of his free hours in the growing seasons were spent here in this garden with Trudy, following her direction on how to divide bulbs, mix soil, tell the difference between foxglove and delphinium. Just one more thing that made him a weirdo—a close friendship with a forty-something-year-old librarian.

"I'll try to find time to help you," he says. "But Dad's still hell-bent on getting me into the store this summer."

Trudy keeps her eyes on the ants drinking sap from a peony bud.

"You know I'd rather—"

"You thirsty?" she asks. "I'm goddamn parched."

They settle on the creaky porch swing with two glasses of iced tea and watch the birds—sparrows in the stone bath, goldfinches on the suet, robins on the lawn, hoping for worms.

Trudy takes a sip of tea, ice clinking against the glass. "How'd you do on finals?"

"Mostly B's. Aced my Intro to Plant Science exam, though."

"Did you? Imagine that."

Across the street at the grade school, there's a burst of happy shouts as kids stream outside for recess, running toward the same wooden castle Greg once collected splinters from when he was that little.

"You pick a major yet?"

"Still undeclared."

"Why don't you just go for horticulture?"

Running his thumb over the beads of condensation on his glass, Greg considers how to respond. Hard to give an answer, though, when you've barely given yourself permission to ask the question.

"Mom and Dad don't think it's a practical degree," he finally says.

His wish to go downstate for college was debated for months before his parents relented, saying they would help pay for it only if Greg promised to come back up north to work in the hardware store each summer. Along with this is the expectation that after he graduates from Orono, he will return to work with his father full-time, eventually becoming the next Fortin man to supply Dalton with its hardware needs.

All his life, Greg has carried an unchanging image in his mind: His father, dressed in faded Wranglers and a corduroy shirt, bent over the counter at the store, surrounded by boxes of nails and thumbtacks. The gold frames of his glasses shine under the fluorescent lights, and his brown eyes squint at the stack of receipts laid out in front of him. Always keeping track of the numbers, always thinking of the bottom line.

Not that he's an old scrooge or anything. His father is friendly and generous, the guy everyone in town goes to for advice on nail guns and dysfunctional garbage disposals. Thanks to him, people can fix their toilets, install linoleum, paint their nurseries, build porches, light their moldy cellars. Every home in Dalton has a piece of Jim Fortin inside it, or so Greg's mother likes to say.

It's not a terrible legacy, or a terrible life. It's just not the life Greg wants.

"What did your father do for a living?" he asks Trudy.

"He and my mother were dairy farmers."

"Did they want you to do the same thing?"

"Oh, no. I was always dropping the milk pails and spooking the cows."

They watch as a robin tries to pull a worm up from the ground, hopping in mad little circles as the worm refuses to loosen its grip on the earth. Finally, with one big yank, the worm is ripped in half, its head disappearing into the robin's beak.

"But Gregory." Trudy turns to look at him with steely, unblinking eyes. "You and I both know you're not the hammer-selling type."

He has never had to tell her he's attracted to both girls and guys, just as she has never had to explain to him that Bev Theroux is a hell of a lot more to her than her longtime best friend. They understand these things—these secrets—with something beyond language, the same way Greg often knows what song is about to come on the radio, or who is calling before he picks up the phone.

"Any hot dates down there at school?" asks Trudy, in her best almost-gentle voice.

He stares out at the maples edging the yard, the sun playing hide and seek behind the new green leaves moving in the breeze. Remembers the swirly sensation in his stomach as he tried to flirt with the freckle-faced girl from English Comp. "The corpse flower," he told her, "smells so bad some people pass out from it." Or the party last month in the Hilltop dorms, when he was pressed into a corner with that guy with the coal-black hair who kept discreetly touching Greg's arm, giving him The Look when no one else was paying attention, and all he could do was yammer on about the differences between peaches and nectarines.

"Here's the thing," Greg says to Trudy. "I'm going to die a virgin."

WHERE THE FOREST MEETS THE RIVER · 19

She lets out a bark of laughter, then points toward a scraggly peony bush whose buds are tighter and paler than the rest.

"See that bastard? Every year, I'm sure it's going to die off. Then every year, weeks after all the others, it blossoms like a sonofabitch."

"So you're saying I'm a late bloomer?"

"I'm saying better a little too late than a lot too early."

He and Trudy sit on the porch long after the school bell rings and all the kids across the street have run back inside, destined for paste-scented classrooms. All around them, thick in the afternoon air, is Greg's favorite smell in the world: newly woken flowers, breathing summer to life.

His mother's constant touch—hugs and shoulder rubs and hair tousles. His father whistling as he sets the table. His little sister, dressed like the ghost of Kurt Cobain. Mustard-yellow kitchen walls; overcooked lasagna; smell of dish soap. Potpourri in the bathroom. TV turned up too loud on a black-and-white western—bad Southern drawls and shootouts, cowboys versus Indians. Crooked lampshade on a nightstand, broken umbrella in the back of a closet. The welcome sensation of comfort and familiarity nestled right up alongside the buzzing, hungry desire to run out the front door, get back in the car, and start speeding south.

In other words, home.

Greg wakes early the next morning. In the pink-orange light of a sun reluctantly rising, he rubs the sleep from his eyes and rolls out of bed. From one of his piles of laundry, he pulls a pair of gym shorts, socks, a Radiohead t-shirt. As soon as he slips on his running shoes, he feels something inside him settle, like a panicked bird finally resting on a branch. When he steps out into the cool dawn air, he takes what feels like his first full breath since he drove away from campus yesterday morning.

The town is still but not at all silent. As Greg jogs down High Street, he hears the boom of lumber dropped from fork-lifts out at the mill, the subtle hum of teethed machinery that chew trees up and spit them out as plywood. Jake-breaks on Route 11; robins and chickadees calling. On Main Street, the only business open is the Store 'N More, lights shining yellow—through the window near the loading dock, he sees the tall form of Bev Theroux behind the deli counter, slicing bread. A few cars and trucks trundle past him, drivers lifting their hands in motionless greeting.

As he heads up Prescott Road, sweat pricks under his arms, and his breath finds its rhythm. The muscles in his calves tighten as his heart chugs along, strong and quick. He half-hopes to catch Angela Muse's mother smoking a cigarette on the front porch of the little house across from the Pinewood Tavern, but there are no signs of life other than a scruffy calico eying him from the driveway. Past the high school, down Winter—Greg smiles to see Trudy's kitchen light on—and back onto Main, pointed north.

By the time he reaches the hardware store, he's drenched in sweat, all his muscles aching in that delirious rush he has come to crave just as much as he once longed for candy bars and mint-chip ice cream. His father's red pickup is parked behind the store, and the office light is on in the back. Greg feels a tug toward that light, that room, where he knows his father is writing out orders at his metal desk. Every Saturday of Greg's life, it was that desk and those order forms and the pencils with greasy erasers that always left smudge marks on his father's palms.

If he were to enter through the back door right now, his father would look up from the desk and grin. *Couldn't resist the siren call, could you, son?* He would offer Greg a clean rag to wipe the sweat from his face and invite him to sit down beside him to review the orders for wood screws and staple guns and copper pipe. Eager to pass along the knowledge he's spent a lifetime gathering.

Greg takes in a deep breath of green air and gold sun and keeps running—past the store, the fire station, down around the Catholic church, up Rich Fucker Road, the town and valley and forest and river spread out behind him. Each time his feet hit the pavement, his calves screech and sing. Bone-deep ache, delicious freedom. Gravity pulling him down to the earth, as the summer wind pushes him forward.

ADAPTATIONS

T rudy is the first person in the post office when it opens on Saturday morning. Marching past the wall of Most Wanted posters—why can't criminals brush their teeth once in a while?—she heads straight for the front counter. Rings the little brass bell once, then twice. She can hear Bev's voice in her mind telling her to be patient for once in her life. But she has better things to do than stand around here all day.

She's about to ring the bell a third time when Gloria Arsenault trudges out from the Employees Only door and steps behind the counter. Her hair, which hasn't moved since the mid-80s, smells of cigarette smoke. There's a shine of sugar on her lips, as though she were out back slamming down donuts before deciding to get to work.

"Help you?" she asks in a bored voice.

"I ordered a dress from the Penney's catalog a month ago," says Trudy, "and it still isn't here, even though it was only supposed to take two weeks."

"Bummer."

"I've called the shipping department twice, and twice they've told me the dress was sent here a week ago. So why haven't I received it?"

"If we had it, we'd've put it in your box."

So this is what Trudy's tax dollars pay for. Incompetence. Ambivalence.

"Can you please just check in the back?" She knows how bitchy she sounds but doesn't care. She knows she could drive twenty minutes to the mall and buy a different dress, but she refuses. This dress from the catalog is the only one she will wear to Greg's sister's wedding. It's the perfect shade of green.

When Gloria sighs, a yeasty smell comes pouring out of her mouth. "I'm telling you it ain't back there, but I'll check if it'll make you happy."

She disappears behind the door, leaving Trudy to flip through a book of stamps that spell out the word LOVE in red letters above cherubs' bored faces. If there really are fat baby angels flying around up there, they must think it tragic their image is being used to mail water bills and birthday cards to distant cousins.

The door of the building opens, and Trudy turns to see Annette Frazier stepping into the lobby. Talk about a tragedy. The woman is wearing sweatpants and a stained shirt. Her badly-dyed hair falls across her face in greasy strands. Seeing Trudy, she pauses in a patch of sunlight pooling on the floor, then inches forward, like a cat ready to bolt at any moment. The closer she gets, the stronger the smell of unwashed skin and sour wine.

So this is what losing a child can do: turn an overly-chatty, image-obsessed woman into something barely human. Something that can only be pitied.

"Hello, Annette," says Trudy, trying to keep her voice soft— that's how Bev would speak if she were here right now. Softly. Kindly. "Nice day out there, isn't it?"

"Bit too sunny. Bit too bright."

"Going to be a hot summer, if you can believe Channel 8."

"Yes. Very hot."

Holding up a small brass key, Annette jerks her head in the direction of the PO boxes, and without another word to Trudy, wanders off toward them.

The Employees Only door slams open, and Gloria huffs out with a roughed-up looking package in her hand. She throws it onto the counter. "Blame Dan," she says. "Dan's the one who sorts everything back there."

On her way out of the building, Trudy gets stuck holding the door open for Annette, whose arms are filled with two heavy-looking boxes.

"You want help with those?"

"No, no."

They step into the grass-scented morning, and Trudy watches as Annette maneuvers the boxes into the back of her car. Then she walks around to the driver's side and stands there blinking up at the sun with mole-like eyes.

For Chrissake, this woman. Trudy wants to shake her, tell her to get a hold of herself. But she should show a little mercy. Keep trying to practice the damn kindness that comes so naturally to Bev.

"That Gloria's a real piece of work, don't you think?"

Annette doesn't answer. She doesn't say a word.

Trudy spends the next several hours in the garden. Hands in the dirt, surrounded by the scent of peonies and roses, she lets her mind wander. First to the new novel she's close to finishing—*Snow Falling on Cedars*—which she's pretty sure she'll assign for the June book group at the library. From there, she thinks of lonely men in lonely places, which leads her to Gregory Fortin, who should be here beside her tearing weeds from the earth. He comes from decent people, but Trudy has little faith his family will ever see that boy for who he truly is. Putting him to work in a hardware store, of all places . . . And with the thought of long hours spent under buzzing bright lights, Trudy's thoughts turn to Bev, who once took so much pride in her job as director at the retirement village, and who now spends forty hours a week tossing pizza dough and assembling Italian subs.

Though it's only been a day since she saw Bev, Trudy already misses her. Nearly twenty years since they met and bonded over books and townwide gossip, and still neither is a whole person unless the other is right there beside her. The love they share is so much deeper and more complex than a friendship, or an affair, or even a marriage. Maybe especially a marriage.

Trudy tosses the weeds onto the brush pile at the edge of the lawn, then rinses her hands off under the hose, pausing to take a sip of the water, which tastes of dirt and warm rubber. The sun has wandered away from the center of the sky, but it will be hours before it reaches the horizon. Longer still before all its light disappears.

Inside the house, she feeds Mycroft—he meows in approval when he realizes she's thrown some sliced turkey in with his cat food—then she steps into the living room, where she finds Richard asleep in his recliner in front of an infomercial for hair tonic guaranteed to restore natural growth in as little as six weeks. His face is tilted back, mouth half-open. One of his slippers has fallen off, revealing a black sock with a hole in the heel.

Irritation tingles in Trudy's veins. Not that a man doesn't deserve a Saturday nap once in a while. But with Richard, it's more than a simple need to close his eyes for a few minutes. He only naps when he's in one of his funks. He's had these bouts of depression for the past five years, ever since Bridget Theroux died. He's a good man, but he has one hell of a god complex—no doubt part of being a doctor. He still blames himself for Bridget's suicide. As though he could have done anything to save that girl.

Richard lets out a low, pained moan in his sleep, as if trapped inside a nightmare, and another familiar feeling, this time of guilt, rushes through Trudy's bloodstream, pooling in the pit of her stomach.

Never, not even in the early days of their courtship or marriage, did she ache for Richard when he wasn't with her. She thought of him fondly, was always glad to see him after a brief separation, but she didn't plan her outfits for him or count the hours and minutes until they were together again.

A better wife, or at least a different one, might open the curtains her husband has pulled shut, let the sun pour in, and sit beside him. Turn the TV off, wake him with a kiss, convince him to start talking. Unburden himself.

Trudy leaves Richard asleep and alone in the darkened living room. Goes upstairs to find the perfect dress. Only one hour, forty-two minutes until she and Bev are together again.

On the surface, nothing has really changed in Dalton since Bridget killed herself. Men still work twelve-hour shifts at the Frazier lumber mill; women still bust their asses working any job they can find—tending cash registers, making Christmas wreaths, watching over the gates into the North Maine Woods. All the same buildings on Main Street. All the same churches; all the same potholes. Evergreens exhale their sharp, fresh scent, and potato fields roll outward to kiss the blue sky. Flowers grow, flowers fade; the maple sap flows, the trees shed their leaves and put themselves to sleep for Aroostook County's long, hard winters.

But there are differences. Some are subtle, like the heaviness that briefly settles on what should be joyful gatherings, such as graduations and retirement parties. As if anything worth celebrating is also something to be ashamed of. As if living is somehow selfish.

Other changes are more prominent, though rarely talked about: Ollie Levasseur, that shit-weasel, turned Bev's beloved Whispering Pines into little more than Death's overpriced waiting room for the old folks in town. Annette Frazier, Bridget's mother, became an alcoholic recluse, only coming down off Rich Fucker Road to buy groceries or pick up the packages that, if rumors are to be believed, are from those wretched home-shopping networks. And Bev's son, Nate Theroux . . . thirty years old now, single father and widower, he's decided he'd rather work as a kiln operator at his father-in-law's mill than go back to the career he's meant for with the Dalton Police Department.

The changes have touched Bev and Trudy, as well. In the immediate months after Bridget died, when Bev quit the Pines and spent all her time caring for her infant granddaughter while Nate had himself a breakdown, Trudy feared she had lost her best friend forever. There was a tension between her and Bev that had never existed before. They stopped their nightly phone calls, their daily coffee visits, their weekly dates to Frenchie's. When they did see and speak to each other, it was like trying to tap into a foreign language. Just godawful.

But Trudy believes that in life, you either adapt or die. And in love, you either adapt or lose everything. Slowly, persistently, she and Bev built a new kind of relationship, one with more grief and unpredictability than what they'd had before Bridget died. When Bev needed a little alone time, Trudy gave her space. When Trudy needed reassurance, Bev promised they would make it through the other side and find their solid footing again.

Things got a little easier once Nate pulled his shit together enough to bring Sophie back home with him the winter after Bridget died. In the years since, Trudy and Bev have almost returned to how they were before—nightly phone calls, coffee visits nearly every day. And they're back to having their weekly dates, too; though, thanks to Bev's acid reflux and Trudy's intolerance for loud drunk people, they've traded Friday nights at the bar for Saturday afternoons at the library.

Adapt, or lose it all.

She wears her pink linen shirtdress with a pair of white tennis shoes. Too hot to leave her hair down, so she pulls it into a loose knot at the nape of her neck. Tiny gold earrings.

When she peeks into the living room on her way out of the

house, she sees Richard is still asleep in the recliner; Mycroft has settled on his chest, a puddle of black and white. Trudy leaves them there and heads out into the sunny afternoon.

Winter Street is in bloom, all the maples budding green. Somewhere nearby, someone is mowing their lawn, and Trudy closes her eyes briefly as she walks the familiar road, inhaling the smell of lilacs. Cutting across the playground parking lot, she hollers at a couple kids to stop hanging off the monkey bars. "Hell of a way to break your neck," she says, unbothered by their snotty teenage eye-rolling.

She pauses outside the redbrick library, admiring the window boxes she installed last weekend—begonias, impatiens, sturdy little flowers that thrive in sunless places. Then, humming a Dolly Parton song, Trudy unlocks the door and steps inside the building.

She's always loved the library best when she is the only person in it. The full and waiting silence among the shelves of books; smell of polished oak and paper, glint of light on the brass pulls of the card catalog. Other than her garden, this is where Trudy feels most at home, most alive, most herself.

The Dalton library, open four days a week, is a happening little place—say what you will about the backwoods of Maine, but the people in this town like to read. Between helping patrons remember the title of "that book with the yellow cover," leading story-times for the grade school classes, and keeping track of all the items that circulate in and out of the library, Trudy is kept plenty busy. She catches a break when Alice O'Neill comes in to help, but Alice and Roger are being gadabouts this summer, traveling the country in a camper van with that dopey dog of theirs. (Trudy suspects the trip is less about inspiration for Alice's perpetual novel-in-progress and more about needing a few months away from Roger's mother.)

Saturdays are the perfect time to attend to things that fall to the wayside during the week: unpacking new books and

VHS tapes, adding them to the catalog, reshelving items "help-fully" put away by patrons. Trudy doesn't mind the extra work, though. Especially not once she and Bev realized a couple years ago that they'd rather have their weekend dates here than at Frenchie's, which always reeks of beer and old sweat. Here in the library, unlike at the bar or any other place in Dalton, she and Bev don't have to pretend to be anything other than what they really are to one another.

Trudy steps behind the circulation desk and begins to un-pack boxes of new books. And in a few minutes, sure enough, there's the tinkle of the bell above the door, and there's that thrill in her blood. Turning, Trudy sees Bev standing in the lobby in cutoffs and a tank top the color of wild loosestrife. The sun shines through the windows, bathing her golden.

"Can't wait two goddamn minutes, can you, Tru? Just have to show me up and get right to work."

"For Chrissake, these books aren't going to unpack them-selves."

"Patience is a virtue."

"Patience can bite my ass."

When Bev laughs, Trudy feels the familiar swoop and soar in her belly, the warm singing tingle in her blood. Because if home is a place, it's right here. And if home is a person, it's her. It's Bev. It will always be Bev.

Every day, Richard Haskell sits at a desk that was built for his father, in a clinic that was built for Dalton, and feels the lifeless eye sockets across the room boring into him. Looks up from his paperwork, and there's the skeleton. Turns from staring out the window at the copse of trees, and there's the skeleton. Trudges into the room on dark winter mornings, and there's the damn skeleton.

He and the bones have shared an office space for as long as Richard has owned the clinic—longer than that, if he counts all the hours he spent in this room as a child and teenager while his father simultaneously charted and quizzed him on the difference between hypo- and hyper-glycemia. His mother had a name for the skeleton—Horace—but Richard's father said it was insensitive to name a body that once belonged to a living person who almost certainly was not named Horace. Better no identity than the wrong one.

Richard is staring down the skeleton one afternoon when there's a familiar knock on his office door.

"Just come in," he says, for the thousandth time since she started working here. "No need to wait for an invite."

Still, Rose Douglas looks tentative when she steps into the room, as if afraid she's interrupting something more important than his half-eaten sandwich. She's wearing the same outfit Richard saw on a mannequin at Sears a couple weeks ago—gray skirt, ruffled white shirt. The sign near the mannequin said *Working Woman*, and he felt there was something offensive in the term, though he wasn't sure why.

Holding out a folder toward him, Rose says, "I forgot to pull this one this morning."

Richard reaches over the desk to take the chart. *Frazier, Annette N.*

"She's coming in today?"

"Marshall called twice to confirm," says Rose. "He swears she'll *absolutely* be here. So I'll put five bucks on her absolutely not being here."

"Make it ten."

It's not good form to joke about patients with your receptionist, but after dozens of cancellations and no-shows, Richard has lost most of his sense of duty toward Annette. There are whispers and mumblings around town about the state she's in, rumors of alcoholism and a shopping addiction. And it's all probably true. And Richard would help her if he could. But she hasn't asked for his help, so there you have it.

A better doctor might call her until she finally agreed to come into the clinic to discuss therapy and AA and antidepressants. And maybe that's the doctor—the person—Richard used to be, or could have been. Before the Down Days.

Tucking the chart underneath the rest of the afternoon appointments, he thanks Rose, then offers her an onion ring, which cooled and congealed even as Bev was ringing him up at the Store 'N More.

"None for me, Dr. H. If I eat one, I'll want them all."

Out at the front desk, the phone rings, and Rose tosses him a smile before hurrying off to answer. God knows where Janine has disappeared—she's a decent nurse, but she takes the term "flexible schedule" a little too seriously.

Richard stares down at the Styrofoam carton, wanting to inhale every onion ring, every crumb of toasted sourdough. It could be worse. It could be steak, or fried chicken. Sometimes it is. But today, he's trying. It's an Up Day. Or at least he'd like it to be.

He used to take good care of himself, used to follow all the dietary advice he gave his patients. But when he hit forty-five, shortly after Bridget Theroux died, all Richard wanted to do was eat terrible, delicious food, all the things he had deprived himself of all his life. He blamed himself for Bridget's suicide, and he was always so hungry, and he was tired of the clinic, the town, the sham of his marriage, everything. So he went on a prolonged binge, hit rock bottom in the form of tainted shrimp, straightened himself out, ate all the right things, threw himself into the work of healing others. But after a while, he grew tired again, and he fell into another binge. And that's been the pattern for the past five years, a constant but unpredictable cycle of Up and Down, tolerable days and terrible ones.

Richard can feel the Down hovering over him right now like wildfire smoke. All that poison circling him. Every time he inhales, he can feel toxic, unseen particles desperate to work their evil magic into his lungs, his blood.

His intercom buzzes—Rose, informing him Janine has in fact left early. "Period cramps again," she says. "Weird how that can happen twice in a month."

"Maybe I should write an article about her for the medical journals."

He hears her laughter twice—once across the intercom, and again echoing down the hall. "For sure. But Dean Buckley is here, and without Janine to take his vitals . . ."

Richard knows. It's up to him. No one else to do the job, this legacy he never asked for. He stores the rest of his lunch in the mini fridge under his desk, then puts on the starched white jacket everyone in Dalton says looks so good on him. So right.

The skeleton, frozen in its perpetual mockery, watches Richard leave the room.

Not-quite morning, Bev leaves the house quietly—Bill has ten minutes left to sleep before the alarm goes off and he starts getting ready for their granddaughter's daily drop-off—and steps onto the front deck, slick with dew. Sky still dark, no birds singing. A peaceful, lonely kind of feeling.

The drive to the store takes less than a minute, not even enough time to hear the full weather report on the radio. End of May, but the temperatures will be more like July, according to the new meteorologist who talks as if he's constantly sucking on a lemon.

When Bev steps out of her car in the store parking lot, she hears a scuffling of paws. Squinting in the halogen streetlight, she sees a raccoon scrambling away into the bushes between the Laundromat and the trailer park on Larch. No doubt looking for someone's garbage, carelessly left untended. Lucky it's only a raccoon—just last week, George Nadeau came into the store for his usual jelly donut and told Bev about the black bear he caught trying to get into the Dumpster behind the Diner. "This close to grabbing my shotgun before the sonofabitch took off," he said.

Bev loves to hear stories like that from the locals, to feel as though their words plop her into the middle of whatever adventures or mishaps they're describing—confrontations with wild animals, cake-baking gone wrong, four-wheelers stuck in the mud all the way up in the nowhere-woods of Barren. She didn't get to hear many of these tales when she was the director at the Pines. There, she was stuck in an office all day, signing payroll, ordering adult diapers in bulk, and calming disgruntled relatives over the phone, assuring them every assisted-living apartment came equipped with washer and dryer.

Trudy thinks Bev belongs back at the Pines, no matter how many times Bev tells her she likes her job at the Store 'N More. "You don't just go from director to deli worker," Tru says. "You don't give up on everything you've spent a life building."

But sometimes the life you built collapses, and you must construct a new one.

Bev unlocks the door outside the loading dock and steps into the store, flicking on the lights. Everything familiar appears in front of her—pizza oven, chest freezer where they keep the live bait, cooler filled with the Fruitopias and Jones sodas so popular with the teenagers around town.

She steps behind the deli counter and gets to work. She loves the rhythm of the store in early morning, the solitary preparation—laying out cold cuts and veggies, slicing bread, getting the coffee pots and Slush-Puppie makers into working order. Sometimes she listens to the oldies station, but usually she prefers to go about her business only hearing the thunk of knife on cutting board, the steaming gurgle of the cappuccino machine. Her thoughts unspool easily—what she should make for supper, how much longer the Lumina can limp along under the weight of its rusted underbelly, whether she remembered to mail the electric bill.

Just after 4:30, Jo Martin comes in to tend the cash register and get the store ready to open. She and Bev used to share a smoke on the loading dock before they unlocked the doors, but that stopped a couple years ago when Trudy finally guilted Bev into quitting.

"Going to be wicked hot out there today," says Jo as she pours a generous amount of sugar into her coffee. Her silver hair shines under the fluorescents. "And did you see the fore-cast for this weekend? Can you imagine standing in a big white wedding gown in eighty-degree heat?"

Bev thinks back to her own wedding day, several lifetimes ago—she wore a blue dress, and Bill wore jeans and a plaid shirt. No need for a fuss if you're only going down to the Dalton courthouse. It rained that day, sheets of it falling from the low-ered sky.

At exactly 5:00, Jo unlocks the doors and flips the store sign to OPEN. And then the rhythm changes, the quiet giving way to a steady stream of millworkers and farmers in for their breakfast sandwiches, coffee, scratch tickets, and Marlboros. Bev likes this, too, the constant movement, the small talk with familiar men and women about lumber prices and potato crops and anything else. Phil Lannigan is worried about his oldest horse. Louise Best can't stop talking about the upcoming wed-ding—"Can you believe it, Bev, my youngest son getting *married*? Makes me feel so old . . . "

When Marshall Frazier comes in, he stands back near the bait cooler while a few of his employees wait for Bev to wrap their Italians, which they'll eat on their lunch break at the mill several hours from now. As they head toward the cash register, they mumble hello to Marshall, and he gives them an apprecia-tive smile. But there's something like guilt on his face, too, and distance. Must get lonesome, being the richest man in town.

"The usual, Marshall?"

"If it's no trouble."

Every morning, it's the same thing—one blueberry muffin, no trouble at all.

Today, though, he looks more tired than usual. Over the years since she started working here, Marshall and Bev have built up a mostly-silent repertoire—that'll happen between two people who have lost the same daughter. Bridget was Marshall's child, but Bev thought of the girl as her own long before Bridget and Nate got married. Considered her the daughter she'd never had.

So she doesn't have to ask Marshall for the details to guess that his exhaustion has something to do with grief. Maybe he dreamed of Bridget's strawberry-blonde hair. Maybe he's dreading the upcoming anniversary of her death. Maybe he was up all night making sure Annette didn't get so drunk that she blacked out. Maybe everything.

Handing him the muffin, Bev holds her gaze steady on Marshall's face. He has Bridget's eyes. Sophie's, too. So much green.

"You want to see a picture of your granddaughter?"

Marshall's face brightens. "You have any new ones?"

Bev reaches under the counter for her purse, emerging with two recent Polaroids of their shared granddaughter. In the first, Sophie is clinging to the tire swing Bill put up in the backyard, her red hair streaming out behind her. It's a blurry shot, but Bev managed to snap it just when Sophie was in mid-giggle, and it's like she can feel the girl's joy vibrating through the still image. Marshall grins when he sees it, holds the picture close like he can feel it, too. Which might be some kind of miracle, given the fact that he hasn't spent more than a few hours with his granddaughter since she was an infant.

In the second photo, Sophie is sitting at the kitchen table in Nate's farmhouse. She's dressed in mismatched pajamas, hair everywhere, chocolate smeared on her face. Perfect. In the background, Nate's lanky form is silhouetted by the light coming through the window—his face isn't visible, but Bev can feel his joy, too, his unleashed love for his daughter.

Marshall studies this picture a few seconds longer than the other. "When did Nate install the hardwood floors?"

"Those have been there all along," says Bev. She knows Marshall and Annette have only been to Nate's place in Milton Landing a few times—never, since Bridget died—but she still can't believe how unfamiliar Marshall is with the house. She feels annoyed and embarrassed for him at the same time.

Handing the photos back, Marshall gives Bev a sad little smile. "Guess I should get out there one of these days. See it for myself."

No shit, Trudy's voice rings through Bev's mind. But what good would a comment like that do? The man has enough on his mind. Running a mill, babysitting his drunk wife, grieving the loss of his daughter . . .

Still, though. He could use a little of the tough love Trudy doles out so easily, the kind Bev now channels as she tucks the pictures of Sophie into her purse. "One of these days isn't good enough," she tells Marshall. "One of these days should be soon. Soon as you can make it happen."

Bev doesn't say Annette should go out there with him. She doesn't want that woman anywhere near her granddaughter. Or her son, for that matter. Bev would rather Nate have to deal with ten Dumpster-diving black bears than Annette Frazier.

Not that Annette is a monster. But even before Bridget died, she was difficult—cold and bitter, too eager to claim her four children's successes as her own, while denying any failures. After Bridget died, she locked herself away in that house on the hill on Rich Fucker Road. Her method of mourning is isolation, self-pity.

Bev never wanted to be that way herself, even though losing Bridget was like having one of her organs yanked up from her throat. So she chose a different way of grieving, one that involves fixing cantankerous coffee pots and slinging sandwiches. Trudy says she's overqualified for this job, but Bev likes to provide for the hungry, grateful people of Dalton. Some of them talk too much, and some of them don't say anything at all, and hardly anyone ever brings up Bridget directly. But everyone who comes in here knows who Bev is and what she has lost— not just a daughter-in-law, but pieces of her own son, her own self. And everyone who comes into this store on the corner of

Main Street gives Bev something she needs, even if it's just a distraction. But often it's more than that. Often it's a knowing smile, and a promise of good weather, and an unasked-for but appreciated update on their oldest horse. He can't run like he used to. But he still loves apples, offered whole on the palm of your hand.

But Wait, There's More

It started off with just a few little things—imitation ruby necklaces, steak knives, grout cleaner. It was late at night, deep in winter, and she had had two or maybe three glasses of wine. The shiny women on the TV made everything look so good. So necessary. There was a thrill in Annette's belly, a rush of *aliveness* in her blood when she recited her credit card number into the phone. As soon as she hung up, the familiar storm clouds rolled back beneath her skull. But the feeling was made a little softer by the promise of a gift in the mail within three-to-five business days (she paid extra for expedited shipping). And sure enough, when the boxes arrived at the post office, she felt another surge of *this-is-living-I-am-alive*. And so she placed another order, and another, and another . . .

Two years later, Annette's purchases fill several rooms of the house that once held an entire family. Snow globes clutter the piano where Craig used to play Debussy. Will's basketball trophies have been pushed aside for a collection of Beanie Babies. The mirrored basement where Penny practiced arabesques and pirouettes is piled with boxes containing everything from *Gone with the Wind* collector plates to hair-crimping irons, and Marshall's den is taken up by pieces of exercise equipment Annette doesn't use. The only space left untouched is Bridget's room. That door has remained shut since Bridget went away five years ago.

Went away. That's the only way she can allow herself to think of it. Because the word *died* is a clod of dirt shoved down a throat, and *suicide* isn't any better—too many syllables, a term trying too hard to cover up the grotesque violence it holds inside it.

Annette tries to avoid any words concerning Bridget's death, or her life, for that matter. She can't remember the last time she spoke her youngest daughter's name.

One night, Marshall comes home from the mill and, as always, sits down on the wooden bench in the mudroom. As always, he removes his steel-toed boots, lines them up beside his lunchbox. As always, he crosses the kitchen to stand beside Annette in front of the stove to land a dry kiss on her cheek. And then he blows the world apart.

"I want to have Sophie and Nate over for supper," he says.

Annette drops the spoon she's been using to stir tomato soup, red drops splattering on the white stovetop. She can feel Marshall's eyes flicking between her unwashed hair and the glass of wine on the counter.

"Why?"

"I need a reason to see my own granddaughter and son-in-law?"

The clouds in her skull are growing bigger, bigger, bigger. She turns the burner off and pours the soup into two new Italian hand-painted bowls.

"We've been in neutral way too long, Annie."

His voice is soft and pleading. He never asks for anything.

"No," she says.

She doesn't sleep much. Up beyond midnight, awake before dawn. First drink around noon, sometimes earlier if she has a headache or it's raining or the morning news anchors have nothing good to say about the world. Maybe just the smallest splash of vodka in her coffee. She only drinks wine in the evenings. Sometimes while she watches the shopping networks, she loses count of how many glasses. But it's got to be a better way to drift off to dreamland than whatever chemicals are in those sleeping pills her husband takes.

Marshall sleeps well, or at least regularly, the same schedule he's kept for the thirty-four years they've been married. In bed by nine, up at four. He hasn't done any grunt work at the mill in over a decade, ever since his father retired and named him manager, but he likes to be there early, to walk the floor and joke with the blue-collars. His way of trying to prove to himself, if no one else, that he might wear a white hat, but he's not so different from them.

He only took a couple weeks off after Bridget went away. Annette was both infuriated and relieved when he went back. It was too soon; everyone in town would accuse them of moving on too quickly. Mourning should last longer. Forever. But it was exhausting having him around the house all day; he listened to the radio too loud and left dirty dishes in the sink, like a teenager. Except when their own children were teenagers, they knew better.

Annette kept a pristine house when the kids were young. She cleaned every day, and they were expected to help. Their chores rotated weekly, listed on a calendar she kept on the fridge. To get them used to unfairness, she often assigned them the tasks they hated the most—toilets for Craig, vacuuming for Penny, laundry for Will. But Bridget found a way to cheat the system by pretending not to hate anything; placidly accepting whichever job Annette gave her, even if that meant hand-scrubbing bath tiles or standing on a ladder to wash all the tall windows.

"You should give them a break," Marshall used to say.

But he didn't understand. He didn't know the discipline it took to keep a life clean.

After Marshall goes to bed, she settles on the sofa with a bottle of wine and orders a Thigh-Master and a dozen gold-plated napkin rings. *But wait, there's more!*

The next day, Marshall opens the bills she has been ignoring all week. He lets out a long exhale when he reads the amount on the credit card statement, but he doesn't say anything. He used to trust her with everything from their weekly incidentals to year-end taxes. He only took over the finances after the packages started arriving on a regular basis. Sometimes Annette fears he'll cancel the card, get a new one and hide it away from her. Instead, he settles on exaggerated sighs. And he always leaves the bill on the table for a while, long enough for her to pick it up and read it. She never reads it.

You can say a lot without actual words. You can see a lot without actively looking.

There was a brief time, after Bridget went away, when Marshall considered selling the mill. A Canadian company would have paid an obscene amount of money for the business his great-grandfather started in the late 1800s. But he decided against it.

"I'd be giving away the family legacy," he said.

Annette once cared a great deal about her husband's legacy. Everyone in Aroostook, and probably as far south as Bangor, knew the name Frazier. Frazier meant lumber, jobs for an entire region. Frazier meant quality, success, and, most importantly, security for her children for the rest of their lives.

But those children have moved on. Will runs a sporting goods store in New Hampshire with his wife and two teenage stepsons. Craig, recently engaged, teaches at a high school down in Brunswick, or maybe it's Bath; Annette can never remember. And Penny is always on the road with the Maine State Ballet.

Maybe if Bridget were still here, none of the rest of them would have strayed so far or stayed away so long. But all the Frazier children, in their own ways, are gone for good. And what's the point of a legacy if there's no one left to claim it?

On this bright morning, Marshall leaves the credit card statement on the table long after he's gone outside to wash his truck. The piece of paper glows in the sun. Annette has a feeling deep in her belly that this time is different. This time she cannot avoid it; if she doesn't look at the bill herself, he will hold it up in front of her and read it out loud. A mortification she cannot endure.

Wine in hand, she wanders over to the table, feeling the same nauseating curiosity she did as a teenager when she stumbled on a neighbor's cat flattened by an 18-wheeler in the middle of the road. She doesn't want to look. She can't not look.

The number is a kick to the diaphragm. So much bigger and so much worse than she thought it would be. Beneath her skull, the clouds grow tall as buildings, heavy as molasses—the kind of silent storm that begs for one more glass of wine, and then perhaps another.

"Okay," she tells Marshall later that night, during the commercial break between *Wheel of Fortune* and *Jeopardy.* In the TV flicker, the wrinkles at the side of his mouth remind her of clean, precise knife slashes. "You can invite them for supper."

It's not that she dislikes her son-in-law. It's that Bridget always liked him too damn much. Starting in second grade and never ending after that, it was always Nate-this and Nate-that.

"Where the hell are you?" Annette once asked Bridget. "Because it seems like that boy has taken every piece of you away from yourself." Her daughter, no more than thirteen at the time, stared at Annette as though she were an orphan or a homeless person—something to be pitied. "That boy," she said, "helps me keep all my pieces together."

So much for that theory.

It's not that she blames her son-in-law. But he should have been home that night. He should have seen the signs. "He was working, Mom," her other children remind her on the rare

44 · SHANNON BOWRING

occasion she calls them, her words slurring. "It's not his fault," Marshall says. "None of us saw it, Annie. None of us saw what she was going through."

But fuck them with their head-shrinkers and sleeping pills and suicide-prevention-fundraising bullshit. Maybe her son-in-law isn't to blame, but she's got to blame something. And, thanks to Marshall hiring him to work at the mill four days a week, Nate's a hell of a lot more accessible than god.

The house is airless, dark, claustrophobic. She wanders each room, staring at the boxes filled with the things she had to have and now cannot remember why. The clouds in her head are as heavy as the moon. She stands on the second-floor landing outside Bridget's room. Every once-bright hope long dead. The rain on the roof sounds like footsteps; no, bullets; no—razor blades.

She used to believe in a capital-G god.

But the capitol-G god she believed in saved no room or mercy for people who chose to go away. He deemed that final selfish act a sin. Sent those sinners down to burn.

No matter how her daughter left this world, she doesn't deserve that torture in the next one. This is the only thing Annette knows for certain.

That and the fact that $19.99 is a hell of a good deal for state-of-the-art, money-back-guarantee, non-stick air-bake cookie sheets.

When Marshall comes home from work that night, he stops inside the mudroom. As always. Takes his boots off. As always. But there are two new voices answering his, one male and overly polite, the other young and chirpy, like a cartoon bird.

Annette has gone out of her way to never see her granddaughter in person. Five years. She doesn't know the girl. Doesn't want to. The pictures Marshall brings home, gifted to him from Nate, are more than enough to haunt her forever. That child looks exactly like Bridget. A living, breathing ghost.

The voices get closer to the kitchen doorway; from where Annette stands beside the stove, she can see a tall man's arm, a flash of blue t-shirt. A swirl of curly copper hair. The sound of a cartoon bird laughing. And then the little voice asking the big ugly question: "Why's this house so messy, Daddy? Why're there so many boxes?"

Bottle of wine in hand, Annette flees the kitchen. Hurries upstairs to her bedroom, slams and locks the door behind her. Every pore is sweating; she removes her dress, collapses on the bed in her bra and panties. Turns the TV on. Takes one sip of wine, then another, and then another. Through the growl of clouds in her head, she hears her husband calling her name down in the kitchen.

She pulls the phone from the nightstand and holds it to her chest, readying herself for the moment the familiar words flash across the screen, where two blonde women are demonstrating how to clap a lamp into life. With each clap, each burst of light, aliveness sparks across their faces and inside Annette's veins. *CALL NOW*, the flashing words shout. *CALL NOW! CALL NOW! CALL NOW!*

DAUGHTER

Sophie is green grass and laughter and fireflies. She is wild strawberries warm from the sun; cricket-choirs on early autumn evenings; Northern Lights in winter skies. She is the sound of footsteps hurrying down wooden stairs, the smell of summer rain.

Depending on the day, her favorite animals are either otters or elephants. She loves to watch the sparrows at the feeders, the bees buzzing on the wildflowers. She hates peas. When she grows up, she wants to be a zookeeper, and a whale doctor (whatever that is), and maybe, if she has time, a magician.

Nate is punched in the chest a thousand times a day with his love for her. He watches her giggle at Big Bird, hears her sing along to her mother's old Springsteen albums, holds her close to feel her hair against his cheek—just wallop after wallop of love and wonder, love and pride. How many blows can a man's heart take?

He often wakes in the night, tiptoes into the hallway, and stands outside her bedroom listening for her sleeping breath, hardly daring to breathe himself for fear of disrupting her good dreams. Her nightlight turns everything in the room a subtle shade of yellow that reminds Nate of Bridget's favorite flower—tall but delicate, it might have been some kind of daisy.

Not so long ago, he would have known the name. The not-knowing is a weight, a betrayal that thrums deep inside his bones.

But he does know this:

Bridget was moon pies, games of Tag, fistfuls of candy snatched from parade routes. She was the roaring clatter of high school basketball games. She was wine coolers spilled beneath a water tower at midnight and the glowing blue of a million stars.

Bridget's hands smelled of canvas and paint. Mascara annoyed her. She hated the sound of motorcycles, though she always wondered what it would be like to ride one. She never remembered to turn off the lights when she left a room. She was a terrible dancer, but Nate let her believe otherwise.

The five years she's been gone feel like both a second and an eternity. Sometimes her presence is still so palpable in the house, Nate expects to open the door of her studio and see her sitting in a pool of sunshine, adding the finishing touches to a landscape. Other times, he can't fathom that she ever set foot in those rooms, which seem as though they have forever belonged only to him and Sophie. And yet there could be no Sophie without Bridget.

But for every return to the proof of Bridget's life, there is also proof of her death: The upstairs bathroom he hasn't stepped inside for five years. The brand of razor he will no longer buy. The Dalton Police Department jacket that hangs in the back of his closet. And in the cemetery, the most unarguable proof—the granite headstone. *Bridget Susanna Frazier-Theroux. March 1, 1964—June 3, 1990.*

For about a year after Bridget died, it was the manner of her leaving that wrecked Nate most, the thought of her alone in the bathtub while Sophie wailed from the nursery down the hall. But over time, that fear has expanded and evolved into what it is now—not so much the terror or the violence of the act itself, but the blankness that grows a little bigger each day now that the act is over, the things about Bridget he is starting to forget. Her favorite flower. The smell of her skin in the morning. The sound of her laugh.

Nate never imagined he could lose her, so he let the details go unnoticed even as Bridget was living them, creating them. He never realized she was capable of drowning, so he didn't bother looking into the black water she silently sank into for months after she gave birth.

All the signs were there; he just didn't see them.

With Sophie, though, he will pay attention. He will never turn away, never stop looking.

Everything he does is for her.

Each meal is made with her in mind—grilled cheese sandwiches cut into triangles, buttered spaghetti, French toast dusted with powdered sugar. After the bills are paid and the groceries are bought, any money left over goes to Sophie, either as a modest amount set aside in a savings account, or as a splurge at K-B Toys.

The old farmhouse that Nate put so much time and energy into making beautiful has crayon marks on the walls, mermaid decals stuck to the windows, scuffs on the hardwood floor. Stuffed animals lay siege from unexpected places—the linen closet, the junk drawer. The TV is always set to cartoons, and the rooms he and Bridget once preferred quiet now echo with the sounds of their daughter's make-believe—cackle of a forest witch, arguments between unicorns and regular ponies.

Mornings when he wakes from dreams of Bridget, feeling as though a thousand-pound boulder has been dropped on his throat, Nate forces himself out of bed to make Sophie breakfast. Moments when the horror comes screaming back, he pushes aside images of Bridget lifeless in the tub and accepts Sophie's invitation to search for fairies in the woods.

That awkward supper at the Fraziers' a week ago, when Bridget's mother hid upstairs, leaving Nate and Marshall to pretend everything was normal as they ate cold soup and listened to Sophie talk about the difference between heffalumps and woozles . . . that was for her, too. Because stilted and strange as his relationship has been with Marshall and Annette since Bridget died, his daughter still deserves to get to know her maternal grandparents.

And because of Sophie—for Sophie—the DPD jacket remains in his closet.

The winter after Bridget died, Nate took the job from Marshall at the lumber mill, and he's been there ever since. The work is mindless, sitting in a glassed-in box above the kiln, hitting buttons that turn the flames on or turn the flames off. And the work is loud, all those huge saws on the shop floor, the constant grinding of metal teeth gnashing through trees that used to be alive. Nate doesn't mind. The pay is decent, and the shift only keeps him away from Sophie for ten hours a day, Monday through Thursday. Even that time apart feels interminable, but it's better than the long hours he would have had to endure had he returned to the Dalton police. That's what he tells people if they ask why he would go from being a cop to being a kiln operator. What Nate doesn't tell them is the darker reason behind the career change: Tommy Merchant. Just his name is like an oil spill, oozing out to infect everything. Tommy Merchant: abuser, dealer, addict.

If Nate hadn't been so dazed by the punch Tommy landed the night he arrested him, had found more evidence of the drugs he was selling, maybe Tommy wouldn't have gotten off the hook so easily. Maybe he wouldn't have been back in Dalton that sweltering July day after Bridget's death, and Nate in his blind grief wouldn't have inflicted on him the kind of violence he thought himself incapable of. The kind of violence a good cop—a good person—would never resort to.

Nate has never told a living soul about that day. There were rumors, and maybe some people believed them. Even if they didn't, though, he still carries the guilt of what he did, the weight of knowing how unforgivable it is to give over to that brutality.

He failed Bridget. He failed himself. He failed the whole damn town. And maybe worst of all, he failed Sophie, too—because of him, because of what he didn't see, his daughter will never know her mother. Never feel Bridget's arms around her. Never hear Bridget's voice whispering encouragement in her ear. Never learn from Bridget all the things only a mother can teach her daughter.

Nate and Bridget's life together was meant to be simple, joyful, predictable in the best ways. Instead, his life without her is pain—penance. But he can deal with that; he can carry that, so long as he knows that he's doing the very best he can do for Sophie.

So he works a job he doesn't care about. He agrees to uncomfortable family dinners. He pretends to be shocked when Mufasa, plastic-nosed and synthetic-furred, stalks him from behind milk cartons in the fridge.

Everything—this mere existence, this often-agonizing act of breathing in and breathing out, moving through another day without Bridget—everything is for his daughter.

MOTHER

While pretty much everyone else in Dalton is getting ready for a wedding, Rose is scraping scrambled eggs off her kitchen floor. In this very moment, in nicer houses, other women are curling their hair, slipping into satin dresses. Rose's dirty hair keeps slipping from its ponytail, and her shirt smells like mildew. Husbands and boyfriends all over town are telling their women how gorgeous they look, while Rose's oldest son tells her she missed a spot of egg near the leg of his chair.

"You should be doing this, Adam. You're the one who spilled the plate."

"Yeah, but you're the mom," he mumbles around a mouthful of toast. She made it just the way he likes—crusts removed, thick layer of margarine mixed with cinnamon-sugar.

"You're nine. That's old enough to clean up your own mess."

"Yeah, and you're, like, forty."

Rose has the ridiculous urge to cry. She's not forty. She's twenty-six. She is so fucking tired.

Suddenly Brandon is crouching beside her under the table, cleaning the last of his big brother's mess off the floor. His eyes are the same shade of brown as hers, and his dark hair has a cowlick in the front, just like hers did when she was his age. He probably cries more than a seven-year-old boy should.

"Mum," says Adam, tapping his glass on the table. "Can I have more?"

Brandon gives Rose a knowing look before opening the fridge, where he grabs the bottle of apple juice for his brother.

They look so similar but act so different. Brandon chews his cereal slow, careful not to bother his loose tooth. Adam eats like all the food on the planet will vanish any second. Brandon, top of his first-grade class, reads the back of the cereal box while Adam stares out the window, squinting at the sun as though daring it to reach down from the sky, grab him by the shirt, and punch him.

Just like his brother, Adam is practically a mirror image of Rose—his face is her face, his hair the same color as hers. But he has his father's eyes.

While the boys watch cartoons, she spreads the bills out on the kitchen table. Rent, water, electric, phone . . . Not so long ago, the numbers made Rose want to take the kids and drive them up to Fort Kent and across the border. She always imagined it'd be easy to disappear in Canada. Go off the grid; build their own cabin, grow their own food. Fuck the Man.

But things haven't been so bad since Dr. Haskell hired her to replace Stacey Trinko as a secretary. At the clinic, Rose has her own swivel chair at the front desk, where she files charts and schedules appointments for thirty hours a week. Dr. Haskell always makes sure she's done in time to pick up the kids from school. The paycheck isn't huge—sometimes she has to take on extra hours at the Diner to make ends meet—but for the first time in her life, she has benefits: health insurance for her and the boys, plus two weeks' paid vacation a year.

As the intro for *Teenage Mutant Ninja Turtles* plays in the background, Rose starts to write out the checks, careful to get every number right. By the time she's sealed and addressed all the return envelopes, the show is halfway over. Peering into the living room, she sees Adam standing too close to the TV while Brandon pushes his Matchbox cars through the gray shag carpet.

God, she hates this trailer. That nasty carpet, the fake wood paneling, linoleum that always feels greasy no matter how many times she mops it. The windows aren't big enough for any good light to come through, and the fridge, oven, and bathtub are a nasty shade of green that reminds Rose of baby shit. Her boys spend too much time in this trailer. And on a sunny day like this, there's really no excuse for it.

Stepping into the living room, she uses her best excited-Mom voice. "Who wants to go on an adventure?"

Brandon raises his hand. Adam gives her a look that could be curiosity or annoyance. Or maybe a little of both. "When my show is over, Mum."

Not the enthusiasm she was hoping for. But she'll take it.

The exercise would do them good, but Brandon is a slow walker, and Adam always wants to stomp on the lines of ants marching down the sidewalk. So Rose packs them into the old Celica, which still reeks of cigarettes, even though her mother abandoned the car three years ago when she left town with Ponytail—a creep like that isn't worth any real name. Last time Rose talked to her mother on the phone, they were living in a duplex near Lewiston. Goodbye to bad trash, or however that saying goes.

"Can we get ice cream?" Adam says from the backseat as they drive past the Shanty.

"Maybe on our way home."

"I don't want ice cream," says Brandon. "I want a milk-shake."

"That's the same thing, dummy."

"Don't talk to your brother like that."

"It's okay, Mumma."

"No, Brandon, it's not okay for him to talk to you like that."

"Stupid dummy, stupid dummy . . . "

By the time they get to the river, Brandon is near tears, and

Adam is kicking the back of the driver's seat. Less than five minutes into this outing and Rose is ready to turn around and park them right back in front of the TV.

Outside the car, she makes them slather sunscreen on their faces, arms, and chests before they run down the slope in their swimming trunks, bought for a buck a piece at the thrift store. Before they can plunge into the river, Rose kicks off her sandals and wades in, testing the current. Even when she walks out deep enough for the cold water to kiss the hem of her shorts, the pull is barely there. Safe.

Still, she insists Brandon wear his life jacket and tells them to stay close before taking a seat on the grass while they run, shouting, toward the shallow water. Adam tries to push Brandon into the reeds, but he manages to flinch away, splashing into the river at his own pace while his brother yells at him for being a chicken.

Maybe pushing and yelling is just part of being a boy. Part of being brothers. Rose doesn't have any siblings. And she never knew her father, so she never learned any of the wisdom a dad can pass down to his sons. Some of what Adam and Brandon need to know is far off—shaving, fixing an engine, driving stick—but so much of what they should have been taught or given by now has already slipped away. They don't have a tree fort. They've never gone fishing or hunting. Rose can try to be a lot for them. But she can't be a father.

After he left town five summers ago, Rose didn't hear from Tommy for months. All sorts of rumors bounced around town—someone knew someone else who'd seen him in Bangor; Mellie Martin swore he'd served her beer in a bar up in Fort Kent. Rose still doesn't have a clear idea where he is or what he's doing (and she doesn't care all that much). All that matters is that he's gone, which can either make her feel so lonely it's like all the air has been sucked from her lungs or like she's finally free of a mountain she has been hauling around since she was fifteen.

When Tommy finally did call, he had nothing to say but sorry. Sorry for everything he did, everything he was. He sounded like he meant it, but he was always good at that. At the time, Rose's mother was living with her and the boys in the trailer, helping as well as her mother ever helped with anything. Rose was busting her ass at the Diner, the Pinewood Tavern, Bergeron's—anything to keep the bills paid. Adam was a little ball of rage, blaming her for Tommy leaving; Brandon's asthma was the worst it had ever been. People in town were always giving Rose that Look: pity mixed with a dose of *No big surprise there*. Because, of course, Tommy Merchant had maybe been selling drugs before he left town. Of course, he was the reason for the bruises Rose used to try to cover. Of course, he turned out to be a terrible father— just look at all the other drug-dealing, wife-beating, terrible fathers in the Merchant family.

Tommy has called a handful of times since the first time— sometimes for the boys' birthdays, or Christmas. Or sometimes for no good reason in the middle of the night. Rose would know that drunk voice anywhere. "I miss you, baby," he always slurs. She always hangs up on him.

"Mumma! Mumma, look at this!"

Shielding her eyes under the sun, she watches as Brandon, sitting safe on a big rock, splashes his hands in the river. She doesn't know what she's supposed to be seeing, what trick he thinks he's mastered. She claps anyway.

"Mum, check this out!"

Adam pulls in a deep lungful of air, puffing out his cheeks, and dunks beneath the water. For a few endless moments, he doesn't reappear, and terror tingles through Rose's body. Just when she's about to run down to the river, Adam's head breaks the surface, and he comes up laughing.

"Did I scare ya, Mum?"

"Dammit, Adam, don't you ever do that to me again."

He laughs and treads water while his brother watches traffic rumbling by on the bridge. A log truck toots its horn, the sound echoing off the water, the pine trees, the sky.

Maybe it's easier for Brandon. He was only two when Tommy left. But Adam was four, old enough to have some good memories of his dad. They watched a lot of cartoons together. Tommy was never violent with the kids, and he never hit Rose in front of them. He was always careful about that, and in some twisted way, she used to think that meant he was setting a good example for their boys. God, it's embarrassing how long she clung to that idea, as if it could wipe out all the other shitty things he'd ever done.

"Mumma!"

Brandon is leaning back on the rock, sunning himself like a mermaid. Or maybe the right word is merman. Too late, Rose notices Adam swimming up behind him, only the top of his eyes visible above water, like that demonic shark in *Jaws*. Before she can shout out for him to stop, he thrusts his arms in front of him, pushing his brother into the river.

She sprints across sharp stones, not feeling the prick and pain on her feet, and splashes into the river, lifting Brandon from the straps of his life jacket. Sobbing, he grasps her around the neck, wraps his wet legs around her waist.

"What the hell, Adam?"

He crouches in the water, staring up at Rose with dark hazel eyes that flicker between anger and guilt.

"I didn't think he'd fall in. I thought he'd catch himself."

"You know he's not a good swimmer."

"He has a life jacket on."

She carries Brandon to the shore, where she sits with him curled in her lap. His body shivers, so she reaches into the beach bag for his Lion King towel, wrapping it around him like a blanket. After a few minutes, his sobs turn to hiccups.

What would a different mother do? Make the problem child engage in some heart-to-heart chat like they do in *Growing Pains*? Or settle the matter with a spanking? Or maybe nothing can easily fix Adam . . . Rose spends a lot of sleepless nights worrying that Tommy passed along some kind of poison that's boiling inside Adam's bloodstream. That one day her oldest son will grow into yet another drug-dealing, wife-beating Merchant boy. Maybe that sort of violence is inherited just like cowlicks and hair color. Maybe it's already started—there were those fights at school this past spring between him and one of the Bergeron boys, and there are the ants Adam loves to crush underneath his dirty heels.

Down in the river, he sits waist-deep in the water, staring downstream. He looks mean and he looks lonely. His shoulder blades, pulled up to his ears, are white as angel wings.

"Adam." At the sound of Rose's voice, he turns, his eyes fixing on hers, asking without words if she still loves him. "Get your scrawny butt over here."

He runs up the shore and plops beside her. Leaning his head against her arm, he mumbles that he's sorry, he doesn't know why he did it, he just thought it'd be funny. He smells like boy—dirt and sweat and summer. Brandon is quiet, watching bridge-traffic again, and Rose is so ungodly tired.

She tells Adam it's okay. They're okay. They're all going to be just fine.

Hours later, after ice cream and milkshakes, after Disney movies and chicken nuggets, after mango-scented baths in the awful green tub and promises that there's no such thing as closet-monsters, after both boys are finally asleep, Rose cracks a beer and settles down on the ugly brown couch. She's trying to decide if she should watch TV or just go to bed when the phone rings.

On the other line, staggered breathing. Thumping bass in the background. A stranger's laugh, coyote-like. And then a slurred, slow confession. "Baby, I miss you, I been thinking about you, d'you miss me too?"

She would know that drunken voice anywhere.

Rose slams the phone down and pulls the cord from the jack. Then she sits there frozen on the couch, staring at the shag carpet. She remembers the time he laid her out on that floor, straddling her hips, pushing her face into the carpet so hard that little bits of grime stuck to her cheek and mouth. Taste of salt, smell of dirty feet. He was angry about the lie she'd told, the way she'd made him believe she was pregnant with their third baby when really she wasn't pregnant at all. She should have been focusing on how to get away from him, how to soften the pain of his fists against her ribs, but all she could think about was how bad a housekeeper she'd turned out to be.

Maybe the worst part of the whole thing is how Rose still remembers the good parts of Tommy. The way he would wake her in the middle of the night by trailing soft kisses down her spine. The way he could always cheer her up with his CBer impersonations and surprisingly good dance moves. The way he could hug her and make the whole world disappear.

She knows it's wrong to miss him even a little bit. She knows he's no good for her or the boys or anybody. But he's the only guy she's ever loved. The only guy who ever loved her back, even if that love did involve fists and threats and fear and loneliness.

It's the same kind of love her mother always accepted from all the different Ponytails she brought back to the trailer out in Barren while Rose was growing up. The only kind of love Rose has ever known.

BELONGING / UNBELONGING

Nothing in the house has changed since Vera was here three years ago for her mother's sixty-fifth birthday. Same sugar bowl on the kitchen counter. Same hand towels in the bathroom. Same pink-and-green quilt tucked over the pillows in her childhood bedroom. The sounds and smells haven't changed, either—persistent, faint hum from the substation next door; cloying aroma of fabric softener. And on the lawn, her mother's garden gnomes, disfigured by decades of bird droppings and snowstorms, along with her father's half-ravaged hammock hanging between two pines.

"Why don't you take that thing down, Dad?" Vera asks her third morning home as she and her parents sit on the back deck drinking coffee.

"Why should I take it down? Not doing anybody any harm the way it is."

Her mother, broken leg propped up on the porch railing, chimes in. "That's right. And we might use it, one of these days."

That damn leg is another perfect example of her parents' apathy. Her father had called Vera from the Dalton clinic a few days ago. "Mom had a little mishap," he said. "Took a spill down the stairs, tweaked her ankle." She demanded to speak with Dr. Haskell, who admitted her mother's fall had been serious enough that he was sending her over to Prescott for additional tests.

That night, Vera sped nearly 160 miles north from Bangor. At the hospital, she spent ten minutes asking a pregnant receptionist to track down her parents before finding them in a windowless exam room, along with a doctor who confirmed her fears—her mother had suffered a closed tib-fib fracture. Long road to recovery ahead.

"Why were you going upstairs in the first place, Mom?" Vera asked that night. "The only thing up there is my room."

"I was bringing fresh linen."

"Why are you changing sheets on a bed no one ever uses?"

"If you really intend on staying the next couple months, then you're going to use it."

"But I wouldn't have had to stay with you for the next couple months if you hadn't gone up there and broken your leg."

"But won't it be nice to have fresh sheets, dear?"

Now, as the sun rises over the town and their coffee grows colder, Vera's mother lets out a contented sigh. "Isn't this nice? The whole family together again. We should take a little paddle down the river."

"Not with a broken leg, Mom."

"Not even if I just sit in the middle and have you two do all the work?"

"Sounds good to me," says Vera's father.

"Dad, no. Not a chance."

Her parents share an exasperated glance, like two kids angry at the babysitter who won't let them eat ice cream before supper. Vera has seen that same look exchanged between many of her older patients at the hospital in Bangor, where she works as a nurse practitioner in the ER. Couples in their sixties with all the desire to keep up with the lifestyles they're used to, not yet accepting the reality of their bodies' limitations. Not yet understanding they have become the elderly people they once pitied.

Vera tries a tactic she usually reserves for toddlers—diversion.

"Tell me again why I need to go to this wedding today."

Her father, as interested in weddings as he is in trimming his salt-and-pepper eyebrows, slumps back and stares out at the lawn, no doubt counting the minutes until the dew dries up and he can get behind the wheel of his ride-on mower.

"Because one of us needs to be there to represent the family," says her mother. "And if you're so adamant that I need to rest, then you'll have to go in my place."

"And how exactly are we related to them again?"

"Before she was a Best, Louise was a Jandreau on my mom's side. And Gareth's uncle married your dad's stepcousin."

Years of calculating complicated medication dosages in her head, and Vera still can't figure out how this makes her related to Ian Best, a decade younger than her.

"Are we related to the Fortins, too?"

"Well, there's that rumor Jim's grandfather had a little *something* going with my great-aunt. Clarence Junior didn't much resemble Clarence Senior . . . "

What would the Dalton family tree look like if someone were to map it out? So many branches overlapping to form loyalties and rivalries that go back all the way to when the town was settled in the 1800s.

Vera stretches her arms over her head, tries to crack her spine. Her muscles ache from sleeping on a too-soft mattress, her skin is dry from her mother's soap, and her stomach, unacclimated to her parents' diet of starch and red meat, is sour and bloated. Nothing about this house fits anymore.

"I don't have anything to wear for a wedding," she says. "Maybe I should drive over to the mall—I could find something quick and still be back in time."

"Don't be silly, dear. You can wear something of mine."

Vera glances at her mother, sitting there in one of her oversized Hawaiian-print dresses.

"Really, I can just zip over to Prescott and find something cheap."

"Nothing cheaper than free."

Then her parents fall silent as they stare at the line of cedars that edge the yard. Several of the trees are turning yellow, drooping under the sun. Vera wants to ask her father why he doesn't water them, why he lets them wither away slowly. But she already knows what he would say. If they live, they live. If they die, they die. Who's he to fight nature?

While her father mows the lawn and her mother stays out on the deck reading the *Bangor Daily*, Vera shuts herself in her old bedroom with her orange rotary phone—the height of cool when she was a teenager in the 70s. She settles on the window seat and dials the number for the hospital switchboard, impatiently waiting to be connected.

Finally, Nurse McMillan answers the line in her usual gruff voice. "Bangor Emergency."

"It's Vera. Just checking in to see how you're doing there."

"Busy. How's your mother? How long until you're back?"

When the now-retired charge nurse asked about your family, it was out of real concern. When McMillan asks about your family, you feel guilty for even having one.

"You know how it goes with these kinds of fractures. Six to eight weeks in a splint, then a brace, likely some physical therapy."

"I suppose we'll just have to limp along without you, then."

As soon as she hangs up the phone, Vera feels as though she can breathe again. She used to love working in that hospital— the pace of the ER, the long hours of nothing but drug seekers and sprained ankles interspersed with mad midnight runs of drunk college kids needing their stomachs pumped, stunned car crash victims, women desperate for a place to hide away from their partners' knuckles . . .

The hospital hasn't been the same since the administration shakeup last year. McMillan is only one part of a bigger problem. Now, patient care is second to revenue, and there's a strain between the staff that never existed before. Vera used to rush to the hospital before her shift began, eager to review charts and catch up with holdover patients. Now she wakes each morning with a sense of dread, arriving at work just in time to punch her card, leaving the minute her shift is over. Her loyalty remains with the patients, but even those relationships have begun to fray. Whenever she spends extra time with an expectant mother or a sudden widower, she can feel McMillan and the shadowy *Them* staring at the clock. Keep it moving. Don't linger.

Outside, the mower sputters to a stop, and Vera watches from the window as her father climbs off the seat and strolls over to a patch of dandelions. He picks a handful of the weeds and tucks them into his breast pocket, their yellow heads like tiny suns against his blue shirt.

When she goes downstairs later, the dandelions are in a jelly jar on the coffee table. Her father denies having put them there, and her mother pretends to believe him. And Vera feels something split apart inside her; from love or loneliness she cannot tell.

In the forgotten reaches of her mother's closet, she finds a two-piece tunic dress. It's a little too big, the extra fabric bunching around her waist, and the color is reminiscent of Pepto-Bismol. But at least it's not covered with giant flowers.

Just before noon, armed with the carefully wrapped punch bowl her mother claims every new bride needs, Vera sets out for the wedding. It's a hot day, sun like a blade. The air conditioner in her Honda is on the fritz, so she rides with the windows down, irritated with the breeze for mussing her hair, irritated with herself for spending so much time trying to straighten the stubborn waves out of it.

She drives past all the familiar places. Half-deserted streets lined with tidy ranches and double-wides. Library, Advent church, Frenchie's bar, Store 'N More. Out of town and up the hill, the road levels out to reveal fields, forest, and, beyond the hills, the silhouette of Katahdin. The sight of the mountain sends a thrill through Vera—*I know you*, she thinks, the phrase popping unbidden into her mind.

Best Family Farms is at the end of a gravel road. She came here as a kid to pick rocks from the potato fields. The Bests were still hand-rolling their barrels to the potato house at that time, and Gareth (back then, he would have been about the same age Vera is now) laughingly encouraged her and her classmates to try to push the barrels through the field.

Vera parks in a grassy lot packed with other vehicles. She checks her appearance in the rearview, smoothing her hair back into place best she can. Then, following hand-painted signs—*Marital Bliss Ahead!*—she makes her way past the farmhouse and into a backyard teeming with people. Dozens of white chairs point to a trellis draped in ivy and pink flowers. From some invisible speaker, a nasal voice croons about true love.

She wanders toward the crowd, nodding greetings to people she vaguely remembers (her grade school secretary, the woman who used to sneak her extra lollipops from the bank) and stopping for the obligatory small talk with several of her mother's friends (Arlene Nadeau's voice has gotten even louder with age). By the time she reaches Dr. Haskell, hovering near a table heaped with gifts wrapped in silver and white, Vera is already counting the hours until she can slip away unnoticed from the reception.

"Hell of a turnout, isn't it?" she says, adding her mother's present to the pile.

"Now, you know it's not a real event unless the whole town is invited."

It's been years since she last saw Dr. Haskell. He can't be more than fifty, but his hair is thinning in random patches; inside his suit, he seems diminished, as though he has been enduring a long, painful process of collapsing in on himself. His skin, damp under the sun, is pale and shiny.

"You feeling okay, Richard?"

"I'm fine. Crowds just aren't my favorite thing," he says. "How's your mom? Must be going crazy in that splint."

"She and I both."

From the hidden speaker, a Bad English song starts to play, and everyone hurries to take their seats. Beneath the arbor, Pastor Ray stands with his Bible clasped in his hands. Beside him is Ian Best, looking young and nervous in his wedding coat.

"Guess it's time," says Vera. "Want to sit together? We can whisper about whatever awful dresses the bridesmaids are wearing."

Dr. Haskell lets out a puff of breath that might be laughter. "Got a bit of a backache, so I'll stay standing. But I'm sure my wife would love to mock bridesmaids with you."

Vera heads for the last row of chairs, where Trudy stands with her arms crossed over her chest. She's wearing a green dress that complements her ashy blonde hair. Towering next to the petite librarian is Bev Theroux, in a burgundy skirt suit, dark curls frizzing around her face.

"My husband still sulking back there? Well, let's the three of us sit down and act like we want to be here." Trudy squints at Vera. "Hell of a thing, isn't it, having to wear your mother's clothes?"

"Stop it, Tru," says Bev. "The poor girl."

When the bridesmaids emerge from the back porch of the house, Vera's face burns. All four of them are in dresses the same shade of pink as the one she has on. Then Sarah Fortin steps out in a wedding gown that resembles a case of toilet paper that's been wadded up and glued back together, and Trudy leans toward Vera.

"Could be worse," she tells her. "You could be wearing *that*."

After Sarah's father has dropped her off at the altar with Ian, there's nothing for the crowd to do but sweat in the sun and watch the couple beneath the arbor staring at each other with wide eyes like cartoon deer. As the maid-of-honor recites a saccharine poem, Vera's mind wanders to the men she never married. There was Leon, who ran marathons. Rick hated the smell of her gardenia perfume. Gavin hummed whenever he tinkered on his Corvette, and he loved the sound of rain on a tin roof.

She thinks of Gavin the most, though she wouldn't go so far as to say she misses him. They lived together for a year in a spacious, sunny apartment on Stillwater. After a few months, she started to feel caged-in. Gavin hogged the bed and left beard trimmings in the bathroom sink. But worst of all, he resented her work. "It's just a job," he'd say whenever Vera volunteered to cover someone else's shift or pored over her old textbooks late into the night, trying to find a rare diagnosis for a patient who came to the ER twice a month with debilitating joint pain. "It's my calling," she would argue. "My life." But Gavin, who worked for a construction company just enough to pay the bills, could never relate.

She could have married him, though. She considered it. But by the time he asked, Vera knew it was just a last-ditch effort to keep the relationship from splintering apart.

Hard to believe it's been three years since she turned down his proposal and moved back to Bangor, into a one-bedroom over a widow's garage near the hospital. Thirty-five, and still alone. There's the occasional man to satisfy the usual needs, but nothing that lasts more than a few weeks. Vera usually doesn't mind—she enjoys her own company, and she relishes the peace of an apartment that belongs only to her.

Sometimes, though, when she calls her parents to wish them another happy anniversary, or when she sees white-haired couples walking arm-in-arm through the hospital, she feels a familiar ache, like a pebble lodged between her lungs.

Beneath the arbor, Ian and Sarah, now transformed into man and wife, kiss each other hard, through grinning mouths, as the crowd breaks into cheers.

"They look happy, don't they?"

"She sounds surprised, Bevy."

"Maybe a little bit, Tru."

Whatever answer Vera might have given is drowned out as the theme song for *Dirty Dancing* begins to play and the guests stand to clap for the newlyweds, rushing hand-in-hand down the grass as though sprinting the last leg of a race where, up until now, the finish line was invisible.

But just before they cross that finish line, they come to a sudden halt. Though the crowd is still cheering, Vera can make out the sound of Sarah shouting something with panic in her voice. *Help.*

Shoving aside a bridesmaid with an unfortunate Rachel-cut, Vera hurries to the couple, now leaning over an inert figure on the ground beside the gift table. Bending down beside Dr. Haskell, she sees him gasping for breath, clutching at his left arm.

"Can you talk through it, Richard?"

He shakes his head.

"Okay. No biggie. We're just going to get you to the hospital, and you'll be fine."

Vera looks up, startled to see what feels like hundreds of people pressed in around them. Trudy and Bev crouch on Dr. Haskell's other side, Trudy pressing a hand to his forehead while Bev fans him with her wedding program.

"Someone needs to call an ambulance."

Before anyone can answer, there's a ripple of movement in the crowd, and then a gangly-limbed, brown-haired man in khakis and a blue Oxford is kneeling beside Vera.

"It'd take the on-callers ten minutes just to get to the station, another ten for them to get out here. I'll drive."

It's the voice that convinces Vera—calm but assertive.

The guy turns to Bev. "You'll stay here, watch Sophie while I'm gone?"

"Of course."

"Thanks, Ma."

It's only then Vera recognizes the guy as Nate Theroux. Several years younger than her, their paths rarely crossed in school or when they were growing up. But she knows things about him. He and his daughter live in the old Donoghue place on the other side of the river. He used to be a cop. His wife killed herself five summers ago.

Nate lifts Dr. Haskell as easily as if he were a sack of flour as Bev hollers at everyone to get the hell out of the way. The song is still playing, ridiculous lyrics about having the time of one's life, as Vera, Trudy, and Nate, with the doctor wheezing in his arms, hurry toward the lot where all the vehicles are parked. Nate gently lays Dr. Haskell in the bench seat of Vera's car with his head on her lap. The doctor's eyes flutter closed, open, closed again. Beneath her index and middle fingers, his radial pulse feels thready.

"Trudy, hand me that bottle of aspirin in my glove box. And Nate, haul ass."

As Vera pushes a pill into Dr. Haskell's mouth and instructs him to start chewing, Nate whips out of the lot, tires stuttering on the dirt road as they speed toward Route 11.

In the passenger seat, Trudy twists around so she can hold her husband's hand. When she speaks, her voice wobbles only a little bit. "Chrissake, Richard. Quite a scene back there. When did you become such a whore for attention?"

Though his eyes remain shut, the doctor's lips flicker slightly upward.

Vera isn't good in waiting rooms. She's meant to be behind the Staff-Only doors, with the hurried squeak of shoes on tile and the beep of heart monitors.

But this isn't her hospital, and as soon as Dr. Haskell is whisked behind those doors, he is no longer her patient.

The Prescott ER is low-ceilinged, the walls painted a distressing shade of jaundice. Vera paces in front of a window that looks out onto a mostly empty parking lot, blanched white in the afternoon sun. The only other person in the room is the same pregnant receptionist who was working when Vera's mother came in with her broken leg.

On her fourth circuit around the room, Vera catches the eye of the woman, who offers her an embarrassed smile. "You want a hair thing?" she asks.

Vera glances at her reflection in the window—half her hair is still straight, but the other half has gone wavy again. Grateful, she accepts the Scrunchie.

"Thanks," she says, pulling the disaster into a ponytail. "How far along are you?"

"Thirty-two weeks. Twins."

"Jesus, you must be uncomfortable."

"You have no idea."

The doors swing open, and a nurse steps out, raising her eyebrows at the three of them—Nate in his rumpled khakis, Trudy in her elegant green dress, and Vera, swaddled in pink like some poorly-wrapped Valentine's present.

"Which of you belongs with Richard Haskell?"

"*Doctor*," snaps Trudy, striding across the room. "*Doctor* Haskell. And I'm coming back there whether you want me to or not."

The nurse frowns but allows Trudy through the doors, which swoosh shut behind them. At the desk, the receptionist hangs a sign—*Back in Five!*—and waddles off toward the bathroom.

Unsure what else to do, Vera slumps into the chair beside Nate. Up close, he looks both older and younger than thirty—his face is kind, open, but there's something wounded, distant, and ancient in those blue eyes.

"I don't mind staying here if you want to get back to the party," he says.

"Honestly, the idea of watching drunk bridesmaids dance around to YMCA isn't all that appealing to me right now."

"But what about the electric slide?"

"Now there's a reason to hurry back."

The receptionist returns to her desk, collapsing into her chair. Pregnant women always make Vera grateful not to have experienced that same torture for herself. Kids are great, but pregnancy and labor? Not for her. Working where she does, she's seen too many episiotomies, too many women nearly ripped in two.

"You were good back there," Nate says. "At the wedding, I mean. With Dr. Haskell."

"You weren't so bad yourself. Almost like you've handled an emergency before."

According to Vera's mother, no one in Dalton talks about what happened five years ago—Bridget Theroux slicing her wrists open in the bathtub, leaving Nate a widower and their young daughter motherless. Absurd. How do you not talk about that kind of tragedy? How do you let that simmer in the background?

Knowing she might be pushing too far, but unable to stop herself, Vera asks, "You're a cop, right?"

As Nate shifts in his seat, the smell of cedar wafts toward her. "Not anymore."

"Shame. You have the instincts."

They fall into a not-uncomfortable silence. Outside, shadows lengthen over the parking lot. When Vera's stomach rumbles, Nate gets up and pushes some coins into the snack machine, returning with a bag of potato chips, which they share without speaking. The quiet wraps around Vera, making her feel drowsy and numb.

Finally, the Staff doors open again, and Trudy emerges, walking swiftly toward them, her flats scuffing against the carpet.

"He's fine," she says. "It was definitely a heart attack, though."

"But it's Dr. Haskell," says Nate, sounding like a kid who has just discovered the truth about Santa Claus. "I mean, I know doctors get sick . . . But it's Richard."

"Well, bad genetics and red meat are a bastard of a combination."

"Will they treat him with medication?" asks Vera. "Or will he need an angioplasty?"

"Hell if I know."

Outside, an ambulance with flashing lights but no siren pulls up. Two male paramedics, in no rush, unload a stretcher with an unmoving figure draped in a white sheet and wheel it to the ER doors. Nate stares at his loafers as the men, deep in conversation about whether Mel Gibson was wearing any boxer-briefs under that kilt in *Braveheart*, walk through the waiting room. He doesn't look back up until after the Staff doors have swished closed behind them.

"You should head back to town," says Trudy. "No use in all of us sitting around here."

"Are you sure you should be alone?" asks Vera. "If he needs surgery, it could be hours . . . "

"I won't be alone. I already called Bevy."

"But I told her to stay at the wedding with Sophie."

"You know your mother never does what she's told, Nathaniel." There's a flicker in Trudy's eyes, like she wants to laugh. Then she glances around the waiting room, and the twinkle fades away. "She drove your truck back to the house, left Sophie with your dad. She's probably halfway here by now."

Trudy takes a deep breath before wandering back to the swinging doors, where she pushes her way through as if she were the one who hung them there. Nate and Vera stand silent, watching her go. At the desk, the phone rings, and the receptionist answers in a chipper voice that quickly turns low, intimate.

"Guess we should hit the road," Nate finally says.

"Guess so." Vera wishes the numb drowsiness from earlier would return, but there is only that itchy desire to sprint through those doors, see what kind of help she can offer on the other side.

"Kicking like crazy in there," the receptionist mumbles into the phone as she rubs her huge belly. "Like they're trying to bust through like the Kool-Aid Man."

The paramedics return with the empty stretcher, still arguing about underwear and kilts. Nate says again they should get going, and Vera again says yes, they should. But neither of them moves for the doors that will spit them out from the cool, antiseptic waiting room and into the parking lot, the almost-summer sun.

For the first hour after Nate speeds away from the Best farm, there's a lingering thrill in the air, everyone talking about how awful the doctor looked and how they hope "that Curtis girl" knows what she's doing (no one seems to doubt Nate can handle the situation). When Sarah and Ian step out onto the fake parquet floor of the wedding tent for their first dance, people seem shocked to remember why they're here in the first place.

As Greg stands near the edge of the tent and watches his sister twirl in the arms of the Potato King to a country song, he wishes he'd been the one whisked off to the hospital. His suit jacket is itchy and uncomfortable, and he keeps imagining the buttons on his shirt are straining against his stomach (once a fat kid, always a fat kid). The music is too loud. There are too many bridesmaids, too many old ladies doused in White Shoulders.

A schmaltzy ballad begins to play, eliciting a wave of sighs from all the mothers and grandmothers. Just as Aunt Arlene makes eye contact and starts to rush toward Greg, he feels someone yank him backward by the fabric of his suit jacket.

Startled, Greg turns to see Charlie Best grinning at him. Though Ian and Lori's older brother must be closing in on thirty, with his untamed black hair and bright eyes, he looks a decade younger. Before the rehearsal dinner last night at the Pinewood Tavern, Greg had never talked to the guy in his life. Over plates of rubbery chicken, Greg, unsure what to say, told

Charlie that the word *tulip* comes from the Persian word for *turban*; Charlie had pronounced him one cool dude.

"These people are nuts," Charlie says now, pulling Greg further into the crowd of half-drunk wedding guests. "Let's get the hell outta here."

Feeling as though he's been swept out of the path of a log truck, Greg follows through the crush of people, hanging back while Charlie grabs four bottles of beer from a cooler at the end of the bar. Then Charlie leads him through the yard, past the spot where Dr. Haskell collapsed, and up to the farmhouse. On the porch, he gestures to one of two Adirondacks, and Greg drops onto it, grateful. His feet ache from standing for hours in stiff dress shoes.

Sitting in the other chair, Charlie leans forward to snap the cap off a beer, which he offers to Greg before opening one for himself. "Cheers, man. Let's send some good vibes to the doc, yeah? Wish him a speedy recovery and all that shit."

"To speedy recoveries," says Greg. "And all that shit."

They watch the swell of people dancing to a Bryan Adams song in the tent across the lawn. The sun is dropping toward the horizon, casting gold light over the potato fields that surround the house. Greg removes his shoes and socks, letting the air kiss his sweaty feet. Then he shrugs off his jacket. Charlie, looking relaxed in the same jeans, shirt, and Birkenstocks he wore to watch the ceremony, smiles but remains quiet.

After a few sips of beer, Greg feels bold enough to ask what's been bugging him ever since Sarah cornered him at Christmas and told him he was going to be her best man.

"Why didn't Ian ask you to stand up there with him today?"

Charlie takes a long pull off his bottle before answering. "Did you know all this was supposed to be mine?"

"What was?"

Holding his arms out wide as if to scoop up the entire vista before them—the yard, the house, the fields—Charlie says,

"This. That's how it goes, isn't it? Oldest boy gets married first; oldest boy gets the farm. Only I didn't want the fucking farm."

"So they, what? Cut you out of the wedding?"

"Nah, man, nothing that tragic. When Ian got engaged, I was on the road, that's all. No good phone number. No way of knowing if I'd be back in time for this whole circus."

For the past few years, Charlie has been living elsewhere. Rumors vary—some people in town say he went south, others say west; a few say Canada. Some people say he's only back in Dalton for the wedding; others are sure he discovered the bigger world isn't all it's cracked up to be and has come back to the County for good.

"What was it like?" Greg asks. "Out there, I mean? On the road."

"Some of it was good, some of it not so good."

"Where'd you go? What'd you do, what'd you see?"

Charlie throws back the rest of his first beer and cracks open his second, laughing. "You ask a lot of questions."

Feeling as conspicuous as the fat freshman he used to be stuck in a too-small desk in high school biology, Greg mumbles an apology.

"Don't be sorry" says Charlie. "You want my opinion, people in this town don't ask enough questions. Anyway, I went all over the place, down to Florida and across to California and back around."

"Did you see the Everglades? The Grand Canyon? The redwoods?"

"All of it, man."

Greg sips his beer, trying to imagine these places that belong to a mythology he used to believe in. He once dreamed of leaving Maine, traveling wherever fate directed him. He wanted to see epiphytic orchids and saguaro cacti; wild blue columbine and giant sequoias that burst from seed pods several millennia ago.

But lately the only place Greg can envision with any real clarity is this town, and the only future he can seem to imagine is one in which he lives out his days giving the people of Dalton advice on how to snake their bathtubs and when to re-stain their decks. His father's slim shadow hovering behind him, gently correcting any mistakes.

Greg finishes his beer in three long gulps and reaches for the second. He tries to imitate Charlie's smooth decapitation of the bottle, but only succeeds in bruising his palm against the porch railing.

"Gotta be a little faster. And put a little more weight behind it."

This time, Greg succeeds, the cap skittering across the porch floorboards as carbonation mists from the mouth of the bottle.

"Old pro, man." Charlie reaches into his back pocket for a baggie and a sleeve of rolling papers. "Split one?"

Greg has smoked his fair share of weed down in Orono, thanks to David, who toked up nearly every night, aiming the smoke out their skinny dorm-room window. He doesn't love the feeling of being high, but he does like the act itself—inhale, hold, exhale; repeat. That crackling orange flame.

"Sounds cool," he says.

Charlie rolls the joint on the porch railing, seals it with his tongue. He offers the first drag to Greg, who pulls the smoke down his throat, deep into his lungs. Releasing the breath of green smoke back into the air, he hands the joint back to Charlie.

They sit there a long time, smoking, not saying much, as the sun falls behind the trees and the sky turns pink, then purple, then indigo. Greg lets his thoughts off their tether, allows them to trip around. He thinks of Dr. Haskell clutching his chest, and Nate carrying him across the yard as if the old man weighed nothing more than an armful of feathers. He thinks of the fine dust that coats every surface of his father's store, dust that sticks to his hands long after he has locked up for the night. He thinks about this country where he lives, this country he has never seen. All the unknown miles, all the unknown sights and smells. And Greg thinks of Charlie, a County boy out there breathing it all in—city smog and mountain snow and dry desert air, and the salt of the Pacific; the green wonder of a tree that has been reaching for the sky since before Vesuvius erupted in 79 AD. And even after that beast hurled its ash across the earth, still that tree kept growing, reaching, knowing the sun was somewhere up there, far beyond the clouds.

The drive to Prescott has never taken so long before. How can twenty-two miles feel like twenty-two years? Bev must age about a decade before she even drives past Bergeron's, where inside people are shopping for pork chops and creamed corn and toilet paper.

Even though the Lumina air conditioner is blowing cold air into Bev's face, she's still sweating through the blouse and jeans she pulled from the hamper in exchange for her wedding clothes. On the radio, a Mellencamp song; outside the car, nothing but woods and fields, streaks of green under a blazing blue sky. All she can think about as she presses her foot to the gas pedal is Trudy, terrorizing those poor doctors and nurses.

In Prescott, Bev blows through two stop signs, unbothered by the honking trucks or the men inside them tossing her the bird. She also doesn't care about the car she cuts off in the hospital parking lot, or even about snapping at the massively pregnant secretary at the ER desk who only lets Bev through the Staff Only doors after five long minutes of begging.

Nearly a century after she left Dalton, she is permitted into a long room filled with a dozen curtained-off beds. Doctors and nurses bustle around, all of them avoiding one curtain in particular. Bev heads straight for it, and finally, *finally*, there's Trudy, still in her green dress, sitting in a chair beside an empty bed.

For a moment, the worst flits through Bev's mind—Richard had a second heart attack, or the first one finished him off after all. Then she remembers what Tru told her over the phone, all the tests the doctors need to run.

Before Bev can say hello, Trudy glances up from her lap, where she's rifling through her purse. Her expression is glazed and frantic. "I can't find any goddamn quarters."

"What do you need quarters for?"

"For the goddamn vending machines."

"Stop poking through that stupid bag. I've got you. Just sit still and wait here."

Bev doesn't need to ask Trudy what she wants, because she already knows. Package of Nutter-Butters, bottle of ginger ale. She craves sugar when she's stressed, empty calories that will fill her up fast. Bev gets her two of each.

Every few minutes, a nurse or doctor pops their head inside the curtain to give Trudy an update—the angioplasty went well, Richard is asleep but recovering, it should only be a little bit longer before they get him into a room for the night.

"And are we supposed to just sit here until you do?" Trudy snaps at a nurse with freckles tossed across her nose. "You could've at least parked us somewhere further away from the bathroom. The guy in Curtain Three better be here for his prostate, because no grown man should be pissing that much."

Soon after, a candy-striper shows Bev and Trudy up to the cardiology wing, where there is an empty waiting room with comfy chairs and soothingly dim lighting. When Bev glances at a clock on the wall, she's surprised to see it's nearly two o'clock in the morning.

"You should go home, Bevy. I can be here alone. I'm a grown woman."

"Shut up. You know I'm here for the duration."

Long minutes pass. Trudy flips through tabloids while Bev tries to concentrate on her knitting. Sophie requested a new sweater to wear for her first day of kindergarten. "Yellow like that dress Mumma's wearing there," she said, pointing at the framed photo of Bridget on Bev's living room wall. In the picture, Bridget is probably six months pregnant with Sophie, smiling in the sunset glow outside the farmhouse. She has a paintbrush in her hand—not the kind she would have used for her landscapes, but the sturdier kind meant for prettying up old porches. Nate took the photo, a sliver of his thumb peeking up from the foliage-strewn lawn.

Damn pity that Sophie has only seen her own mother in pictures. No memories of the woman herself.

But aren't borrowed memories better than nothing? That's what the counselor Bev saw for a while a few years ago would say. *Shouldn't you focus on the things you* can *give your granddaughter, rather than the things she's lost?*

Trudy doesn't know about that head-shrinker. It's the only secret Bev has ever kept from her, and sometimes she feels so guilty about it that she gets queasy.

It's not that Trudy would judge Bev for going to therapy—unlike a lot of other people in Dalton, she isn't categorically opposed to psychiatric intervention. It's that Tru would feel betrayed to learn Bev had shared the most private parts of herself with someone other than her. For so long, they've been each other's everything.

But it was easier for Bev to talk about Bridget's death with someone who didn't know her or her family, and that someone happened to be a therapist whose toner-scented office is only one floor below this very waiting room. Bev stopped going after only a dozen sessions—it was helpful, talking to someone like that, but without the insurance she used to get from her job at the Pines, she and Bill just couldn't afford it.

At quarter to three, Trudy tosses the magazine onto the end table. "What kind of place are they running here? Did they leave him in some back hallway? Just look at that nurses' station—not one goddamn nurse."

"Maybe they're short-staffed."

"Maybe they're idiots."

"If no one comes to talk to us in the next fifteen minutes," Bev says, "I'll march around this entire hospital until I find someone who isn't an idiot. Someone who can actually tell us something."

For the first time since they saw Richard breathless on the ground at the wedding, Trudy almost smiles. "Make it ten minutes."

"Deal."

Just a few moments later, a gray-haired nurse appears to tell them Richard has been peacefully sleeping in a room down the hall for the past two hours. Before Trudy can start spouting off about administrative incompetence, Bev whisks her down the hallway. The overhead lights buzz, and there's a smell of sour medicine, bleached linens.

They stand in the door of the room. Trudy's breath comes out in ragged little bursts when she sees Richard lying in the hospital bed, hooked up to machines. Every nerve in Bev's body is tuned into Trudy's desire to be led away from this room, this building. They could get in the car, hit I-95 out of Houlton, drive south. Be free.

But it doesn't matter what Bev wants, because their lives are bigger and more complicated than that. There are layers of loyalties and jealousies, unspoken regrets and desires . . . Bev has Sophie and Nate, and Bill. And Trudy has Richard—she will feel responsible for him now, driven by her guilt to prove she's capable of caring for him, that she wants him to stick around for the long-haul. In her own way, loving him. It will be a long, intolerable summer, Trudy preoccupied, giving Richard all that attention Bev wants for herself.

"It's all right," says Bev, gently nudging Trudy's shoulder. "Go sit next to him, tell him you're here. Tell him you're not going anywhere."

Trudy gives her a look that contains more than any language ever could. These moments when the steel melts away and all that's left is Tru, vulnerable and softhearted, Bev falls in love with her all over again.

"Don't worry," she promises. "I'm not going anywhere, either."

Richard sleeps. Bev knits. Trudy stares out the window as the sky outside the hospital turns from black to gray. All she can hear is the clink of aluminum needles and the regular, irritating beep of the heart monitor next to Richard's bed. She wishes it would stop—but no, that's the wrong way to feel; if that sound stops, everything else does, too.

"Quit it, Tru."

"Quit what?"

"Thinking what you're thinking. He's all right."

Bev has let the half-finished sweater pool in her lap, needles crossed on top of the plush yellow yarn. She looks almost as exhausted as Trudy feels.

"He could've died, Bevy."

"But he didn't."

The monitor keeps beeping as Richard's chest rises and falls in a smooth, easy rhythm. He looks so helpless. So small. Trudy's mind flashes back to him lying on the ground at the wedding, curled up like a wounded animal, gasping for breath. Her first thought when she saw her husband like that wasn't compassion, or even concern. It was rage. In those seconds before she understood he was having a heart attack, she was angry at him for writhing around on the grass, in front of the whole town. For causing a scene, embarrassing himself.

"Stop it, Tru. The important thing is the way you reacted once you saw it clearer."

She's not surprised Bev knows what she's thinking now and

what she was thinking then. What does surprise her is the lack of relief she gets from Bev's words. Even though they're sitting close together, Trudy feels far away. Floating in a cold, white limbo.

At the wedding, after the anger and before the worry, there was a brief but painfully bright moment when Trudy felt a spark of relief—no, worse than that. Something like hope. Seeing Richard struggling to breathe on the ground, she knew how close he was to whatever afterlife he might believe in, and a tiny part of her silently urged him toward it. *Go*, she thought, only for a moment. *Go and free us both*.

She's not a churchgoer, and she doesn't believe in a god who sits on a golden throne deeming every person worthy or unworthy of mercy. But if there ever was a moment for a lightning bolt from the great blue beyond, that would've been it.

What kind of woman wishes for her husband to die so she can give herself completely to someone else?

Trudy listens to the monitor and watches Richard breathing. His eyelids flicker and he sighs in his sleep, and for the first time in decades, she wonders what he dreams.

She knows Bev can feel the new distance between them. The not-thereness. They rarely speak of envy, but it's here in this room with them now, and it was in every room with them after Bridget died, when Bev had to focus all her attention on her own family.

Another person might grasp Trudy's hand harder, fight like hell to keep her from drifting away. But Bev squeezes once and pulls away. Then she begins to knit again, needles clicking to the same rhythm of Richard's heartbeat. It goes like that for hours. Bev doesn't say anything else. Just sits there. Lets Trudy float.

Axis

The next morning, Nate wakes on his parents' couch to the chatter of Sophie and his father in the kitchen. It takes him a few seconds to remember why he's waking up here rather than at his own house. Then it all comes back to him—Dr. Haskell laid out on the ground at the wedding, the gray sheen of his skin that made him look like a mannequin, or a corpse. Nate had been certain the guy was going to die before they got him to the hospital, and he had readied himself for the inevitable, rehearsed silently what he would say at the funeral. Better, he has learned, to be prepared than blindsided.

Groggy, he stands and curls his toes into the nap of the carpet as he stretches his arms above his head, fingers brushing the ceiling. He's still dressed in his wedding clothes, khakis twisted around his knees, Oxford shirt too tight around his wrists.

When he enters the kitchen, Sophie grins at him over a bowl of Frosted Flakes.

"You snore, Daddy."

"Not as bad as your Bampy."

His father fakes a pained expression. "Don't mock the elderly."

Usually, Nate would assure his father he's miles away from old age. But in the morning light, he notices new wrinkles around his father's mouth, a spattering of silver at his temples. In the kitchen chair, he sits canted off to one side, probably the only position that doesn't make his spine shriek in pain.

"Where's Ma?"

"Still at the hospital, I 'magine."

"She didn't come home last night?"

"You know your mother. She wouldn't leave Trudy alone like that."

There's a faint but familiar strain in his father's voice. Nate has always been aware his parents don't have the most romantic marriage—he can't remember ever seeing them hold hands, let alone kiss—but he's never understood why his father acts so cagey whenever he mentions his mother's friendship with Trudy.

"Daddy, can we go to the river today?"

It's Sunday, Nate's day to do laundry and clean the house and plan out their meals for the week. He should go grocery shopping. He should fix the wobbly spindle on the porch railing. He should drive to Prescott, check in on Dr. Haskell.

"Of course we can go to the river," he says. "We can do whatever you want."

After breakfast, his father gives Sophie a hug goodbye. "Till tomorrow, kid."

"Don't forget, Bampy, you promised we'd play Go Fish."

"I'll be warming up that deck of cards before the sun comes up."

Nate isn't the only one who does everything for this kid. There's his father with his trashed spine, up early four days a week so Nate can drop off Sophie at the house before heading to the mill. There's his mother, who left her job at the old folks' home so she could care for Sophie in the months after Bridget died. By the time Nate was steady enough to bring Sophie home, it was too late for his mom to get her job back, so she started working the morning shift at the Store 'N More. Happy to sell millworkers their cigarettes if it means she can get home before noon to spend the rest of the day with her granddaughter. Marshall could have found a more experienced guy to operate the kiln at the mill, but he chose his son-in-law instead.

If only Sophie knew how this broken world has shifted for her, how she has become an entire family's rotational axis.

Back at the farmhouse, she dashes upstairs to change out of her PJs, her feet stomping like iron pegs on the floorboards. How can such a small creature make so much noise? She's back within one minute, dressed in sneakers, zigzag leggings, and a Rugrats shirt.

"Let's *go*, Daddy."

"Patience, Soph."

Nate goes into the downstairs bathroom, where he splashes water on his face and swaps his dress clothes for shorts and a t-shirt. By the time he steps back into the hallway, Sophie is bouncing on her feet, body wiggling with excitement.

Her obsession with the river is new. It started when Nate brought her down to see the ice go out in April. He held her a safe distance from the bank as they watched the slabs of winter roaring down the river, water splashing up toward the pale blue sky.

Since then, as spring has opened into summer, Sophie has been tracking the river, the subtle changes in its depth and speed, the various colors it can turn from one minute to the next, depending on sun and wind and cloud. She has a special interest in the animal tracks pressed into the pebbly mud on the shore; can already tell the difference between fox and coyote, squirrel and chipmunk.

He lets her run in front of him, though he calls out for her to slow down whenever she gets a little too far ahead. They make their way through the fields, the spruce-scented woods, and onto the shore, where the river flows slowly.

Sitting on a patch of sun-warmed grass, Nate watches as Sophie attempts to skip stones across the water. He's shown her how a dozen times, but she's never gotten the hang of it. After a few minutes, she gives up and plops down beside him, resting her head against his arm. She smells like river water. After her bath tonight, Nate will have to bribe her into letting him comb out the tangles in her hair—a fudgsicle might do the trick, or another viewing of their *Aladdin* VHS tape.

"Are we going to have supper with Grampa again?"

"Do you want to?"

"I think so. But can we do it at our house instead? I don't like his house. It's too messy. It feels all wrong."

"Whatever you want."

Nate is secretly relieved—he doesn't like that house either. Bridget always hated it, too. "It just doesn't feel like a home," she always said. And he understood it wasn't the house itself (way too big, way too clean), it was also the people inside its spacious rooms: her mother with her cold, detached discipline, her moody siblings. Maybe Marshall would've brightened the place up a bit, but he spent most of Bridget's childhood at the mill.

In the trees around them, birds call back and forth. Up in the sky, clouds come together, fall apart, come together again.

"Six days," Sophie suddenly says. "We'll be there, right, Daddy?"

There is the cemetery, next Saturday morning. Before the town wakes up, as the sun rises and throws pink light across the town and valley. Their morbid, annual father-daughter tradition. June 3rd. The day Bridget died.

"That's right," says Nate.

Sophie is quiet for several moments, then she pulls slightly away from Nate so she can look into his eyes. "Why'd she die?"

And there's another wallop, straight to the chest.

"She was sick, remember?" says Nate. "Sometimes when people get sick, they die."

"Yeah but why was she sick?"

He has been dreading this moment since he found Bridget in the bathtub, water stained pink with her blood. How do you explain suicide to a child? How do you explain postpartum depression, and colicky infants, and husbands who didn't see what they should have seen, didn't save what should have been saved?

As soon as Sophie started talking, Nate and his parents agreed they needed the same story to give her when she inevitably began to ask why she didn't have a mother. They settled on a story vague enough but close enough to the truth: *Your mumma loved you very much, but she was sick, and she died when you were still a baby.* As for the off-limits upstairs bathroom, Nate has only ever told Sophie that it was the last place he saw her mother, and he doesn't like to go inside it—"It makes me too sad," he's always said, and Sophie has always accepted this.

The older and more curious she gets, however, the more Nate worries these stories won't be enough for her.

For now, he decides to stick with the usual half-truth. "I don't know why she got sick," he tells Sophie. "Sometimes bad things happen to the best people."

She stares at him, the wind blowing her hair around her face. Nate does his best to keep his eyes steady on hers, to appear trustworthy, even as every cell in his body pulses with fear that his daughter has reached the limit of this narrative, that she has outgrown the lie.

Then Sophie nods, and she lays her head back against Nate's arm, and his body relaxes. He's bought himself some time; the story will hold a little bit longer.

The river flows on, steady north.

The Other Side

There's a grenade in his chest, heavy and ticking, but all he can think about are battleships he never built; hulking thousand-ton beasts that still somehow manage to glide across the surface of a slate blue sea, untroubled.

Here is a vaguely familiar face, hovering above him. There are sketches of ships, drawn out in his own hand. There are solid arms lifting him from the ground. Here is the taste of the ocean, salt on his lips. Thunderclouds on a watery horizon, black sinking into gray.

He is in a dimly lit room humming with machinery. His limbs are strapped to a table. Commanding voices mutter phrases like *ready to tilt* and *balloon just in case*. Plasticky smell. White coats press in around him, someone's soft belly pushing against his elbow. Prick of needle, rush of heat, taste of ink in the back of his throat. A pause. A nothing. Then another rush, cold this time, and he is drifting back out to sea.

Something is ebbing away from the center of him, rushing out to the very edges of his being, vibrating there, begging for release.

Someone keeps calling his name.

* * *

Richard wakes in a white room, tucked beneath white blankets. Beside him, a monitor beeps; a burnt-chemical stench makes his nostrils itch. When he tries to pull the cannula from his nose, a hand tugs his arm away.

"You leave that damn thing right where it is."

Turning his head, Richard sees Trudy, still in the dress she wore to the wedding, sitting in a chair next to him.

"How long . . . ?" he asks, the words rasping out of his dry mouth.

"All night."

A galloping fear rips through him, the certainty that while he was sleeping, he was sliced open from sternum to navel. The monitor beeps faster.

"It's all right, calm down. You're fine. They did some kind of angio-something."

He can't remember the last time he heard so much tenderness in his wife's voice. She must have sat in the waiting room the whole time they were running tests, the whole time he was in the cath lab. Hours and hours, wondering if she was going to be a widow.

"Richard."

He meets her gaze, those eyes he knows better than his own. The whirl of spun silver, the flash of feeling that could either be love or resentment—for Trudy, those two emotions are braided together like rope.

"You scared the shit out of me."

Maybe there is something new in her gaze—or perhaps it is something old. A softness Richard hasn't seen in so long. A flicker of their early days. Trudy could be twenty-one again, pulling him toward the river as a summer moon turns the whole world blue. She could be that bride on their wedding night, laughing as rain kissed the windows of their honeymoon cottage on Portman Lake.

"I'm sorry to put you through all that worry," he says. "You must be wrecked, hanging around here alone all night."

"I wasn't alone," says Trudy, shifting her eyes to the metal bed frame. "For the first of it, Nate and Vera Curtis were here with me. And then . . . "

Now there's a different sort of ache in Richard's chest—the low, faint thrum of a familiar kind of loneliness. Only then does he notice the two Styrofoam cups of half-drunk coffee on the table beside his bed.

"Bev?"

Trudy steels her slim shoulders. "I'm sorry."

Not that this should come as any great shock. He and Trudy have had a silent agreement for years. Their marriage is civil but strained, always shadowed by the bigger, truer love between her and Bev Theroux.

"Where is she now?"

"Ran down to the cafeteria. Should be back any minute."

The choices they have made, the compromises he has given into . . . All to avoid a divorce that would end in townwide spectacle and disgrace for everyone involved—himself and Trudy, Bev and Bill, Nate. And now Sophie, too, and by extension, the entire Frazier family. The roots run deep. The secrets run wide.

Trudy opens her mouth as if to say something, but then she and Richard hear the rhythm of Bev's footsteps, moving quick toward them down the sterile hall.

Though he spent countless hours at Maine Med as part of his education and residency, Richard has never been hospitalized himself. He always had sympathy for the patients confined to their beds, but until now, he has never understood how vulnerable they felt, or how time warped, shrank, and expanded around them.

One second, Bev is welcoming Richard back from the brink, sounding genuinely relieved to see him awake; the next second, she's gone, the only evidence of her having been there her coffee cup and the cellophane-wrapped muffin she brought Trudy from the cafeteria.

Nurses come in and out to monitor his vitals, check his urine output, rehang fluids for his IV. A different woman every time—there's the one with gray hair, and the one with a voice like a bird, and the one with a bleach stain on her scrubs.

"Where the hell is the doctor?" asks Trudy, and Richard, half-asleep, tries to say that he is here, right here, but then he's standing at the prow of a ship, staring at a swath of starry heaven, the Milky Way a crooked incision splitting the sky in two.

He wakes to eat lime Jell-O. Trudy flips through channels on the TV mounted to the wall, a quick succession of weather maps, televised sermons, toothy women selling diamond bracelets. The light in the room changes, hours marching on. Finally, there's a knock at the door, and a man in a white coat steps into the room, studying the chart in his hands.

"Richard Haskell?"

"*Doctor*," corrects Trudy, a hard glint in her eyes.

"Yes, that's me, Dr. Capaldo."

Looking up from the chart, he reveals a young, handsome face untouched by wrinkles or worry. And Jesus, all that hair. Like that kid on *ER*.

Ignoring Trudy completely, the doctor walks straight to the bed and gestures for Richard to lean forward so he can press a stethoscope to his back. "Hear you had yourself a little heart attack," he says. "Must have been pretty scary."

Trudy's eyes could set the room on fire.

"Well, I knew what was happening. I'm a physician myself, and my father . . . "

"Yes, I saw in your family history that he died of cardiovascular disease. Can you take a deep breath for me now? That's it, that's good."

Dr. Capaldo gently pushes Richard back against the pillows, then scratches out a few notes on the chart. The heart monitor beeps. Down the hall at the nurses' station, a phone keeps ring-ing, unanswered.

"Okay, so let's first of all discuss what exactly happens during an MI—excuse me, heart attack."

"You really don't need to explain. As I said, I'm a physician—"

"What we're dealing with here is a partial blockage . . . "

Do ships still have planks? Much as he hates violence, Richard wouldn't mind seeing this guy pushed from one into a churning sea, sharks circling.

" . . . so, we performed an angioplasty—and what that means . . . "

Trudy's face is turning red, and her breathing comes in angry bursts.

Richard musters up as much authority as he can with a plas-tic tube shoved up his urethra. "*Doctor*. The only thing my wife and I want to know is when I can get back to work. I run the clinic in Dalton."

"You're looking at a recovery period of anywhere from a few weeks to a few months, Richard. Your heart needs to rest, and your body will need to adjust to the medications we're putting you on."

"What medications?" asks Trudy.

Dr. Capaldo launches into a list Richard knows well—statins, beta blockers, antiplatelet agents . . . He feels as though his bones have been replaced with wet bags of sand, and the only thing he wants is to drift away, dream of ships and seas and starry skies. He closes his eyes, imagines the salt spray, the moonlight on water . . .

"Ah, I see our patient is a little sleepy. That's normal—"

"For Chrissake, we know it's normal, you snide little shit."

Still with his eyes closed, Richard smiles. *Tell him, Trudy. Give him hell.*

"Now, ma'am—"

"Don't you *ma'am* me. I don't need that crap from a snively prick who skipped the class on bedside manner. Who the hell do you think you are?"

"Mrs. Haskell—"

"You have no right to talk to my husband like he's missing half his brain. No, we've heard enough. Time for you to leave. Go tease your hair or shoot hoops with George Clooney, or whatever the hell it is you do. *Doctor.*"

There's a rustle of clothing, quick strides across the floor. Richard opens his eyes to see Trudy glaring at Capaldo's back as he lets the door swing shut behind him. She turns to Richard, ready to let more venom fly.

"I know," he says. "But I really should get some sleep. Why don't you call Bev or Nate, have them drive you back home? Take a nice long bath, eat a real meal."

Trudy absentmindedly runs a hand through her hair. "Fine. But I'm not calling Bev or Nate. I'm calling the Curtis girl."

"Vera?" asks Richard, vaguely remembering the pressure of steady fingers against his wrist, counting his heartbeats. "Why her?"

Under his wife's stare, Richard feels his body shrinking, dissolving into the mattress.

"You heard what that jackass said. It'll be weeks before you go back to work. And in the meantime, what's going to happen to the clinic? All your patients?" Trudy pauses for a breath. "You need someone to step in and take your place."

"But Vera's only a nurse practitioner—"

"So she sends the more difficult cases here to Prescott. But she's fully capable of doing the rest of it, and she'll have Rose and Janine there to help her out. And Christ knows she needs something to do while she's stuck in town all summer with her parents."

Richard has a flashback to being six or seven years old, fighting with Pauline Bergeron at recess over who had the rights to the monkey bars. He didn't even particularly like the monkey bars, but damn if he was going to let her have them.

Then he remembers the relief he felt when Pauline won the fight and dangled upside down, pigtails swinging in the breeze. The shame in knowing he never would have dared such a feat himself.

"All right," says Richard. His voice sounds very old and very far away, echoing across the span of an ocean, the width of a star-drunk universe. "Vera it is."

PRODIGAL

When Trudy calls to ask for a ride back from the hospital, Vera is glad for the chance to leave the house. In the living room, her mother is fretting over Jeff Goldblum's bare chest ("I just don't understand *why* he has to take his shirt off after almost getting eaten by a T-rex") while her father grouses about how impossible it would be to clone dinosaurs ("let alone intelligent ones"). Ever since he retired from the mill a few years ago, he and Vera's mother devote a couple hours each weekend to watching movies rented from the library. "Sunday matinee," they call it. The tradition might be cute if they didn't spend so much time yelling at the TV or arguing about each movie's finer plot points.

After making her mother promise not to walk around the house without her crutches, and after denying her father's request that she bring back KFC for supper, Vera steps out of the dim, cool house and into the glare of the afternoon sun. Not even June, but the thermometer mounted on the porch railing hovers just below 75 degrees.

Vera's first sensation on entering Dr. Haskell's room up in the cardiology wing of the Prescott hospital is an ache of homesickness. The white walls, the beeping heart monitor, the smell of antiseptic . . . all of it makes her long for her own hospital, where she served an actual purpose in the role of patient care beyond fetching cups of coffee and fast-forwarding through previews on a VCR.

Dr. Haskell is a tall man, but you wouldn't know it looking

at him as he sleeps in his hospital bed. After all her years working in medicine, Vera's breath still catches in her throat each
time she sees a once-strong man diminished to infancy in one
of those beds. It's the metal frame that flanks the mattress, reminiscent of a crib.

"Thought you got lost on the way here," says Trudy from a
chair beside the window.

"I haven't been away from the County that long."

Vera settles into a vinyl chair near the head of the bed. From
this vantage point, she can see the plastic of the cannula misting
each time Dr. Haskell exhales. She studies the monitor, noting
his vitals.

"Good enough for you?"

She snaps her gaze back to him, who smiles at her through
bleary but bemused eyes.

"Sorry," she says. "Old habit."

"Ask her, Richard."

"I'm getting there, Trudy."

"Get there faster."

As Dr. Haskell lays out his proposal for her to run the Dalton
clinic while he recovers, Vera feels herself torn between the desire to shout yes and the fear of what saying yes might mean.
It's not the job itself—she can handle the job, no problem—but
something else that makes her hesitate.

Ever since she was a kid, Vera has only wanted freedom.
Purpose. Movement. And for her, those things lay beyond
Dalton. She always loved the landscape of the County, the expansive views of valleys and forests and meadows. All the billion clear, bright stars. But she also always longed to discover
other horizons, to see the moon from a new angle.

Bangor isn't exactly exotic, but for Vera, it's always been
different enough to keep her content. Old brick buildings, department stores, Chinese restaurants, a used bookshop ruled
by a tabby cat named Pudge . . . Only a couple hours south of

Dalton, but the city feels like it exists within an entirely separate universe.

There, the streets are busy with traffic and people out walking, running, biking, always on their way somewhere.

Here, the roads are thick with log trucks, moose, and deer.

There, Vera can have pizza delivered to her apartment at 10:00 at night.

Here, everything other than the Store 'N More is closed by 6 P.M., and good luck asking one of the women who works there to drive a pizza out to someone perfectly capable of getting off their ass to get it themselves.

There, Vera is her own woman, wholly independent.

Here, she will be reclaimed by every single person who has ever known her or her parents or her parents' long-dead relatives.

"I know it's a lot to ask," Dr. Haskell sums up. "If you're not up for it, no hard feelings. But if that's the case, I need to start rescheduling folks and referring them to other places."

Vera stares out the window, watching robins swoop through the sky. The monitor beeps; down the hall, the nurses' station phone keeps ringing.

Say yes.

It's a clinic, a real clinic where she can be of use, where she can help people. But it wouldn't be like Bangor, where every patient coming into the ER is a stranger she will only need to interact with for the duration of their time in her unit. Even though she's been gone nearly twenty years, Vera still knows the people of Dalton. She would be treating teachers who taught her the ABCs. Postal workers who stuffed *Teen Beat* magazines into her mailbox. Grocery clerks who sold her tampons with conspiratorial looks. Girls she used to have sleepovers with turned into wives and mothers; bright-eyed boys she once kissed transformed into hard-faced men worn down by years of physical labor in lumberyards or farm fields.

Older people in Dalton will remember her as the toddler who carried a stuffed octopus everywhere, or the eight-year-old who threw up at the Advent Church Easter party after eating too many Cadbury Crème Eggs, or the fifteen-year-old caught kissing Harry Arsenault in the softball dugout. The men and women closer to her age will remember her as a teenager who faked migraines to get out of gym, a snob with all the answers in class, a mouthy show-off who made sure everyone knew she wasn't just another townie; she was a young woman destined for bigger places, bigger things.

Say no, hire your mother a temporary live-in nurse, and get the hell out of the County.

But there are practical, pragmatic matters to consider: Without her paycheck coming in from the Bangor hospital, there are still bills to pay, rent money her landlord will still expect to collect even if Vera isn't in the apartment. And an entire summer stretches before her in which all she has to look forward to is trying to make her mother sit still and listening to her father argue with the weather channel.

On the other side of the room, Trudy gazes out the window at the cloudless sky. "Going to be a long summer," she muses, letting out a sigh. "Heat like this."

Vera's thoughts return to her parents' house. A bed designed for a child, crammed beneath a south-facing window and a low ceiling with no fan. The reek of dryer sheets. The sound of her mother singing all the wrong words to old doo-wop songs. The iron taste of the rib-eye steak her father loves so much.

"Okay," she tells Dr. Haskell. "I'll run the clinic."

JUNE

"I decided to leave here. Stern resolution.
Grasp the world. Then I found
the Village Virus had me, absolute."
—SINCLAIR LEWIS, *Main Street*

ON PORTMAN LAKE

Vera Curtis looks the way Rose likes to think she might have if she'd never had kids. Her black hair is smooth and shiny, and she's nailed that trick of wearing makeup so it looks like she has none on. Not one wrinkle on her face, even though she's ten years older than Rose. She wears nice dresses paired with flats that squeak a little whenever she walks into the front office to ask another question about the clinic.

At first, Rose is annoyed by all these questions: *Can we schedule a patient before checking with their insurance? How do you fax an out-of-state number? Where do we keep the coffee filters?* But after a couple days, she starts to look forward to them. Vera could get the answers from Janine, who's been a nurse here for about a hundred years, or she could call Dr. Haskell and ask him. But she doesn't. She comes to Rose, who feels a giddy sense of pride every time she can rattle off the answer: *Dr. H. sees anyone even if their shitty plan says he can't. Dial 9 before the area code. In the break room, cupboard above the sink.*

Vera's always just so grateful after Rose offers her one of these explanations. And not in a fake, snively way like Janine. A *real* way. Rose gave up on getting approval from older women when she was still a kid, right around the time her mother started bringing home a new Ponytail every other week. But whenever Vera smiles at her and thanks her for "helping make this transition smoother," Rose feels the way she imagines Brandon does whenever Mrs. Rafferty gives him a gold star on a spelling test.

When she gets to the clinic on Friday morning, Vera is

already there, standing outside her car with a grease-splotched paper bag in one hand. She's wearing a purple dress today, her hair pulled back in a twist.

"Token of appreciation," she says, handing the bag to Rose, who can tell by the yeasty-sugar smell that it contains cinnamon donuts from the Diner. "I couldn't have made it through this week without you."

"You'd've been fine. But thanks." Rose pretends to search through her purse for her key to the building so Vera won't see the blush of joy on her face. The gesture seems like something women do for one another when they're real friends, the kind who borrow each other's clothes and keep each other's secrets. The closest thing Rose ever had to something like that was Suzie Howe, back in sixth grade. They had sleepovers, talked about boys they liked and teachers they hated. But it was short-lived—Suzie moved away the summer before junior high.

In the waiting room, Vera fans out the magazines on the tables as Rose stacks rainbow-colored blocks for the kids. Then Vera gets the coffee going in the breakroom while Rose organizes things in the front office—all the day's charts in order by appointment, radio set to 96.1, window open to catch the summer air. She puts the donuts in her purse, thinking she should bring them home for the boys. Then the breeze blows the smell of cinnamon at her, making her stomach rumble, and she takes the bag back out, setting it beside the phone.

Vera comes into the office with two cups of coffee—plain black for herself, cream and sugar for Rose.

"Will Janine be in today?"

"She better be. It's the boys' last day before summer break, and I promised to take them swimming as soon as school lets out. Janine said she'd cover the desk for me."

As she says it, Rose realizes Vera might not be as generous with the schedule as Dr. Haskell always is. As if Vera Curtis, with her perfect makeup and fancy nursing degree, could ever understand what it's like to be a single mother. Sure, Rose has to work, but she also has to be with her kids. Pick them up from school. Teach them how to swim. Doze away with them under the sun, all their sunburnt, mosquito-bitten limbs tangled up in hers.

The phone beeps, turning itself off from night-mode—eight o'clock, time to open the doors. Rose grabs her keys and heads for the lobby, but before she can leave the front office, Vera places a hand on her arm.

"Even if Janine doesn't show up," she says. "I want you to take off early. Spend time with Adam and Brandon."

Relief, surprise, and the stupid urge to cry rolls through Rose in an unexpected wave. "That'd be nice," she tells Vera. "Thanks."

After she unlocks the clinic doors, Rose settles back down at the front desk. She reaches for the pastry bag and holds her face above it, breathing it in—all that warm sweetness. She takes her time eating the first donut, savoring the flecks of cinnamon-sugar that collect on her lips and fingers. Just as she reaches for the second donut, she thinks better of it. She'll save that one for Vera. It's what a real friend would do.

It was a nice plan she and the boys dreamed up last night, talking about how much fun they'd have splashing in the lake and grilling hotdogs on the shore. The kind of family outing Rose never had as a kid with her own mother.

But it seems like every damn person in Dalton had the same idea for the last day of school. When Rose pulls into the parking lot, the lake shore is packed with too many people, too much bare flesh burning under the sun.

"I don't know, guys. Maybe we should go back to town. Swim in the river instead."

"I don't mind the river,' says Brandon.

"No, Mum," Adam whines, "you promised."

So they get out of the car, pavement scorching the soles of Rose's feet through her flipflops. Adam takes off running for the water, while Brandon hangs back with her to look for an empty space high up on the shore.

She lays out towels on the ground and strips down to her bathing suit, a mismatched tankini she bought at the thrift store. The bottoms fit all right, but the top is a little too plunging for a family beach day. Funny—back when she was a teenager, she would have stripped down naked in front of all these people and been proud of it. Now, she keeps fussing with the top, uselessly trying to make it cover her cleavage.

"Go ahead and swim with your brother, buddy," she tells Brandon, who hovers around her in a way that's both sweet and annoying.

"I need my life jacket."

Shit. Rose knew she forgot something.

"You'll be fine," she says. "I'm right here if something happens."

"Do I have to?"

Part of her thinks she should take him by the hand, walk him into the lake, and stand there with him until he figures out how to hold his breath, tread water. But when Brandon looks at her with his eyes wide with fear, something inside Rose slips and shatters.

"You don't have to do anything you don't want to," she says. "Let's just sit here, okay? Do some people watching."

Brandon's tiny shoulders fall away from his ears. Then he lies down beside her, resting his head in her lap so she can stroke his hair. All around them are the sounds of kids laughing, water kissing the shore, power boats whining across the lake. Squinting, Rose recognizes several girls she went to school with down the shore—typical, bitches pretend they don't see her when she waves at them. She sends silent curses in their direction, willing their tanning lotion to stain their white bikinis.

And Jesus, it's hot—Rose can't remember it ever being this hot on the second day of June; the kind of heat that slaps you in the face and makes you want to sleep till September. Every few minutes, the nearby outhouse door slams open, releasing the stink of other people's crap.

In the lake, Adam finds a group of boys his age and swims out with them toward the line of buoys that separates the shallow water from the deep. Rose keeps a close eye on him, feeling a jolt of fear every time he plunges underwater to do a handstand.

"Your brother's a daredevil," she says, pressing her hand to Brandon's sweaty forehead.

"Do you want me to be one, too, Mumma?"

"I think one's enough."

"Good."

A minute later, Rose hears her name and looks up to see Nate Theroux standing above her, so tall he almost blocks the sun. Standing beside him holding his hand is Sophie, in a pink bathing suit, her hair pulled back into pigtails.

"Thought that was you," Nate says, sitting down so Rose doesn't have to keep bending her neck to look at him. He smells like winter trees, and his eyes are bluer than the water. Not so long ago, that combination would've knocked Rose flat. But her old crush on him wobbled a bit after his wife offed herself. Hard to imagine a romance with someone that tragic.

Plus there was that whole thing with Nate going off on Tommy in the yard of the trailer a few weeks after Bridget died, punching him until his face was a mess of blood and bruises.

Rose has never told anyone she witnessed that scene. Tommy lied about it; told her it was one of his asshole cousins, and she let him think she believed him. Truth is, she was glad to see him get hurt the way he'd hurt her so many times before. It felt like karma, even if it wasn't the good kind.

She knows Nate knows she saw what happened that

day—their eyes caught as she watched out the window of the trailer—but they've never talked about it. Some things are better left silent.

Sophie sidles up to Brandon, whispers something in his ear, and smiles; to Rose's surprise, he giggles and grins back. The kids have met a couple times, at the Diner and the Store 'N More, but they've never played together—Sophie's two years younger, not even in school yet. That doesn't stop her now, though, as she leads Brandon a couple feet away to watch a spider scurrying across some rocks.

Without Brandon in her lap, Rose feels over-exposed in her bathing suit. Not that Nate's looking at her boobs, though—the guy might as well be a monk.

"How are things at the clinic without Dr. Haskell?"

"Kinda weird. Vera's got her shit together, but it's his place, you know?"

"I should swing by his house this weekend."

"He says he doesn't want any visitors."

Sophie and Brandon drag twigs through the dirt, making tunnels for the spider. Adam comes running up the shore, crouching beside them to see what they're doing. Water drips off his hair, splashes on his brother's bare feet.

She and Nate watch for what feels like a long time as the kids play. Neither of them says much, and usually that kind of silence drives Rose crazy, makes her feel like she's supposed to fill the empty spaces. But it's okay with Nate, under the sun. They both laugh when Adam and Brandon scamper backwards from Sophie as she holds the spider out toward them.

"They're great boys, Ro."

The nickname is like a shock of cold water—Nate hasn't called her that since she worked at the police station. Back when Nate was still a cop. Back when Bridget was still alive, and Rose was still jealous of her.

"Sophie's pretty great, too," she says. "Lots of spirit."

Nate gazes at his daughter with so much love Rose can feel it radiating off him like a magnetic field. "Spirit's a good word for it. Bossy could be another."

"Girls hate being called bossy. Just so you know."

"Yup, sorry about that. Felt wrong as soon as I said it."

Rose hasn't met many men who can apologize quick and easy like that. They're usually so sure they have all the answers, and god forbid a woman try to put them in their place. There were so many times Rose disagreed with something dumb Tommy said, or tried to explain why he was wrong about something, only for him to lose his shit and smack her across the face. Or call her a stupid cunt, which sometimes felt worse than any physical violence.

Rose would bet a million bucks Nate has never said the word cunt in his life.

The outhouse door slams open and shut once again, just as a cloud finally rolls in to cover the bright sun. Sophie is telling the boys all about Charlotte, the spider who can write messages in her web, and Adam is pretending like he's never heard the story before, even though it was his favorite when he was her age. He can be sweet like that with his brother sometimes, too, when he's not stealing Brandon's toy cars or convincing Brandon there's a monster named Mr. Baldy who lives under their bunk bed.

"Maybe you could bring the boys out to the house sometime," says Nate, as if he's seeing something new in Sophie, too, some glimmer that isn't there when it's just her alone. "Lots of space to run around. Good swimming spot down at the river."

Rose can't remember the last time she drove out to Milton Landing. She's never really wanted to see the farmhouse where Nate and Sophie live, which has got to be haunted with the kind of shit that happened there with Bridget. And suicidal ghosts are probably the angriest, scariest kind of ghost.

All that land out at his place, though—huge yard, endless

fields, stands of forest . . . The boys would love to play in that kind of openness after a lifetime of trailer-park lawn, which is more dirt than grass.

"That sounds all right," Rose says. "But is the river shallow? Brandon doesn't swim too good."

Nate smiles as the kids start giggling about a group of teenage boys and girls who walk by with huge boomboxes and tiny bathing suits. The cloud disappears, and the lake and shore are smacked with eyeball-bruising sun once again.

"It's a safe river, Ro," he promises. "And I can teach him how to swim."

Anniversary

They leave the house while the sun's still rising. In the passenger seat, Sophie sings along with the radio, a song about life in a northern town. Nate knows the song was written for another place in another country, far away, but the feel of it is Dalton. As he drives down Davis Road, the lyrics play for all the familiar things—Judy Warren's cabin, Harvey Trinko's butcher shop, the Pritchard Farm. All the known forest and all the known fields, and the Aroostook River winding its way through the middle of it all.

When they get to the cemetery, Nate trundles down the narrow dirt road, all the way to the end of the lot, where the hill drops away to the valley below. The sun casts the land in a rosy-gold glow that makes even the biomass mill on the horizon look romantic.

He does his best to smile at his daughter, to appear calm. "Okay, Soph. Let's go talk to Mumma. Tell her all the good things you've been up to."

The morning air is cool, and the world smells sweet and alive. Sophie, dressed in rainbow overalls and an orange shirt, leads Nate to Bridget's plot, where they sit on the grass under a maple tree bursting with new leaves. She leans forward to touch the stone, her fingers tracing the letters of her mother's name.

"Hi, Mumma."

Nate lets her talk uninterrupted for a long time, hearing every word but pretending not to so she can feel like all these stories belong only to her mother. Stories of the river, stories of the sky. Terrible knock-knock jokes. Observations about the spider she and "those skinny boys" watched yesterday at the lake.

"What were their names, Daddy?"

"Brandon and Adam Merchant."

"And who was their mumma?"

"Rose Douglas."

"If she's their mom, why don't they have the same last name?"

Before he can explain about unmarried mothers and absent fathers, she turns back to the gravestone to carry on with her stories. Nate lets the words flutter and fall away from him as he stares toward the distant blue of Mount Katahdin. His hands feel tingly and leaden, the same way they did that day not long after Bridget died.

It's not like he set out that day looking for Tommy, back in town so soon after Nate put him in jail. It's not like he saw Tommy tinkering with his truck outside his trailer and just decided to beat him up. It was the heat of the sun and a loud Fourth of July parade. It was knowing what Tommy was capable of, the bruises Nate had seen on Rose's arms. It was the horrific things Tommy said about Bridget, who'd only been dead a month.

The whole scene is still a blur; Nate can only really remember hot blood on his knuckles, and fear in Tommy's eyes.

Every time he's run into Rose at the post office or the Diner or Bergeron's over the past five years, Nate has wanted to tell her he's sorry for what he did that day. Sorry he lost control, sorry she had to be a witness to it. He isn't sorry Tommy left Dalton afterward, though, because he can't smack Rose around anymore. And Nate's sure it's hard for those boys, not to have a father around, but maybe it's better than their growing up with that particular father, who would no doubt teach them it's okay to treat women the way Tommy always treated Rose.

"Daddy," says Sophie. "I'm gonna go look for flowers for Mumma."

After she's run off toward the edge of the cemetery, Nate rests his palm against the cool granite headstone and imagines what Bridget might say about Tommy. Something about how men who hit women deserve whatever violence they get in return. But maybe that's just fantasy, an attempt to excuse his own behavior.

Occasionally, Nate will have nightmares of that July afternoon, dreams so real it's like he's right back in the moment. The worst thing about those nightmares isn't the blood or the crack of bone beneath his knuckles; it's the thrill of power he feels as Tommy begs him to stop. The dark satisfaction of seeing Tommy hurting. As long as he lives, Nate never wants to have that kind of power over anyone again. Never wants to feel that way again—the same way, no doubt, Tommy felt all those times he wielded his strength against Rose.

Nate isn't sure what prompted him to invite her and her kids out to his place as they sat on the lakeshore yesterday. Maybe it's his attempt at atonement. It could be a terrible idea. But Sophie lit up when she was showing Brandon and Adam how to build spider tunnels, and Nate hasn't done enough to expose her to other kids, give her the chance to make friends.

She returns with a handful of lilacs, laying them on the stone before turning to face him. "Did Mumma have a bad heart?"

Surprised and confused by the question, Nate says, "No, Mumma had a very good heart. She was one of the nicest people I've ever known."

"Not like that. I mean was it her heart that made her get sick and die?"

How is he supposed to say that yes, in a way, Bridget's heart *was* infected—not with any sort of disease, but with a blackness bigger than anything she or he could have ever imagined?

"No," he tells Sophie. "That wasn't Mumma's kind of sickness."

His daughter chews on her lower lip, frowns. Before she can ask him anything else about Bridget's death, Nate stands up and reaches for her hand.

"Want to help me on a mission?"

"What kind of mission?"

"We need birdseed."

Sophie's eyes brighten. "Okay, but we have to get the big bag. There were so many birds last night I couldn't even count them."

Nate's own heart is a bruised and bloodied thing, a lump of muscle stubbornly beating.

As soon as he parks outside the hardware store, Sophie hops down from the truck and skips toward the entrance, and he has to shout at her to wait for him. "There are cars," he says, even though theirs is the only vehicle in the lot.

The bell above the door tinkles as they step into the store, which smells of sawdust and oakum. Jim Fortin glances up from the register and nods before turning back to a stack of receipts. In the Lawn & Garden aisle, as Nate silently curses the price of the fifteen-pound bag of sunflower seeds, Sophie ogles the display of bell-shaped hummingbird feeders.

"Can we, Daddy?"

"How much do they cost?"

He and his parents have been teaching her numbers ahead of when she starts school this fall. She's had the alphabet down for nearly a year already, thanks to Nate's father, who takes her to the library at least twice a week.

"Five," says Sophie. "Almost six."

"Go ahead. Careful, though—that's real glass."

Halfway to the register, she lingers in front of the lit-up wall of paint samples, her eyes starry at all the different colors spread out before her. She reaches for a swatch of yellow.

"I want this in my room."

"You don't like the green?"

She waves the strip of paper in front of her. "This is better."

Bridget chose the color that covers the walls of Sophie's room, back when they were setting it up as the nursery. Verdant Veridian. She said it was the color of Dalton in summer, all the trees and fields. Safe places. Home.

"We'll talk about it later, okay?"

"Are you saying no I can't paint it?"

"I'm saying we'll talk about it later."

She pouts all the way up to the register.

"This is a good one," Jim says, scanning the barcode on the bird feeder. "Especially if you put it up near some red flowers. You have any of those?"

Sophie frowns. "No red flowers."

"We sell some, you know. We got a section outside behind the store. But hold on, let me call up the real expert—he can tell you a lot more about this stuff than I can."

Jim hits a button on the intercom, his voice crackling through the speakers. "Need some assistance up front, son."

Greg emerges from somewhere deeper in the store, stepping around boxes of nuts and bolts to join his father behind the register. Nate still can't believe how thin the kid has gotten, how strong and healthy he looks.

"This little lady here," says Jim, "wants flowers that will attract hummingbirds. I told her we have some red ones that should do the trick."

"Any bright color should work," Greg says. "Petunias are good, but those are annuals—you'd do better to plant something that will come back every year so the birds will, too."

Sophie looks up at Nate, begging silently.

"Sounds good," he says. "But I don't know the first thing about gardening."

"You can help them out, can't you, son?"

Nate has no idea why Greg would say yes—he must have friends he wants to hang out with, better things to do. But something flashes in Greg's eyes, and he nods. "I can help," he tells his father. "I'll need some time off from here to do it, though."

So, while Sophie bounces around the marked-down bags of charcoal, Nate negotiates how many plantings he'll need and what kind (whatever Greg thinks) and how much they'll cost (whatever price Jim thinks is fair, though a bulk discount might not be asking too much).

By the time he and Sophie get back in the truck, Nate feels swindled but several pounds lighter than when they walked into the store. It might be the idea of a garden—Bridget always wanted a garden, and he tried to make one for her, before and after she died, but none of his efforts turned into anything real. Or maybe the almost-buoyant feeling is from the grin on Sophie's face, the way she holds the glass feeder to her chest as though it were a hummingbird itself. All tiny hollow bones, and wings that never settle.

Promptly at 5:00 that evening, Marshall's black GMC pulls into the driveway. Sophie, stationed at the windows in the front hallway, shouts updates as Nate sets the table. "Grampa's out of the truck! Walking past the big bush!"

"Is Nana with him?"

"Just Grampa."

When Nate extended this invitation to his in-laws a few days ago, it felt like the right thing to do. Why shouldn't they all spend time together on the anniversary of Bridget's death? And why shouldn't Nate use the awful occasion as an opportunity to see if his in-laws are ready to be grandparents to Sophie? Now, though, the whole idea seems stupid, and the significance of the date, as well as Annette's absence, adds another layer of vulnerability to an already loaded situation.

He watches from the kitchen as Sophie opens the front door, moving back to let Marshall enter the house. If it were her beloved Bampy, she'd be wrapping her arms around his waist. But hugs like that are for grandfathers you know, grandfathers who haven't ignored your existence for the past five years. She chatters happily with Marshall, however, even offering to line up his shoes beneath the coat rack before leading him into the kitchen.

Marshall, who hasn't been inside the house since just after Sophie was born, gazes around the room as if he's been dropped on an alien planet. He's wearing pressed trousers and a green Oxford, an outfit more appropriate for the parties he and Annette used to host than for a supper of baked mac and cheese. Then again, maybe Nate should have worn something nicer than jeans and a t-shirt, and he probably could have insisted Sophie wear real clothes instead of polka dot pajamas.

"Place looks good," says Marshall, nodding at the cupboards. "Those didn't even have doors last time I saw them. Dean Buckley come out and fix them up for you?"

"Did them myself."

"No kidding."

"Annette not feeling well tonight?"

"Headache." Marshall opens and closes a cupboard. "Smooth hinges. Nice."

As Nate finishes setting the table, Sophie drags her grandfather into the living room, describing the décor with the confidence of a guide in an art museum: "That's a Mumma painting, but that's by some guy named Awe-bah-don, and this is my Rafiki drawing . . . " To Nate's surprise, Marshall tells Sophie that he likes Pumba better than Timon.

"Pumba's funnier, isn't he?"

"Way, *way* funnier."

By the time they all sit down at the table, Sophie is deep into sharing her theory that Nala should have been the Lion *Queen*.

"Actually," says Marshall, "girl lions control social structure and hunting in their packs. And they're always the first to eat."

"So the movie got it wrong?"

"Movies get a lot of things wrong."

Nate feels himself relaxing as Sophie and Marshall chat about other things Disney didn't get right: Carpets can't fly, and cats, unfortunately, can't play musical instruments.

"What about mermaids, though?" says Sophie, her voice wobbling between hope and worry. "They're real, right?"

Remembering how Bridget never believed in Santa or the Easter Bunny as a kid, thanks to Annette's refusal to instill what she called *false beliefs* into her and her siblings, Nate has another flare of nervous dread. Before he can interject to soothe his daughter's fear, Marshall fixes a serious look at Sophie over his glass of ginger ale.

"What kind of question is that?" he asks. "Of course mermaids are real."

Marshall insists on helping with the dishes, drying each plate and piece of silverware carefully. He and Nate talk about yesterday's Red Sox game—won by just one point, but that's all the points you need.

When the kitchen is clean, Sophie leads them outside into the warm June night. As she runs barefoot toward the swing set, Nate and Marshall wander around the lawn, trying to guess where Greg Fortin might try to plant new flowers.

"Any idea what he'll put in?" asks Marshall.

"He mentioned some names, but damn if I know what they are."

Marshall stares up at the second story of the house—Sophie, as usual, has left her bedroom light on. "I bet Bridget would have known," he says.

It's the first time all night they've mentioned her. Nate expects to have to fight back the familiar urge to collapse under the weight of her absence. Instead, he feels an airy sense of relief at hearing her name. Across the lawn, Sophie swings higher, hurls her laughter up to the purpling sky. The sun is just starting to set, casting pink light across the fields and forest.

"Do you happen to remember," Nate asks, "what her favorite flower was?"

Marshall crouches down and grazes his palm over a patch of grass as if waiting for the earth to give him the answer. "Wish to hell I did," he says. And then, a breath later: "It was yellow, though, wasn't it?"

Gone Away

M arshall asks several times if she's sure she doesn't want to go with him to supper out at Nate's. "I really think it'd make you feel better," he says. "Get out of the house, spend some time with family."

"What family?" asks Annette, pouring a glass of wine, spilling a little on the sleeve of her bathrobe. "Our kids are nowhere to be found."

She's never seen so much disappointment on his face before.

"You're not even looking, Annie," he says. "You're not even trying to see what's right in front of you."

Get out of the house.

As if she's one of those crazy people afraid to step outside their own front door. But Marshall has no idea what he's talking about. She leaves the house plenty. Early every Monday morning, she does the grocery shopping at Bergeron's. She goes to the post office three times a week. And sometimes when she can't sleep, Annette takes long walks. She likes to wander up near the water tower and the substation. There she can feel the electricity hum in the night air, can feel the vibration beneath her sternum, the not-quite-silent whine inside her skull. In the valley below, Dalton dark and sleeping. All the people in the town floating in good dreams, or nightmares, or maybe if they're lucky no dreams at all.

After Marshall leaves, Annette settles on the sofa in front of the TV. Nothing good being sold tonight—sports memorabilia, some-assembly-required dollhouses. The house is stuffy and warm, but she doesn't like to open the windows—too many allergens floating around in the air. So when she begins to sweat, she simply starts shedding clothes. Bathrobe. T-shirt. Satin pajama bottoms. Never in her life has she sat on the couch in her underpants. She hasn't showered in a few days, and an acidic, greasy odor radiates off her skin. The woman she used to be would have been horrified. Humiliated.

But wait, there's more!

Baseball cards signed by the third baseman.

The woman she used to be wore cashmere and smelled like vanilla. She hosted parties. She donated money to animal welfare organizations, Republican campaigns, St. Mary's. She cooked *coq au vin*. She raised her children to look after themselves, mind their manners, keep their grievances to themselves. "No one likes a whiner," she'd tell the kids whenever they complained about chores or homework or rainy days. "Whiners get nowhere in this life, you mark my words."

But wait, there's more!

The dollhouse comes with top-of-the-line wood glue, for all the thousand shingles.

On the first-year anniversary, the remaining kids gathered here at the house. Marshall made lasagna and worried out loud about the decline in lumber prices. Penny and Will argued politics and war. Craig wouldn't stop talking about a plane that crashed in Thailand the week before—*two-hundred twenty-three people*, he kept saying. *Broke apart in midair.* Finally, Annette had enough. "No one wants to hear these ugly things," she said. "Can't we all just eat dinner and talk about something pleasant?" Nobody mentioned Bridget. The family never got together on any of the following anniversaries. But Marshall makes it a point to call each of the kids on the third of June, to tell them he loves them and misses them. He always offers

Annette the phone. She never takes it. If her children don't want to talk to her, she doesn't want to talk to them.

Besides, what is there to say?

Halfway through the salesman's memories of a homerun during a high school baseball game, Annette rises from the couch. She barely feels her feet on the carpet as she walks across the living room and up the sweeping staircase. She's still so damn hot; there's no air in here. She unclasps her bra and drapes it over the banister. Never in her life has she walked half naked through her own house.

One by one, she steps into the children's abandoned bedrooms, staring beyond stacks of boxes and late-night purchases into what the spaces used to be. Will's trophies, gold and silver soccer balls. All of Penny's retired pointe shoes strung across her wall. Craig's bookshelves stacked with volumes about musical theory. Successful in all the ways they wished to be, thanks to the discipline Annette taught them. The opportunities she gave them.

She wanders up to Bridget's closed door. She doesn't have to step inside to know what it looks like. Custard-colored walls, easel in front of the window, paintings everywhere. Life and color and movement caught on canvas, left behind, forgotten—all the pieces Bridget didn't bring to that wretched, drafty farmhouse out on the edge of town.

"What am I supposed to do with them?" Annette asked. "Do you think this is a storage facility?"

"Do whatever you want, Mom," said Bridget. "If they're that much of a bother to you, toss them on the lawn and burn them."

Five years ago, she called her youngest daughter for the last time. "You should get out of that house," she said. "Join the living once in a while."

Had she heard Sophie screaming in the background? Maybe.

But that's what babies do. They scream and they cry and they shit and then they scream some more. Mothers from the beginning of eternity have coped with it; there was no reason her own daughter couldn't find the strength to cope with it as well.

Hours later, the phone rang in the middle of the night. Marshall answered, half asleep. "Nate?" he mumbled into the phone. "What do you mean, gone? What are you saying?"

He dropped the receiver and turned to tell Annette. But she already knew. Something under her ribs pulsed with a kind of pain she'd never known before, as if someone had taken a serrated knife and sawed her heart into slivers.

Get out of that house, she told her daughter. *Join the living once in a while.*

She slides down the wall outside Bridget's bedroom. Never in her life has she sprawled in her underpants on a hallway floor.

Does she blame herself? Yes. Does she blame Nate? Yes. Can Sophie be blamed—not as she is now at five years old, but as she was then, an infant with colic? Sure. Does Annette blame Marshall? Maybe a little.

Does she blame this whole damn town? Might as well.

Growing up, the imagined world was Annette's for the taking. She spent her childhood dreaming about what she could do after she escaped this nowhere-town that her parents, who valued deep roots and cheap property taxes, would never abandon. The Diner and the Store 'N More and St. Mary's every Sunday morning was enough for them.

But Annette would leave. She would see New York City skyscrapers and drive Route 66 in a pink Cadillac. She would settle in California and marry a dashing tall man who made his money from something more dignified than lumber or potatoes—film, maybe, or advertising, whatever that entailed.

Then Annette accepted her kindhearted but short-statured

classmate Marshall's invitation to their Senior prom, and by the time they danced the last slow song of the night—Earth Angel—she was unexpectedly smitten. He was a good listener, and when he laughed it sounded like relief. He would be staying in this town forever just like Annette's parents, but at least he was a Frazier. They would never be without money. Three months after her twentieth birthday, they were married. Just under a year later, Will was born, and then in quick succession came Craig, Penny, and Bridget.

Soon after her twenty-fifth birthday, Annette's parents moved to Florida. Haven't been back since. Only call on Christmas, and birthdays when they remember.

Those early days of motherhood come to her in flashes: blue moonlight shining through the window as she rocked her babies, smell of formula, lukewarm bathwater on her wrists. Until all the kids were in school full-time, she had help, a rotation of nannies who drove over from Prescott every morning and then drove back after supper. Annette knew people in town disliked her for that—good mothers don't pawn their children off on strangers—but she and Marshall could afford it. And god knows she needed the break. Four children. All of them constantly needing, wanting, demanding time and energy Annette couldn't always give.

She should have hired Bridget a nanny. Not that Bridget ever would have accepted the help. That girl was so stubborn. Behind Annette's sweating spine, behind a closed door, is a whole room of stubborn. Clothes and shoes and toiletries Bridget chose not to bring with her into her married life with Nate.

"Take them with you," Annette insisted. "This house isn't a museum for your unwanted things."

"This house is nothing but a museum," her daughter said.

When Marshall gets home around seven, Annette is on the couch and dressed again, though she left her bra hanging over the banister. The TV flickers blue and white.

"Have you eaten anything, Annie?"

"Not hungry."

He sighs, then reaches for the cordless phone on the coffee table. Without thinking, she lunges forward and slaps his wrist, trying to grab it away from him.

"If I want this dollhouse with no shipping and handling, I need to call in the next five minutes."

There's shock and anger in Marshall's eyes. Then his expression changes to pure, clear pity. Gently, he pulls the phone from her grasp. "I need to call the kids," he says. "You can use it when I'm done."

He steps into the kitchen. She pours another glass of wine.

Her parents did come back for the funeral. They looked nothing like the mother and the father Annette remembered. When they hugged her, she felt like she was wrapping her arms around two stiff ghosts. They left immediately after the reception, taking a dozen deviled eggs along with them. Annette wondered if they ate them on the plane, popping them into their old dentured mouths one by one, watching the earth and the ocean roll on all those miles beneath them. A landscape she has only ever imagined.

That first day Trudy brings him home from the hospital, Richard is stunned to see she has thought of everything. The downstairs guest room is set up with a TV, radio, books from the library. Reading glasses on the nightstand. Vases of forget-me-nots on the windowsills. His favorite pajamas are in the bureau, his slippers lined up beside the bed. There's even a bell for him to ring in case he needs something and can't get it himself.

The bathroom is stocked with toilet paper and magazines; the fridge full of fruit and low-fat yogurt. Trudy prepares his meals and snacks every day, a thoughtful rotation of veggie soup, brown rice, egg-white omelets, almonds, blueberries. For the first time since she had that nasty bout of pneumonia a decade ago, she closes the library, only going in early each morning to empty the book drop and dust the shelves. Then she's right back home, puttering around upstairs or out in the garden.

Once every hour, she pops her head into the guest room to check on him. "Are you hungry? Do you want water? Should I bring you a few more John Grishams?"

For so many years, Richard has longed for this kind of attention from Trudy. Now that he has it, all he wants is to be left alone. Sleep. Watch daytime television. Draw sketches of ships that will never see the ocean. Sleep some more.

But there's Trudy, fists on her hips as she asks why he didn't finish his soup, how long it's been since his last bowel movement. There she is, scolding the cat for getting into the kitchen cupboards; cursing at telemarketers; trailing the smell of potting soil through the house; sneezing too loudly; jazzercising too enthusiastically. She's everywhere, all the time, and Richard would welcome another heart attack if it meant getting away from her.

There's a family of birds living in the forsythia underneath Richard's window. They dart in and out of the bushes, fly all around. They make a goddamn racket.

He wonders if death is quiet, if it is peaceful—not the act of dying, but what comes after.

Most of the time, he feels as if his real self—what some people might call a soul—is floating around the room while his body lies on the bed, useless as a lump of clay. He's always tired. Some of the meds make him bloated; others make him piss every twenty minutes. Walking to the bathroom leaves him gasping for breath, and everything he eats tastes beige.

One night, as Trudy snores in her bedroom upstairs, Richard finds an old movie on TV. A platinum-blonde in a clingy evening gown is in serious trouble; luckily, she knows how to handle a gun. He likes her confidence. He reaches under the waistband of his pajamas and works at it. Gives up after a quarter of an hour. He's disappointed but unsurprised. That part of him hasn't been all-the-way alive in a very long time.

But to think about the body, and whatever soul is attached to it, is to consider how it relates to other bodies, other souls. Richard recalls how things used to be with Trudy. They made love often in the early days. There was undeniable craving. Heat and electricity.

Then there was Bev.

"Do what you need to do, Richard," Trudy told him, giving him permission to step out of the marriage just as she had done. And he did, but only one time, with a pediatrician he met at a medical conference in Portland in the early 80s. The topography of a stranger's body, all those unknown curves and valleys, wasn't thrilling. The only heat was a smolder of shame and regret. That's when he knew that for him, there had to be love, or at least a familiarity, an affection, an intimacy beyond touch.

He and Trudy have never talked about whatever physical relationship she and Bev might share. Richard never wanted those details; he only ever wanted to know what would happen to his body without his wife's. Where all that unspent desire would go.

It was simple, really. If you don't fan a spark, the flame will never catch.

He used to like birds, in an abstract sort of way.

Now he fantasizes about shooting the birds outside his window with a BB gun. *Pop, pop, pop*, one by one, blasting them out of the forsythia bush.

There are constant phone calls from patients and neighbors and friends. People drop by the house with no warning; at Richard's instruction, Trudy turns them away at the front door. "Give him another week," he hears her say, her voice carrying from the kitchen to the bedroom where he lies emasculated on a pale blue quilt. *Get Well* cards clutter the desk beneath the window that looks out onto Winter Street. It's summer, all the trees full and green; kids riding bikes and chasing each other across the wooden drawbridge at the playground. There's laughter out there. Sunshine. Flowers. Joy. But every day is a Down Day.

He wonders if this is how Bridget felt before she killed

herself. So much love and life all around her, but she was sinking, sinking, sinking, deep below the ground.

One night, as he watches another old movie, Richard hears
Trudy's footsteps coming down the stairs, and then she appears
in the doorway of the guest room. She's in a white nightgown,
hair flat on one side.

She nods toward the TV. "Is that Mr. Blandings?"

"It is."

"Mind if I watch for a bit?"

Not waiting for him to answer, she settles beside him on the
bed, though she stays on top of the sheets. She smells like Ivory
soap. When she laughs, the bed trembles.

During a commercial break, she turns to face him. "Richard,"
she says, reaching out to place her hand on his. Her skin is so
warm. So alive. "I'm glad you're not dead."

Is he supposed to thank her? Agree with her? Before he can
decide, Trudy leans toward him, and Richard watches the scene
from the other side of the room—his body lying motionless on
the bed, his wife pushing her lips against his, squeezing her eyes
shut while his remain wide open. It reminds him of the time in
junior high when Eugenie Best was forced to kiss him during a
game of Spin the Bottle. No heat. No anything.

As soon as Trudy pulls away from him, Richard is back in
his own body, stuck there with her. In the TV glow, her eyes are
dark and unreadable.

"I'm not dead," he says. "But I'm not a charity case, either."

"What the hell's that supposed to mean?"

"You know exactly what it means. I've got no interest in
your pity."

She surprises him again by not saying anything—all their
lives, it's been Trudy with the last word, Trudy with the parting
remark. But she just falls silent and gets off the bed. Scoops up
the cat from the windowsill and carries him upstairs.

Beneath the sheets, every part of Richard is lifeless. Outside, the wind blows, scratching the forsythia against the window-pane.

That first week, Vera stops by the house every evening to sit beside his bed and recap whatever happened at the clinic that day. She talks about Phil Lannigan's hemorrhoids, Jo Martin's eczema, Gloria Arsenault's migraines. Within a few minutes, her voice starts to sound like white noise—crashing surf, or a river swift and steady. The first couple days, she asks for Richard's opinions on these patients, but by the middle of the week, she only seeks his signature for prescriptions.

Friday, she spends extra time talking about the Vietnam bullet that's finally worked itself out from George Nadeau's bone and muscle and sinew to brush up against the surface of his thigh. She talks about the pain George has had all these years, not just in his leg where the bullet buried itself, but every-where—hips and spine and shoulders, nothing aligning where it should. All that pain from one small piece of lead.

"Hell of a thing," says Vera, "what a little bit of trauma can do to a body."

T rudy returns to work a week after Richard comes home from the hospital. If he's going to be ungrateful for all that she's done for him—the cooking, the cleaning, the pretending he doesn't stink like an old man—then she's going to let him wallow all alone in that house. It's summer, the library's busiest season, and the people of Dalton need their books. And Trudy needs her sanctuary.

As soon as she enters the little brick building, she feels calmer, and the nerves that have been churning in her stomach since Richard's heart attack finally start to settle. The guilt's still there (*Go and free us both*), but it's softer now, stifled enough that Trudy can get on with all the things that need to be done before patrons begin to arrive. Emptying the book drops. Organizing the card catalog. Turning the date stamps from May to June.

Ten minutes before she opens the library, the phone rings; even before she answers, she knows it will be Bevy, calling from the Store 'N More.

"Jo's going to fire you if you keep making these personal calls."

"She'd never get rid of me. I'm the only one whose arms are long enough to clean the back of the pizza oven."

Trudy grins against the mouthpiece. Crazy, how just a few words spoken in that warm, familiar voice can make her feel as though the world has slowed its mad spinning.

"So," says Bev, "back at work, then?"

"Obviously."

"Just for the day, or for good?"

An image of Richard lying in front of that damn television flickers through Trudy's mind. *Withered.* The man is withered and bitter as a rotting apple.

"For good."

"Listen—oh shit, hang on a sec," says Bev, and Trudy hears her set the phone down while she takes someone's order for a BLT. Heavy on the B.

As soon as she comes back on the line, Trudy asks, "Who in the hell's ordering lunch at this time in the morning?"

"Dean Buckley."

"It's not even ten o'clock, for Chrissake."

"Well damnit, Tru, the man's been up since four."

In the parking lot outside the library, a silver minivan pulls up, and Trudy watches through the window as Molly Lannigan and her three youngest kids pile out of it. Jesus, that's a lot of blonde hair. Nearly blinding under the summer sun.

"I've got to open things up here, Bevy."

"I know. But listen, you want to pop by for a visit tonight? I've got a bottle of coffee brandy with our names on it."

Bev's house is another kind of sanctuary, particularly her kitchen. The Moosehead table, the yellow tiles . . . how many hours have they spent there together, drinking and gossiping about all the other people in town? The room always feels sunny, even on cloudy days.

Trudy is about to say yes, she'll go over just as soon as she closes the library at 4:00. But then another image of Richard floats to her mind, this time of the disgusted look on his face the other night when, in a surge of confused guilt and affection, she had tried to kiss him and he had turned away. Denied her.

"I don't want your pity," he said. But something in his eyes or in his voice told her she sure as hell owed him something.

"Maybe tomorrow," she tells Bev. "Maybe I'll swing by to see you tomorrow."

A few hours later, Trudy watches from the circulation desk as a strange scene unfolds in the children's corner of the library between one of the Bergeron boys (she can never keep them straight, but this one has an overbite) and two of his female friends. The kids, all around seven or eight years old, are preparing for an epic journey, readying their boat for whatever they might meet on the high seas.

No surprise, the boy has appointed himself captain. He proclaims the trip will take twelve years, maybe nine if the weather's good. Megan Cyr assures the others she has packed enough provisions for their adventure, including a sandwich bag filled with graham crackers and two handfuls of Hershey kisses. Ashley Wilkins offers to act as lookout, patrolling for sharks, pirates, and mermaids.

"The ocean's rough today, ladies, so be careful." The boy walks the perimeter of the green area rug, newly christened the S.S. Potato Boat. He turns an about-face when he reaches the edge, careful not to place his feet on the worn blue carpet of his imaginary ocean. "If you fall in, I ain't coming back for you."

"But that's not fair," whines Megan. Her brown eyes swim with the same terror Trudy is sure floods in after nightmares of monsters under her bed. "You're s'posed to take care of us. That's what good captains do."

"Don't worry," Ashley says, tucking her hair behind her ears. "If you fall in, I'll jump in after you. I'm a real good swimmer."

The boy stands tall at the prow of his imaginary ship and sets his eyes on a horizon past the card catalog, which glows like spilled gold in the midday sun.

"No stops until Arctanica!"

The girls take their places beside him, tentative grins on their faces. "Arctanica," they cry. "Arctanica!"

Trudy wonders if she should tell them boys rarely have a reliable sense of direction. But they're young. No need to wreck their illusions just yet.

After supper—more damn chicken, more steamed vegetables—she sits alone on the front porch. The warm evening air smells slightly decayed, thanks to the viburnum bush on its way out, all the tiny white flowers shriveled and brown at the edges. Chimney swifts dart from oak to maple, chirping as they go.

"Nice night for porch-sitting."

Trudy pulls her eyes from the birds to see Vera walking up the driveway. She's wearing a white blouse with a flowy skirt the color of lupines. Miles better than that Pepto Bismol disaster she wore to the wedding.

"Mind if I join you?"

"It's a free country. Or so they'd like us to believe."

Vera settles on the porch swing beside Trudy and kicks off her sandals before resting her feet on the porch railing. Her bare calves are shiny in the sunset light. She smells like the clinic, vaguely antiseptic.

"So how's the new job so far?" Trudy asks.

"It's going well." Vera hesitates. "I mean, I think it is. Have you heard different?"

Usually, Trudy would tell her to get a grip; she's a grown woman who doesn't need anyone else's approval. But she's grateful for Vera—not a lot of people would agree to take on an entire town's medical problems with no warning. And she has sympathy for Vera, too, because it can't be easy to earn professional respect from the grade-school teachers who taught you how to tie your shoes.

"Haven't heard any complaints," says Trudy. "Though I doubt anyone around here would be stupid enough to bring them to me in the first place."

"Fair enough."

As the sun sets, casting long purple shadows across the lawn, they watch finches making their last trips to the feeders before calling it a night. There are nests hidden in all sorts of nooks and crannies around the yard and the garden. Lots of good places to make a safe home.

"How's our patient?" Vera asks.

Trudy thinks back to supper, how Richard refused to eat more than a few mouthfuls of broccoli. How he clenched his jaw when she asked if he'd rather have boiled carrots and then got up from the table and harrumphed his way back into the guest room, slamming the door behind him.

Some wives wouldn't reveal their husband's delicate mental state, especially in this town where the term *depressed* is considered more problematic than a racial slur. But Trudy isn't just some wife, and she's not afraid of any word, no matter how ugly.

"He's in a fester," she says. "Moping around, feeling sorry for himself."

"Yeah, a heart attack can have that effect on people." Vera pauses, watching sparrows splash in the bird bath. "Especially men. But he needs to get outside, Trudy. He should be getting fresh air and exercise. A walk around the yard, or up and down the street."

"I keep telling him that, and he keeps telling me he needs more time to heal."

Now Vera turns to face Trudy. "If he doesn't get out of this house soon," she says, "he's going to end up so far gone no one will be able to help him."

Trudy thinks of Bridget Frazier, the shock of her death. How sudden it was, and how final.

The look on Richard's face when Trudy tried to show him that she still cares for him despite everything—the secrets, the unspoken strain of this long, false marriage. That look, and Richard's refusal of her kiss, made it clear he doesn't want anything to do with her. Chrissake, the humiliation of being turned down by one's own husband . . .

But he needs something from Trudy, even if he'll never admit it. And after all she's put him through over the years, at the very least, she owes him an honest attempt at rescue. Or at least the chance for him to rescue himself.

"I'll find a way to get him outside," she promises Vera. "Even if I have to drag him out by what's left of his hair."

S ummer is always a little different in the store. There's still Bev's quiet alone-time, followed by the burst of blue-collar regulars. But the teenagers come in later, many of them with sleep-mussed hair and breath that smells like last night's party out at the gravel pit. Stay-at-home mothers come in with kids to pick up gallons of milk and candy bars they insist will *not* be eaten for breakfast.

And sometimes tourists stop in during the summer, too, though not so many as in fall or winter, when out-of-state hunters and snowmobilers drive through town on their way into the woods. They come in with breathless stories about spotting moose on the side of Route 11, and they're usually dressed in new L.L. Bean jackets and boots that cost more than most people in Dalton earn in an entire week. They make a lot of jokes about lobster, missing the point that the County is hours north of the ocean.

Bev doesn't mind the tourists, though. She likes showing them how to scoop live bait out of the cooler and assuring them there are no wolves or grizzlies in the North Maine Woods. She knows some of these strangers view her as some backwoods specimen, a thing to either be admired or pitied, but that's their problem, not hers. For her part, Bev loves to hear where they've come from, to try to imagine places she doesn't have any interest in seeing for herself—New York and New Jersey, Boston and Philly. This past fall, a group of hunters came up all the way from Mississippi, and she loved hearing their thick Southern accents, the way they made one-syllable words sound like entire sentences.

One morning in June, as Bev wipes down the deli counter during a lull, she hears the bell over the front door open and looks up to see an unfamiliar family walking into the store. The father heads for the Delorme display as identical twin boys run toward the soda coolers. The mother, dressed in overalls and a floral shirt, trudges toward the deli. She has flitting blue eyes, hair that's trying hard to be blonde.

"Do you make fresh sandwiches?" she asks in a voice that could belong to a twelve-year-old girl.

Bev forces herself to smile, even though she has the strange, sudden urge to bolt from the counter and hide in the bathroom. "We can make whatever you like," she says. "What're you thinking?"

The woman squints up at the menu posted on the back wall. She lets out a big sigh, as though everything in the world, including this menu, has never done anything but let her down. In the back of the store, her kids are bickering over who should get the last Sprite—Matt won rock-paper-scissors, but Evan is three minutes older, and that trumps the rules of any stupid game.

"We'll just have four ham Italians, I guess. One with no olives, two with extra pickles, and one without oil."

"You got it."

The woman wanders toward her husband, who shakes the book of maps at her as if to say he has enough to deal with; she can police the boys, who are now throwing boxes of maxi pads at each other.

As Bev assembles the sandwiches with shaking hands, she wonders what's wrong with her. She sees iterations of this same family over and over again, tired parents desperate to get their kids away from TV and into the woods for the summer. What is it about this family—this mother—that makes her feel as if she's breathing out of a dirt-filled straw?

Jo returns through the loading dock door, reeking of cigarettes from her twenty-minute smoke break. "Take these,"
says Bev, pushing the wrapped sandwiches into her hands, then
bolts outside with no further explanation.

The air is muggy and still, the sky a sickly shade of white-
blue. Beneath her shirt, sweat rolls down Bev's spine. She paces
the loading dock, desperately craving a Virginia Slim, until she
sees the family walk out of the front of the store, headed toward
a minivan with Connecticut plates parked near the gas pumps.
The kids are still fighting, and the dad yells for them to shut
up. After the rest of them have gotten into the van, the mother
stands outside, staring back toward Route 11. Then she gets in
the passenger seat, slams the door closed, and the van heads
north on Main.

Bev leans against the building with her hand pressed on her
clavicle until her breath comes easier. It's a trick the Prescott
shrink taught her. *When you're panicked, just stand still and
breathe, breathe, breathe.* It takes nearly ten minutes of breathing for her nerves to settle enough to go back inside, where Jo is
waiting for her near the Slush-Puppie machines.

"Everything okay?"

"You know how it is. Hot flash, that's all."

"Sure," says Jo, but she watches Bev carefully for the rest of
her shift.

It's not until she's driving home, imagining that family tooling around the County with no sense of how to read their new
maps, that Bev realizes the woman reminded her of Bridget.

She thinks back to that night five years ago when everything
shattered. The call from Nate in the dark hours when everyone
in Dalton was sleeping, unaware of the life that had just ended
on the edge of town. Her and Bill's numb, blind drive out to the
farmhouse, and the hoarse cries ripping from Sophie's throat,
and the smell of metal that clung to Nate's hands, hands that
had tried and failed to resurrect the only woman he'd ever

loved. He stained his DPD jacket with bloody bathwater, and Bev took it upon herself to sneak it out of the house before the funeral, to have Chief Halstead exchange it for a new one, which she snuck back into Nate's closet soon after. She's never had the heart to tell Nate about that—he didn't seem to realize in the moment how ruined the jacket was, how irreparable it would end up being.

For a long time, Bev was too angry at Bridget to miss her. Angry that it had fallen on her to watch Sophie, to deal with the colic that had driven Bridget to the brink. Angry that it was her burden to witness Nate collapse inside himself. Angry that she couldn't work, couldn't see Trudy, couldn't sit out on her back deck with a beer to watch the sun sink behind the trees on summer nights without a worry in the world.

Easier to rage about the life Bev had lost than to grieve the life that had ended alone inside that bathtub.

It wasn't until after Nate took the job at the mill and started to pull himself together that Bev's anger fizzled away, evolving into a mix of regret, pain, and disbelief. She'd loved Bridget for as long as Nate had, since the first day he brought her over to the house when they were in second grade and Bev spent a laughing afternoon teaching them how to play Crazy Eights. It wasn't long before she considered Bridget the daughter she and Bill never had. And Bill felt the same way, beaming with pride whenever the girl presented him with another crooked drawing of his 18-wheeler.

Bev drives past the parking lot of the Advent church, waving to Pastor Fields as he mows the rectory lawn. The air is sharp and green, the sun nearly up to the center of the sky. She isn't sure if she believes in heaven, though she's not quite as opposed to the idea as Trudy is. But Bev is certain Bridget isn't flying around up there in some celestial realm with the angels, as so many people in town said at the funeral and still say now. She's also sure that if angels do exist, they were never once human.

Her daughter-in law was as human as they come. Much as Bev loved her, she recognized the tiny cracks that later became wide fault lines. Bridget was over-sensitive and moody, though she always tried to pretend that wasn't the case. She was smart and talented, but she would be devastated if she got a C on a geometry test or couldn't paint a landscape the way she thought it should be painted. She feared failure the way other people feared heights or deep water, and Bev blamed Annette for that. There was nothing warm or loving in the way that woman mothered Bridget and her siblings.

At the intersection of Russell Street, Bev pauses to let Mellie Martin speed through the yield sign in her VW Beetle. As she waits, she thinks again of the woman at the store. What about her reminded her of Bridget? There was no physical likeness, no echoes of Bridget in her childish voice.

As Bev pulls into the driveway, she sees Sophie waving a yellow plastic bat under the birch trees. Bill stands a few feet away, preparing to lob a ball in her direction. Bev can tell by the way he's standing, slightly stooped, that his back is killing him. But he grins at Sophie, and he laughs as she swings the bat and misses the ball but starts sprinting, anyway.

"Home run, home run!" she shouts, face bright, curly hair bouncing with each step over the grass.

All these tiny perfect moments. All these pieces of Sophie that Bridget will never witness, all the life she decided she didn't have the right to anymore.

That's when Bev understands. The woman in the store didn't resemble Bridget, but she sure as hell *felt* like her—the lightless eyes, that air of disappointment that hovered around her like a foul odor. Bridget carried around that exact same air after Sophie was born. And Bev had noticed it then, but she didn't have a name for it, or maybe she didn't want to find a name for it. Maybe she thought naming it would give it too much power. So she chose to ignore it, until it was too late.

"Hopeless," says Trudy when Bev calls her that night. "This diet I've got Richard on is hopeless. I'm goddamned tired of steamed vegetables."

Bev stares out the window at the setting sun, the light brushing the tops of the trees. She's thirsty, or maybe she's hungry, or maybe she just needs to take a scalding hot shower. Wash the grief away.

"If I see one more piece of broccoli . . . "

"Tru."

"What? *What*, Bevy?"

She could spill the whole story. Tell Trudy about the boys tossing maxi pads and the dad looking in the wrong section of the Delorme and the mother who ordered four sandwiches as if she was preparing for her last meal. She could tell Trudy how impossible it sometimes feels just to keep breathing. How much she misses her daughter-in-law. How much she misses everything, all the ways their lives were so much easier before Bridget died.

"Try cauliflower," Bev suggests. "I've always liked it better than broccoli."

Known Topographies

O n the last stretch of road before she returns to her parents' house, Vera takes her sandals off to feel warm ribbons of tar on the pavement squish beneath her toes, just as she used to do as a kid. The sun, tucked halfway behind the distant hills, lights the air bronze. The air smells of flowers and soil. A few cars and pickups pass her as she walks, trailing Garth Brooks, Ace of Base, Nirvana. Moments like this, Dalton feels far preferable to Bangor's seemingly constant stream of traffic and wail of sirens.

When she left the house earlier to take a walk, Vera's parents promised they'd stay on the couch watching the news until she got back. But as she steps into the kitchen, she's smacked in the face with a haze of smoke. Her father stands on a chair waving a dishtowel at the smoke detector while her mother stands at the stove trying to balance on her crutches as she tosses burnt bacon onto a grease-splotched paper towel.

"What the hell happened?" Vera shouts over the incessant beeping.

Her mother lays four pieces of fresh bacon in the skillet. "Nothing to worry about, dear."

With a final wave of the dishcloth, the alarm falls silent, and Vera's father steps off the chair, dragging it toward the table. "No harm done," he says, then sits down and takes a drink of his Bud Light.

Vera rushes around the room, opening all the windows to let the smoke roll outside. "You guys could've burned the house down."

"Really, there's no need to be dramatic."

"You shouldn't even be cooking, Mom."

"Your father was craving bacon cheeseburgers."

"So wait for me, or make him cook. You have a broken leg."

"Exactly—a leg. Not an arm. I can still use both of those."

Vera feels more exhausted than she ever has at the end of a twelve-hour ER shift. What will she have to say or do to make them take anything seriously?

She drops down into the same chair at the table she sat in all during her childhood and adolescence. Every family dinner, every birthday, every angsty teenage morning—the view from this chair never changed. Golden Harvest stove and refrigerator, brown linoleum, giant wooden spoon and fork hanging on the wall.

Her mother turns off the burner and hobbles over to the counter, where she begins assembling burgers, layering bacon over beef. "Who wants mayo and who wants ketchup and mustard?"

"You seriously can't get her to stop, Dad?"

"She's an independent woman, Vera."

"She's damn stubborn, is what she is."

"This broken leg hasn't turned me deaf, you know. And just for that, I'm giving you extra bacon."

Vera's father lets out a snort of laughter as his glance flicks between her and her mother. "So which of you's the kettle," he asks, "and which of you wants to be the pot?"

That night, she dreams of the apartment she once shared with Gavin. The rooms are bigger and brighter than they were in real life, filled with lemon-scented sunshine. Vera walks each room trying to find her anatomy textbook—she can't remember which direction the blood flows in a normal heart, and she's furious with herself for forgetting. If she could only find the book, she could find the answer, and the anger would vanish. But the longer she looks, the bigger and brighter the rooms get, until she is standing inside a blinding, endless cavern, sur-rounded by nothing but silence.

When she wakes the next morning, Vera lies in her child-hood bed for several minutes trying to envision the heart, its arteries and atriums, but all she can bring to mind is a vague outline of a diagram she's looked at thousands of times. Blue for the blood that flows in one direction, red for the blood that goes elsewhere. But which is which? How could she forget something so fundamental?

Suddenly the thin sheet on top of her feels like the lead aprons used for x-rays. She gets out of bed, dresses hastily, pulls her hair into a ponytail. Doesn't bother with jewelry or makeup, or with any kind of breakfast—if she leaves the house now, she can get out before her parents wake up.

She makes the quick drive to the clinic, down the hill, past the high school and the soccer fields, damp with dew that glim-mers in the first light of morning. She passes no other cars, but she does see Greg Fortin running down the shoulder of Howard Street—he lifts his hand in a wave as she makes a wide, slow swerve around him.

At the clinic, Vera heads straight for Dr. Haskell's office. The yellowed skeleton greets her, one hand lifted in an impersonal wave. She steps to the bookcase, scanning the shelves until she finds the volume she's looking for, the same thick textbook she used to pore over before her nursing exams.

Her dream is still so close, and she fears she won't be able to find the answer—but to her relief, her hands land on the right chapter almost immediately, and she stares down at the familiar diagram.

As soon as she sees the two-dimensional heart laid out on the page, Vera remembers all its parts and functions. Blue for the blood that moves from the pulmonary to the lungs; red for the blood carried out to the body. Atria, valves, ventricles, all in harmony. Constant in-flow, out-flow, steady rhythm.

In the corner, the skeleton mocks her with his toothy smile. He had a heart once, too. Where is it now? Burned a long time ago, probably. Or preserved in a jar only to one day be brought back out, laid on a table, and dissected by students just like Vera, who need to see inside a thing before they can understand how that thing works.

Forget the soul, forget romantic metaphors. The heart is a muscle inside your chest powered by electricity and blood. Only when it stops beating, only when you cut it open, can you appreciate how simple the function, how elegant the design.

All the panic of the dream is gone, and Vera feels a twinge of shame that she allowed herself to worry in the first place. She returns the textbook to the shelf. Eats the apple and the yogurt she left in the office's mini fridge. Is there in the front lobby to open the doors for Rose when she pulls in at quarter to eight. Unlike Janine, that girl is always punctual.

The ER could be so demanding, so physically and mentally exhausting—hours on her feet without a break to eat or pee or think; beeping monitors, blood-stained floors, combative drunks, family members reeling from the grief of a loved one's sudden death. In her twenties and early thirties, Vera more than thrived on that chaos; she craved it, needed it. What was the point of life if she wasn't constantly moving?

Growing up, she equated Dalton and the County with claustrophobia, inertia. The only thing that ever changed was the weather, and even that followed a regular pattern—five months of good sun, six months of snow, and one month buried under mud. Potatoes were planted, reaped, sold. Trees were felled, sawn, sold. The geese flew north, the geese flew south; the people stayed where they were. Vera swore to herself she would never be one of them—better to die, she always thought, than become a townie.

But as she closes in on the end of her second week at the clinic, she feels something inside her shifting slightly, like clouds pulling closer to the sun. Thanks to the schedule Dr. Haskell established for himself long ago, Vera's days follow a steady, workable pattern: five or six patients in the morning, an hour for lunch and paperwork, then four or five more patients in the afternoon, plus an additional hour for charting, processing prescription requests, and all the other necessary administrative details. Just a few years ago, this routine would have felt tedious; now, Vera finds it reassuring. She's always home in time for supper (whether her mother will let her cook is another matter). She and her parents watch *Wheel of Fortune* and *Jeopardy*, programs she once considered lame and now takes a secret delight in, especially when she gets a word or answer before her mother. Sometimes she helps her father with his jigsaw puzzles, another hobby she never wished to take on for herself but that feels strangely satisfying, fitting all those pieces into their perfect places.

Even the part of the job at the clinic that initially gave Vera the most anxiety—treating people who watched her grow up or who grew up alongside her—hasn't been as bad as she feared. There have been a few old teachers who treat her like a ten-year-old acting the role of a nurse in a grade school play, and a couple catty mothers Vera went to school with. For the most part, though, the people of Dalton seem to accept her as their temporary caretaker. To be sure, she's no Dr. Haskell—every patient or patient's parent asks how much longer it'll be before he comes back at work—but Vera hasn't yet sensed any outright animosity.

"It's like they're taking me seriously," she tells her parents one night. "Trusting whatever I have to tell them."

"What'd you expect?" her father asks, the television reflecting off his bifocals. "Rioting villagers?"

Vera, who can't imagine anyone in Dalton having the energy to organize any sort of rebellion, shakes her head as she watches Alex Trebek give a pitying stare to a baby-faced man who buzzed in only to draw a blank.

"More of a passive aggressive protest," she says. "Jumping ship at the clinic and going over to the Prescott doctors instead."

"Who the hell wants to drive all the way to Prescott for a tube of hemorrhoid cream?"

"Jerry."

"It's not crude if it's true, Gretchen."

In the recliner, Vera's mother sighs. "Dad's right, though, dear. No one's going to go out of town when they can get what they need right here."

Not so long ago, that statement would have proven Vera's theory that the people of Dalton would rather stay somewhere with limited resources—she doesn't even have a lab at the clinic—than take a chance on something new, somewhere less familiar. But there's comfort and pride in knowing that she is the one they choose. Sure, she has to send out their bloodwork to the lab at the hospital, and sure, she has to refer more serious cases to doctors in Prescott or even Bangor. But she can remove splinters, recommend exercise and better diets, order medication refills. She can give the people of Dalton enough of what they need. Heal them enough to carry them through another boring, same-old day.

"You should know this one, dear," says her mother, squinting at the TV.

Vera turns her attention to the clue on the screen. *This is the measurement of the amount of blood your heart pumps each time it beats.* She sees the blue and red diagram in Dr. Haskell's anatomy book. The blood that flows out of the ventricles, the blood that leaves the heart with each squeeze.

"Ejection fraction," she says. One second later, Baby Face gets it right, too, and Alex beams at him like a bespectacled, silver-haired god, offering redemption.

BLOSSOM

G reg has driven past Nate's place on Davis Road countless times, always thinking what a waste it is that so
many acres go unplanted, unused. The farmhouse
itself is nice—blue shutters, wraparound porch—but other
than a few anemic-looking rhododendrons and lilacs, there's
no landscaping to speak of. The grass is dying to grow high
and wild, but Nate's an old-school guy; he probably thinks he
should mow at least once a week.

Greg unloads the flowers from the bed of his father's
pickup. His father didn't have a great selection at the hardware store, so Greg drove all the way out to a greenhouse in
Prescott, gleefully charging the store's business card for all
sorts of new life. Bee balm, columbine, butterfly weed. Red
impatiens, pink petunias. Begonia, iris, bleeding heart. All of
it waiting to either take root underground or in the hanging
baskets he brought to place around the yard. The rain from
the past couple days has left a sweetness in the air, and puffy
clouds float through a cobalt sky.

It takes a long time to figure out where everything should
go, weighing up what needs sun and what needs shade, which
colors will look best together, ease of access for watering and
weeding. Once he's mapped out in a sketchpad where all the
new flowers belong, Greg begins to clear out the few plots
where someone with no idea what they were doing, maybe Nate
or Bridget, tried to plant other things. Daffodil bulbs mashed
up against tulips; scraggly roots of daylilies duking it out with

gladioli. If Trudy saw this mess, she'd have a heart attack just like her husband.

Greg loves the rhythm of this work, carefully dividing root systems, placing them in a bucket of water in the shade until he's ready to plant them elsewhere. He loves the smell of dirt, the wriggle of earthworms against his fingers, the sound of his trowel scraping off buried rocks. He loves the ache in his shoulders, and the sweat that slides down his spine.

It doesn't take long until his thoughts begin to float free as the passing clouds. He thinks of the last name Theroux, wondering which long-ago citizen of Dalton decided to do away with the proper pronunciation (*The-roo*) and make the name sound instead like it belonged with Henry David Thoreau, who once traveled all over Maine in search of some mythic wilderness. Then Greg thinks of a book he stumbled across on a shelf in Fogler last winter, a thin volume of Thoreau's observations of the plants and wildflowers he found around Concord—bluet, shadbush, trillium, hundreds more. Greg remembers one line in particular: *Whorled utricularia very abundantly out, apparently in its prime.* That sentence has stuck with him all these months, like poetry, or lyrics to a favorite song.

As he begins to plant the new flowers, his mind skips back to all the hours he and David spent sharing joints in Cumberland Hall Room 219 while listening to David's endless collection of mixed tapes. All the songs Greg had grown up hearing on the radio in Dalton were country, classic rock, or pop bullshit that made him want to rip his ears off his head. David's tapes were filled with everything great and unfamiliar, from smooth sliding jazz to driving angry grunge, which he swore was being played everywhere other than Aroostook County. Greg figured David would know—he grew up near Boston, an entirely different world with three-lane highways and stores open past dark.

Before he got to college, Greg had been petrified of sharing a dorm room with a stranger. He worried that he'd be paired up with some John-Stamos lookalike, that he'd pop a boner one day while the poor guy was changing. Thankfully, though, Greg never felt a physical attraction to David, never had anything even close to a crush on him—he cared too much about his pecs, and he had a nasty habit of leaving toenail clippings strewn across the floor. But there are worse things in a roommate, so Greg was happy when David suggested they rent a two-bedroom together in Orono for sophomore year. Good to have a solid living situation lined up, better yet to have the assurance of not developing a crush toward the guy he'd be living with.

Greg hasn't had a serious crush on anyone since high school, when he liked Angela Muse and Henry Covington at the same time. Talk about a shit-show. And what made it even more confusing was the couple's dramatic on-again, off-again relationship, and the fact that Greg was friends with them both. He acted as their reluctant mediator all the way through eleventh grade, when Angela left Dalton to live with her father down on Indian Island.

As Greg hangs the petunias on shepherd's hooks in front of Nate's porch, he thinks back to how miserable he felt during those in-between years. How he used to stuff his face with junk food in an attempt to ignore his fantasies of kissing Henry and Angela. These days his imaginings are vaguer and less specific—the girl from English Comp, the dark-haired guy at that Hilltop party—but his fantasies are still heavy with the weight of shame and fear.

Unlike in high school, Greg now knows there's a word for people like him, an actual definition beyond *faggot* or *fucking homo*. He also knows there's a specific hatred reserved for people like him, a silent simmering kind that often erupts in violence, or worse. Just look at the gay man who was thrown by a bunch of asshole teenagers off that bridge into the Kenduskeag.

That guy drowned eleven years ago, but all that intolerance still lives on today—and now it's accompanied by AIDS jokes.

Focus on the flowers. The burst of color against the over-manicured lawn. The sensation of cool breeze on hot, damp skin. Smell of soil, sound of chickadees. All of it nearly as effective as a half-dozen Kit-Kats, or a sprint down an empty road.

After a while, Greg stands, stretching his spine, and steps back to assess his progress. The yard looks better, no doubt, but so much of it is still so empty, begging for attention. Things need weeding, trimming, edging—and if someone doesn't do something about the lupine patch soon, the bastards will take over the entire lawn.

Just as he starts to pack up his tools and bags of potting soil, Greg sees a ruby-throated hummingbird dart toward a hanging basket of petunias. The bird hovers there, beak thrust into the flower to lap up the nectar. Wings so fast they're barely even a blur.

He checks his watch—nearly four-thirty. He's already been here longer than he told his father he would be; not much harm in lingering a few more minutes. Soon, Nate will be home from work, and he'll have Sophie with him, and Greg can show off all he has done here. Tell her about the hummingbird. The way all that new color brought it down from the trees, just as he promised it would.

He's sitting on the front porch when Nate pulls into the driveway, tires of his truck popping against the dirt. As soon as he kills the engine, the passenger door opens, and Sophie hops out, runs toward the house with her tiny arms held open.

"Flowers!" she shouts, reminding Greg of his little sister. He used to get such a kick out of Aimee when she was that age, how she'd get so excited over things like heart-shaped rocks or mud puddles deep enough to jump in.

Nate steps down from the truck, lunchbox in one hand and Thermos in the other. He stands still for several moments, blinking at all the unfamiliar flowers like Dorothy when she's dropped in Oz and everything turns to color.

"How many?" Sophie asks Greg.

"What do you think?"

She surveys the yard with a serious expression. "Sixteen."

It was eighteen, but he knows better than to argue with a five-year-old.

While she flits from flower to flower, Nate joins Greg on the porch, sitting beside him on the top step. He smells like sweat and sawdust and looks dazed as he asks, "You did all this in just one afternoon?"

"It's no big deal. I mean, you've got a huge yard. I'd love to do way more."

"Like what?"

"Roses and peonies would be nice," says Greg. "Shrubbery would be good, too—maybe forsythia or spirea. More lilacs. And no offense, but your rhododendrons are some of the saddest things I've ever seen."

Nate gazes at Sophie as she stoops to sniff each flower. "She always wanted a garden," he mumbles. Then he shakes his head as if warding off a blackfly and looks at Greg. "I'll give you free rein—plant whatever you want wherever you think it'll grow best. I can't pay a lot, but I'm sure we could work out a fair deal."

With Trudy, Greg has only ever maintained a garden already in existence. He's never had the chance to design his own land-scape with curves and lines and colors of his own choosing. But he's here for the summer to work at his father's store, not play in the dirt. And even though he's managed to find a few hours over the past couple weeks to weed Trudy's garden, there's no way his dad would give him the time off necessary for a project this size.

"I want to," he says, "but my parents . . . "

Nate considers this for a few moments. "I could talk to your folks," he says. "Find some way to convince them."

Greg knows they're both thinking about that winter day five years ago when Nate pulled him from the icy river. That was a whole other shit show—waddling over the ice to help Angela after she fell into the water, then getting stuck out there himself, like a frozen, beached whale. If Nate hadn't been at the river that day, Greg might be dead. Or so his mother says. She's basically built a shrine to Nate since then—no way she'd let his father turn the guy down if he asked for this one small favor. The move seems kind of ballsy for Nate, though, who's always struck Greg as a hopeless rule follower.

"Are you sure? That won't violate some kind of ethic code for you?"

Nate, almost smiling, keeps his eyes on Sophie, now absorbed by a white moth fluttering around the butterfly bush. "She really, *really* wants a garden."

Later that night, as Greg and Aimee wash and dry the dishes, the phone rings. Greg's mother answers in the living room; through the wall, he hears her tell his father to mute the TV. He pauses with his hands in the hot water, trying to hear their words. Beside him, his sister, dressed in yet another baggy flannel shirt, lets out a theatric sigh.

"Keep it moving, loser. Some of us have other places to be."

"You used to be such a sweet kid."

"Bite me."

A minute later, his parents appear in the doorway of the kitchen. His mother is smiling, but there's a look of deep disappointment on his father's face that makes Greg feel as though he's done something terrible, like stealing an old lady's money or running over the neighbor's one-eyed cat.

"Gregory," his mother says. "How would you like a second job this summer?"

Over the next couple weeks, the land around Nate's house transforms from a boring swath of grass to a carefully orchestrated explosion of color and texture. Purples and reds and pinks; foamy blossoms alongside sturdy foliage; dense shrubs shading delicate groundcover. One day, he and Sophie come home to find a curving edge of white stones around the freshly pruned lilacs; another, the bird bath is surrounded by tall grass and orange flowers, and there are lush green ferns hanging from the porch eaves. New scents float on the breeze—lavender and peony; catmint and rose.

Is this what the place could have been like all these years? Is this the vision Bridget had when they bought the house right after they got married? Nate has a sense that she and Greg would have gotten along well, that the two of them could have talked color theory or design or whatever it is artists talk about for hours. And that's exactly how Nate thinks of Greg—as an artist. Who else could have seen this sad plot of land and known how to bring it to life? He's amazed by how much Greg has managed to accomplish in just a few hours each afternoon; the amount of change that's happened in so short a time.

"I'm not paying you enough," he says one afternoon as he and Greg stand admiring the new patch of hostas tucked up beside the front porch.

"Honestly, I'd do this for free."

Bridget used to say the same thing about her paintings. People around town bought her landscapes at modest prices, and she sold a couple pieces to the university over in Prescott for a more-than-generous commission. But most of the time, Bridget gave away her work for free, saying no amount of money was worth more than seeing someone light up when they recognized their own potato fields, or their favorite stretch of river. Nate often wonders how many houses in Dalton have Bridget's paintings displayed on walls beside stuffed deer heads and pictures of their own kids.

Imagine if all the backyards in Dalton were filled with Greg's flowers. Much as Nate likes Jim Fortin, he can't help but feel the man is wasting this kid in a hardware store. Selling tools is one thing; creating a garden like this—so much color, so much life under the sun—is something else entirely. Not as conventional, maybe. Not as steady or predictable. But maybe just as necessary.

Every night after supper, Nate and Sophie amble around the yard, admiring all the new things. "What's that one, Daddy?" she often asks, pointing at flowers whose names he can't remember. The rare times he can tell her what something is—yarrow, somehow he knows yarrow—and she gives him that wide grin, Nate feels as though his body is filled with helium, that he could lift up and float high above all the bright color, all the known world.

Fridays are Nate's one day off during the week, and he always uses the time with Sophie doing pretty much anything she wants—river walks, swims at the lake, endless games of Candy Land. Sometimes, though, there are less fun, more necessary things to attend to, errands that can't be run during the weekend—trips to the bank or post office, oil changes for the truck. Doctor appointments.

"Do we really have to?" asks Sophie one Friday morning in mid-June.

"We really do," says Nate, stacking dirty dishes beside the sink. "You want to go to kindergarten in the fall, don't you?"

"I guess."

"Then you need booster shots. And a checkup to make sure you're strong and healthy."

Sophie pushes away from the table and stands in the middle of the kitchen, curling up her arms to show off her tiny biceps. "But look, see? Strong and healthy."

Trying not to laugh at the sight of his daughter flexing in her bright pink nightgown, Nate says, "You're right. But guess what? You get to see someone new at the clinic today—a *lady* doctor."

"Where's Dr. Haskell?"

"He's been feeling sick, so he's taking a little vacation."

"Is he going to die like Mumma?"

Has Nate done this to her? The half-truths about her mother's death, the annual visits to Bridget's grave . . . Has he given Sophie the fear that anyone around her could die at any moment?

"Dr. Haskell is going to be just fine," he says.

Sophie squints at him, tilts her head. Nate gazes back, eyes wide open, until she nods. She returns to the table, thoughtfully chewing the last of her French toast, while he continues washing dishes. In the living room, the radio is on, playing some Hootie and the Blowfish song. A warm, floral breeze pushes through the open windows.

As Nate starts rinsing the silverware, Sophie says, "We never have vacation."

Everything he does is for her, but nothing will ever be enough.

At the clinic, Sophie hurries to the kids' section of the waiting room while Nate steps to the front desk, where Rose sits behind a closed glass window in the middle of a phone call, cord wrapped around her wrist. Her long hair is pulled back in the kind of braid Nate's never been able to manage for Sophie.

While she finishes her conversation, he flips through one of the Dalton Daze pamphlets stacked on the desk, feigning interest in the town-wide festivities planned for the week of July Fourth.

Rose hangs up and slides open the window. "It'll be a few minutes. Janine left us in the lurch again, and Vera's still on lunch break."

"No rush," says Nate, holding up the pamphlet. "Can I take this?"

"What they're there for." She hesitates, then adds, "Is that offer still good, by the way? To have me and the kids out to your place for a playdate with Sophie?"

"Of course," says Nate. "Anytime."

He walks past the half-wall of glass blocks to sit on a couch near Sophie, who lies on her stomach on the carpeted floor, absorbed in a picture book.

"Any luck?"

"Waldo's too good at hiding, Daddy. He's *too good*."

While she flips pages, Nate studies the pamphlet, scanning for typos like Bridget used to do. *Firework diplay. Firemans Muster.* "Doesn't anyone proofread these things before they print them?" she would always say, laughing, and Nate would tell her she should call the town office, point out the mistakes. But she never wanted to embarrass anybody.

After a few minutes, the door to the back hallway opens, and Vera steps into the waiting room. She's in a yellow shirtdress, her hair falling to her collarbone in a mostly-smooth curtain. She looks content, at ease.

"Check near that beach umbrella, beside the lemonade stand," she says to Sophie.

"He's so sneaky."

"He sure is. I'm Vera, by the way."

"Are you the lady doctor?"

"Technically I'm a kind of nurse, but I can do almost everything a doctor does."

"So you're a super nurse?"

"I like that idea. You ready to come back here with me?" Only when Sophie jumps up to follow her down the hall does Vera look at Nate. "You too, Dad."

He hangs back while Vera has Sophie step onto the scale and then against the wall, noting the numbers in her chart. "Up four pounds and two inches from your last visit. Very nice."

"Will I be tall like Daddy?"

At 6'4", Nate's height has always made him feel conspicuous—when he was a kid, he was constantly slouching, trying to make himself more invisible, until one of his teachers told him he'd end up with a hunchback.

"Maybe not that tall. You might take after your mom instead."

"My mumma's dead. Did you know that?"

"I did," Vera says. "I've heard good things about her, though. Actually, I think my own mother might have one of your mom's paintings hanging up in her house."

"We have lots."

Nate wants to describe which paintings they have and where they hang. But he can't bring himself to interrupt their conversation, which Vera deftly steers toward happier things as she steers Sophie into an exam room and onto the cot: "What vegetables do you eat? How many sugar snacks do you have in a day? Which do you like better, dancing or swimming?"

He sits in a chair beside the window and watches as Vera listens to his daughter's heart. He knows exactly what she's hearing through the stethoscope, the familiar *thump-tha-thump-tha-thump*. How many times has he stood in the dark listening to that sound as Sophie sleeps? By now he knows that heartbeat better than his own.

Vera steps back and gives Sophie a serious look. "We've put it off as long as we can," she says, "but it's time for a couple shots. Do you get scared of them?"

"A little. But Daddy says I need them if I want to go to school." Sophie sighs. "Actually, I think I'm scareder of school than shots."

Wiping Sophie's upper arm with an alcohol swab, Vera says, "Kindergarten isn't so scary. You'll already know all the other kids from head-start."

"I didn't go to that."

"Oh?" Vera's gaze flicks over to Nate, then her attention is right back on Sophie. "Well, if you can handle shots, you can handle school no problem. Look at you. All done, and you didn't even flinch."

Both Sophie and Nate blink, surprised to see Vera depositing a syringe into a container on the wall. Dr. Haskell always makes so much of a production out of the whole thing, counting down the seconds until the needle pierces the skin.

After placing a purple Band-Aid on Sophie's arm, Vera asks her to go back to the waiting room while she talks to her dad. "See if you can find Waldo at the skating rink," she says. "It's a tough one, but I think you can handle it."

Nate steps into the hallway with Sophie and watches her skip away from him. Only after the lobby door falls shut behind her does he return to the exam room, where Vera stands in front of the window. Cracks of sun come through the closed blinds.

"So why'd you want me to hang back?" he asks. "Is there anything I should know about? Is she okay? She's been a little stuffed-up lately, and I thought it was just allergies, but could it be something—"

Vera holds her hands out in a gesture that says *quiet*. A gesture that says *enough*.

"Sophie's perfectly healthy. I just wondered if you had any questions or concerns for me. Sometimes it's easier for parents to ask when the kid isn't right there listening."

Nate could stand in this room all day asking Vera if he's

doing everything right, and still not come away with a satisfactory answer.

"Sophie's mom was allergic to bees," he says. "Does that mean she is, too?"

"It's possible. If she gets stung, keep a close eye on her."

"What could happen?"

"Anything from mild skin irritation to anaphylaxis."

"How can I know how bad it might get?"

"You can't." Vera opens a cupboard door and rummages through some bins, emerging with a white and yellow box, which she hands to Nate.

"Two EpiPens," she says. "Just in case."

It's a professional gesture, he knows. But there's also a shine of understanding in her pale-blue eyes, the sort that goes beyond a nurse's responsibility to her patients. The sort that exists between two regular people who know that terrible things can happen at any moment, with no fair warning.

Back in the waiting room, as Sophie flips through the last of the Waldo pages, Nate steps up to the front desk, twenty dollars ready for the usual copay. Rose slides open the window and accepts the bill.

"Sorry, by the way," she says. Her eyes are bright with worry.

"For what?"

"Inviting ourselves to your house earlier. Putting you on the spot like that."

And there's that memory of Tommy again, cowering under Nate's fists. Rose's face in the window of the trailer, watching the violence unfold.

Then Sophie comes running up to the desk, bobbing on her tippy toes to accept a lollipop from Rose, and she looks so happy when Rose tells her how smart she is for finding Waldo in all those busy places.

"Don't be sorry," Nate says. "We're free all day tomorrow if you want to bring the boys around. Say noonish?"

The worry in her eyes fading slightly, Rose smiles. "Okay. Sounds good."

Sophie pushes her lollipop to one side of her mouth. "I like your braid. Daddy tries hard, but he can't do hair very good."

As Rose, smiling bigger now, prints out a receipt, Nate pulls the Dalton Daze pamphlet out of his pocket.

"Are you and the kids going to any of these things?"

Rose takes the red paper from his hands and scans through the events. "What makes a baked bean super?" she asks. It isn't until she laughs and winks at Sophie that Nate gets the joke, that he realizes she's found the one mistake he didn't see.

Later that afternoon, down by the river, Sophie looks up from the house of rocks she and Nate have been assembling for the better part of an hour. The sky is deep, and the river flows low, slow, steady. Somewhere nearby, a white-throated sparrow is singing.

"Daddy?"

Her hair is a mess and her clothes are filthy and Nate's love for her is so big he might burst into pieces one day. Maybe that's all spontaneous combustion is—so much love the body just can't hold it in anymore.

"What is it, Soph?"

"Bampy said his dad had cancer and died. Is that how Mumma died, too?"

Punch to the heart. Ribs turned to shrapnel.

"No," says Nate. "Mumma didn't have cancer."

Sophie squints so hard in the sun the green of her eyes disappears. She's never looked at him this way before, with so much disbelief. She's too smart for her age, unrelentingly curious. The clock is running out on the lie. But is the moment for truth now, here on the riverbank under the hot blue sky?

Then Sophie's face changes. Shy little smile. "I really like Rose," she says.

"I'm glad. She's a nice lady."

"And she's pretty too, don't you think?"

Long dark hair, brown eyes. That mismatched bathing suit at the lake, pink and orange. And the way she handed his daughter a grape lollipop, as if she somehow knew it's her favorite flavor.

"Sure," says Nate. "I guess she's kind of pretty."

Sophie nods as if something important has been settled, then turns her attention back to the rock house. Gravel for shingles; stones for siding; a smooth purple pebble beneath the front door. Only the smallest creatures could live here, but they would live here well.

A couple hours after Nate and Sophie leave the clinic, Vera steps into the front office and leans against the desk. "Any more today?"

"Arlene was the last one."

"If you want, you can take off. I can cover the desk while I work on paperwork."

The idea is tempting. Rose could go home, collect Adam and Brandon early from Marian Gallagher next door. She could catch some sun on the lawn behind the trailer while the boys jump around in the sprinkler. But it seems selfish to leave Vera here all by herself. Not the kind of thing a friend would do.

"I can stay a while."

"Actually, here's a better idea," says Vera, massaging the back of her neck with one hand. "How about we both leave at four and grab a drink at Frenchie's?"

Rose feels the same thrill in her belly she'd get whenever Suzie Howe would invite her to a slumber party back in grade school.

"That sounds good. But it's real short notice to get a sitter . . ."

"Oh, shit, of course. Well, I'll just bring the drinks to you. If that's okay."

Other than her mother, no one has visited Rose at the trailer over the past few years. She'll have to do some frantic cleaning, the kind that involves throwing laundry and toys into her bedroom and shutting the door.

"It's okay," she says, hoping she sounds casual, like the kind of normal person who has friends over all the time. "Let's aim for after the boys' bedtime, though. That way we can watch *Unsolved Mysteries.*"

As soon as the words are out, Rose gets the feeling her Friday ritual of watching that kind of garbage television might not be considered normal at all.

Then Vera grins. "I love that show."

That night, for once, when she tells the kids it's time for bed, Adam doesn't argue. She tucks both him and Brandon in, inhaling their familiar scents of dirt and grass and something sweet she's never been able to put a name to.

"Mum?" Adam asks from the top bunk. In the bed below, Brandon curls around his teddy bear, already half-asleep. "Did you mean it when you said we're going to Sophie's tomorrow?"

"Of course I meant it," says Rose. "Do you think I'd lie about that?"

Adam presses his face to his pillow, so his words come out all muffled. "You lie about Dad missing us. If he missed us, he'd come back home."

"We're going," says Rose. "Twelve o'clock, on the dot, we'll be in the car."

"We'll see, I guess."

It's a shitty feeling, knowing your kids don't believe the things you tell them. The things you wish were true.

She leaves the room, closing the door behind her. Though there's still a little sun left outside, she turns the hallway light on for when Brandon will inevitably have to get up later in the night to pee. Then she turns on the TV, gets the right channel. Stupid, but she feels as nervous as if she were about to invite frigging royalty into her house. She's wearing pajama shorts and a Garfield sweatshirt—not exactly the outfit one might wear for a king or queen.

There's a knock at the door, and Rose rushes to answer.

Vera is standing on the cracked cement slab outside, dressed in sweatpants and a Bangles t-shirt. Her hair is wavier than usual, poofing out in random places. She's holding a bottle of gin in one hand and tonic water in the other. Her Honda is parked behind Rose's car, engine ticking.

"Sorry if you're a wine or a beer person," says Vera. "But it's been so long since I had a good G&T, I just couldn't resist."

"I'm not picky."

"Thank god."

In the kitchen, Vera mixes the drinks into Hamburglar jelly glasses while Rose pours some chips into a bowl. Then they go into the living room and plop down on the couch just as the intro song for *Unsolved Mysteries* begins to play.

"It's eerie, isn't it?" says Vera, nodding at Robert Stack. "All these people disappearing with no explanation?"

Rose thinks of Tommy. One day he was here, next day he wasn't. But maybe the creepier part is the phone calls in the middle of the night, which have been happening more often lately—three times last week. Twice last night. Reminders that he hasn't disappeared forever.

"Eerie's a good word for it." Rose takes a gulp of her drink, booze burning her throat all the way down. "I don't buy the alien abductions, though."

It's weird, feeling the weight of someone other than the kids on the other end of the couch. Is this what normal people— normal friends—do? Sit around watching TV, getting tipsy in cluttered living rooms?

At the commercial break, Vera turns to Rose. "So tell me," she says. "What's the hardest part of being a single parent?"

No one has asked her the question before, and Rose isn't sure if she should be offended. But the look on Vera's face is all kindness.

"I mean, other than the daily grind of making sure they do their homework and don't choke on a Fruit Roll-up," says Rose,

"I guess just knowing that everything they have or don't have is all on me. That I'm the only one they can depend on. It really sucks for them, you know? Kids need more than just a mom."

"I don't know. I think if they have one rock-solid parent, whether that's a mother or a father, kids can thrive."

"Like Sophie Theroux?" asks Rose, thinking of how effortless Nate makes parenthood seem despite the shit he's been through. "You think she'll do all right, growing up without her mom?"

"I think any kid with a dad like Nate would grow up just fine." Vera gives her a knowing look. "He's a great guy. Kind of handsome, too."

Rose laughs, the sound coming out louder than she'd like—damn gin always goes straight to her head. "Yeah, he's a good guy. And no, he's not terrible to look at. But that's all you're getting out of me."

"For now," says Vera, and she winks—the kind of teasing thing real friends do, the kind of easy familiarity real friends share.

Later, 2 A.M., the phone rings, waking Rose from gin-soaked sleep. She unplugs it from the wall. Falls back into dreams of men in trench-coats, men in police uniforms.

Rose still thinks of Nate's house as the Donoghue place, which was known around town when she was younger as being haunted. It was always unclear if someone lived there before Nate and Bridget bought it—some people swore Trent Donoghue did, but Rose can't remember ever seeing signs of life in the old place. When she was a kid, the porch was all rotted out, the lawn untamed, and the dormer windows always looked like the blank eyes of a dead person.

Now, though, as she pulls into the driveway, Adam and Brandon giggling in the backseat, Rose is just about smacked in the face by how different the house looks. The white siding stands out against the blue shutters that flank the once-empty windows, where curtains billow in the breeze. On the front porch are two Adirondacks, a glider, hanging ferns. And there are flowers everywhere, so many flowers and colors covering the lawn that when Rose steps out of the car, she feels like she's fallen into a painting.

As Adam and Brandon jump around making lightsaber noises, she spins in a slow circle to see the forest rolling down to the river, an endless green field, Mount Katahdin, faraway hills, more woods and fields. The air smells sweet, and the sky stretches for a big blue forever in every direction.

Sophie is standing on the porch, bouncing from one foot to the other. Her hair is held back in curly pigtails, and her romper is the color of lemons. Knees covered in mosquito bites. She says a polite hello to Rose, then turns to Adam and Brandon.

"You need to see this anthill I found," she tells them, and just like that, they're off the porch and running toward the edge of the driveway.

The screen door squeaks open, and Nate steps onto the porch. Rose tries to remember if she's ever seen him in cargo shorts before; she can't decide if the look is ridiculous or endearing on his gangly frame.

"That'll keep them busy for a few minutes," he says. "If you want, come on in, and I'll give you the grand tour."

The inside of the house is just as nice as the outside. Hardwoods creak under their feet. Old cast-iron sink in the kitchen; built-in shelves in the living room. On every wall, in every room, are what Rose guesses must be Bridget's paintings, brightened versions of the landscape that lies beyond the windows. All the decorations, and all those colors, along with Sophie's toys, books, and stuffed animals scattered all over the place, make the house feel alive in a way Rose has never felt inside a house before. Or is she only imagining the sensation of breathing in each room, the faint thrum of a heartbeat behind the walls?

Funny, you'd think that kind of thing would feel uncomfortable. But Rose actually likes it—it's like everyone who's ever had a good life inside the house is somehow still living it. Like maybe in some ways their lives never really ended. A good kind of haunting.

Upstairs, Nate walks past two closed doors without comment—Rose wants to know but gets the sense she shouldn't ask—then he shows her his room (no clutter, windows open, matching brass lamps on either side of the neatly made bed) before leading her across the hall to Sophie's.

On the daybed, Mufasa snuggles up against the pink pillows. Books on all the shelves. More of Bridget's paintings, as well as Winnie-the-Pooh posters on the walls, painted a shade of green that reminds Rose of leaves right after a rainstorm.

"It's a happy room," she tells Nate, and he grins like it's just what he was hoping to hear. That's a good feeling, too—making him smile like that. Knowing she's said something exactly right, for once in her life.

Back outside, they gather up the kids, as well as two bags stuffed full of towels, snacks, bug dope, and sunscreen, then head toward the river. Rose and Nate let Sophie lead the way, the boys close behind her, as she skips through the backyard, down a grassy field hot under the sun, and into the woods, where everything turns dim and cool. Rose breathes in the smell of spruce and cedar and old bracken. A woodpecker is tapping a tree trunk nearby, and a chickadee keeps shouting out its *Cheeseburger* sound. Good smells and good sounds, some of Rose's favorites, but they bring back lonely memories. As a kid, she spent hours by herself in the woods behind her mother's trailer out in Barren. Hoping for fairies but never finding any.

The river is tucked between two sides of the forest, a nice shock of blue in all that green. Sophie leads them to a shallow spot near a stand of alders, where she and Adam waste no time in stripping down to their bathing suits—thrift store trunks for him, what looks like a brand-new one-piece for her, shiny and purple.

"Be careful," says Nate, keeping his eyes on Sophie as she walks into the water.

While Rose helps Brandon put on his lifejacket, he leans in to whisper into her ear. "I don't know this part of the river. I don't know if it's safe."

"It's safe," she tells him. "I wouldn't've brought you anywhere that isn't."

But the way Brandon looks at her as she nudges him toward the water makes Rose feel like she might as well be pushing him off the edge of a thousand-foot cliff. Maybe she should let him sit on the shore and just dip his feet into the water, feel minnows nip at his toes.

Suddenly, Nate is pulling his shirt over his head and tossing it onto the rocky shore. His white-as-milk stomach is mostly flat, and there's a patch of dark hair on his sternum that Rose wasn't expecting. He probably won't be a model for any paperback romances anytime soon, but there's something about the way he looks that makes him seem solid. Grownup.

"What about this?" Nate asks Brandon, crouching down so they're eye-level. "You go out as far as you want, and I'll stand right next to you."

"The whole time? Because sometimes Adam likes to play tricks and push me in."

"No one's playing any tricks on you on my watch."

Rose hangs back on the shore, watching as they walk into the river. They've only taken a few steps when Brandon shrieks out that it's deep enough. Nate, water barely above his ankles, stands guard as promised while Brandon splashes in the slow river. Just upstream, in a calm green pool, Sophie and Adam are swimming in circles around each other, making up some complicated game called Crocodile. *Jaw open!* Sophie shouts, and Adam, giggling, shouts back *Jaw closed!* Rose doesn't get it, but they're laughing, so it must be all right.

The sun is blinding and heavy, and the woods smell so lonesome, and Rose has bills to pay and errands to run and a useless, abusive ex who left her to do it all on her own, in a trailer that reeks of mildew and old carpet. Maybe he'll call her again tonight, or tomorrow, or the next day.

But sitting on the shore with the river trickling past and birds singing, and the big sky above, and Nate keeping watch over her boys . . . with all that goodness, mostly everything feels okay. A lot of things feel almost possible.

Regimen

It starts with Trudy dragging him by the elbow around the yard one evening. Clouds like spun sugar. Birds chirping and shrieking in the forsythia bush.

"I'm not a pony," says Richard, trying to break free from her grasp.

"You're right," she says, "you're more of a jackass. But you need to get out of the house. You need to exercise."

It's the exact thing, minus the part about the jackass, Richard would tell his own patients post-MI. The heart is a muscle that needs to be trained. If he keeps lying in bed watching TV all day, he risks permanent damage. Without movement, the heart grows thick and the blood festers, pooling to form clots that could travel to his lungs or his brain. Kill him.

Richard hasn't yet decided if he wants to be alive—if, in fact, he even *is* all the way alive—but that kind of certain death isn't particularly appealing. So he allows Trudy to corral him around her flowers, follows along as she scowls at her climbing hydrangea, which isn't so much climbing the fence as it is slumping up against it, like a heat-weary farmhand gasping for breath.

"Bastard thing," Trudy says, weaving the white flowers around each other, forcing them in the direction she thinks they ought to grow.

He wants to tell her to leave it, let nature take its course. But his wife has never backed away from a fight until she can be certain she will come away the victor.

The next night, he barely finishes his chicken before Trudy drags him outside. There was rain earlier, and the damp grass tickles his bare feet. Everything smells of wet pavement, dying peonies. Across the street at the playground, kids clamber on the jungle gym. Trudy instructs Richard to make a lap around the yard while she goes back inside to feed the cat, whose yowls can be heard from the open windows in the kitchen.

"The whole perimeter. No cutting corners."

After she's gone, he walks slowly around the lawn, shamed and frightened by the resistant burn in his calves—already his body has begun to atrophy. His heart races; sweat prickles under the thin hair on his scalp. The cuffs of his sweatpants collect rainwater. He's so tired he could lie down beneath the maples and sleep until morning.

The screen door slaps shut, and Trudy yells at him from the porch, her voice loud enough to make the kids at the playground look over toward the house.

"Pick up the pace, Richard. You can do a hell of a lot better than that."

Under his breath, he curses. Then he moves a little faster. Walks a little further.

His days begin to follow a pattern he doesn't have the energy to fight. He wakes early, either from the forsythia birds or Trudy's hands slapping at his feet. After breakfast (low-fat, low-cal, low-taste), Trudy heads off to the library. While she's gone, Richard watches game shows, soap operas, talk shows with celebrities he's never heard of. The endless shiny faces and insipid chatter has a numbing effect, and he often falls asleep in the middle of it all. He dreams of salt-crusted ships, and white rooms, and hands pressing against his face. Sometimes, not quite asleep or awake, he dreams of his own detached body unmoving on the bed.

Every day, as soon as Trudy gets home shortly past four, she comes into the guest room and snaps off the television set. "Do something with your brain," she says, throwing yet another discarded library book at him, or a crossword puzzle. One day, she brings him an Audubon field guide and tells him if he's going to swear at the birds who have made a home under his window, he should at least know their names.

Supper is ready by five thirty, and Trudy won't let Richard leave the table until he's eaten everything on his plate.

"Were you a nun in another life?" he asks as she stands over him, watching him stab the last of his brown rice onto his fork.

"Ask more stupid questions and I'll make you eat more spinach."

And every night after supper, Trudy leads him outside to circle around and around like prisoners confined to a courtyard. Some nights they hear the crack of a baseball bat and the applause of a dozen devoted fans over at MacGregor Field. One night there's a thunderstorm, and they walk through the stinging rain, Richard petrified by the sizzle of lightning while Trudy throws a middle finger up at the slate gray sky.

"It isn't safe out here," he says.

"It isn't safe anywhere. Four more laps."

By the second week of their new regimen, Trudy has him walking up and down Winter Street. Richard can't help but imagine all the neighbors pressing their noses against their windows, watching as he hobbles like an old man past their houses. All his weakness on full display. But maybe that was Trudy's plan all along, because he's more motivated to push a little harder, just to get the pity parade over with.

"Soon enough," she says, "we'll have you circling the whole block. Work our way up to Rich Fucker Road."

She walks so fast, talks even faster.

Richard has lost count of how many days he's been away from the clinic. He doesn't miss it. With all his parents' expectations, and with his sense of responsibility for this little town, he never had the chance to be anything other than a doctor. But it's not a job that has ever felt quite right to him or for him, even on the best days. Without it, though, he feels unmoored, unsure of who he is and who he wants to be.

On their walks, he and Trudy often run into people they know, all of them his patients at one time or another. Not so long ago, Richard would have listened to their hurts and ailments, offered them some kind of healing. Now, he can't bring himself to care about Gloria Arsenault's clogged sinuses, or Louise Best's vertigo, or even George Nadeau's new lease on life now that the 'Nam bullet is gone from his thigh. As these familiar friends and neighbors tell Richard these things, all he wants to do is sprint away from them. Take their prayers for his speedy recovery and toss them like pebbles down a deep, black well.

With each forced march along street, his body feels stronger, more solid—but if there is a soul rattling around in there, Richard still can't feel it.

He finds the noisy forsythia birds in the field guide. Not wrens or sparrows as he suspected. They're catbirds, with sleek gray bodies, black caps, patch of russet beneath their tail feathers. When they call to one another, they sound like Mycroft meowing, asking irritating questions. They imitate the songs of other birds and can sing without rest for over ten minutes. An entire winged lifetime of mockery.

"Those damn things are laughing at me," Richard says one night as he and Trudy sit on the porch after their walk. He's out of breath, covered in sweat.

"What damn things?" asks Trudy, deadheading petunias.

"The catbirds."

"For Chrissake, Richard. They're birds. They don't give a shit about you or me or anyone."

And that's how the June evenings go. The two of them

sitting on the porch, not talking much, while the sun drops behind the town, casting copper light over all the trees and rooftops. Trudy fusses over her flowers, grumbles about the state of Helen McGreevy's rose bushes next door. And Richard tries to find his breath, hopes to settle his heart. Listens as the catbirds trill their songs, their lifelong imitation.

Full sun, bright morning. Air alive with honeybee buzz. Trudy is wrist-deep in weeds, angry with herself for letting them get so out of control.

"It's your fault, you know."

Beside her, bent over the dianthus, Greg plucks blades of grass crowding out the pink flowers. "Don't blame me," he says. "Blame my dad."

Trudy rests on her heels and watches him work his way through the flower patch. His cheeks are sunburnt, nose peeling.

"How many hours does he have you putting in at the store?"

"Seven until noon, Monday through Saturday." Greg pauses as a white butterfly hovers around him, not moving again until it flies off toward the roses. "Then I spend a few hours out at Nate's place, two or three times a week."

"And here with me when you can."

"Here with you when I can," says Greg, giving Trudy a smile with no trace of their usual sarcasm behind it. "Wish it were more often."

He's a sweet boy, kind and smart and earnest, and if Trudy were a softer sort of person, she might tell him all those things. Tell him she's proud to know him. The person she is, though, has to bite her lip from telling him he deserves better than this town, that store. He deserves the whole goddamn world, and everything in it.

She points toward a spot he missed, where the dianthus bumps up against the yarrow. "Getting sloppy, there, Gregory."

That evening, as Trudy and Richard are about to leave for their walk—he doesn't want to go, but too bad—there's a knock at the front door. She doesn't need to look out the window to know who is standing on the other side. After all these years, she can feel Bev's presence like the promise of rain.

Glancing at Richard, who's trying to tie his sneakers as Mycroft weaves around his ankles, Trudy tells him to hold on a minute. "But only a minute," she adds. "You're not getting out of this, so drink some water before we hit the pavement."

When she steps onto the porch, Bev is sitting on the glider, staring out at the bird bath, where two goldfinches perch on the rim. She's dressed in a tank top and a pair of jeans she's had for a decade. Her dark hair piled on top of her head.

Trudy canceled their usual date night to take Richard out walking, and when she tried to call Bev yesterday, she wasn't home. Out shopping, Bill said over the phone. He sounded surprised to hear from Trudy, as though he had assumed she was at the mall with his wife.

Too many missed opportunities.

Settling beside her on the glider, Trudy breathes in Bevy's familiar scent of rosewater. "Our timing has been hell, hasn't it?"

"Yup. As soon as I drove up, I realized you two were probably on your way out." Bev pauses, eyes flicking toward the open window, behind which they can hear Richard scolding the cat. "He doing any better?"

"Physically, I think so."

"And mentally?"

"I'm not sure about that one yet," she says. "But I can't imagine the fresh air and exercise is working against him."

"Can't imagine."

The sun is falling lower each minute, tossing tarnished light across the town. It's hot and humid, and tomorrow is supposed to be even worse; no rain in the forecast for the next week.

She'll need to water the flowers when she and Richard get back tonight. Probably again in the morning.

Such a strange summer, just begun and already a thousand years old. Time warping, stretching, not following any of its usual patterns. Trudy wishes Richard would hurry up and get better so she and Bevy could skip town, leave everyone and everything behind. Let the rest of the sun-scorched season roll on without them.

"In the fall," says Bev, "we'll go have ourselves an adventure."

"Bangor again?"

"Why don't we go somewhere on the coast instead?"

"You hate the ocean."

"But you like it."

There's so much in that voice, so much in those words. All the things they would give one another, and all the things they have never been able to, living in a place like this.

"The coast sounds good," says Trudy. "But I won't eat any lobster rolls."

Bev laughs, the sound startling the birds and making them fly away on tiny yellow wings. "No oysters, either."

It's the same sort of conversation they've had a million times before. But there's a shadow hovering between her and Bev, a sense that something has shifted. The same feeling lingered after Bridget died. Back then, it was Bev pulling away. But Trudy knows it's her now; she's the reason for this distance, for the glint of hurt in Bevy's blue eyes.

The door opens, and Richard steps onto the porch, scowling at Trudy. "I drank all that damn water, so if you're still hell-bent on going, we better go now before I have to piss it all back out."

"Chrissake, Richard," says Bev, stealing the words from Trudy's mouth. "You're starting to sound just like us."

HAVE & HAVE NOT

From Trudy's front porch to her own back deck. Their houses aren't even a half-mile apart, but Bev feels as though she might as well be on her own planet when she settles in her patio chair that evening. The sun is gone; the sky a sickly orange like cantaloupe flesh. Bev can't stop imagining Trudy and Richard walking together, strolling through all the familiar streets of Dalton.

The kitchen door opens, and Bill comes out onto the deck. He's always been so thin, and there have been times that's given him a starved appearance, like he was a man always hungry for some specific meal he couldn't find. But he looks good these days—clear, bright eyes, hair still thick despite turning more silver at the temples. Being a grandfather agrees with him, keeps him young. If it weren't for the lean he's got from the bad back, Bev could swear he's still in his forties. Nowhere near his actual fifty-eight.

Lighting a cigarette, he nods toward the beer in her hand. "That gonna give you heartburn this time of night?"

"Probably."

"Good thing I picked up more Rolaids today, then."

"Yup. Good thing."

Bill settles into the seat beside Bev, who closes her eyes to better inhale the smell of his Marlboro smoke—she's been missing the habit lately, desperate to pull that poison into her lungs, just for a moment of pleasure, relief. Life's harder without a vice or two.

Back when she first met Bill in the early 60s, he smoked weed instead of cigarettes. He had a thick mustache. He was against the Vietnam war, and he would've slipped off to Canada if he hadn't gotten lucky with his draft number. When Bev got pregnant a year after she and Bill started dating, he could've slipped off then, too. But he asked her to marry him instead. He wasn't great with emotions (he stepped out of the room anytime she started crying from pregnancy hormones), but he was kind to her, and a great father from the moment he cut Nate's umbilical cord—a rare thing for a man in 1964. He drove massive trucks unfathomable distances, seeing places Bev could hardly believe existed, deserts and miles-high mountains, swamplands and sandy beaches.

She and Bill were apart often because of those long-haul trips, and she suspected he found other company on the road. Part of her was upset by this, almost jealous. But when he was home, she didn't crave his body in the ways she should have. The times they did have sex, it was mostly fine, but Bev found herself thinking of other things—what color to repaint the kitchen, how many pounds of decaf she should order for the cafeteria at the Pines. Outside the bedroom, she and Bill got along, but there wasn't a lot of humor between them, nothing that sent her blood tingling.

Wasn't until she met Tru that Bev realized it wasn't normal to be so disengaged with the person you're supposed to be in love with.

She knows Bill knows about her and Trudy, even though they've never talked about it, just like they never talk about the affairs he likely had out on the road. Some things don't need to be discussed, brought out into the open.

Halfway through the beer, sure enough, Bev feels the acid deep in her throat start to boil. She hands the bottle to Bill, who accepts it without a word and finishes it in three gulps.

Maybe their marriage isn't about passion, but they do share

a life together. They finish each other's drinks, pick up extra Rolaids, admire Sophie's artwork on the fridge. That's the most important part—Sophie. In all their years together, they've never been more in sync than they are when they're with their granddaughter. As soon as Bev comes home from the store on days they watch Sophie, the three of them have lunch together, Bill making her and Sophie laugh with his Eeyore impressions. In the afternoons, they color, watch Disney movies, try to make brownies in Sophie's Easy Bake oven.

In the hours when their granddaughter isn't here at the house with them, Bev and Bill are still thinking about her, talking about her new obsession with rivers, trying to decide if it would be too much to buy her one of those tiny pink Jeeps. They start Christmas shopping in October. They've been setting aside money for her college fund.

So they might not have an ideal marriage, but from the moment Sophie came into the world, they made an unspoken promise to be a strong, united front for her. That they'd do anything to keep that girl happy, to make her feel special and loved and wanted in a world that can be so damn cruel.

Trudy and Richard will never have that kind of unity, Bev thinks as Bill lights another smoke. They can walk around the block as much as they like, help each other heal from heart attacks, talk about every kind of bird there is in the sky. But they'll never know what it means to be grandparents. To know that they played a part in bringing new existence into life.

POTATO CIRCUS

The twenty-ninth of June has always been a big deal in the Fortin family—Greg guesses that's just how it goes when your father and your older sister share the same birthday. Years past, celebrations have included backyard barbecues, cabin rentals on Portman Lake, even a trip to New Brunswick that ended abruptly when Aimee, six at the time, came down with a stomach bug that included Exorcist-levels of projectile vomit.

If Greg thought the birthday festivities could finally end now that Sarah is a grown-ass married woman, he was wrong.

"We have even more to celebrate now," his mother says as she pipes frosting onto a carrot cake. "Ian's birthday was three days ago, can you believe it? Really, what do you think the odds are?"

"Well, there are almost six billion people in the world, so . . ."

"Gloomy Gus. Go tell your dad we're leaving in twenty minutes."

He finds his father down in the mildew-scented cellar bent over his latest project, a replica of a Pullman steam engine painted a deep, rich red. As a kid, Greg thought it was cool that his father built model trains and railroads. They would spend hours down here together, painting houses no bigger than Greg's thumb, laying circular tracks that took the moving trains around and around a village that looked remarkably like Dalton. Same streets, same store and post office, same trees; even the river was there, a shiny blue ribbon alongside the tracks. But the older he got, the sadder Greg thought it was—his father could build any town or city in the world, or even create his own, but instead he chose to copy the very place where he had spent his whole life.

"Your mom ready?" asks his dad, peering at Greg through his glasses. His eyes look huge, owl-like.

"Just about."

"Good 'nough. But first, come here. Come see this."

Greg crouches to study the train's working headlight, the precise brushstrokes spelling out BANGOR & AROOSTOOK.

"What exactly am I supposed to be seeing?"

His dad points at the tiny conductor in the engine room, complete with striped hat and overalls. "This guy looks just like you."

Though he tries to recognize himself in the flat painted grin, Greg only sees a child's plaything, a plastic fantasy. He wants to tell his father he's gone nuts. He wants to tell his father he's predictably boring. He wants to tell his father about the boy at the party the last week of school, and the cute girl in English Comp, and the strange behavior of Cook pines, which slant toward the Equator, tilting more the further south or north they grow.

"Don't you think he looks like you?" prods his dad. Graying hair, same Wranglers and corduroy shirt he's worn for two decades. Blood blister on his thumb nail from where Greg accidentally dropped a can of varnish on it yesterday at the store.

"Sure," he tells his father. "I guess we look a little alike."

Sarah and Ian have set up house in a whitewashed cottage at the edge of the Best farm. Every window looks out over potato fields, and the floors are covered with braided rugs made by Ian's mother. Chintzy paintings of farm animals line the kitchen walls.

"Why not some Edward Hoppers? Maybe Monet?"

"Don't be a snob, Greggic," says Sarah, stirring iced tea into a ceramic pitcher. "Just because you went off to college like a little smart-ass doesn't make you better than the rest of us."

She's only been married a month, but she already looks older, not quite familiar—fuller in the face, wiser in the eyes. Her engagement ring and wedding band glint in the sun streaming in through the window. When Ian steps into the kitchen, she wraps her arms around his neck, kisses him softly on the lips. Ian lets out an embarrassing moan of happiness as he pulls her back for more.

Feeling like he might as well be standing behind their bedroom creeping on them through a peephole, Greg takes the pitcher out to the backyard, where his parents and Ian's, Gareth and Louise, are deep in a conversation about potato blight. He sets the iced tea on the picnic table and turns to Aimee, dressed in jeans and a flannel shirt despite it being nearly ninety degrees. Her blonde hair is up in a sloppy bun, and she's got so much eyeliner on she looks like a raccoon after a bar brawl.

"If we run fast enough," Greg says, "we could get to the minivan and steal it before Mom and Dad even notice."

Aimee snorts. "Like tooling around with you would be much better."

Lunch is fried chicken, green salad, and—surprise—mashed potatoes. Sarah and Ian entertain everyone with stories of their honeymoon in Quebec, where they stayed in a giant hotel overlooking the St. Lawrence River. Ian talks about his bad French, and Sarah assures him it wasn't as terrible as he thought— "Though he did ask for butter in his coffee instead of cream." All the adults laugh too much and too loud while Aimee and Greg stay mostly silent under the dappled shade of the oak that reaches toward the sky with gnarled fingers.

When lunch is over, Greg's mother and Louise ferry the empty dishes back inside, insisting everyone else stay where they are. They return with the cake, cream cheese frosting halfway melted from the heat inside the cottage. Then the mothers insist everyone sing three rounds of Happy Birthday, and Greg wishes Charlie Best were here to pass him another joint under the picnic table. But the guy took off soon after the wedding, back on the road to places Greg can only dream about.

Before Louise starts cutting the cake, Ian and Sarah exchange a bright, laughing glance.

"We have some news . . . "

It's just like in the movies, the mothers weeping, the fathers shaking hands. The baby is due in December. No one says anything about the timing—clearly it happened before the wedding, but it's not the 1800s, and none of them are practicing Catholics, so who the hell cares? Greg even catches a glimpse of excitement on his little sister's face when Sarah tells her she'll be Auntie Aimee from now on.

He's not against babies, or the people who have them. And it's nice to see Sarah so happy with the guy she chose as her husband, even if that guy does smell like fertilizer and look like a scarecrow. But after a few minutes of celebrating, all Greg wants to do is shift the conversation to something else. He'd much rather talk about the oak tree sprawling above them. He could tell everyone here that oaks don't start producing acorns until they're at least twenty years old. That one single tree can produce ten thousand acorns during a mast year. That of those ten thousand, only one acorn might go on to become a new tree.

Why don't they talk about the odds of *that*?

The last day of June is scorching and sticky, temps near ninety degrees with eighty-five percent humidity. The moment Vera steps out of the cool shower, she's drenched in sweat again—her parents never felt it necessary to install air conditioning. "It's only hot thirty days a year," her father has always said. "Why would I waste money on an air conditioner?" There are fans placed in windows throughout the house, including Vera's bedroom, but they don't do much more than move fetid air around.

It's a relief to walk into the icy-cold clinic, where Rose sits at the front desk shuffling through a stack of charts. She seems on edge, dark circles under her eyes. Her skort is rumpled, as if she just pulled it out of the dryer.

"No offense," says Vera, "but you look like hell."

"It's this fucking heat," Rose says. "No one's been sleeping in our house."

"Tell me about it—I feel like I've had PMS for two weeks. I'm going crazy."

"Speaking of crazy." Rose takes a chart from the bottom of the stack. "Annette Frazier's supposedly coming in today."

Vera has been back in Dalton for a month, but she's only seen Annette a couple times, once at the post office, struggling to carry a large box, and once at Bergeron's—Vera was at the cash register, Annette across the store in the produce aisle, where she knocked over a display of limes. Stood there while all the green fruit bounced over her feet and onto the floor, didn't even make a move to pick any of them up.

Glancing through the chart, Vera sees Dr. Haskell left a note on a date of service from two years ago: *Complains of insomnia, occ. brain fog. Denies alcohol use but slurred words t/o appt. Recommend antidepressants, out-patient Tx at Prescott hospital. Pt. refused all.*

"She hasn't been back since this last visit?"

"That'd be a big fat no," says Rose. "Her husband keeps trying to get her in, but she always either cancels the appointment or just doesn't show up."

Vera has seen Marshall Frazier once here at the clinic this summer, for a refill on his sleeping pills. He looked smaller than she remembered him, but he seemed to be coping with his daughter's death as well as possible—he didn't avoid using Bridget's name, and he talked about wanting to take Sophie to see *Pocahontas* in the Prescott movie theater. Hurt in his eyes but hope in his voice.

As she and Rose go through their now-regular opening routine, moving room to room, straightening everything up before the patients arrive, Vera's thoughts wander to the Fraziers. She, Will, Craig, and Penny were all in high school around the same time. They were nice kids, popular, top of their classes. But Vera always felt bad for them. They seemed lonely, and at every soccer game, band concert, and dance recital, Annette called too much attention to herself by cheering too loud or bragging too hard about their many talents.

According to Vera's mother, Marshall could have married anyone in Dalton, and not just because he was loaded. "He was sweet. Why he chose Annette Morse, we'll never know."

But maybe there's just no accounting for who a person falls in love with, or why.

Vera and Janine are halfway through lunch when Rose hurries into the break room. "It has arrived," she whispers dramatically, her eyes wide.

"You're shitting me," says Janine. "Annette actually showed up?"

"She looks awful. Smells like a redemption center, too."

Feeling like she should discourage this kind of gossip—professionalism counts, even in Dalton—Vera interjects. "I thought her appointment wasn't until one-thirty?"

"Good luck asking that woman to leave and come back in an hour."

Janine gulps down the last of her sandwich and pushes away from the table. There's a splotch of grape jelly on her Minnie Mouse scrubs. "I'll get her into a room," she says. "Weigh her in and everything. If she'll let me."

After the nurse hurries down the hallway, Rose gives Vera a conspiratorial look. "Last time Annette was here, she made Janine cry. Just so you know."

As soon as Vera opens the door of the exam room a few minutes later, she's smacked in the face with the reek of wine-soaked sweat. Forcing herself to keep a neutral expression, she steps into the room, where Annette paces in front of the window. Despite the heat, she's dressed in thick gray sweatpants and a bleach-stained sweatshirt. Her hair is ginger at the roots, turning splotchy brown near the tops of her ears, and her face is sallow, cheeks sunken in like a prisoner who hasn't been fed in weeks.

Vera closes the door softly behind her. "Scorcher out today, isn't it?"

"It's summer," says Annette, sounding surprised and irritated at the same time.

Vera picks up the chart, looking for Janine's usual Post-it. But there's nothing except for Dr. Haskell's notes from two years ago. "Did Janine take your vitals?"

"I don't need that nonsense. I just need some of the sleeping pills you give my husband."

"I can't prescribe medication unless we do a full exam."

Annette collapses into one of the chairs parents usually sit in. She stares at Vera. "You're Gretchen and Jerry's girl, aren't you? I thought you moved down to Belfast."

Seeing her opportunity, Vera grabs the blood pressure cuff off the wall. "Bangor," she says as she wraps the cuff around Annette's thin arm. "I'm just here for the summer. Till Dr. Haskell comes back to work."

"What makes you so sure he's coming back?"

Though Vera has wondered this same thing, she's careful not to let any doubt show on her face as she waits for the cuff to wheeze out one last breath and reveal Annette's numbers. Not terrible, but not great.

"May I?" asks Vera, holding up her stethoscope.

"I'd rather you didn't."

Down at the hospital, Vera could distract patients into complying, or charm them, or, with the right person, lay out the truth, however plain and ugly. Though she wants to use this last trick on Annette, something twists in Vera's gut, warning her to tread lightly.

Draping the stethoscope back around her neck, she asks, "How about you tell me what brings you in today?"

"Like I said, I need sleeping pills."

"Have you tried natural remedies?"

Annette slumps in the chair as she peers between the closed blinds, squinting in the crack of sun. "I told Marshall this would happen," she says. "God forbid a woman ask for a little help from a medical professional."

Vera takes a few deep breaths, reminding herself of all Annette has lost, all the grief she's suffered the past five years.

"I want to help you," she says. "I just don't feel comfortable giving you meds without trying some other things first."

"What kinds of things?"

"Gentler, more natural remedies. Chamomile, light exercise. And oftentimes insomnia is psychological. I could recommend a couple good therapists over in Prescott."

It's a fumbling attempt to catch a speck of dust in the dark, and Vera knows it has failed as soon as the words are out of her mouth. Annette grips the arms of the chair so hard her knuckles turn white.

"You want to lock me up in an attic, too? Like I'm some kind of hysteric?"

From what Vera has heard, Annette has already succeeded in locking herself away from the world. But no use pointing that out now.

"I think you've been through a lot since your daughter died, and counseling might help."

Annette rises from the chair, releasing another wave of boozy sweat. "I don't know why I bother," she says. Then she pushes past Vera, throwing the door open and letting it slam shut behind her.

The room feels small and hot and rancid, as if the fermented breath from Annette's mouth has contaminated every surface, oozed into every nook and cranny. Vera spritzes a can of air freshener around the room, then disinfects everything Annette might have touched. She feels guilty, as if she has contributed in some small but irredeemable way to the erasure of a woman already on the verge of disappearing.

S he can't have sleeping pills, so she just won't sleep. Every bit of food turns to sour poison in her mouth, so she just won't eat. She can't remember the last time she showered, so why not let it go one day longer? She doesn't need any more late-night purchases, but she orders more Beanie Babies, more collector plates, the entire boxed set of *Bonanza*.

When Marshall sits beside her on the couch in the glow of the television, his words sound far away, like she's stuck at the bottom of a swimming pool filled with syrup. Sound travels all wrong. His face is just a blur, a dark shadow.

"Annie."

That's the one word she hears clearly, and it's how she almost remembers he used to say it, before Bridget went away, before everything ended.

Annie—they were eighteen, kicking pebbles down Main Street late one autumn night.

Annie—he was holding Will as she lay panting and elated in the hospital bed.

Annie—the surprise fifteen-year anniversary trip to the Bahamas, where every bit of sun-soaked air smelled like coconut and pineapple.

All those things belong to a different woman; all of that happened in some other distant universe.

If she holds her breath and moves very slowly, she can swim the whole length of the pool, all the way down to the bottom where no sun reaches.

JULY

"Someones married their everyones
laughed their cryings and did their dance
(sleep wake hope and then) they
said their nevers they slept their dream"
—E.E. CUMMINGS, *Anyone lived in a pretty how town*

G reg runs silent under summer trees. This hour of day usually belongs to him alone, but today the town is alive and buzzing. It's the first of July, the beginning of Dalton Daze.

On Main Street, he slows his pace to take in the red, white, and blue bunting tacked onto every telephone pole. In the parking lot outside Frenchie's, people are setting up picnic tables for the strawberry shortcake sale this afternoon—a handwritten sign assures *ALL PROCEEDS GO 2 FIRE DEPARTMENT.*

Every summer of his life, it's the same old shit. Dalton Daze. Four days of patriotism and town pride in the form of bake sales, a Fourth of July parade and fireworks, and the street dance, where the local tribute band, Buck Fever (or Fuck Beaver, depending on who you ask), plays bad covers of Lynyrd Skynyrd and Foreigner.

Greg jogs down the dirt path that leads to the baseball diamond. Here there are no people; only the birds, singing, and the big wide sky, painted pink and orange. He does laps around the bases—closest he's ever come to any kind of home run—each stride forward an almost delirious pain, a burst of happy misery. Every muscle aching. Every nerve awaking.

When his breath starts sticking near his kidneys, Greg collapses in the grassy outfield. Lying on his back, he slows his breathing until his heart settles and the cramp subsides. There is a clump of red clover near his head, a buzzing honeybee. Already the sky is turning bluer, the day slipping forward.

He's supposed to be at the hardware store in twenty minutes to help his father with the ordering. Then he's supposed to sit at the lemonade booth outside the store to bring in Dalton Daze customers. Like a little kid. But all Greg wants to do is lie here in this grass, watch the bees on the clover (*trifolium pratense*), and try to calculate the amount of nitrogen those sturdy little flowers have added to the soil beneath his spine.

His reward for agreeing to the lemonade stand was a guarantee from his father he could leave the store early and help Trudy pull weeds. It's been a few days since he was last in Trudy's garden, and he misses the flowers more than he's ever missed an actual human in his entire life. That's probably not normal. But nothing about Greg, that he can tell, anyway, has ever been normal.

Turns out, not a whole lot of people want to pay a buck for powdered lemonade when they can buy a cup of fresh-squeezed for fifty cents just up the street. In the two hours he has been sitting at his table in front of the hardware store, Greg has netted exactly six dollars, plus a quarter tip from his Aunt Arlene.

"It's not about the money, son," his father says when he steps outside to check on Greg. "It's a way to get people in the door. I sold two hoses and three quarts of varnish in just ten minutes."

By noon, the pitcher of lemonade has begun to bake under the sun. Greg sits sweating in his folding chair, bored as hell. He can only see a tiny bit of Main Street from here. There's a lot of people out walking, but he can't recognize anyone from this distance. From inside the store, his father's music plays—Hank Williams, or Boxcar Willie, one of those dinosaurs.

A gold pickup with a busted muffler pulls into the parking lot, filling the air with the reek of motor oil. The driver's door opens, and a guy with dark, wavy hair steps onto the pavement. Greg doesn't pay much attention, until—

"Shit, Fortin. Is that you?"

Henry Covington is in front of the table, grinning down at Greg. In the bright midday light, his eyes are more blue-green than ever, like a tropical ocean. No doubt about it, the guy is still cute, but there's a droop to his shoulders that wasn't there just a year ago at their high school graduation.

"How's it going, man? I didn't know you were in town."

"Just for the summer." Then, feeling like a little boy staring up at a man, Greg pushes his chair back, metal scraping on tar, and stands so they are face-to-face.

"Jesus. You start taking diet pills or something?"

Henry had left Dalton the week after graduation to stay with relatives down in Mass for the summer, so Greg's weight loss must be a real shock. Something about the reveal feels staged and awkward, and Greg has the sudden desire to be fifty pounds heavier, just so he can have something to hide behind.

"No diet pills," he says. "Lot of aerobics, though. You know, those tapes with all those dudes in leotards. Works wonders."

Laughing, Henry claps Greg on the shoulder. "You haven't changed a bit. I got to grab a few things for my old man right now, but let's hook up later. You going to the street dance tonight?"

Bad music, cheap beer, sloppy drunks—the stuff of Greg's nightmares.

"For sure," he says. "I'll be there."

Henry reaches into his pocket, takes out a crumpled dollar bill, and drops it in the nearly empty jar with the rest of the day's profits. Then he pours himself a cup of lemonade, and Greg watches, holding back his own laughter, as Henry takes a swig, screwing up his face at the taste. Full body shiver as he swallows. "Shit, man. You're selling hot piss out here."

When he gets to Trudy's house a couple hours later, the first thing Greg notices is the new patch of daylilies that have opened since the last time he was here. They wave in the breeze, their yellow throats gulping light.

The second thing he notices is Dr. Haskell sitting on the porch in a pair of sweats that have been cut at the knees, revealing startlingly white calves. He leans back to shout into the open kitchen window, "The kid's here," which is answered with Trudy's directive to hold on a minute, she can't do two things at once.

Dr. Haskell turns back to Greg. "The cat threw up."

"Yikes."

"Do you have cats?"

"My dad's allergic."

"Lucky."

Standing in the heat, watching Dr. Haskell twirl a glass of water between his palms, Greg feels nearly as uncomfortable as he did at those college parties. Is he supposed to chat about the weather? Ask how the old guy's doing since his heart crapped out on him?

"Listen," he says, "can you tell her I just went ahead and got started?"

Before Dr. Haskell can answer, Greg hurries off toward the gardening shed.

By the time Trudy joins him near the rose bushes, he has already ripped out several handfuls of weeds. For a few minutes, they kneel side-by-side without talking while Trudy gets to work pruning the roses. High in the maples, cicadas whine.

Greg can't stop thinking about Henry. How many thousands of hours in high school did he fantasize about kissing the guy, running his fingers through that hair? But even as he imagined those things with Henry, he also dreamed of wrapping Angela Muse's thick, black braid around his wrist, trailing his mouth along the curve of her hips. All those thoughts jumbled up with the craving for candy bars, Oreos, anything sweet. The memory is so vivid Greg's mouth waters. But also tangled up with those thoughts of Henry and Angela, and the need for junk food, is the shame that has swirled in his belly for as far back as he can remember.

"All right, Gregory. What the hell's bothering you?"

He isn't surprised Trudy can sense his mood—but he is unsettled by his own bleak response.

"I told Henry Covington I'd meet up with him at the street dance tonight even though I'm pretty sure I'd rather you jam those pruning shears through my hand."

"Are you nervous about the Henry part or the dancing part?"

"Take a wild guess."

"True. Only drunk old women dance at those things."

Shifting so that he's sitting cross-legged, Greg looks up at the branches above, all those green leaves swaying under cloud and sun. "I don't even know if I like Henry anymore," he says. "It's just—"

"It's just that you ever did in the first place?" says Trudy, giving him a rare, soft smile.

And there's that shame, and that fantasy of Henry's lips against his own, and the old need for chocolate cake.

"Exactly."

Trudy tosses the shears on the ground and plucks a pink rose from the bush, maneuvering her hand around the thorns. Wordlessly, she holds out the flower for Greg to smell; wordlessly, he does, closing his eyes to savor the spicy-sweet aroma.

"Not a very common rose, Dart's Dash," she says. "Had to go all the way to Bangor to buy it when it was just one puny little shrub. But can you imagine this garden without it?"

Greg takes the flower from her palm. "I get what you're saying. But sometimes it really sucks, you know?" He traces the smooth petals with his fingertips. "Not being like the rest of them."

Now Trudy fixes him with her usual steely stare. "For

Chrissake, Gregory. Why the hell would you want to be like the rest of them?"

After spending a half-hour trying on different outfits, Greg settles on jeans and a Velvet Underground t-shirt. His running shoes, too, in case he needs to make a quick getaway. Before he leaves the house, he steps into the living room, where his parents are curled on the couch, his father rubbing his mother's feet as they watch TV.

"Where are you headed off to?" asks his mother, glancing at the clock.

"Meeting Henry at the street dance."

"You know, son, usually a guy would meet a *girl* at a shindig like that."

It's probably just a throwaway comment, one of those dad-jokes his father loves so much. But Greg wonders if there's real fear under the surface of the laughing words, if his father has figured out his virgin son beats off to thoughts of both men in gym shorts and women in cork wedges.

"Henry and I might find some girls there," says Greg.

"Just be careful, sweetie," his mother says, and maybe there's something behind her words, too, some subtle warning about all the terrible things that could happen to a boy like him. Or maybe she's just a mom, worried about everything and nothing in particular.

By the time Greg heads down High Street, the sun has dropped below the horizon, but gold light lingers on the distant fields and forest. The sky is deep purple, and the air smells of fresh-cut grass and spruce.

Half of Main Street has been cordoned off for the eighteen-and-over dance, the area in front of Frenchie's a mass of people—twenty-something girls clad in short shorts; middle-aged women with teased hair; millworkers in their usual blue denim. The natural scents of summer have been replaced with those of beer and cheap perfume. On a makeshift stage, Buck Fever plays a shitty rendition of Simple Man. Greg tries not to stare at the lead singer—too damn depressing to see your grade school gym teacher dressed in ball-tight pants, wailing into a microphone.

He feels a tap on his shoulder and turns to see Henry grinning at him, holding out a red plastic cup.

"How'd you manage to get that?"

"Don't worry, Fortin. No cops are going to nab anyone underage tonight. Half the DPD is already drunk off their ass."

Greg accepts the cup, clunking it against Henry's before taking a few hurried gulps, eager to get the taste out of his mouth.

They find a patch of empty sidewalk in front of the furniture store, where they lean against the window. The golden light is gone, replaced with a dark-blue sky punched through with stars. The neon OPEN sign above the door at Frenchie's is on the fritz, blinking in a rhythm that almost matches up with the opening bars of Hot Blooded.

"Jesus," says Greg, "can't they find some better music?"

Henry gazes toward the stage, where Mr. Arsenault is waggling his hips at a crowd of women who drunkenly sing and dance along. "I mean, *that's* embarrassing," he says. "But I like the songs they play."

Greg feels a surge of disappointment toward Henry as he thinks back to all those nights in the dorm room with David's mess of mixed tapes, all the music that puts this kind of overplayed crap to shame. He sips his beer, stays quiet.

"Hey," says Henry, "you ever run into Angie down at UMO? Indian Island isn't too far from there, right?"

It could be sophomore English class all over again, Angela pointedly choosing a desk on the other side of the room from Henry, who pleads with Greg to find out what he did wrong and how he can fix it.

"I never saw her," Greg says. "One of the guys in my dorm

grew up on the reservation, and I asked if he knew her. He said she left her dad's place last summer. Wasn't sure where she ended up."

Henry's shoulders sag. In the erratic neon light, he looks like he could be forty years old, another worn-out millworker. "Refill?" he asks, nodding toward Greg's cup.

"I'm all set."

"Part of that new diet?"

"Something like that."

"Be right back."

Greg used to love to watch Henry walk away—the guy could really wear a pair of jeans—but tonight all he feels as he watches Henry's white shirt swallowed up by the crowd is a sense of boredom. And then a fair amount of disgust when he hears the unmistakable sound of a girl puking onto the curb a few feet away. She wipes her mouth, pushes her hair out of her face, and straightens up. Only then does Greg realize it's his baby sister, standing there alone in her oversized plaid shirt, eyeliner smudged halfway down her cheeks.

He ditches his cup and walks toward her, careful to stop before the splatter of her vomit. "Your mother would say it's not very ladylike to blow chunks in the street, Aimee."

When she scowls, she looks just like she did as a toddler after their parents told her she couldn't color on the walls. "What are you doing here?" she says. "You're usually holed up in your room by now."

"I'm here with Henry. What about you? How'd you even get in? You're only fifteen."

"No one cares, Greg."

"Didn't you tell Mom and Dad you were hanging out with Danielle tonight?"

"I was, till the bitch decided to go give Travis Wilkins a handy behind the bar."

Then Aimee is bent at the waist and puking again. Greg

catches a whiff of regurgitated peppermint schnapps. When she stands up, all the fight is gone from her face.

"Come on," he says. "Let's go for a walk."

"What about your hot date? You're just going to leave him behind?"

If there's anything other than sarcasm behind her words, Greg can't tell. He pulls her along through the beer-soaked crowd. As they turn onto Winter Street, the band slides into Sweet Caroline, and the people go wild. Another perennial favorite.

For the second time today, he finds himself at MacGregor Field. He leads Aimee to the bleachers, where they sit beneath the yellow glow of one lone light attached to the fence behind home plate. They can still hear Buck Fever, the drums and the rhythm and the screaming crowd. But there's breathing room here. Millions of stars, and the smell of dirt and clover.

"I'm not drunk, you know," says Aimee.

"You were puking in the street."

"Yeah, because I hate schnapps."

"Then why were you drinking it?"

"Because, Greggie, all the cool kids were doing it."

He can't help but laugh. She really does seem sober, and she was only doing the sort of thing normal teenagers normally do.

Aimee squints toward the baseball diamond. "Think we can find any?"

"I don't know. It's pretty dark."

"Race you."

Before he can answer, she sprints off toward the field. He chases after her, savoring the warm wind against his face, the solid earth beneath his shoes. Gaining speed easily, he passes Aimee, smacking her on the shoulder as he runs by. When he reaches the pitcher's mound, he holds up his arms in victory. There's a bouncy, buoyant feeling in his chest.

She catches up to him, pulling in deep breaths. "Forgot to

tell you," she says. "Winner has to go finish off that bottle of schnapps I hid behind the store."

Under the single light, they squint at the ground, searching for the dark orbs. Aimee finds the first one, shouting "Puffball!" before stomping on it hard enough for the fungi inside to come exploding out in a tiny dust cloud.

They run from base to base, stomping all the mushrooms they can find. By the time they collapse in the outfield, Greg's cheeks and stomach hurt from laughing, and Aimee is threatening to hurl again. After a while, their giggles fade. Down on Main Street they're playing the Stones, the notes drifting up to the stars, the fingernail moon.

"You won't tell Mom and Dad, will you?" asks Aimee, tapping the toe of her knockoff Docs against Greg's shin.

"No narcs here," he promises.

Except for the hours he has spent weeding Trudy's garden and landscaping Nate's yard, this is the happiest he has felt all summer. Or possibly forever. He has the sudden, unexplainable, probably stupid urge to tell his sister who he really is. To give a voice to all the hidden desires, all the lonely wonderings.

"What if I had actually been on a date with a girl tonight?" He pauses, heart throwing itself against his ribs. "Or what if I'd been on a date with Henry? What would you have said?"

Greg forces himself to pull his eyes from the stars and watch Aimee's reaction. Her profile is just like their mother's—upturned nose, round forehead. She takes a moment to answer. Then another. Then she turns her face so she's looking right back at him, and she holds her gaze steady on his.

"I'd have told you that no girl in Dalton is good enough for you," she says. "And you can do a whole lot better than Henry Covington."

"What's that supposed to mean?"

"He might be cute now, Greg, but have you seen his father? That hair isn't going to last forever."

Then she grins and taps her foot against his shin again, lighter this time. His sister, of all people—his badly dressed, eyeliner-smeared, puke-smelling sister. The relief is instant, and far better than any junk food binge, any runner's high.

But the fear is still there, too, soaking in his cells, like the nitrogen constantly released by the clover into the soil beneath them.

"Don't tell Mom and Dad, okay?"

"No narcs here," Aimee promises. "But honestly, Greg, they're so wrapped up in Sarah's stupid baby news they'd probably just forget if you did tell them."

"Babies aren't stupid," says Greg, in a perfect imitation of their mother's mushy voice. "Babies are *miracles*."

"The only miracle will be if that kid comes out *not* looking like a potato."

His sister.

They lie there on the sweet-scented grass, watching the stars and moon glide through the sky long after the band stops playing.

Date Night

While the rest of the town gets drunk down on Main Street, Trudy lets herself into the library. She flicks on the desk lamp in the windowless office, where she keeps the boxes of new books, then goes back out to the lobby, watching out the window toward the parking lot. For once, she doesn't have to wait long—because here comes Bev, right on time, walking to the library door. When she steps inside, a burst of terrible music from the street dance sneaks in after her.

"For Chrissake, hurry up and shut that."

"It's just a song, Tru. It can't bite you."

In the office, Bev grabs the boxcutter and starts ripping through cardboard. She looks like she usually does—cutoffs and a purple shirt, hair pushed back in an alligator clip—but something feels different.

"What's wrong?" Trudy asks.

"Just trying to get this done fast," says Bev, already slicing into another box. "Jo and I are opening the store earlier than usual tomorrow to get ready for the firemen's muster."

"You didn't have to come here."

"Only way I was going to see you."

Feeling as if Bev might as well have jabbed the boxcutter into her spine, Trudy falls silent and starts unpacking the books, sorting them by fiction and nonfiction. While she inventories the books by author, Bev finishes up with the last box and drops down into Trudy's swivel chair. The room is too quiet for too long, the only sound the faint rhythm of bass on Main Street.

When Bev finally speaks, her voice is conciliatory, tentative. "You want to hear about Sophie's new obsession?" And she tells Trudy all about *Pocahontas*, and how Marshall has promised Sophie he will take her to see the movie.

"And you're really going to let her believe whatever inane love story Disney's trying to sell?"

"I figure I'd wait to tell her about Native American genocide until she's at least seven." Bev picks up the pressed four-leaf clover Greg gifted Trudy at the beginning of summer and runs her fingers along the edges of the glass, holding it up to the lamp so she can study the delicate veins running through the leaves.

"Give him some credit, Tru. He's been out to Nate's for supper twice a week for the past month. Sophie likes him."

"I just don't think—"

Bev slams the block down so hard on the desk that Trudy is sure the glass has shattered, that the tiny clover inside is ruined. "Damn it, not everything is your business. It doesn't matter what you think about the situation, because it has nothing to do with you."

"I'm sorry," says Trudy, feeling like a kid getting yelled at for sneaking sweets before supper. "You're right."

"Yes, I am. And I'm tired, so I think it's time I head home."

It isn't the words, but the frostiness within them that scares Trudy most.

"You told me, Bevy," she says, "you told me you weren't going anywhere."

"And I meant it, but I'm not a saint. You remember what it's like, standing on the outside of a tragedy."

Trudy knows they're both thinking of Bridget five summers ago, of the horrible months afterward when nothing made sense and everything was uncertain. They got through it that time, and Trudy wants to promise Bev they'll get through it this time, too. That things will be better for them soon.

But who knows how long Richard is going to mope around, how long he's going to need her. For the first time, Trudy wonders if everything really is salvageable for her and Bev, and the idea that it might not be makes her so panicky that her legs start to shake.

She doesn't follow Bev into the darkened lobby. She listens to the door open—loud burst of Lynyrd Skynyrd—and slam shut again, bell jingling violently. Then she stands there in the lamplit room for a long time, staring at her four-leaf clover. The glass is scratched, but not quite broken.

Sunday morning is bright and blue. Nate wakes with his feet tangled around the sheet. For several minutes, he lies on his side of the bed—he still can't bring himself to sleep where Bridget slept—and stares at the crabapples outside his window. He slept badly, dreams of driving around in a DPD cruiser, chasing a black car down Route 11 when suddenly the brakes stopped working. Sixty miles an hour, seventy, eighty . . . no way to slow down. Fear like he's only ever felt the night he came home to find Bridget gone.

By the time he drags himself into the kitchen, Sophie is at the table with a bowl of cereal. She's changed out of her pajamas into a sequined teal dress and has tucked several paper towels into her collar to keep the outfit safe from any spills. Her hair curls around her face. One of the bracelets Nate's mother bought for her dangles from her wrist, dangerously close to the milk in her bowl.

"Looking good, Soph. Fancy."

"It's my movie outfit."

Smiling, Nate switches on the coffee pot. Ever since Marshall made the plan for Sophie to go see *Pocahontas* with him at the Prescott theater today, it's been all she can talk about.

"How many hours?" she asks.

Nate glances at the clock, surprised to see it's already after 8:00. "I'm dropping you off at Grampa's at 11:00."

"Do we have to go inside when we get there?"

She doesn't need to say anything else for Nate to understand—

that one supper at his in-laws' house earlier this summer was enough to make him hope he and Sophie never have to go back in there again. All Annette's boxes from the home shopping network, all those bottles of wine in the fridge, the uncomfortably intimate scent of unwashed body . . . Nothing happy can live in a house like that.

"We can wait for Grampa outside," Nate assures Sophie, who lets out a sigh of relief before attacking her cereal. Turns out the paper towels were a good idea—with each bite, half the milk misses her mouth. His daughter is a lot of things, but graceful isn't one of them.

Nate takes what Bridget always called the scenic route into town, turning left out of their driveway rather than right. As Sophie nods her head along to a Three Dog Night song on the oldies station, he drives past woods and fields, the unmarked road that leads to the radio tower, the white church near the train tracks. During his year on the force, Nate was called out to that church once. He was still riding with Bruce Rossignol then, and the whole drive over, Bruce wouldn't shut up about what they might find when they got there. "Whaddya think, Boss? Someone stab a sinner with a crucifix? Or maybe someone collapsed during that spooky *speaking with tongue* business." Turned out just to be Helen McGreevy needing them to jimmy her car, though. No danger, no one to save, but Nate felt sure he'd done a bit of good in the world, getting that cranky old lady back into her Pinto.

"Daddy, what're they singing about?"

Years spent listening to this song, and Nate still doesn't know what Shambala is, or where to find it, or what happens when you get there. "A fairy-tale kind of place," he tells Sophie.

"Is that where Mumma went when she died?"

A better father would have an answer ready. Nate pretends he didn't hear the question and keeps on driving, even though he can feel Sophie staring at him from the passenger seat long after the song turns to local commercials—Independence Day Sale at Prescott Chevrolet; don't miss it.

When they get to the Fraziers', they hop out of the truck and stand in the driveway. From here, they can see the whole town, forests and fields stretching hundreds of miles in each direction. Foamy clouds scud across the sky.

"There's us, Daddy," says Sophie, pointing at the outline of their farmhouse on a smaller hill in Milton Landing, three miles away. How many times did Nate and Bridget stand on this very spot when they were children, then teenagers, and look out toward the old Donoghue place, swearing it would be their home one day? Funny, the dreams that come true and the ones that fade to nothing.

Footsteps behind them, and Nate turns to see his father-in-law loping their way with a smile on his face as he takes in Sophie's outfit. "Guess I underdressed," he says, twirling so she can assess his jeans and polo shirt.

"You can borrow my bracelet if you want to fancy it up a little."

Without hesitation, Marshall holds out his hand so Sophie can slip the plastic beads onto his wrist. "What do you think, Nate? Should I debut this look at the mill next week?"

"Only if you want all the guys to be jealous."

Sophie tugs her grandfather's hand, saying they're going to be late. When Marshall asks if she's forgetting something, she looks confused, and Nate feels a jolt of betrayal. Is this how it will be when she starts kindergarten? Will she run right onto that school bus without so much as a backward glance?

"Hug your dad goodbye, kiddo."

She hurries to Nate and jumps up in his arms.

"You promise you'll be good for Grampa?"

"Only if you go do something fun."

"Does going home and mowing the lawn count?"

"You're boring, Daddy," Sophie says. "But you don't have to be."

She leaps down from his arms and sprints toward her grandfather's truck. Marshall reaches out to give him a firm handshake, the same kind they've given each other since Nate took Bridget to their first Spring Fling in sixth grade. The kind that says not to worry, your girl is safe with me. The panic eases slightly.

After they're gone, Nate stands in the driveway staring out toward the river braided through a thousand trees. Above him, the house looms like some imposing fortress.

Before he gets in his truck, he glances up at Bridget's old bedroom. He almost thinks he sees the white lace curtains gently swaying. But it's been years since those windows were open. Years since any breeze moved inside that room.

With Sophie's words running through his mind—*You're boring*—Nate decides to check out what's going on downtown, where Main Street is closed to vehicles so people can walk around to all the different booths set up by local artists and businesses—Corinna Getchell selling pottery, Ted Bergeron manning the fried dough cart, giving the treat away for half-off to anyone who shows their latest receipt from the grocery store.

He parks in the lot across from the Store 'N More, watching the crowd, recognizing several people even from a distance. There's Dean Buckley walking out of the Store 'N More, and there are George and Arlene chatting it up with Pastor Fields, and there, last in line at the Girl Scouts' Sno-Cone stand, is Rose. She's wearing a white sundress, and her dark hair is loose, flowing down her back.

She turns toward his truck and waves, beckoning him over. Telling himself it would be rude not to, Nate steps down from the truck and crosses the street toward her. The crowd is thick and loud, everyone laughing and talking over the country music that spills out from the doors at Frenchie's.

"Where's Sophie?" asks Rose as he joins her in the line.

"Went to the movies with her grandfather. What about Adam and Brandon?"

"Some other kid's birthday party. God, have you been dragged to one of those things yet? They're the *worst*."

She insists on buying him a Sno-Cone, but Nate can't stop himself from adding a couple bucks to the tip jar held out to him by a gap-toothed girl he doesn't recognize wearing a Brownies sash. He and Rose find a picnic table outside the bar, and they sit there not saying anything for a while, letting the flavored ice melt on their tongues while people stream around them in a blur of noise and color. Nate keeps glancing back at the girl in the sash, feeling more frustrated each time he can't think of her name.

"Caitlyn Stephens. Paul and Marnie's girl."

Startled, he turns his attention to Rose, who's watching him over her paper cup. "Who the heck are Paul and Marnie?"

"They moved here from downstate last month. Bought that old Christmas tree farm out on Poor Man's Road."

"How do you know all this?"

"Marnie brought Caitlyn in for booster shots last week," Rose says. "Which I technically shouldn't tell you—patient confidentiality and all—but I doubt you'll rat me out."

Nate flicks his eyes around the crowd, wondering how many other strangers are moving around him. "I used to know everyone in Dalton," he says. "Everything that was going on."

"No one can know what's going on all the time."

Before Nate can respond, the air is split with the shriek of sirens, and there's a ripple of motion as everyone hurries onto the sidewalks. He and Rose stand to watch the ladder truck, newly washed and shiny red, easing its way down the street.

"Damn it. This is the stupid muster, isn't it?"

"I don't see any buildings on fire, so it must be."

They could leave. They could walk away, Rose toward her trailer, Nate back to his truck. But something seems to keep them rooted to the curb.

When the red truck stops in front of the hydrant on the corner of Main and Larch, several firefighters jump down onto the pavement. Gordon Martin starts in on his usual recitation of the rules—two groups of three will be timed from the second they start pulling on their gear to the second they hook up the hose to the hydrant. No pushing, no shoving, no cursing.

"I don't remember the no-cursing rule."

"That's because no one ever follows it."

Urged on by the crowd's cheers, the first team does well, from gear-up to hose-down in under three minutes. Not surprising—Larry, Gwen, and Bob have been fighting fires around Dalton for over a decade. It's the second team the crowd roars for. Ronny is solid, but Kevin and Jason are in their early twenties, practically untested.

As soon as Gordon starts the clock, it's a mess. Jason trips over his boots and Kevin struggles to get himself strapped up to his O2 tank. That's when the cursing starts, good-natured heckles of *goddamn jackwagon* and *fuckin' send it!* Beside Nate, Rose laughs and leans into him, accidentally or on purpose, he can't tell. Her bare arm is warm and solid against his own, and he feels a strange little twist in his stomach.

It's when the team gets to the hydrant that things really fall apart. Ronny is screaming at the rookies, telling them to get their shit together, but something goes wrong—Nate can't see what, through the mass of people—and suddenly water is spraying up to the sky like one of those geysers out west. The firefighters are shouting, but the crowd is shouting louder as water comes falling in shiny-prism sheets, splashing onto the pavement.

All around them, people yell and laugh inside the unnatural rain as Rose, eyes closed, tilts her face up to the sky, letting the torrent wash down on her. Nate tries to step away from the spray, but it's useless—his clothes are immediately soaked. He wants to tell Rose he has to leave, get back home. That the porch light needs to be replaced, that the lawn needs mowing, that the twist in his stomach reminds him of jumping off a steep riverbank into the cold black water below.

But Rose, eyes still shut, is moving her hips slowly, as if swaying to a song Nate is almost certain he's never heard before. And he stands still, and watches.

The orthopedics wing at the Prescott hospital smells like overcooked noodles, and the windows catch the sun full force, effectively turning the waiting room into an oven. The TV in the corner is set to the Springer show. To the audience's delight and the husband's shock, the paternity results confirm he is *not* the father of Junior. The wife manages to sob without ruining her makeup as her tattooed, muscled ex-boyfriend appears from backstage.

"How do these people have time for all these romances?" asks Vera's father, who's been riveted to the screen since the nurse came and whisked her mother down the hall. "Don't they have jobs to go to?"

"It's scripted, Dad. You can't believe any of it."

Vera is using all her willpower not to leap off the chair, run down the hall, and burst into the exam room—she wants to hear everything the doctor has to say about her mother's leg. The progress of her healing.

Even though Vera closed the clinic for the day so she could be here with her parents, her mother insisted on going into the room alone to have her cast removed. "I don't need you, dear," were her words. But how much information about aftercare is the doctor giving that she will forget as soon as they leave the hospital?

"Look at this chowderhead," her father says, pointing at the TV. The jilted husband is shaking his fist at the ex-boyfriend's glowering, steroidal face. "That's not a fight he's gonna win."

Unable to sit still any longer, Vera begins to pace in front of the windows as the show cuts to a commercial.

"Why are you so riled up? It's only a leg. And if they're taking the cast off, that means it's healed, right?"

"She's not out of the woods yet. She'll still need a splint, maybe some physical therapy. A broken leg at your age can be lethal."

"*At our age?*"

"I hate to break it to you, Dad, but you and Mom are almost seventy."

"So do you want to shop around for nursing homes after this? I hear Meadowbrook serves pudding instead of Jell-O."

Vera turns to look at her father, sitting there as relaxed as if he were in his own living room. His hair has gone completely white, but his eyes are as clear as they were when she was a child.

"I'm just saying you and Mom need to take things a little more seriously."

At the front desk, the bottle-red receptionist ignores the phone. On the TV, an ad warns about the dangers of asbestos.

Vera's father gives her a long look, and she suddenly feels as nervous as the first time she had to start an IV line on a sobbing three-year-old.

"You know Mom and I are proud of you," he says, "and we're glad to have you home for the summer. But you're driving us nuts."

The phone at the desk rings again, gets ignored again.

"We're not your patients. We're not invalids. I know you don't wanna believe this, but Mom and I can take care of ourselves."

Vera sinks into the chair beside her father. "I worry about you guys."

"Maybe it's time you start worrying about your own stuff."

"And what do you mean by that?"

"You're not getting any younger yourself. And you've gone an awful long time without a fella."

Vera can't help but laugh. "You're starting to sound like Mom."

Her father laughs, too, the same back-of-the-throat rumble that plays in the background of her childhood memories—family canoe trips, Root Beer Float Fridays, Monopoly games at the kitchen table as snow ticked against the windowpanes. It was a predictable existence, not terribly thrilling (most of the time, Vera was sure she would die of boredom), but growing up, she never doubted her parents loved her or each other. She's seen enough through her work to know not everyone is so lucky.

Back on the show, the ex has the husband in a headlock while the wife screams about what a sham the marriage has been ever since her husband got slapped with that lawsuit for running over his mistress's Pomeranian. It's ridiculous, unreal.

"Okay," says Vera's father. "Maybe you don't need a fella. But it sure as hell seems like you need something you're not finding down there in the city. Mom and I both know you hate it at that hospital."

True, Vera has mentioned to them that things have changed in the ER, that she feels more like a robot than an actual nurse. But she's never gone into detail about how useless she feels, and how lonely, and how disconnected from everything around her in Bangor.

"It's not like I can just quit, Dad. It's my job."

Her father gives her a brief look that contains so many big things—impatience, empathy, frustration, understanding.

"Jobs aren't spouses or children," he says. "You can leave them whenever you want."

From any other man, it might sound as though he is trying to say he has spent a lifetime secretly hating everything from his work at the mill to his time spent with Vera and her mother. But then he laughs again, the sound conjuring up more specific memories of those childhood moments—him always knowing how much paper money Vera was hiding under the Monopoly board, her mother expertly paddling around unseen rocks in the river, both of them pretending Vera hadn't already snuck a giant spoonful of vanilla ice cream before asking for another on top of her root beer.

"Yup," her father says, as the bodyguards break the husband free from the ex's grasp. "I might not be as addled as you think."

After supper (a takeout bucket of KFC to celebrate her mother's newly braced leg), Vera leaves her parents at the house and walks down to the bandstand, where she's supposed to meet Rose for the Dalton Daze concert.

It's early evening, humid, clouds like stretched pink taffy. Cars and trucks are parked along High Street, and people line the sidewalks; kids eating cotton candy, adults not-so-discreetly sipping out of flasks or brown bottles. Up in the bandstand, the high school brass band is playing a trumpet-heavy song.

Vera says hello to several people, many of whom have been into the clinic to see her over the past few weeks. She marvels with George Nadeau about how much better his posture is without that shrapnel lodged in his thigh. Phil Lannigan assures her, quietly, that the hemorrhoid cream is doing the trick. Gloria Arsenault asks if she can come in next week to talk about better migraine medications; Vera promises she'll have Rose call after the holiday to book her an appointment.

She settles down on a bench beneath the lone elm that survived the plague of the 70s and waits for Rose to find her. As the band launches into the Blues Brothers' rendition of "Gimme Some Lovin'," she spots Nate and Sophie at the face-painting booth. Sophie, dressed in red overalls, claps her hands as she sees her reflection in the mirror Molly Lannigan holds up for her. From here, Vera can't be sure, but she thinks it's a butterfly painted on the girl's face. She watches as Sophie hops off the chair only to push Nate down onto it. Laughing, he holds his hands up as she instructs Molly what to draw on his cheek.

Vera has always admired that easy-yet-everything surrender parents offer up to their children. She hasn't aspired to motherhood herself, but she can understand the appeal—the tiny faces that look like your face, the family legacy that will carry on long after you are gone. The little daily wonders of what kids say and how they think.

If she were to ever change her mind about having children, Vera knows she would go about it in a way not a lot of people here in this town would understand. She doesn't think a husband is necessary, for one thing, or even a boyfriend. Single parenting is damn hard, but not impossible. Look at Rose. Look at Nate. They struggle but they make it work, each in their own ways. Vera could do the same, should she ever choose to.

The band segues into a Kansas song, and the crowd cheers. At the face-painting booth, Nate glimpses himself in the mirror and grins. Then Sophie grabs him by the hand and pulls him toward the bench where Vera sits beneath the elm, under dappled evening shadow. When Sophie sees her, she drops Nate's hand and runs at her, hair bouncing. As she gets closer, Vera sees it's not a butterfly on her face after all, but a delicate flower, purple-petaled.

"You like it?" Sophie asks.

"I love it."

"It's an enemy."

Nate laughs. "Anemone, is what she means. Greg Fortin has been teaching her all about flowers."

Sophie's name is shouted over the crowd and the music, and they turn to see Marshall Frazier waving at his granddaughter from the sidewalk.

"Can I, Daddy?"

She's off and running before Nate can answer.

"Good thing I was going to tell her yes," he says, and he laughs again, but there's a hint of sadness in the way he stares after her. The hurt of being left behind.

That must be the worst part of being a parent, single or not. The certainty that for the rest of their lives, in ways both small and huge, your child is going to sprint away from you without looking backward.

Then again, Vera has to chuckle as she sees Rose walking toward her and Nate with Adam and Brandon in tow. The boys are arguing about which Power Ranger is best, and Rose looks as if she'd gladly pay money to have a grandparent swoop out of nowhere to take them off her hands for a while.

"Sorry I'm late," she says. "These two didn't want to leave the house."

Rose hands Vera a paper plate of fried dough—somehow, she guessed how Vera likes it, with just a hint of cinnamon. Vera has had close friends before (though not so many since she's been at the ER), but never anyone who intuitively understands her the way Rose does. Even though they've only hung out a few times since that first night Vera went over to watch *Unsolved Mysteries* at Rose's trailer, it's as if they've known each other forever. It's a nice feeling, homey and unexpected.

Also unexpected is the way Nate stares at Rose as she kneels to tell Adam and Brandon they can like different Power Rangers; the yellow one is just as good as the blue one, so please, *please* stop fighting. She might as well be giving away secrets of the universe, judging by the expression on Nate's face—a blend of admiration and respect, and a fair amount of awe.

It's the same way Vera's father stares at her mother when she answers correctly on Final Jeopardy. The same way her mother looks at her father when he surprises her by cooking waffles on weekend mornings.

No one, not even Gavin back when they were at their happiest, has ever looked at Vera like that. And up until now, she never thought she needed anyone to look at her that way. Always believed she was better off alone.

What can be lonelier than realizing—amid the crescendo of a Journey ballad, in a crowd of people who watched you grow up and move away from this little nowhere town to prove you could evolve into something more than the girl they knew—that you have never been in love? That you have never given yourself willingly to another person, trusting them to help you evolve into the person you are meant to be?

Nothing. Suddenly Vera can think of nothing lonelier than that.

INDEPENDENCE DAY

The morning of the Fourth, Bev steps out of her car and into the parking lot of the Store 'N More. The sky is low and black. No birds singing. But there is a strange noise, some sort of animal snuffle, over near the Laundromat. Bev squints into the pool of light cast by the halogens as a solid shadow emerges from the scrub brush.

Her first instinct when she understands she's staring at a black bear isn't fear, or even shock. Instead, Bev feels a cool sense of detachment as she and the bear look right at each other. Too large for a cub, too small for a full-grown adult. Mangy-looking thing. Its eyes, glossy under the streetlamp, are comically tiny for its big, blocky head.

"Hey, bear." Bev speaks softly.

The creature's ears perk toward her, and his nostrils test the air, tasting the witch hazel toner she splashes on her face each morning. Only when he takes a lumbering step toward her does Bev come to her senses. Bear attacks are pretty much unheard of here in the North Maine Woods, but this one might have rabies, or brainworm. Or maybe only moose get brainworm. Either way, there's no predicting what a wild animal might do.

Bev draws herself up tall, puffs out her chest, and yells in a deep voice, "Hey, bear!"

His eyes go bright with fear as he startles backward, then he takes off running toward the patch of woods behind the Laundromat. As soon as his fuzzy rump disappears behind the brush, Bev feels abandoned. Unaccountably alone.

*

All morning, it bothers her. She slices deli meat and worries about the bear. She cleans up spilled coffee grounds and wonders if the bear has a family. She listens to millworkers bitch about having to work on a holiday and imagines the bear wandering alone through the woods, desperate for company.

"You okay, Bev?"

The question comes from Marshall, of all people, standing there waiting for his usual muffin. Only today, he's not dressed for work, because as the boss of the mill, he *does* have the holiday off. He also gave Nate the entire week off, which Bev is grateful for—her son needs time with Sophie before she goes off to kindergarten at the end of summer.

"Why would a bear come into town this time of year?" she asks.

"There was a bear hanging around here?"

If he doesn't lower his voice, half the men rummaging through the beer cooler will hear him and make a plan to go out poaching tonight, when all the cops and game wardens are either asleep or drunk.

"I didn't see a bear," Bev says, loudly. "It's just one of Sophie's hypothetical questions."

"Our girl does ask a lot of questions, doesn't she?"

Bev feels a twinge of annoyance. Does he have the right to call Sophie *their* girl when he's just now getting to know her? It's the sort of ungenerous thought Trudy would blurt out loud. The sort of thing Bev would tell her not to say.

Up at the cash register, Jo breaks into a peal of laughter with Molly Lannigan, who's buying sparklers for her, Phil, and the kids to light at their house later tonight, their annual Fourth of July tradition.

Handing Marshall his blueberry muffin, Bev says, "You should come out to the fireworks tonight. Nate, Bill, and I bring Sophie every year. I know she'd love it if you were there."

He doesn't have to tell her his answer. His grin tells it for him.

Nearly every Fourth of July since Nate was a teenager, Trudy and Richrd have joined Bev's family down at the river for the fireworks, the official end of Dalton Daze. Five summers ago, there was nothing to celebrate so soon after Bridget's death, so none of them went. And this year, in the wake of her and Trudy's tiff the other night, Bev doesn't feel a strong desire to meet her there. The last thing she wants is to watch Trudy scowling at Marshall as the sky lights up green and gold, determined not to have a good time.

But disinviting her would be petty and childish. Cruel.

So when Bev gets home from the store, while Bill, Nate, and Sophie lounge around on the back deck eating bomb pops, she takes the phone off the wall and dials Trudy's number. It rings several times before Richard answers, sounding slightly winded.

"Trudy's in the garden," he says. "She asked me to tell you she doesn't feel up to going to the fireworks tonight."

Feeling as though she's been slapped across the face with a wet dishtowel, Bev can only ask him why, though she imagines she already knows the answer.

"Says she has a headache. Plans on lying down as soon as she comes inside."

Maybe Richard doesn't know a lie when his wife tells it, but Bev sure as hell does. Headaches are Trudy's go-to excuse when she doesn't feel like leaving the house, when the only company she can abide is Mycroft curled up on her lap while she reads one of the dozen books stacked on her nightstand.

So it will be like that between them now, Bev thinks as she hangs the phone back on the wall. The exact kind of lies in the exact kind of marriages she and Trudy have always longed to escape. Different desires, similar distance. Lonely, independent living.

Rose hates the Fourth of July. Too many flags, too many undercooked hotdogs. But Adam and Brandon love barbecues and fireworks, so once every year, for their sake, she pretends to be patriotic for a few hours.

This year, Adam insists they leave the house long before the parade starts. "We gotta get good seats, Mum," he says, as if they'll have to duke it out with thousands of people rather than dozens.

"They always throw lots of candy near the Post Office," adds Brandon.

When they set out from the trailer just after 9 A.M., the sky is thick with gluey clouds, no sun anywhere, but it's still over eighty degrees. Rose, loaded down with three folding camp chairs, is sweating before they even reach the end of the gravel driveway. So weird to think that on this exact day five years ago, the boys were with her mother watching the parade while Rose sat inside the trailer watching Nate lay Tommy flat on this same dirt they're walking over now. Sometimes she wonders if any of his blood is still there, hidden under pebbles, poisoning the ground.

He called again last night. "Why don't you want to talk to me, why don't you miss me?" he slurred, and Rose nearly told him to shove the phone up his ass. But she just hung up, because she wasn't brave enough to say those words. He might be hundreds of miles away, but he's still Tommy. He's still got reach.

By the time they get to the sidewalk outside the Post Office, Rose's heels sting with blisters—damn sandals are cute but impractical—and her hair has worked itself loose from its ponytail. Her tie-dyed dress keeps clinging to her in unfortunate places. She feels grimy, disgusting, nowhere near beautiful. Just a badly-dressed, under-showered mother, begging her kids not to belch so loud in public.

She settles in her chair while Adam and Brandon hover close by. It doesn't take long for Main Street to fill up with people. Rose recognizes pretty much everyone lined up along the route, kids already sugared-up from morning pancakes, parents bleary-eyed from hangovers. Lots of people wave hello to Rose, shout greetings—Molly and Phil Lannigan with all their blonde kids; the Fortins; Dean Buckley . . . Everyone used to know her as Tommy Merchant's poor, abused fiancée, but ever since she started working at the clinic, most of the people in Dalton seem to think of her as simply Rose Douglas. There's a good feeling in that, like she's finally aced a test she's been studying for her whole damn life.

Rose is staring down toward the Store 'N More when she hears a familiar voice behind her. "Looks like we picked a good spot, Soph."

Turning, she sees Nate grinning down at her. She looks like she just walked out of a hobo camp; he looks nice and put together. White shirt, faded jeans, eyes bluer than the river. Standing beside him, Sophie is dressed in pink leggings and a zebra-striped shirt. Hair wild in the muggy air.

Leaning in so close Rose can smell her Froot-Loop breath, Sophie says, "I told Daddy this was where to be. It's where they throw all the candy."

"Great minds think alike. Adam and Brandon said the same thing."

"Yeah, because who do you think told *them*?"

While the kids hop around on the sidewalk, Nate unfolds

his chair and settles beside Rose. Their elbows knock together, and he apologizes before shifting so his body is angled further away from hers. She feels a trill of the same nervousness she used to get when they both worked at the cop shop.

She's not the same girl who used to fantasize about shirtless warriors on horseback. She threw her vibrator away long ago, afraid the boys would find it. She's slept with a few townies since Tommy left, but she never wasted time thinking about them after the night was over.

What is it about Nate? What about him makes her feel so anxious and so at ease all at once? How can those two things even exist at the same time? And how does he always smell so good? And why didn't she ever thank him for punching Tommy in the face?

Maybe it's time they talk about that, and about everything that led up to it: Nate arresting Tommy. Nate coming home after and finding Bridget dead. Tommy getting out of jail a few weeks later. Nate beating Tommy until he was a puddle of useless bones in the driveway. Rose letting it happen, pretending it never happened.

The wail of sirens rips through the morning, bouncing off the buildings. Down on the other end of Main, people cheer as the ambulance turns the corner, flashing its red and blue lights and honking its horn.

Nate leans in close to Rose, bringing the smell of cedar with him. "I don't know about you," he says, "but I really hate parades."

Over supper that night, Rose tells the boys she has a surprise for them. But they have to eat their peas and their pork chops if they want to actually get it.

"That's a bribe, Mum."

"Yup, it sure is. But trust me. It's a bribe you want to take."

Adam and Brandon eat everything on their plates. They help

wash and dry the dishes, and for once they don't interrupt Rose while she's on the phone with Vera, whose only Fourth of July plans include eating the s'mores her parents insist on making in their backyard—"You'd swear I was ten years old," she says. "But if it keeps them happy . . . "

Finally, just after 8:30, Rose gathers the boys in the living room. "You want to see the fireworks, right?" she asks, feeling nearly as excited as they look.

"Yes!" they shout, and run toward the trailer door, ready for her to get them in the car and head to the river.

"What if I told you the surprise is that we have VIP seats to the show?"

"What's VIP?"

"Very important person. Like a celebrity."

Brandon's eyes grow wide. "Are we celeries?"

Usually this flub-up would prompt Adam into teasing his brother. But he just giggles and goes along with it. "I think Mum's saying we *are* celeries. For tonight, anyway. Right, Mum?"

"Right. So come on, then. We don't want to be late."

She grabs a blanket off the couch and leads them out into the yard. Next door, Marian's lights are off, an added bonus— it will make this better. This crazy idea that came to Rose as she lay awake last night unable to sleep after she hung up on Tommy, hand on the phone in case he called again.

Behind the trailer, she has already got the ladder in place, and she tells Adam to go up first. He looks at her like she's nuts, but in a good way, then makes his way up and onto the flat roof.

"Go ahead, Brandon," says Rose, worried his fear of heights will ruin this whole thing. But he climbs up slow and careful while she holds the ladder steady.

As soon as she's sure he's safe beside his brother, Rose makes her way up awkwardly with the quilt slung over one arm. Once she's on the roof, she lays the blanket out, tells the boys to settle down and get comfy.

The three of them snuggle close and wait while the sky, still cloudy, grows even darker. Darker. There's rain in the air, that's for sure, and probably later tonight, Rose will be tiptoeing through the house while the boys sleep, putting out buckets in the spots the roof always leaks. Like some kind of trailer trash Santa.

But for right now, the roof is sturdy, and the rain is holding off, and her boys are pressed tight and warm against either side of her, and Nate hates parades just as much as she does, and Vera is her friend, her real friend, and the world is dim but also tolerable.

When the first firework bursts low in the sky, reflecting blue and green over the trees and fields and river, Rose closes her eyes. Sees the flickery light lingering there long after the sound of the explosion fades away.

Below them, under a plywood roof without enough insulation, the phone starts ringing.

E nough."

This is what Marshall tells Annette when he comes home to see her unboxing another Thigh-Master. There's more than that, though; she is sprawled in the middle of the living room floor, surrounded by new boxes. A rice cooker. Bamboo cutting boards. A foot bath with tiny bottles of essential oils, some of which spilled in the box and now fill the room with the smells of eucalyptus and sweet orange and clary sage, whatever that is.

"Look at me," he says.

She sips her wine and opens another box, the some-assembly-required Victorian dollhouse. She will glue each roof shingle in place. She will build the spiral staircase. She will paint the siding pink or yellow or blue.

There have been clouds gathering all day, hanging heavy above Dalton. When she was a child, Annette's parents used to each take one end of a quilt and hold it over her body while she lay giggling on her bed. They'd slowly bring the blanket down closer, closer, closer, until the tiny hairs on her legs and arms stood up straight, grazing against the wool. The clouds are like that, but instead of warmth they will bring rain; instead of joy they will bring all the pollution from all the world right back down to earth. All those invisible toxins flooding the rivers, rooting deep in the soil, choking the seeds that maybe one day could have birthed a tree.

He tells her he has cancelled the credit cards and hidden the checkbook. There are no more joint banking accounts, only his name on everything. Frazier, Frazier, Frazier. The name was hers to borrow, and now it has been taken back. Marshall swears it isn't permanent, and it isn't punishment, but Annette doesn't know what else you could call it, ripping a woman's entire identity away like that with no warning.

"Come with me," he says.
And then, "You used to love fireworks."
And then, not so soft, "You need to leave the house."
And finally, soft again, as he's walking out the door, "I won't be gone long."

After Marshall has left the house to meet *them* down by the river, Annette creeps through every room and every hall. Packages everywhere. Useless merchandise everywhere. She remembers a story she read a long time ago about a woman locked in a room. The woman was sure the wallpaper was alive and breathing, watching all her movements. Annette felt disgusted by the woman, mortified for her. But now, after a few glasses of wine, dressed in nothing but her bra and underwear, sitting in the hallway outside her *gone-away* daughter's bedroom, she thinks maybe that woman had it right. Who's to say what's alive and what isn't, who watches and who doesn't?

They say each birth gets easier. But Bridget was number four, and she was the hardest of them all. With the others, Annette had time for an epidural. With Bridget, there was no time for any numbing agent. She woke on that cold March night drenched from the waist down. The digital alarm clock read 2:01. They called in Marshall's parents to be with the other children, all sleeping, then they sped to the hospital, sleet falling like silver needles in the headlights of their station wagon. Every bump agony; every contraction an iron fist squeezing her womb and her spine into pulp. By the time they got to the hospital, she was fully dilated. When Bridget came ripping and tearing and howling her way into the world, Annette was staring at the clock. 3:03. Sixty-two minutes from start to finish, flood to harvest. All their other babies were born bald. Bridget's skull was covered in thick whorls of hair. Annette couldn't stop stroking her fingers gently along that hair, as if it were a rabbit's foot that would give her all the good luck she'd ever need.

They, whoever they are, say fire is as cleansing as rain. Annette is sure she has heard this somewhere, or maybe she read it in one of the books she used to keep, the ones that promised to decode her dreams.

Sure, she used to love fireworks. She used to love a lot of things. Clean white carpets and canapes, church on Sunday mornings, parties. She loved Debussy rhythms, gold-plated soccer trophies, pointe shoes shaped to the precise contours of her eldest daughter's feet. Freshly painted canvas, so many shades of green and yellow and blue, colors that seemed to hold all other colors inside them.

One day ago, or maybe two, or who the hell knows, Annette stepped inside Bridget's room for the first time since she went away. She stood behind the curtain and watched the scene in her driveway. Marshall and Nate and Sophie on one planet, Annette floating high above. She saw the laughter between the three of them. The love. She wanted to rush down to them and beg them to show her how to be like that, open and new. She wanted to close her eyes and say a magic word and make them disappear—them, and then the town, and then herself and the house and everything inside it. Will the world into disintegration. Nothingness.

The Curtis girl at the clinic recommended therapy.
Annette will make her own therapy.

She takes many trips in and out of the house. Each time she steps outside in her underwear, she is shocked by the grass against her feet, the pebbles that catch between her toes, the greasy air licking at her skin. It is so dark, and the clouds are so low, and down at the river, the whole damn town is crowded together, gazing up at the sky, waiting for the first burst of color, the gun-metal reek of carefully controlled explosions. Annette carries boxes, and more boxes, and when she's tired of carrying those, she makes the long trek up the stairs and down the hall, into Bridget's room, and she grabs an armful of paintings—they're too heavy, so she opens the windows wide, kicks out the screens, and hurls the paintings down onto the ground, far below. Heavy hollow thunks like carcasses dropped from the sky.

"Join the living," she told her daughter.

"Burn them all," her now-dead daughter said.

As the first of the fireworks start to boom down at the river—too far away to see the burst, but the faintest imprint of their color bleeds up into the clouds—Annette strikes the match. The pile of unneeded things is as tall as her head; she could easily throw herself in, make her own funeral pyre. The real punishment, though, the one she deserves, is remaining alive. Bearing witness to the carnage. There is the dollhouse, the Scarlett O'Hara collector's plates, the exercise equipment (unlikely to melt), the tiny vials of oil that will thickly scent the night. Fake rubies, glittering. Small stuffed bears, reaching for rain. And there are the paintings, frozen images of living landscapes. River and forest and meadow and mountain. Deep-dark blue and spring-bright green; new-growth yellow and peony pink.

The boxes burn first, but Bridget's colors burn brightest.

Richard can walk around the block three times without a rest now, four if it's not too hot and humid. His pace is still slower than he'd like, but his heart no longer tries to vault itself out of his throat whenever he climbs a hill. Most nights, Trudy walks beside him. Sometimes he doesn't mind her presence—she takes care of the small talk whenever they run into people—but more and more, Richard longs to be alone, to mosey, to look up at the sky for however long he wants without her telling him to pick up the pace.

"It's a marathon, Trudy. Not a sprint."

"You think they meander like that in a marathon?"

So it's a relief on the last night of Dalton Daze when she tells Richard he's on his own. She's going to lie down before her headache turns into a migraine while Bev and pretty much everyone else in town goes to the river. Even with the threat of rain, it's still the Fourth of July, and that means fireworks.

"You should go join them," Trudy says.

Richard imagines his patients and friends and neighbors down in that field behind the Aroostook Lodge, the river running just a few yards away. Every year it's the same—lots of chatter and lots of laughter as the volunteer crew flubs the first few rounds of fireworks. Always the elated fear that the explosions are too near the earth, that all the embers will go spinning through the crowd.

"Think I'll pass," he says.

"For Chrissake, don't just sit in that recliner while I'm upstairs sleeping. You get out and walk."

"That's my plan."

"Planning and doing are two different things."

As usual, her voice is stern, but there's a softness in her eyes as she gazes at him over the kitchen table. Outside, the catbirds are singing, trying their best to sound like robins.

"I promise, Trudy. I'll walk, just to get away from those damn birds."

Then he offers her a smile, and she gives it back to him. He has been sitting out on the porch every day, binoculars in hand, trying to catch sight of every movement those birds make. Sometimes Trudy joins him. Even went down to the hardware store the other day and bought herself her own pair of binoculars. They're smaller, and metallic, and she swears their focus puts Richard's to shame.

Dalton is quiet and still. No traffic. No one else out walking. It's like the town has been frozen in time. Richard remembers an episode of *The Twilight Zone* he and Trudy watched when they were younger, when their bodies fit together easily. In the show, the apocalypse came in the form of a nuclear bomb. The only survivor was a man who happened to be down in a bank vault. When he came up from the underground, his whole world was flattened, razed. No survivors other than himself and all the hundreds of books that for the first time in his life he would finally have uninterrupted opportunities to read. When the man broke his glasses, Richard swore out loud, and Trudy cried. "All those books," she said, "and no one to read them." At first, Richard felt concerned that his wife was misplacing her empathy—surely a human deserved more sympathy than any story. But eventually he understood that while his wife only voiced her grief for the books, the mourning inherently extended to all the people who would never read those books. And as he walks the empty streets of Dalton under the gray sky, Richard remembers something

238 · SHANNON BOWRING

else Trudy said that night, as she curled her limbs around his. *What's a story without a reader?*

Ever since his heart attack, he has been asking himself a similar question: *What's a body without a soul?*

The past few weeks, he has felt his own soul hovering closer, following him around like an extra shadow on these evening walks. Sometimes he could swear he feels it brush against his face while he's watching the catbirds twitch their tails, sing their songs. But that soul or spirit hasn't quite settled yet, and his body still feels void of something essential.

He is just about to make his third loop down High Street, back toward Main, when he changes his mind. If he heads up Rich Fucker Road, he might be high enough above the town to see the fireworks down at the river.

Calves aching, he eases his way up the gradual incline, past Ted Bergeron's house, the Vances' place with its fenced-in tennis court. As he nears the top of the hill, he catches a whiff of something acrid—someone must be burning trash.

At the foot of the Fraziers' long driveway, Richard turns to face Dalton. And there it is, the town spread before him. He knows every bend in the river, every rooftop. He has stood inside each of those three churches for weddings, baptisms, funerals. He has walked and driven each street, each unpaved road. This time of day—nearly night—and with all these clouds, Mount Katahdin is invisible, but Richard knows where she lies on the southwestern horizon, all the curves of her familiar face, the graceful swoop of her spine.

Down at the river, the fireworks begin with a crackle and a boom. The bursts of green and blue against the low clouds remind him of the bruises that Rose used to come into the clinic with as a patient after getting in Tommy Merchant's way after he'd been drinking.

The wind shifts, and Richard again smells something burning—not grass, not wood, something unnatural. Manmade.

Turning, he glances up at the Fraziers' house perched on top of the hill, its huge windows reflecting the clouds and the fireworks' muted colors. Then he sees a glimmer of brighter shades, orange and red.

At the top of the driveway, a fire. Inside the fire, boxes of all shapes and sizes piled at least five feet high. Standing beside the fire, too close to the fire, Annette Frazier, wearing only a beige bra and underpants.

Before Richard can make sense of the scene, he's running up the hill, heart rattling, feet pounding against pavement, toward the inferno. As he gets closer, he sees paintings on fire, too, and he nearly chokes on the reek of turpentine and scorched canvas.

"Step back, Annette!" he yells over the roar of the flames, but she just stands there, skin pink from the heat, and stares at the writhing flicker.

Richard rushes to her, nearly tackling her to the ground. She tries to squirm away from him, back toward the flames, but he wraps his arms tight around her body, lifts her into his arms, and carries her across the lawn, only setting her down when they reach the ivy-covered trellis Bridget and Nate stood under on their wedding day. Richard and Trudy were here that day, a lifetime ago. There was a bright blue sky, two violinists from away playing something sweet and somber, and Bridget in her lace gown, holding a bouquet made by Trudy. Richard can't remember what flowers she carried, but they were yellow and white, a nice contrast to the dark green foliage his own wife had so carefully chosen.

Both hands on Annette's damp shoulders to keep her from running back toward the fire, Richard asks, "What happened?" But that's a ridiculous question, because it's pretty damn clear what happened. This woman decided to burn her life to the ground.

At least she didn't set fire to the house. Or herself.

"I couldn't get it all," says Annette. "There's so much left inside. I just got so tired."

There's a giant pop, then a steaming hiss of wood splitting apart—a frame on one of the paintings beads with flames. Sparks scatter all around.

"Annette." Richard keeps his voice gentle, even though his heart is hammering and sweat stings his eyes. "We need to call the fire department."

"They're busy," she says, pointing vaguely toward the river.

"Someone will be at the station; they'll radio in for backup."

Down at the river, the booms come louder and closer together, building toward the first grand finale—they always do at least two, sometimes three. The clouds have rolled in closer, thicker, but still the first splatter of rain is unexpected, hitting Richard's scalp like a piece of cold shrapnel.

"Annette. Please. Let me help you."

She lets out a breath that reeks of fermented wine and unflossed teeth. "It caught so fast." Flames tall and bright in her eyes. "Just one match."

Richard makes her promise to remain beneath the trellis while he goes inside to call for help. Hard to trust she'll stay put, but what other choice does he have? Giving the flames a wide berth, he sprints onto the side deck and into the kitchen, which smells of smoke and something rotten. Every surface is cluttered with dishes and papers; the floors are so filthy the soles of his shoes keep sticking. He can barely believe this is the same pristine house he was in for a New Year's Eve party five years ago.

Not taking his eyes away from the window—Annette still stands beneath the trellis—he makes the call to the fire department. Thank Christ, it's Gil who answers, and he promises he'll have people up there "quicker than a hooker can count pocket change." Richard slams the phone back into its cradle and sprints outside—on the way out the door, he sees one of Marshall's shirts hanging on a chair, and he grabs it—then he's racing past the flames all the way to Annette, who is sitting cross-legged on the ground, leaning back on her elbows as if watching nothing more dramatic than a campfire.

He sits on the ground beside her and pulls Marshall's shirt over her shoulders, ignoring the stench of her body, the skim of sweat and oil on her skin as he tugs her arms through the sleeves. Without any resistance, she lets Richard button the shirt up the front, past her bony ribs and small, sunken breasts.

The rain is coming harder now; the fireworks rolling in an unrelenting rhythm. Richard can hear the claps and cheers of Dalton carried on the wind.

Then the alarm bell outside the fire station is wailing, as if the town is under threat of nuclear annihilation. Annette won't stop staring at the fire she made. She's been preparing to light that spark for years, Richard realizes, since the moment she got the phone call her daughter was dead. All the days she has spent alone inside that house. No one to witness her minute-by-minute unraveling.

What is a story without a reader?

What is a body without a soul?

What is a mother without all her children?

Down at the river, bursts of light and roars of wonder. Here on the hill, a fire burning, resistant to the rain.

I t could have been worse."

This is what Nate mumbles into the phone a couple hours after the fireworks, as Sophie sleeps upstairs. "It could have been the house," he says.

"But it wasn't." His mother's voice on the other line is wide awake and alert despite it being well past midnight. Nate doubts that anyone in Dalton is sleeping much tonight—too much excitement, too much to gossip about.

He opens the fridge, grateful for the slice of light that spills onto the kitchen floor. With the rain and the clouds, it's far too dark outside.

"If Dr. Haskell hadn't been there . . . "

"But he was."

"If Annette had stepped just a little too close . . . "

"But she didn't. Don't dwell on things that didn't happen."

Dwelling on what really did happen tonight doesn't seem much better, though. Imagining his mother-in-law striking a match and lighting Bridget's paintings on fire, watching them burn a hole in the sky—no better at all.

"Go to bed, Nate," his mother says. "Take advantage of having the week off and sleep in tomorrow. Do something fun with Sophie."

Here it is, nearly 1:00 in the morning, and his mother is comforting him just like when he would call from sleepaway camp in the middle of the night as an eight-year-old. Here he is, thirty—a widow, a father—and still in need of his mother's consolation.

"I'm sorry, Ma. You've only got four hours till you need to get to the store."

"Well then, it's a good thing I can function on only three hours of sleep."

After they hang up, Nate stands in front of the fridge, feeling the chill on his bare feet. He stares at the cartons of milk, the clementines Sophie swore she would help him eat but hasn't touched since he brought them home a week ago. Something green and fuzzy catches his eye, and he shifts the mesh bag over to see a tiny, stuffed hummingbird staring at him. Sophie brought it back from the movies the other day, explaining the bird was one of Pocahontas's best friends. She told him the name, but Nate can't remember.

Morning light punches its way through the curtains, blinding him as soon as he opens his eyes. He listens to a pair of cardinals outside his window and wonders if Marshall and Annette are waking up right now to the smell of charred grass and melted plastic. Or maybe they never slept at all.

While Nate stood with Sophie, Marshall, and his parents, watching the fireworks last night, the world seemed almost good again, filled with possibility. Marshall held Sophie on his shoulders as the lights twinkled above. His mother and father laughed as they passed a can of beer back and forth. If Rose was somewhere in the crowd, he couldn't see her, but he was thinking of her, remembering how she lifted her face up to the hydrant spray on Main Street. Bridget was there with him, too, but she felt softer than usual, more a light breeze than a hulking thundercloud.

When Nate heard the sirens begin to wail in the center of town, he was surprised by his reaction to them. For the first time since Bridget died, rather than feel paralyzed by the sound, he felt a strong impulse to get in his car and speed toward it. To help in whatever way he could, even if that was just

244 · SHANNON BOWRING

to direct traffic so the paramedics and firefighters could work their magic.

What also surprised Nate was hearing his phone ringing when he and Sophie got home twenty minutes after the fireworks ended. More shocking to hear his father-in-law on the other line. "It's my fault," Marshall said. "Annie's been needing more help than I can give for a long time." Nate didn't say much in response—not because he blames his father-in-law, but because he knows there's no way to stop a man from blaming himself for a thing like that.

Outside his window, the cardinals stop singing. Nate gets out of bed, pulls on a pair of sweats and a shirt covered in paint spatters, and heads downstairs. He finds Sophie in the living room, curled on the couch with Mufasa. Her hair is wild, curls in every direction, and there are dark purple shadows under her eyes.

"I slept like a lightning storm," she says. "All flickery."

There's no reason for her to be upset; Nate hasn't told her about the fire. To explain why Grampa was calling so late last night, he said Marshall had a question about work (as if he could ever tell his father-in-law something the man doesn't already know about his own mill). Sophie had accepted the lie and skipped off to bed.

A little while later, as Nate washes the breakfast dishes, Marshall calls again. "Hell of a night," he says.

"I bet," says Nate. "So what's the plan?" Aware of Sophie watching him, he turns to face the window. Outside, all the flowers are in bloom, brighter after last night's rain.

"Dr. Haskell and Vera Curtis got us into an inpatient clinic at the hospital in Bangor. I'm driving her down today."

"Good. That's good."

"They say it's a nice place. Not like the nuthouses you hear about on the news. But I'll get a hotel room nearby for the next few days, till she gets settled in." Marshall pauses. "Which means I can't come out to your place tonight."

"Don't worry about that. I'll talk to her."

Nate hangs up and turns to see Sophie staring at him over the table, crayons and coloring book abandoned. "What's going on?" she asks. "Who was that?"

"It was Grampa. He's really sorry, but he has to go out of town, so he can't have supper with us today."

"But he promised."

"Sometimes things come up."

Sophie's expression turns from doubt to panic. "Is Grampa dead?"

Jesus, the look on her face. The betrayal in her voice.

"He's fine," says Nate. "But Nana's feeling a little sick, so he's taking her down to the hospital in Bangor."

"So is Nana going to be dead soon?"

"No one is dead and no one is dying. Everyone's okay, I promise. I wouldn't lie to you."

"Would so."

Before Nate can reply, Sophie scrapes her chair back and hurries from the room. Every footstep on the staircase as she stomps upstairs is loud as the crack of a rifle. Nate feels each blow.

Over the next two days, she's like a different child. She hides in her room with the door closed, refuses to walk down to the river, barely eats. By Friday afternoon, Nate has tried almost everything to get back in her good graces—whoopie pies, all her favorite movies, an outing to the lake, where she refused to put on her bathing suit and sulked on the shore. Marshall has yet to call from whatever hotel he's staying at, so Nate calls the Bangor hospital to ask for Annette's room number, thinking he can ask her to put Marshall on the phone if he's there visiting her. But the receptionist won't give out any information, and her prickly voice makes Nate feel ashamed for even asking.

The only option left is to do what he should have done from the beginning.

While Sophie listlessly eats a PB&J in front of the TV, Nate leans against the kitchen counter and calls the clinic. Rose answers, sounding much more professional than she ever did when she was taking calls at the police station.

"Dalton Clinic, how can I help you today?"

"Ro, it's Nate."

"Yikes. You sound like hell. What's going on out there?"

"Just parenting," he says. "You know how it goes. But listen, is Vera busy? I wanted to talk to her about something."

"I'll grab her." Rose pauses, and Nate imagines her at the front desk, staring out at the glass block wall in the waiting room. "Sorry about your mother-in-law, by the way. Sometimes life can be a real bitch, can't it?"

Despite the exhaustion, and the worry, and the fear he's the world's worst father, Nate can't help but feel a little relieved. It's the one thing he wanted to hear after Bridget died, the one thing everyone seemed too afraid to say.

When Vera comes on the line a few seconds later, he barely starts talking before she offers him the favor he spent all morning gathering up the courage to ask.

"I should have called you before now," she says. "I'm heading to Bangor tomorrow to check on Annette. I thought you might like to come along."

Nate peers into the living room and sees his daughter slumped over the couch cushions, clutching the hummingbird Marshall bought her last weekend.

"Can Sophie come, too?"

"I thought that was a given. Aren't you two a package deal?"

The road south is long and winding. Vera takes Route 11, then 212, thick forests giving way to farm fields and vistas of distant hills. She keeps changing cassette tapes, classical music with lots of peaks and valleys. With each mile further away from Dalton, Nate feels more untethered. He doesn't know the music. He doesn't recognize that trailer, that barn, that gas station. Mount Katahdin looks much more imposing from the interstate than it does from the hazy distance between it and Nate's house.

Bangor is too much traffic and too much noise, heat vibrating off the asphalt between cars pumping out fumes of exhaust. In the backseat, Sophie keeps whipping her head around to take in all the unfamiliar sights. Vera navigates past hotels, restaurants, and the mall where Nate's mother took him shopping for a suit for his Senior prom, then drives down a confusing array of side streets, some crowded with Victorians, others with shoddily built apartment buildings. Outside a neat white New Englander, she slows, gazing up toward a balcony on the second floor of a detached garage as though expecting to see someone she knows standing up there.

At the hospital, she parks in an Employees Only lot, pulling an ID badge from her purse and hanging it on her rearview. "Perks of the job," she says, winking at Nate.

The clinic is in an annex overlooking a river dotted with bits of trash. The white floors and walls are broken up by splashes of what Bridget would call motel art—apples falling out of baskets, boats leaving harbor. Nurses in purple scrubs whisk up and down the hall in soft-soled shoes. It's quiet, and with the sun shining in through the windows, almost peaceful.

While Nate and Sophie wait near an aquarium filled with tropical fish, Vera speaks to the receptionist, who nods before picking up the phone. A couple minutes later, Marshall appears in the hallway. Dressed in jeans and a Frazier Lumber sweatshirt, he looks younger than his age, though his eyes are bleary, his face dotted with stubble. As soon as Sophie sees him, she lets out a shriek that makes the receptionist jump in her chair.

"Grampa! You're not dead."

"Not yet," Marshall says. "Got a few more good years left in me."

"What about Nana? Is she dead?"

"No, she's just down the hall. We can go see her, if it's okay with your dad."

Nate wants to say no, it's not all right, his daughter shouldn't be exposed to whatever state Annette is in. But he's kept enough from her for one week. One lifetime.

Marshall leads them down to the end of the hall, where a door stands propped open. He and Sophie enter the room first, while Nate takes a few moments to collect himself, unsure what to expect. It's been months since he last saw Annette at the post office, and she looked so terrible he barely recognized her.

Vera lightly taps Nate's heel with the toe of her sandal. "No use putting it off," she says. "You go in. I'm going to pop down to the ER and check in with my old boss."

The room is brighter than Nate imagined, well-lit by a large window. Marshall and Sophie stand at the foot of the bed, where Annette sits propped against pillows, silently gazing back at them. She looks old and fragile. Nate can see the bones in her collar poking out through her nightgown.

"Told you," says Marshall, squeezing Sophie's hand. "Nana's just fine."

Maybe Marshall has shown Annette the pictures Nate gives him, but this is the first time Annette has seen Sophie in person since she was a baby. Most grandmothers would have some kind of response—tears, maybe, or even just a blush of recognition. But the only expression on Annette's face is a kind of blankness, like clean porcelain.

"Annie," Marshall prods.

Nate wants to rush across the room, scoop his daughter

in his arms, and get her out of here, away from this dull-eyed woman.

"Annie . . . "

"Yes, I hear you. Hello, Sophie. It's nice of you to come visit."

Her voice is flat. Her hands lie completely still on her lap.

Marshall smiles down at Sophie. "Would you like to give Nana a hug?"

No, Nate thinks, *no way this woman is touching my child.* But before he can interject, Sophie is backing away from the bed, dropping Marshall's hand.

"It's all right, Grampa," she says in an overly polite voice. "Maybe later."

That's when Nate knows Sophie can see it, too. Her grandmother might not be dead, but she isn't all the way alive, either.

A few minutes later, Vera returns to the room. She asks Annette questions about tremors and nausea. Annette's responses are terse, and it's not long before Vera gives Nate a pointed look and asks if he and Sophie are ready to go have some lunch.

"Want to come along, Marshall?" asks Nate.

His father-in-law glances from Sophie, bouncing on her heels in the doorway of the room, to Annette, staring out the window.

"How about a rain check?" he says, apology in his voice. "Soon as I get back in town, I'll come out for that supper I missed, okay, Soph?"

"Okay, Grampa."

Vera guides Nate and Sophie through a maze of hallways and stairwells. Several times, they run into people she knows, and she stops to chat while Sophie makes Nate read her the donor plaques on the walls. He recites the words, but he's thinking about Annette back in that bright room, sitting there silently staring out at the sun-blanched sky. He wonders if there's any hope for a person like that. If that's the kind of person Bridget would have eventually turned into, had she chosen to stay alive.

During her visits with patients, Vera spends most of her time gathering clues about their lives outside the exam room. Worries confessed and unspoken, cholesterol levels, plans for family reunions, plum-colored bruises flowering across ribs . . . all these details draw a sketch of the person in front of her. Helps her see their values and desires, the hurts they've suffered, the joys they look forward to.

From the moment she picks up Nate and Sophie for their trip downstate, Vera does the same thing with them; collecting lots of little details to try to understand the entire picture of who they are. Sophie's sticky fingers and the smell of maple syrup. Nate's tote bag filled with snacks, water bottles, and a pair of what he calls his "just-in-case" socks. The way he tilts his head toward the car speakers as if trying to gather the Danube waltz into his brain so he can pull each note apart and put them all back together. The way he holds his breath and presses an invisible brake each time Vera speeds up to pass someone. The light in Sophie's eyes whenever she looks at her father.

Sweet and cautious, curious and loving—this is who they are, who they have helped each other become. All those things add up to one big, lasting, essential thing: stability. And with every mile away from Dalton, Vera finds herself growing more desperate for a piece of that stability. That steady love and living. Not that she wants those things with them—Sophie is cute, but Nate reminds Vera of the younger brother she never had.

There's something there, though, something they have built

together that Vera finds as comforting as it is miraculous. All that tragedy, and still something good can endure.

In Bangor, she feels irritated with all the traffic, all the noise, all the pavement. She drives past her apartment, expecting to feel the usual burst of warmth seeing the balcony where she has spent so many bright hours alone with a book and a glass of wine. Instead, she feels something close to pity for the woman who used to live above that garage. There are so few windows. She had so few visitors. It's a relief to keep driving down the building-jammed street, to leave the lonely place behind.

The hospital is exactly how she left it two months ago. Construction is still underway on the north wing. Med students scurry around with panicked expressions. Surgeons in scrubs and skull caps stride importantly on their way to the recovery wing to tell their patients they removed the tumor, cleared the artery, fused the bone. Every room smells industrial-clean, with a faint after-whiff of amoxicillin.

After she leaves Nate and Sophie in Annette's room, Vera takes a series of back staircases down to the ground floor, where she ducks into a bathroom to check her appearance. Nurse McMillan is a stickler for personal tidiness, and Vera used to be, too. Used to spend so much time before each shift straightening her hair, applying tasteful layers of makeup, choosing scrubs that made her look professional, approachable.

The woman staring back at her in the mirror now has no makeup on other than some lip balm. She gave her hair a half-hearted pass with the straightener this morning, but in all the humidity, it's turned wavy in odd places, as though she's decided to go for a sort of punk-rock look. Her sleeveless green sundress has half-moons of sweat under the arms.

Nothing she can do about it now, though, so Vera leaves the bathroom and heads for the Employees Only doors that will allow her entrance into the ER. It takes three swipes of her

ID card before the doors unclick and swing open. She has a moment of confusion when she realizes that in her absence, the triage desk has been walled in, forming a barrier between the staff and the patients. She used to be able to see the entire floor from here; now Vera can only see desks beneath windows that give barely any view of the waiting room.

She finds Nurse McMillan huddled over some paperwork in her office. The woman looks older and meaner than when Vera left nearly two months ago. A face like a bulldog, with hair like a pageant queen.

Glancing up from the desk, she squints at Vera. "Back so soon, Ms. Curtis?"

"No," says Vera, feeling a surge of *so-thereness* at the displeasure on McMillan's face. "I'm here visiting someone and thought I'd check in. See if I have any mail."

"We're not a post office."

"But you still keep staff inboxes, don't you? Or did you do away with those when you put up the wall?"

Maybe it's a step too far, the kind of backtalk McMillan hates. But Vera doesn't care today, and she doesn't wait for Nurse McMillan to answer. She doesn't want to hear anything the old bitch has to say.

Nothing in Vera's box other than two flyers for a Subaru sale and an embossed invitation to join the annual fall pharmaceutical conference. She shouldn't be surprised. Early in the summer, she had all her real mail—mostly bills and magazines she never reads—forwarded up to her parents' house. But there's something sad about seeing all the emptiness in the slot above her name.

Before she goes back up to the clinic, Vera ducks into the waiting room, where over twenty patients either pace in front of the vending machines or slump across hard plastic chairs. One man presses a bandage to his forehead. A toddler is repeatedly smacking his mother's calves. Two college-age girls with vomit stains on their clothes are bickering about a guy named Tony—*I kissed him first, no* I *kissed him first.*

Not so long ago, Vera would plunge in and start helping whoever and however she could. But there are too many people crowded in this room, too much desperation all at once. She steps away. Heads back upstairs.

She used to feel so at home here. So herself here. But walking the white halls, Vera feels a strange sense of detachment, as if she's floating through a dream. She briefly comes back to herself when she's speaking with Annette about alcohol withdrawals and treatment plans, but as soon as Vera starts escorting Nate and Sophie downstairs, the disenchantment returns. Doctors, nurses, and imaging techs stop Vera to say hello, ask about her summer up in the County. She's had break-room birthday cake with these people, celebrated the graduations of their grandsons, chipped in for their wedding registries. But none of those relationships ever extended beyond the walls of this building. She might as well be talking to strangers.

After she disengages from a chat with a radiologist whose name she can't remember, Vera turns to see Nate and Sophie staring out a window that overlooks the Penobscot. Polluted, of course, like nearly everything else in this city.

"The cafeteria here is depressing," she says. "How would you guys feel about grabbing lunch off campus instead?"

"Whatever works for you," says Nate, looking as relieved as Vera feels at the prospect of escaping the hospital.

So it's back out into the corneal-burning sun and into the car, hot as a bread oven despite the fact Vera left the windows cracked. She heads down State Street, toward downtown. More traffic. More pedestrians who trudge across the street when they're not supposed to. More red lights. Parking is a nightmare—she has to circle the block three times before zipping into a spot that might not technically be legal. But to hell with it.

By the time Vera ushers Nate and Sophie into the Queen City Café, she feels strung out and on edge. The restaurant is crowded with people talking too much, laughing too loud; the only seats available are three stools at the counter, right next to the cash register.

"Is this all right?" Vera asks Nate, having to raise her voice so loud she feels like she's yelling at him.

He looks wary of how tightly packed everyone is—maybe he's imagining the chaos of an emergency, what might happen if every person surged toward the exit at once—but he offers her a kind smile as he lifts Sophie up onto the middle stool. "All right by us."

Vera's favorite waitress has been replaced by a bubblegum-popping teenager who rolls her eyes when Nate asks for poutine. "That's a County thing," she says. "I can give you plain French fries or onion rings or coleslaw for fifty cents extra."

It takes half an hour for their meals to arrive, and then Vera's pastrami is dry, and Nate's bread has turned soggy from poorly placed pickles. Sophie barely touches her grilled cheese.

They don't talk much while they eat—even if they wanted to, there's no way they could hear each other over the noise of the lunch hour. Each time someone comes up to the register to pay their bill, they stand too close to Vera, bumping into her shoulders without so much as an *Excuse me*. Nate picks up ten bucks dropped by a tourist in a *Bahhh-Hahhbahh* t-shirt, who rips the money from his hands as if she expects him to try to run off with it.

And to top the whole thing off, their final bill, after three waters and three sandwiches, comes to $26. "City prices," says Nate, staring at the receipt with raised eyebrows. But he refuses to let Vera pay.

Outside, they head back to the car, weaving between people who throng outside the shops Vera used to find so charming. Looking at them now, she only sees sagging bricks around the facades, overpriced moose- and lobster-themed souvenirs in the windows. A busker plays a Dick Curless song in the wrong key.

Despite the heat inside the car, Vera feels a wave of relief as soon as she closes the door behind her. Nate, in the passenger seat, leans forward to crank the AC, aiming two of the vents at Sophie in the backseat.

"So," he says, gazing at his daughter. "What do you think of the big city?"

Sophie stares out the window at all the buildings blocking the sky. "Not enough trees."

Vera wants to defend this place she has called home for so long. Tell them about some of her best memories here. Delicious meals in low-lit Italian restaurants. Walks along residential streets, past stately old houses. All these buildings lit up green and red and gold in winter, the entire city dressed up for Christmas.

But all Vera can think about are the wide-open spaces around Dalton. The enormous sky filled with a million stars that she could never hope to see here.

"That's just what you get in Bangor," she says, putting the car in reverse, steeling herself to back blindly into traffic. "Now what do you say we book it back home?"

It takes close to three hours to get to Dalton, and by the time they coast down the hill toward the Store 'N More, they all agree they could use some actual food. Some real sustenance.

"I know exactly what we need," says Nate as Vera pulls into the parking lot.

"I'm paying this time," she says, reaching into her purse and coming out with a twenty. "Is this enough? It's all the cash I've got on me."

Nate takes the money and laughs, tells her not to worry.

While he's inside the store, Sophie tells Vera the entire plot of *Pocahontas*, even singing some lines about painting with the colors of the wind, whatever the hell that means. They sit in the car with all the windows rolled down, cool breeze blowing in. Outside, there are only the sounds of wind through trees, Jake-breaks as log trucks trundle down Depot Hill. The air smells clean and green.

Nate comes back a few minutes later with two paper bags. In one, bottles of lemonade and Humpty Dumpty chips. In the other, three BLTs in pillowy-white sub rolls. As soon as she inhales the scent of the bacon, Vera feels hungrier than she has in weeks. Maybe years. Nate hands her back four dollars in change.

They eat in the car, between the loading dock and the Laundromat. Grease gets under Vera's fingernails. Mayo shines on Sophie's lips. Juice drips from the tomatoes onto the pale upholstery of the passenger seat, and Vera tells Nate not to worry about it. It doesn't matter. All that matters is eating every bite of this perfect meal, savoring it the way it deserves to be savored. Slowly, with reverence.

TALK MORE ABOUT THAT

The group sessions are the worst part. Far more uncomfortable than the full-body booze detox shakes. Way more unsettling than the skeletal, patchy-haired figure that frowns back at Annette in the mirror.

There are six of them in the circle every morning and every evening. Annette is the oldest; the youngest is a seventeen-year-old named Maura who's always pulling her sleeves over her bony wrists. Jackson and Bradley are in their thirties, and both of them drank their marriages to death. Keith, closest in age to Annette, started hitting the bottle after he broke his back in a car crash. And Dawn (who seems vaguely familiar, but that's probably just because she has that look Annette imagines all young native women carry, especially with her long black braid) doesn't seem to have a good reason to drink, other than that she wants to. She's tough, that one, always glaring out the window with her arms crossed over her chest.

Then there's the facilitator, a twenty-something woman named Polly with a man's short haircut. She sits like a man, too, legs sprawled wide in her chair as if inviting the world to dare tell her to close them. Sometimes in the middle of a session, she'll light a cigarette and stare at the person talking with such an intent gaze that everyone starts to squirm. "Tell me more about that," she likes to say.

What Annette really wants to tell Polly is to put out her cigarette, close her legs, and fuck off. All these broken, desperate people can fuck right off.

*

The one-on-one sessions are with Dr. Reiman. With his silvering hair and unwrinkled face, he could either be sixty or thirty. He wears polo shirts patterned with anchors or boats, even though the last time Annette checked a map, Bangor was an hour inland from the ocean. She asks him about this during one of their sessions.

"I grew up on the water," he says. "I loved sailing."

"So why'd you give it up?"

"Who says I gave it up?"

"You're stuck here with us crazy drunks all day. How could you have enough time to float around on a boat?"

"If I didn't find time to float around on that boat, I wouldn't have the patience it takes to stick around here with all you crazy drunks."

"Are you allowed to say that?"

"Oh, I get a pass," Dr. Reiman says. "I used to be one of you."

The walls are too white, and the air is always a little too warm, even when the AC is on high. The food they bring up from the hospital cafeteria is bland but not terrible; every other night, there's chocolate cake or soft vanilla ice cream. It's not like the movies, no Nurse Ratched or forced lobotomies or locked doors; patients can leave the clinic at any time. When the weather is nice, Polly takes the group outside, to a grassy pavilion overlooking a river that reeks of chemicals.

Each patient has their own room, small but bright enough. Annette's looks out over the city, which seems more like a giant parking lot—so many cars, too much pavement. There's one scraggly hemlock she can see from her bed. In the upper branches, an eagle has made a nest. Every morning before group, Annette watches the bird step to the edge and stretch its wings, push off toward the river. Sometimes she sees the eagle returning, catches sight of fish dangling from its huge talons—flash of silver against dark claw; the hunted and the hunter, inseparable.

"Let's talk about control," says Polly, smoke puffing out of her mouth. She's in a men's shirt, cuffs rolled up to her shoulders. "What are some things we can control, and what are some things we can't?"

There's a stretch of silence while everyone in the group looks at one another, hoping someone else will speak. Polly aims her gaze at Keith, who shifts in his chair before answering, using the language they've been trained to use.

"I can't stop bad things from happening," he says. "But I can stop myself from using bad things as an excuse to drink."

Now they take turns, each repeating back the words they're supposed to start believing in. They can't control the weather, but they can pack an umbrella. They can't stop anyone from dying, but they can choose to keep living.

Dawn is the last to speak. She hurls her words like a fistful of rocks. "I can't control shit, and I never been dumb enough like the rest of you motherfuckers to think so."

Polly puffs on her cigarette, leans forward. "Tell me more about that."

Marshall comes every day for lunch. He has a hotel nearby. When Annette says he should go back to Dalton, he tells her he's just fine right where he is. What about work? What about the mill? He says that's not anything she needs to worry about. Plenty of other white-hats can run the mill for a week or two. Now could she please pass the salt?

The shakes have subsided, and the headaches. But she feels queasy at random moments, as if she's been strapped into a Tilt-o-Whirl against her will. And she's still sweaty all the time, like a fire smoldering beneath the surface of her skin.

"Interesting you'd choose that particular metaphor," says Dr. Reiman. "Have you been thinking much about the fire?"

Annette considers telling him what he probably wants to hear—she regrets her actions; she's humiliated by the spectacle she created, the damage she caused. But she doesn't like all the happy lobsters on his shirt, and she's too tired to lie.

"I hardly ever think about the fire."

"Even though that's what brought you here?"

Closing her eyes against the glare coming in through the window, Annette sees six-year-old Bridget in a ruined dress, standing over the kitchen table with a grin on her face and paint all over her hands. On the table, dozens of pieces of paper, some still wet, splotched with pink houses, yellow suns, fat green trees. The colors bled onto the cherrywood table, drying into stains that would take Annette forever to get out. *Mom*, Bridget said. *Look what I made.* In Annette's mind, she hears her own voice, angry and shrill, telling her daughter the only thing she could see was a disaster. *Clean it up*, she said. *Just look at this mess you made.*

"The damn fire isn't what brought me here."

Dr. Reiman nods. Steeples his fingers. "I'm relieved you understand that."

She made Bridget clean the table. Wash her hands until they were red and raw. Bleach all the color out of her dress.

When Marshall steps into the too-white room with Sophie, Annette feels a great eruption beneath her skull. The storm clouds finally breaking. Sending hot tingles all the way down her body. Or maybe that's the detox. The absence of the thing that used to keep those clouds from rolling in.

The girl hovers too close to the bed, staring with green eyes that blink too slowly. And now Nate is here, too, standing beside the doorway as if ready to bolt at any moment. Good. Let him bolt.

262 · SHANNON BOWRING

The clouds are so heavy; the rain burns holes through her veins. Annette makes herself pull in deep, slow breaths as she stares at the child who looks exactly like the child she lost. It's not just the hair, or the eyes. It's the expression on that girl's face as she stares back at Annette. A little too much knowing; too much intuition.

Maura tries to teach Annette how to crochet. Jackson and Bradley sit with her and watch *The Price is Right*, thrilled every time she correctly values the worth of speedboats or elbow macaroni. Keith offers unasked-for advice on bleeding old radiators. Dr. Reiman explains the difference between the word *tack* as a noun and as a verb, and why that difference matters when you're on the sea, in the wind. Polly offers Annette a cigarette that burns like cold peppermint all the way into her lungs. Dawn steals Annette's slippers.

During an evening group session, Polly announces everyone is going to go around the circle and say one thing they admire about the person sitting beside them. She goes first, telling Keith she loves to see how he smiles when he talks about his nephew. Keith compares Maura's singing voice to "that bald-headed chick who shat all over the pope on TV." And on and on, until Annette has to say something nice about Dawn, who sits fuming beside her in a white sundress that contrasts with her brown skin, as well as with the braid draped over her shoulder.

"I like your hair," Annette says.

"Yeah? You want to scalp me for it? Claim it as your own?"

"You don't have to be so caustic."

Dawn turns all her focus on Annette. Such a hard glimmer in her eyes. "You rich, white twat," she says, "you really have no idea who I am, do you?"

Now everyone is staring at Annette, who feels like an

abandoned boat in a storm. Sinking fast. "How could I know you?" she asks. "We're from two different places."

"Except that we're not. I grew up just a few streets away from your snobby-ass mansion. I bagged your groceries at Bergeron's for an entire summer when I was sixteen."

Annette is about to say no, that's impossible, but then she looks at the girl a little harder, and she finally understands why she looks so familiar. It's because she *is* familiar. A piece of her life in Dalton, thrown into this strange world of white rooms and dirty rivers. Cindy Muse's girl, all grown up. *Too* grown up.

Feeling completely upended, Annette says, "I thought your name was Angela?"

The girl—whoever she is—lets out a snort of disgust and stands up so fast her chair falls to the tile floor. Then she stalks out of the room, slamming the door behind her.

For a minute after she's gone, the room is sharp with silence, like the woods after fresh snowfall. Polly clears her throat. "Annette," she says. "Tell us more about that shit-show."

Dr. Reiman asks about her children. Annette talks about Will's basketball record, his #19 jersey they keep preserved behind glass at Dalton High. She talks about Craig's ability to hear a song once and play it back forever. She talks about Penny's first ballet solo, how everyone in the audience gave the ten-year-old a standing ovation for her dizzying set of fouetté turns.

"But what about who they are now, as adults?"

"Hell if I know."

"Okay, we'll leave that for now . . . so what about Bridget?"

Look at the mess you made.

"She was talented," says Annette. "She was smart. She was offered a full scholarship to Colby, but she didn't want to leave Dalton. Couldn't leave that boy behind. They got married. She had a baby. She gave up on all of it."

"Is that how you see it?"

For the first time, Annette allows herself to use the word, even though the clouds are leaden and she wants a drink and she wishes she could pick up a phone and order another one of those do-it-yourself dollhouses. The Greek Revival this time.

"What else is suicide if it isn't giving up?"

"Suicide is just a moment," says the doctor.

The morning after her outburst, Dawn/Angela is gone. While the rest of them were sleeping, she took her one suitcase and walked out into the night.

"Shouldn't someone go out looking for her?" Maura asks. "What brought her here in the first place? Does she have somewhere safe to go?"

"Where she came from or where she's going isn't your problem," says Polly. "Or mine. Or even Dr. Reiman's. We can't save everyone."

The next time Marshall comes for lunch, Annette passes him the salt before he can ask for it. "I miss you," she tells him.

"Annie," he says. "Please."

Her body is stronger, more weight in the belly, not so bony in the face. Maura helps wash the remaining dye from Annette's hair, her fingers strong under the warm rush of water in the bathroom sink. When she looks at the mirror after Maura has dried her pale ginger hair, she feels a pulse of recognition. She knew this woman a long time ago. A long time ago this woman was her.

Keith quits the program.

Rumors get tossed around that one of the night nurses saw him staggering through the park down the road with a brown paper bag in hand. A few days later, a different nurse sees Dawn/Angela bumming for a ride off Stillwater.

"Sure, it's sad," says Polly. "But it's nothing we can control, is it?"

Annette is thinking about leaving, too. Dr. Reiman tells her that would be premature, but it's her decision. No one can force her to stay somewhere she doesn't want to be.

"When you leave here, though," he says, "the work keeps going. Actually, the work out there is way harder than anything we put you through in here. And a lot of people can't handle it."

"Aren't therapists supposed to be encouraging?"

"I encourage you not to fool yourself into thinking things get easier after this. Even the sturdiest boat can splinter apart in rough water."

"Tell us, Annette," Polly says one rainy morning. "Have you found a god of your own understanding?"

Last night she dreamed of I-95 all the way up to Houlton. That's the route they used to take with the kids when they were driving back from their summer vacations in New Hampshire. The kids complained, tired of each other after a week cooped up in a mountain cabin, but Annette insisted they have that extra time together, those extra miles. Marshall flicked through radio stations. Will and Craig always sat in the furthest reaches of the minivan, airing their dirty feet out the windows. Penny, who got car sick, sat in the front passenger seat with a plastic bag clutched in her hands. Annette and Bridget sat in the middle row, their arms pressed together over the center console. Sometimes, Bridget would fall asleep and slump onto Annette's shoulder, and she would close her eyes and wrap her arms around her youngest. Her baby. Silently wish the ride would never end, so she'd never have to let her go.

"The god of my own understanding is dead."

In her room that night, she changes into the silk pajamas Marshall brought her from the mall. Maybe tomorrow she will skip the morning session and call him at the hotel and tell him she's healed as much as she can for now.

Outside, the sun is gone but the light remains in shades of rose and lavender, with only a few indigo clouds scudding across the horizon. In the hemlock, the eagle stands at the edge of its nest, dangling one talon in the air. Only when the wind is right does the bird push off, plummeting sharply before catching itself in a current and floating, weightless, back up into the sky.

AMBLE

Richard walks all the way down High Street and Depot Hill the last evening of July. He says hello to the people who walk past him, who slow their vehicles to stick their heads out the window and tell him about their cures. Phil Lannigan can ride his horse again. Gloria Arsenault's headaches have eased since she cut back on sugar. Jo Martin has bought a self-hypnosis tape to help her finally stop smoking. Or at least cut back to a pack a day.

To each person, Richard says a different version of the same thing—*Glad you're feeling better, but I can't take credit. It's Vera Curtis you should be thanking.*

By the time he gets to the river, he feels tired but strong. Full of good breath. Only the expected amount of perspiration for this sort of exercise in a post-MI man his age. His calves ache, though, and there's a cramp in the arch of his left foot.

He sits on the shore, takes off his shoes and socks, and stretches his feet in the dense air. The sky is the color of rubies; clouds like whipped concrete hang on the horizon. There will be weather tomorrow, maybe rain. Maybe thunder. Even though there's a month of summer left, already the leaves are turning pale green, starting to wither at the edges.

"Dr. H?"

Glancing up, he sees Rose walking toward him, Adam and Brandon beside her, both of them carrying different colored rocks.

"What're you doing here?" asks Rose.

"Taking a walk."

She gives him one of her half-smiles. "Doesn't look like that. Looks like you're taking a break."

"Just until I get walking again. What about you?"

"The boys wanted to look for arrowheads. Even though we never find any."

Behind her, Adam tosses one pebble at his brother, who doesn't move quick enough.

"Go use the holeys. I don't want to get to the Shanty and hear that you have to pee."

They go running off toward the outhouses, and Rose sits beside Richard, tucking her skirt over her knees. In the maples, birdsong—robin and blue jay, cardinal and chickadee. Some kind of sparrow.

"So when're you coming back to work?"

"That has yet to be decided."

"By Trudy? Or your doctors over in Prescott?"

"By fate."

"Is fate something you believe in?"

Does he? He thinks of his father, his pre-determined career path—most children receive family heirlooms and acreage when their fathers die. Richard inherited a town, and all the people in it.

"Sure," he says. "Don't you?"

"I think I'd rather feel like I'm making all the big decisions myself."

She looks across the lot, where Adam and Brandon have decided to pee against two trees.

"Damn it. I swear I taught them better than that."

"Are you kidding? They've got the right idea—no one ever cleans those outhouses."

Rose laughs. "I better get them their ice cream," she says. "Come back to work soon, okay? Vera's great, but it's just not the same there without you."

After she and the kids are gone, Richard sits alone on the bank, nothing but bird chatter and the rustle of leaves. He imagines Annette Frazier wandering the halls of the clinic hundreds of miles away. He's glad he and Vera could pull some strings to get her in there. But it's a place that requires honest work, hard reflection, and Annette was so far gone the night of the fire . . . There are redeemable actions and unsalvageable ones, and Richard has no idea how to tell which is which.

He feels a strange pull toward the river; the need so desperate and urgent it's like thirst, his entire body craving water. Before he can understand this thirst, or talk himself out of satisfying it, Richard hurries down the shore, feeling pebbles bite at his feet, and wades knee-deep into the river, still wearing his clothes.

Pushing forward through the water, up to his thighs, hips, waist, he thinks back to when he and Trudy would come here when they were young. They'd sneak down while Dalton slept, take off all their clothes and swim in the dark, their laughter swallowed up by the moon. "Stop mucking around and kiss me already," Trudy used to say, and Richard would do as directed. Their separate bodies became one eternal, amorphous form on those nights. Moving together, breathing the same rhythm.

Immersed up to his chest now, in the middle of the river, he closes his eyes and feels the water rushing around him, making room for him, accommodating his presence in its gentle but unceasing rush forward.

Can a person share a soul with another person?

Maybe.

Can a person share a soul with a river?

Maybe not.

But maybe he can borrow the river's soul, at least for a little while, until his own folds itself back inside his body.

Richard pulls in a breath, holds the oxygen in his lungs, plunges beneath the surface of the cool green water.

AUGUST

"In that high place in the darkness the two oddly
sensitive human atoms held each other tightly and waited.
In the mind of each was the same thought.
'I have come to this lonely place and here is this other,'
was the substance of the thing felt."
—SHERWOOD ANDERSON, *Winesburg, Ohio*

The flowers are still blazing in bursts of pink, purple, white. Monarchs have appeared, splashes of orange against green.

"Next year, you should put in more milkweed," says Greg, watching one of the butterflies write itself like a scroll of cursive through the shimmery air.

"I should?" Nate asks. "Why not you? You won't be back from school again next summer to help your old man at the store?"

Greg leans against the porch railing. He's nearly as tall as Nate, and with the shadow of stubble on his jawline, they could be the same age. But when he answers, he sounds young and unsure.

"I mean, Dad wants me to. But I don't know. Next summer feels far away."

Under the birches, Sophie is trying to cartwheel. Sometimes she sticks the landing, but mostly, she stumbles. Every time she plants her hands on the grass and kicks herself upside down, Nate holds his breath, waiting for her feet to land back on the ground.

In a few weeks, she'll be spending half of every weekday in kindergarten. She'll sit in the same classroom where Nate once sat, skip through the same gymnasium, eat off the same plastic cafeteria trays. She'll make friends with kids whose parents grew up with Nate, in the same rooms, the same halls. She will be taught by several of the same teachers who taught him.

Those experiences should bring them together, give them more to bond over.

But Nate has a looming fear that as soon as Sophie gets onto that bus the first day of school, he will have lost a piece of her forever.

There's just so much he'll never be able to understand or do for his daughter. He can't fathom what it's like to be a girl without a mother—or just to be a girl, motherless or not. He can't know every thought and fear and feeling that will churn through Sophie's mind as she navigates the new rules, spoken and unsaid, of a new environment. He can't stop bullies from teasing her; he can't pick her up if she falls during recess; he can't stand guard outside the school every second she's in there, just in case she needs something. A hug. An unbruised apple. A human shield for any virus-ridden kid who doesn't sneeze into their elbow. Jesus, he'd give her anything.

"Cool thing about milkweed," says Greg. "Its sap contains toxic chemicals. So when the monarch larvae eat it, they become toxic, too. Unappealing to predators."

Nate wishes he could give Sophie some of that magic, keep all the bad things and all the bad people away from her. Lately he's been waking in the middle of the night panicking about how long it will take before one of the kids at school pulls her aside and says something about her mother, or her grandmother. "Is it true your mom killed herself?" these mean-spirited children might ask. "Is it true crazy runs in your family?" And there's nothing Nate can do about it. No way he can be there to give his daughter the right answer. Or any answer at all.

On the first weekend in August, for the first time since he brought Annette back to town, Marshall comes out to the house for supper. Nate is happy for the excuse to make real food—caprese salad, chicken piccata—but there's the same restless feeling in his belly he used to get while he was patrolling Route 11.

"Are you sure he's not bringing Nana?" Sophie asks as Nate sets the table.

"He says she's going to stay home."

"Good. She's too mean and scary."

"It's not nice to call people that."

"Even if that's what they are?"

He considers telling her something about giving people second chances. But it's not like Annette was warm and kind before Bridget died—that woman has always been, as Nate's own mother might say, *difficult*. So instead of answering Sophie's question, he asks her to lay out the silverware beside each plate.

When Marshall pulls into the driveway, Nate and Sophie greet him on the front porch with hugs and handshakes, then they all move into the kitchen, which smells of lemon sauce and browned butter.

Marshall asks Sophie all sorts of questions about what she might buy when Nate takes her school shopping next week, and she rambles off a list of pencils, light-up sneakers, lunch box. When Marshall talks about how much fun she's going to have in kindergarten, something in his words jostles the nerves Nate has been feeling all day.

After dessert (chocolate ice cream with rainbow sprinkles), Sophie runs outside to wait for the hummingbirds that always come to the feeder this time of evening. Once the screen door has banged shut behind her, Marshall turns to Nate with a pained expression on his face.

"Okay," he says. "No use dragging this out, so here it is: I'm selling the mill. Already have a buyer lined up."

"But it's *Frazier* Lumber," says Nate, too stunned to say anything else.

"And our family's benefited from it for a long time, and we will for a long time to come." Marshall looks toward the

window, where Sophie's voice can be heard singing about dig-
ging for treasure. "But I've got to take care of Annie. I've got to
help her get better. And I don't see that happening here."

Nate doesn't need more of an explanation. Dalton has always
been and will always be his home. But everything here—every
building on Main Street, every field, every tree in the forest—
reminds him of Bridget. Most of the time, it's comforting, this
feeling that she exists within the landscape around him. But on
his low, dark days, all those constant reminders are an assault.

"Where will you two go?" Nate asks.

"I don't know yet." Marshall spins his beer glass in front of
him but doesn't take a drink. "Christ, I never thought I'd leave
this town. And Sophie . . . "

His voice breaks, and Nate looks away to give him a bit of
privacy. Pretends not to see him pressing his hand to his eyes.
After a few minutes, Marshall clears his throat and speaks again.

"It's a good company, out of Quebec," he says. "But these
kinds of transitions are never easy. There might be some changes
to health insurance, PTO, schedules . . . "

The rest of the thought goes unsaid. Nate remembers what
happened when the mill in Portman Lake was sold to a company out of Mass. Layoffs. Men there for thirty years forced to
quit so they wouldn't be owed their pensions. If the same thing
happens to the Frazier mill, half of Dalton could be at risk of
unemployment, welfare, worse.

"You should also know," says Marshall, "one non-negotiable
condition of the sale is that you keep your job."

This promise should put Nate's anxiety at ease. A guaranteed livelihood. But suddenly the idea of sitting in that booth
above the kiln for forty hours a week for the rest of his life
makes him feel as though he's trapped inside a coffin with the
sides pressing in on him. Stealing all his breath.

Yes, he remembers these nerves from his brief time on the
force. This weightless, flickering feeling like gnats swarming

inside his stomach as he waited to pull someone over for speeding or running a stop sign. The glimmering hatred on Tommy Merchant's face when he arrested him.

But he also remembers the expansive swell in his chest as he used to drive the DPD cruiser along the back roads of Dalton, through familiar fields and forests. The sensation that the entire world was rolling out and open in front of him. The weight of the gun on his hip was so heavy . . . but it was also an anchor that kept him from floating up into the endless sky. A reminder of his responsibilities to the town that raised him, all the people he loved.

He turns to Marshall, who has become one of Sophie's favorite people this summer. Who will soon be leaving her behind.

"Do you think there might be a way you could un-negotiate that part of the deal?" Nate asks, then hurries to explain once he sees the confused hurt on his father-in-law's face. "Don't get me wrong, I appreciate the job, and everything you've done for me and Sophie. I'm just not sure it's the job I want forever."

Marshall's expression turns softer. "Whatever you want," he tells Nate.

There's a lot more they could say; about the impossible choice between one's wife and one's granddaughter. About loss. About what happens next to them, and their families, and their town.

They don't say any of it. They shake hands, go out onto the porch, and watch Sophie chasing butterflies.

The next evening, while crickets hum and the sky turns gold, Nate follows Greg through the garden. Greg points out the roses that need to be deadheaded into the fall, the shrubs to prune, and Nate tries to lock the instructions in his mind, but he worries all the new plants and flowers will die as soon as Greg leaves for school in a few weeks.

"Don't worry," says Greg. "I made this garden resilient.

Almost foolproof. And you can always have Trudy come out to take a look if you think it's getting away from you. She'll set you straight fast."

The idea of Trudy pacing around his lawn, hands on her hips and a frown on her face, is as intimidating as it is comforting. Nate has always thought of her as his aunt, or even a second mother. One who loves him just as much as his own but who won't mollycoddle him if she has a hard truth to dole out.

Greg leads Nate back toward the porch, where Sophie is sprawled out on the glider with a coloring book—nothing inside the lines, and it's beautiful, perfect. Bridget used to color like that, too, back when she and Nate were in grade school. "Lines are stupid," she would say, which felt so completely wrong to him. Like she was breaking a rule as set in place as the position of the moon in the sky.

As he got older, he realized the moon was never fixed but always moving. And now he understands there are people like Bridget, and Sophie, who chase that light, and people like him, who stand still and wait for it to come back around.

Nate's gaze falls on an empty patch of earth in front of the porch. Earlier in the summer, Greg offered to keep it bare in case Nate or Sophie came up with a flower they wanted planted there. Something that would thrive in full sun.

"This spot here," says Nate. "Don't you think something yellow would be nice?"

Greg assesses the dusky purple of the globe thistles, the creamy white of garden phlox. "Yup, yellow would be a good contrast. You have something in mind?"

"I don't know the name, but it was Bridget's favorite. It sort of looked like a daisy."

"Tall or short?"

Nate sees it so clearly in his mind: Bridget walking among the yellow at the Prescott Community Garden. She wore an aqua-blue dress; her skin was brown from a summer outdoors.

They were nineteen, maybe twenty, and everything good was ahead of them.

"Tall. Kind of grew in clumps."

"Hold that thought," says Greg, and he jogs back to his father's truck, parked crookedly behind Nate's own. When he returns, he has a gardening book in hand, open to a page near the end.

"Is this the one?" he asks, holding out the book.

And there it is. He might as well be seeing Bridget herself, laughing up at him from the glossy pages.

"That's the one," says Nate. "What is it?"

"Heliopsis," Greg says. "Also called false sunflower."

Funny, how a name can be just right. How two names can be so perfect. Nate turns his gaze to Sophie, who has decided to create her own picture on a separate sheet of paper. Swirls of green and swaths of blue. Both his favorite colors.

Bloom

On a muggy evening, Greg walks through the garden he planted from scratch. There are a few things he'd like to change—more alliums would be good, and maybe fewer lilies—but overall, it's exactly the way he wanted it to be. Flowers in every color; flowers that will bloom in a steady wave from May until September. Varied heights and textures. Aromas ranging from subtly sweet to the spicy kick of Christmas candy. No sharp edges along any of the borders, because nature hates right angles, and a planned landscape should meld into the world around it. Three seasons from now, this garden will almost look like it's been here since the farmhouse was built nearly a hundred years ago.

Nate keeps saying he feels bad, that he didn't pay Greg enough for all this work. But no amount of money could feel better than standing among all the colors he added to the earth himself. Or looking around to watch hummingbirds and honeybees flutter around the blossoms they love best. Or seeing the blush of relieved happiness on Nate's face when Greg told him the name of his dead wife's favorite flower and promised to plant some before the summer ended. No amount of money could give Greg that rush of pride, that sense that he's given something good and something beautiful to someone who deserves it.

Is that how his father feels when he's standing in the hardware store, among the copper pipes and socket wrenches? Does he get this same nearly drunk buzz from staring at the fluorescent-lit wall of paint samples? Showing flustered house-wives to the floats that will stop their toilets from running all day and all night?

Greg wants to love the same things his father does—hard-ware, meatloaf, cowboy movies. Things would be simpler, and probably more comfortable. Lots of other men just like his fa-ther here in Dalton and in the County are happy living that same sort of life. And there is something to be said for predict-ability—even these wild blooms follow a consistent schedule of growth and death every season.

Stopping at the edge of Nate's yard and staring out toward the silhouette of Katahdin, Greg tries to imagine himself twenty years older, still living in this town. Aching feet and swollen knees from standing behind the store counter all day. Vitamin-D deficiency from being indoors most of the time. Maybe he and the wife—because if he stays in Dalton, it will have to be a wife—and the kids take a vacation down to Moosehead Lake every summer, just like Greg's family did throughout his child-hood. Maybe Friday nights are reserved for board games and take-out pizza from the Store 'N More. There are tough days but also good ones, things to mourn and things to celebrate; maybe even times of almost dizzying happiness.

But no matter how hard Greg tries to imagine that life, to put himself here in Dalton in the future, it's not himself he sees. It's his father. They are different people, meant for and made for different things.

The breeze shifts, carrying with it the smell of an oncoming storm. The sky is darkening off to the west, Katahdin turning to shadow. All around him, flowers shiver in the cool air, ready for the rain, ready to drink up all the water they can, water that will flow along their petals and down inside their stamens, all the way underground, into their root systems. In this way, they are already preparing for their autumn death, their winter hiberna-tion, their spring rebirth.

Whorled utricularia very abundantly out, apparently in its prime.

Greg wants to be part of a continual rebirth, a cycle of brighten, blossom, bloom. He wants to be like the flowers, opening their throats wide to receive the rain, gathering strength for the next season. Throwing all their color unashamedly back into the world.

When he gets home, his mother is elbow-deep in Dawn-scented suds. "There's a plate of chicken alfredo for you in the fridge," she says. "I can zap it in the microwave."

Just the idea of eating that congealed mess makes Greg want to vomit. His stomach keeps twisting around, and his heart zips along as if he's just finished sprinting up Depot Hill. He needs to tell them both, but the idea of sitting them down at the same time is too much. He could tell his mother alone right now. She might be easier, or at least a little softer.

Then the phone rings, and she reaches to answer it. *Your sister*, she mouths at Greg, and pinches the receiver between her ear and her shoulder as she continues scrubbing alfredo sauce off her Fiesta-Ware plates.

So it'll be his father, then.

Telling himself it's like ripping off a Band-Aid—*just do it, just do it*—Greg descends the stairs into the cellar, where his father is bent over his model railroad. Wranglers. Corduroy shirt. Gold-rimmed glasses.

He looks up, grinning, and holds out a tiny ranch the color of melted butter. "Looks like the Pelletiers' place on Howard Street, doesn't it?"

"Sure," says Greg, taking a seat on the fake-velvet wingback where their mother used to pose him and his sisters for holiday photos. "You nailed it, Dad."

"You hear they're selling the place?"

"Nope."

"Guess they're going to become snowbirds. Why anyone would ever want to go to Florida . . . " His father shakes his head as he lovingly sets the house back where it belongs, just a few centimeters away from the middle/high school.

Greg wants to launch himself across the room and hug his father as tight as he used to when he was a kid. He wants to gently but firmly suggest his father invest in better sneakers. He wants to run around the block twenty times. Or eat an entire box of Ring-Dings.

Just fucking do it.

"Dad. I need to talk to you about something."

His father keeps his eyes on the train circling his perfectly reimagined town while Greg lets the words pour out, a slurry of sentences spoken too fast and too loud.

"I'm really grateful, you know, for all you do for us, for me, but . . . You should see the garden I planted for Nate, Dad, you should see it, how happy it made him, and that's what I want to do. That's what I want to learn how to do better, and UMO has a good horticulture program, and I know our deal was you'd pay for school if I worked in the store, but I don't fit there, and I don't want to keep trying."

He sits there for what feels like a hundred years, nothing but the sound of the toy train humming around and around the town, before his father looks up and holds his owl-eyes on his. And Greg could deal with anger, or even flat-out refusal, but he can't deal with this—all the betrayal on his father's face. All the hurt.

Just as he's about to say he didn't mean it, he'll live inside the store forever if it would make his father happy, the basement door opens, and Greg turns to see his mother trudging down the stairs as if she has chains attached to her feet. When she steps into the light, the look on her face is even worse than the one on his father's. Greg has a moment of panic, wondering how she could have heard his confession all the way from the kitchen.

"What is it, Cheryl?" his father asks. "What's wrong?"

"I just got off the phone with Sarah," she says in a shaky voice. "She was spotting, so Ian took her over to the hospital. The doctor . . . they couldn't find a heartbeat."

Greg's father lets out a little gasp of shock, then he stands to wrap his arms around her. They rock each other back and forth, in their own parental bubble, leaving Greg to piece together what it all means. The loss of something he could barely imagine in the first place. The baby his older sister will never have. The life that didn't take.

Like Father

Rose and the boys have a perfect rainy Sunday. Waffles for breakfast, thanks to the five-dollar waffle iron they found at the thrift shop. A morning movie marathon—cats and dogs lost in the wild, cartoon lions made king, pumpkins turned into golden carriages. Adam teaches Brandon how to do a headstand (with lots of pillows, and plenty of support from the fake-wood-paneled wall); Brandon shows Rose the best way to build a tower during a game of Jenga (slowly). The three of them go outside and splash in mud puddles as rain comes slanting down. Rose closes her eyes, holds her face up to drink from the sky.

Then, as she is washing dishes after supper while the boys play in their bedroom, she hears a scream that reminds her of the sound her dead uncle's pigs used to make right before he stuck a knife in them.

She sprints down the hall and into the boys' room, where Brandon is lying on the carpet with blood streaming from his mouth, dripping onto his pajamas. The look in his eyes is a mix of pain and terror, and Rose understands without him having to say anything that it was Adam. Adam, who keeps his back turned so she can't see his face. Adam, who's building a Lego castle like his nine-year-old life depends on it. Adam, who has blood on his fingers.

Snatching Brandon off the floor and holding him tight while he sobs, Rose races to the bathroom, where she sits him up on the sink as she gets the water flowing. Fuck, there's so much blood, and it's so red, and it smells like tarnished copper, and she wants to puke but knows she has to keep it together or Brandon will start puking, and then it will be even more of a mess for her to clean up.

She dabs a washcloth gently on his face, wiping away the blood until she can see his mouth, which she coaxes him to open. "I need to see, baby," she says. "I need to see where it's coming from."

Two gaping holes—one where his formerly loose tooth used to be, and another beside it. One that only started to wiggle a day ago.

"Don't be mad at him, Mumma," Brandon whimpers. "They were bugging me and I wanted to pull them out but I was too scared so I told him he could do it. And the first one didn't really hurt that much, and—" He's crying so hard he can't even finish the sentence.

It takes a long time to get the bleeding to stop. A long time for Rose to consider what she should say to Adam, how she should punish him. Pushing down flares of something close to hatred when she thinks of one of her children hurting the other. Or maybe it isn't hatred—maybe it's fear. The same kind of fear she used to feel whenever Tommy would lay her out with one punch or knock her flat with just a few rage-filled words. A powerless kind of feeling. The worst kind of surrender.

Eventually, Brandon's mouth stops oozing, and Rose gets him out of his ruined pajamas and into one of her own clean shirts. "You can sleep with Mumma tonight," she says, carrying him into her room, tucking him into her bed. She sits with him, rubbing his back, until he falls asleep, curled around her pillow.

When she goes back into the boys' room, Adam is still sitting on the floor, though he's abandoned his castle and is staring at his feet, scabbed with bug bites.

"Why?" asks Rose, staring down at this child she helped

create. The son she had when she was little more than a child herself.

"He kept whining about his stupid loose teeth," Adam says. "I just thought I could yank them out and get it over with so he'd stop being such a baby."

He holds out his blood-smeared fist and opens his fingers to show Rose the two teeth lying on his palm. Then his jaw starts to shiver, and suddenly he's the one crying, big ugly sobs that seem so loud for such a small room.

Part of Rose wants to let him sit here alone with his tears, let him feel scared and ashamed of himself all night long. He can't grow up thinking it's okay to hurt people. She can't let him be like that. Like his father.

But then she remembers something Tommy told her a long time ago, back when they were teenagers, back before they'd even slept together. He was talking about his parents, the way his father would get out the belt and whip Tommy senseless while his mother just sat in the other room pretending not to know. "You didn't cry?" Rose asked, and Tommy gave her such a sad look that all she wanted to do was hold him. "No point in crying if no one wants to hear it," he said.

She sits on the floor beside Adam. Gathers him in her arms. Holds him close and lets him cry as long as he wants.

RECOVERY

On the second Wednesday of August, Trudy closes the library early so she can drive Richard to the hospital. "You really don't have to," he tells her. "I can do this myself."

"Just because you can doesn't mean you need to."

When she gets that look in her eye, it's pointless to argue. He sits in the passenger seat and watches the scenery flick by—woods and meadows, tote roads and more woods. Trudy hates air conditioning, so they ride with all the windows down, the warm wind slapping their faces, knotting her hair into something like a half-formed birds' nest.

Richard has been thinking a lot about birds. According to the field guide, his catbirds will be migrating south soon, taking their meowing cries and mimicking songs with them. All sorts of other birds will be on the move, too, destined for warmer climates and brighter skies. In the meantime, they flood the yard with fluttering wings, pecking at the feeders Richard refills at least once a day. He's been keeping a log of all that avian life, sitting on the porch for hours with a pencil and a notebook. *Grackles bullying sparrows again. Robins fattening up for journey south. Catbirds loving the half-oranges w/ grape jelly.*

He never imagined he'd turn into one of those old men who go crazy for birds. They're only birds, he used to think, just another part of the landscape, the ambient noise. Now, Richard wakes each morning wondering if he could make friends with the crow that likes to perch on his roof. Tempt it with shiny objects.

And each night, he puts himself to sleep by counting over the birds he witnessed throughout the day. *Starling, goldfinch, chickadee, cardinal, nuthatch, blue jay, evening grosbeak . . . .*

Sometimes he still thinks about the ships he might have built in another life. The seas he could have sailed. Mostly, though, Richard spends his hours watching all those different colored wings, hearing all those varied songs, wondering nothing more than where those birds have been and where they're going next.

"You just wait," Trudy says as she pulls into the hospital parking lot. "That cocky little shit is going to try to take all the credit for your recovery."

"We'll just have to set him straight, then, won't we?"

She glances over at Richard, returning his smile. She looks so much softer when she grins like that, so much like the young woman he fell in love with that he feels flooded with gratitude and regret, all at the same time. The things they could have had together. The life that was almost theirs.

In the cardiology wing, the secretary squints at the computer screen in front of her for so long that Trudy asks her if she needs glasses.

"It's a new scheduling system. Takes a while to find what we're looking for . . . Okay, here he is—Haskell. Confirm his date of birth for me?"

"Eight-nine-forty-five."

The girl blinks a few times, then perks up, finally pulling her eyes away from the screen to look at Richard. "Happy Birthday, sir," she says in a voice meant for a toddler. "The big 5-0, huh?"

"Happy Birthday, *Doctor*," Trudy corrects. "And don't make such a fuss of it. We can all do the math."

They sit in the waiting room for twenty minutes beyond when the appointment should have started. A Muzak is set to a Beach Boys compilation. Fun, fun, fun. Good vibrations. Surfin', surfin', surfin'. By the time a nurse steps into the room and calls his name, Richard is feeling nearly as on edge as Trudy looks.

They go together to the exam room, Trudy sitting primly in a chair while the nurse takes his vitals. Blood pressure good. Resting heart rate good. He's down ten pounds from when Nate and Vera carried him into the ER back in May.

Before the nurse leaves the room, she promises the doctor will be along in another little minute. Then she lets the door slam shut behind her.

"Imagine if you pulled this crap at the clinic, Richard. Making everyone wait an hour just for a checkup . . . "

"It's a different pace here, Trudy."

"It's bullshit is what it is."

Another quarter-hour later, there's a rap at the door, then Dr. Capaldo breezes into the room, carrying the cloying smell of aftershave in with him. His dark hair is even thicker than it was back in May. He nods hello, then plunks down on the stool, scanning through Richard's chart.

After a few moments of silence, Trudy clears her throat. "Reading a novel there?"

"Just being thorough, ma'am."

More waiting, lots of rustling papers, and finally Capaldo closes the chart.

"Well, Richard, you're bouncing back faster than we could have hoped for. Vitals are great, bloodwork is good. Looks like you're being a good patient and following my advice to eat right and exercise."

Behind his back, Trudy raises her eyebrows at Richard. *Didn't I tell you?*

"Keep it up," Capaldo says, "and it'll be like you never had a heart attack at all."

Every medical professional knows this is just a pretty lie given to patients to ease their worry. The body heals, but it never forgets. Trauma gets trapped in the cells, rewrites a person's entire wiring. Sure, Richard's heart is now unclogged— but it will never function in quite the same way again.

Capaldo presses his stethoscope to Richard's chest and back, nods in approval, then asks if either of them has any questions, his eyes flicking to the door. Done with them. Ready for the next billable patient.

Before Richard can say anything, Trudy is standing next to the cot. She smells like books and flowers. Her hair is a mess from the drive, but she's just as attractive as she was in her early twenties.

"When can my husband go back to work?"

"Remind me what he does? Some kind of rural clinic?"

Her eyes could slice through metal. Maybe Richard should help this guy out. But he likes the draw of Trudy's shoulders, the glimmer of intimidation on the young doctor's face as he tries to edge his stool closer to the door.

Trudy steps in front of him, blocking his way.

"*Rural* clinic? Like he's some house-call horseback-doctor in an Appalachian outpost?"

"I didn't—"

"Where are you from, anyway? Where did you go to medical school, and why didn't they teach you how to treat patients with a little goddamn respect?"

"I grew up in Hartford. Went to med school in New Haven. And you really don't need to use that tone—"

"I'll use whatever tone I like. Now do you see this man sitting here?" Trudy gestures at Richard as if he's a prize on *The Price is Right.*

"Of course I see him, I just—"

"*This man* is a real doctor. *This man* has sacrificed his whole life—his time, his money, his health—to take care of an entire town. He'd never treat any of his patients with the disregard you've shown us."

"Really, ma'am, I—"

"For Chrissake, just take your Prince Charming hair and your fancy *New Haven* degree and shove it."

For a few moments after Capaldo has left the room, Trudy and Richard stay where they are, blinking at each other like two kids who have managed to run off with the cookie jar. Then they both start laughing.

"That poor kid."

"Think I brought him down a couple notches?"

"At least for the rest of the day."

"I should have taken it further. Told him his aftershave makes him smell like a pimp."

Richard's stomach hurts from laughing, and his cheeks feel stretched too wide. Trudy grins, her own cheeks slightly flushed, and lands a quick peck on his lips. Before she can pull away, Richard cups her jaw in his hands and presses his mouth firmer on hers. She is warm and alive, and he is, too, and the soul that's been following him around like a shadow the past few weeks finally settles back inside him as he kisses her, its return to his body like a wave of light flowing from his scalp all the way down to the soles of his feet.

Trudy pulls away, taking his hands in hers. There's love in her eyes, but also apology.

And yet Richard is wrapped in the kind of peace he hasn't felt since they'd fall asleep in each other's arms after making love. So long ago, but the body remembers.

"I'm sorry, Richard."

"It's okay, Trudy. You are who you are. You love who you love. No sense in me being angry at you for that."

She squeezes her fingers against his. "I just . . ."

"Stop." Richard smiles at her as the sun peeks around the blinds. "Just listen, okay?"

Pulling in a deep breath, Trudy nods.

"For you, it's Bev," says Richard. "I know that. But for me, it's you."

Arctanica, Revisited

Strong year for sunflowers, and soon the Purple Dome asters will cover the ground, lend their energy to the humming-birds before they make their way south. As Trudy and Greg pull weeds one hot morning, grasshoppers jump over their hands; crickets chirp all around. Only a few weeks left of summer.

"I need to tell you something," says Greg, wiping sweat from his forehead.

He's been here more often the past few days, during hours he would usually be at the hardware store. He told Trudy about his basement confession to his father, and about his sister's miscarriage. And they've intuitively understood each other's deeper selves without words for years, so this must be some-thing new on his mind.

"What is it, then?" Trudy asks.

"I'm thinking about leaving town earlier than I planned. Heading downstate a couple weeks before school starts back up."

"I thought that lease on your and David's apartment didn't start until September first."

"It doesn't," says Greg. "But I thought maybe I'd take some time and just drive around by myself. See some new places here in Maine."

There's a lot of doubt in his eyes, a lot of worry, but there's also a flash of something Trudy usually only sees there when he's doling out all those anecdotes about plants—excitement. Wonder. Hope.

Truth is, she couldn't be prouder of him if he were her own son. Finally telling his parents he didn't want to inherit the family business, carrying the secret of who he might one day love, and now this decision to strike out on his own, even though Trudy can tell the idea scares him enough to nearly shit his shorts . . . . The whole town used to think Greg was some kind of hero because he pulled that airheaded Angela Muse out of the river when he was fourteen. But Trudy has always known it's something else that makes him heroic. A different kind of courage, one far more admirable and much less common.

If she were a softer, more maternal kind of woman, she might offer up a pearl of wisdom about lessons he should seek on the road or nag him to always carry extra bottles of water and never eat chicken salad prepared in a gas station.

"You do know," she says, "that this will really leave me in a bind here."

Greg's face shifts again, breaking into the kind of sardonic grin they so easily swap back and forth. "I know," he says. "Sorry about that."

"I'm going to get arthritis if I keep slaving over this garden."

"I'll send you some aspirin and bag balm."

"Little shit."

Soon he will be god knows where, driving through this great big state, finding whatever there might be to find.

"Get back to work, Gregory," says Trudy. "This sun won't last forever."

Since the scene with Richard in that exam room at the hospital, the tension that has sizzled in the air between them for years has eased, giving way to a feeling of acceptance. He has known about her and Bev since the beginning, but only now, all this time later, does Trudy feel as if he has forgiven her.

They sit on the porch and watch the birds. They walk around Dalton in the apple-scented evenings, up and down streets they have known their whole lives. They agree boiled cauliflower is an abomination and decide to treat themselves to baked potatoes instead. With sour cream, and just a little cheddar cheese.

Maybe there's no heat, no romance. Maybe she doesn't know his dreams, and maybe they're more roommates than husband and wife. But there is still something between her and Richard. There will always be something.

The next morning at the library, between checking in Molly Lannigan's stack of horse dressage books and putting together a list of new titles to order for fall, Trudy finds time to call Bev down at the store.

When she comes on the line, Bev sounds winded. "You won't believe this. Some tourist just gave me his winning scratch ticket."

"Did he make you do fifty jumping jacks for it?"

"No, damn it, I just had to run all the way from the register to the deli."

Trudy nestles the phone closer to her ear and steps into her office, staring at the glass-encased four-leaf clover Greg gave her at the beginning of the summer. She buffed the scratch out of it from the last time Bev was here, and it looks almost new again.

"Meet me here tonight, Bevy."

"But it isn't Saturday."

"For Chrissake, I don't care. I just want to see you."

There's only the slightest pause before Bev answers. "Okay. I'll be there at seven."

The relief that floods through Trudy is like a wash of sunlight after months of rain. So much sudden warmth.

"So what was the scratch ticket worth?"

Bev laughs. "Hold onto your ass, Tru, because you're rolling with the proud winner of seven bucks."

Later that afternoon, Ashley Wilkins and Megan Cyr come skipping into the library. They hurry over to the children's section, where Ashley unloads a sheaf of ratty-edged papers from her backpack, then the girls bend their heads together over the table underneath the window closest to the picture books.

"What have you two got there?" Trudy asks.

"Plans for our new house in Arctanica."

"We're gonna have a pool *and* a basketball court *and* a place to practice dances."

Trudy thinks back to the last time the kids were in here with the Bergeron boy, about to set sail on the S.S. Potato Boat. "Where's your friend today?"

The girls exchange a glance filled with impatience, pride, resignation. Then they start giggling.

"Well, the thing is, once he got us to Arctanica," says Ashley, "we really didn't need him anymore, so . . . "

"So he mighta fallen overboard." There's a mad little gleam in Megan's eyes. "Or maybe it was scurvy. The official record was lost."

Two young girls leading their own mutiny. Trudy can't help but laugh along with them.

Ashley tosses her hair over her shoulder and reaches out to take Megan's hand. "He was just a silly boy," she says. "We can make our own world without him."

Give Me Shelter

After Bev hangs up with Trudy, she turns to see a woman standing at the deli counter. Her hair is down, and her eyes look focused on something far away. Behind her, twin boys squabble in front of the Fruitopia cooler.

"You again," says Bev, feeling as if she's been handed some kind of redemption.

The woman frowns. "I'm sorry. Do we know each other?"

"You came in around the Fourth of July. I made you four Italians. Your husband was buying a map, and your kids there decided maxi pads make for good ammo."

Now the woman laughs, her eyes brightening unexpectedly. "Yeah, that sounds like us, all right. Sorry about that."

"Don't be. I had a boy that age once." Not that Nate ever would have acted up like that in public (or at home), but this young mother doesn't need to know that. "So where's your husband today? Did you leave him up in the woods?"

She says no—Teddy would like that, but they have lives they have to get back to. He's outside gassing up the minivan for the long drive back to Connecticut. The kids stop arguing just long enough to exclaim to Bev they saw not two but *three* bears in the woods, all thirsty for blood. Bev and the woman share a glance, agreeing silently to let the boys think they faced down sudden death and came away the victors.

Bev makes the family four more sandwiches, pretending not to notice the way the woman's smile fades when she turns to tell her kids to calm down as they start fighting again, louder this time, about the differences between black bears and brown. "Please, you two," she says. "Let me have *one minute* of peace."

Then Bev thinks of all the times she pretended not to see how exhausted Bridget was after she had Sophie. The haunted look in her green eyes that came whenever Sophie started crying. The heavy cloud that seemed to hover around her.

Holding out the sandwiches, Bev holds her gaze longer than a stranger in a small-town convenience store should. "It'll get better," she tells this mother she doesn't know. "They'll get through this phase, and you will, too."

Relief and recognition ripples across her face. "Thank you," she says, and it's just two small words, but that's enough to say all the things they're not saying. All the hard work and hard love that goes into being a mother.

But Bev wants to offer more. So she hands over the seven-dollar winning ticket. "Cash it out up front and get yourself whatever you want."

She watches the woman wander her way toward the register. She picks up two Charleston Chews and a pack of cigarettes. Bev can't help but laugh—one day, a lifetime ago, she would have bought the exact same thing herself.

That night, when Bev steps into the library, Trudy is waiting for her in the dark lobby. She's in a pale-pink dress, hair loose around her shoulders.

"I've been an ass to you this summer, Bevy."

"You've had a lot on your plate."

"I'm still sorry."

"I'll still accept that apology."

For a long strand of moments, they press together in the dark, surrounded by books, other people's stories. Trudy knows every author, every title. Bev has watched her write down all the books' information on the 3x3 cards that litter her office like confetti after a parade. How many days of her life has Trudy spent typing only the pertinent details on those cards? Author, title, number of pages. For fiction, a synopsis of the plot; for nonfiction, a description of the subject matter, along with Dewey decimal number. She can tell just by looking at the titles in front of her what those numbers will be, where the books will find a home on the shelves—a numbered mystery Bev has never been able to solve.

When Trudy takes her by the hand and leads her into the stacks, Bev willingly follows. She knows Tru doesn't need the lights on to know where she is in this building—there is the potted fern that Alice O'Neill always overwaters, and there's the stain on the carpet where some teenager spilled the soda they weren't supposed to bring inside in the first place, and here are the shelves of classics no one ever reads.

Trudy brings Bev all the way to the end of the nonfiction stacks. The 900s: islands, Antarctica, extraterrestrial worlds. Stopping before the recessed window, which lets in a warm orange light from the streetlamps outside, she asks Bev to do her a favor. Push the window open. Let in the night air.

They sit on the floor with the books' spines pressed against their own.

"Tell me everything, Bevy."

So Bev does, a long stream of words that flow like the river after the winter ice comes free. She tells Trudy about the bear she stared down outside the store last month, and the laundry detergent that turned Bill's skin red as cherries, and the unique torture of a kids' song played on repeat ("We get it," she says, "the wind has colors"). She tells Trudy about how excited Sophie gets whenever she talks about Marshall, and how it makes her and Bill feel both relieved and a bit like they've been replaced. They want her to have as much love as possible, but they would selfishly prefer to be the favorite grandparents. And that leads Bev to talk about jealousy and loneliness, the nostalgia of growing old, of remembering everything that's been lost, and from there, without meaning to, she tells Trudy about the counselor she saw after Bridget died.

"You had your head shrunk?" asks Trudy, gazing at Bev with an expression she can't quite read in the semi-darkness.

"Only a little."

"By a man?"

"No, it was a woman."

"And it helped?"

"It did."

For what feels like a hundred years, Bev waits. Breathes, breathes, breathes.

Then Trudy laughs, a sound almost like wind chimes. "Chrissake," she says, "maybe you ought to give Richard her number."

A summer-scented breeze blows inside the library. Bev closes her eyes, savoring it. She feels lighter than she has in weeks. Brighter.

Here they are, safe inside this dark sanctuary, while out there, out in this town they call home, people drink and smoke and work and sleep; laugh and yell, kiss and love, fight and hate and love again. Not far away, Bill is home alone, probably asleep in front of the TV, and closer still is Richard, maybe sitting out on the front porch watching the birds Trudy says he's obsessed with.

Bev's hand finds hers, their fingers twining together in an act as natural as breathing.

"He's okay, Tru. Or at least he will be. I have a good feeling about that."

"And what about us?"

Bev can't believe that tiny word—*us*—can contain so much. All their love and all their stories. All their hopes and all their sorrows. There is so much she wishes she could change, for themselves and for each other. She wants Bridget back, and she wants Nate to have the kind of happiness he deserves, and she wants to hold Trudy's hand on the sidewalk and not feel any sort of shame about it.

"We'll just keep carrying on," she says.

"Good thing we're stubborn like that."

"Yup. Good thing."

They lie close together on the floor between shelves of books that stand above them like guarded sentries. They stare up at the window, the outer orange glow, and they breathe in the ripening-apple scent of late summer, ink on paper. Listen to the unceasing trill of crickets, the murmur of ten thousand pages.

PURGE

A
t night, sitting out on the deck or at either end of the sofa, Marshall tells Annette their plans. First, they'll visit Craig in Brunswick, meet his fiancée. Then Portland, to see Penny in rehearsals for this winter's Nutcracker season. Then New Hampshire, for Will and his chosen family. And after that, maybe Niagara Falls, or D.C., or all the way along Route 1 to the Keys. Once the house sale goes through and the mill isn't their responsibility anymore, anything is possible; they can do anything they want.

Annette doesn't know what she wants. Maybe nothing. Maybe everything.

The one thing she does know is that when he told her, on the drive north from the Bangor clinic, that he sold the mill and wanted to sell the house, get out of Dalton for good, she felt like she could breathe again. Almost.

This town is too small, too filled with people who know too much about their lives. The pain they've suffered, the damage they've caused. Razor blades and front-yard fires.

It's different for Marshall. He will actually miss this place. "What happens to this town," he asks, "once we're not the ones employing it?"

Annette doesn't reply. His is a question bigger than she can answer. Maybe capital-G god could tell them. But she still doesn't feel ready to ask Him any big questions just yet.

During the long days, while Marshall is at the mill tying up loose ends and finalizing details with the Quebec white-hats,

Annette works her way through each room of the house. She will not think about it; she will not feel it. She loads up all the boxes of all the things she doesn't want or need, only occasionally pausing to look through the contents—hand-painted plates and gilded snow globes, so many Beanie Babies. She feels a writhing sort of pity for the woman who sat in the dark and ordered these things.

Once all the boxes are in neat piles, she cleans like she hasn't cleaned in years. She vacuums and mops, dusts and polishes, scrapes gunk and bleaches stains. She works hard and steady, but when she's done, none of the rooms look even half as nice as they once did, back when she was teaching her children how to keep a home looking right.

She remembers the tour Bridget gave her of her and Nate's house a week after they closed on it. The floorboards were warped; the ceilings water-stained. There was a skim of dust on every floor and wall, as if the entire home were trapped inside a sepia photograph. Everything smelled of must and mildew.

"It's filthy," Annette said.

"It's just a little dirt," said Bridget.

They owe a jaw-shattering amount to the credit card companies. That's what she feels guiltiest about—not for leaving her hometown, or for setting fire to her daughter's paintings, but for letting down her husband. He's giving up everything for her, and she knows it.

A few times a week, she and Marshall sit down together and go over the budget. The sale of the mill and the house will take care of the debt, but there is still so much living that needs to be done after that. So much to plan for. So much to consider. It feels like a second chance, but also like a burden Annette isn't sure she's strong enough to carry.

Mid-August, out on a walk as dusk turns to dark and the stars blink into sight, Annette runs into Richard Haskell up on the hill near the water tower. He is walking alone, too. He smiles when he sees her, and she wishes she were twenty years younger so she could sprint away on quick, confident feet.

"Nice night," he says, nodding toward the town spread out below them. Yellow lights in square windows. "You look like you're feeling better."

What she feels is old and exhausted and resigned. She still craves the acidic burst of wine, and she still wants to turn on the TV and order things she doesn't need, and she still wakes in the middle of the night remembering the flicker of flames, the heat of a fire burning all the way down to her bones.

"It's a process," says Annette, falling back on the vocabulary Polly made them use during group sessions. "I'm getting there."

"Where is *there*, anyway?" Richard asks. Below, more lights flicker on in more houses. "And how do we know once we've reached it?"

Annette hears Polly's voice again. *Tell me more about that.* But it's late, and she's tired, and there are only so many questions and answers she can handle at one time. Let capital-G god take that one, too.

"It's late," she tells Richard, and she leaves him there, watching over Dalton.

And suddenly one day all the boxes have been schlepped by Marshall to the Salvation Army in Prescott, and the rooms in the house are clean enough for the realtor to come take her professional photos.

Except for one room. The last and the biggest. The worst and the brightest.

It's a Friday morning. The air smells like rain on pavement. A cool breeze blows through the house, making all the curtains inhale and exhale like lacy white lungs.

The door to Bridget's room swings open easily. Many of the paintings are gone. Annette forces herself to push beyond the guilt, the memory of fire. Yes, most of her daughter's paint ings are gone—but not all of them. Half a dozen still hang on the walls, and several are propped against the iron headboard. What is she supposed to do with them; why is it up to her to decide where they should go?

For the first time since Bridget moved out, Annette makes herself look through every piece. It's all so shockingly familiar: There are the blossoming potato fields on Old Prescott Road, and there's Portman Lake at sunset, and there's the ice going out of the river. Her daughter captured all of it. Annette can practically smell the sweet dirt, hear waves lapping at the shore, feel the frigid spray of river water.

Then she spots a splash of yellow, the corner of a small can- vas. She frees it from the stack and holds it out in front of her. A little stunned, a little breathless.

Nothing but heliopsis. All heights and all sizes, all crowded together. Just like the patch of the wild-growing flowers Annette used to walk Bridget to in the days before she started kindergar- ten. It was just the two of them. Bridget would pick the yellow flowers and giggle as she plucked petals, throwing them into the air. *Loves me*, she would say with each toss. Never *loves me not*. She didn't know that was supposed to be part of the game, and it was one of the only instances Annette thought it was better to let the girl believe what she wanted to believe. All those perfect afternoons, it was always only ever *loves me, loves me, loves me.*

After Bridget's suicide, on the worst of his Down Days, Richard considered closing the clinic, going to work at the Prescott hospital instead. There would be better money there, less responsibility. More anonymity. But in the end, he decided he wasn't ready to abandon all the people who needed him in Dalton. Or maybe it was less about abandonment and more about penance, sticking around in a job he didn't want in order to make amends for the life that was lost in part due to his own negligence. The things he didn't see in Bridget. The ways he didn't help her.

Now, five years and one heart attack later, he feels daunted by the same decision: Return to work at the clinic, or make some kind of change.

"I don't know what I should do," he says one night as he and Trudy sit on the porch.

"Maybe you're asking the wrong question," says Trudy, watching a house finch hopping in the bird bath, water droplets splashing in the evening sun. "Maybe you should be asking what you want to do."

"That's beside the point."

"No, Richard, that *is* the point. What do you want?"

And for a quick shining moment, he sees himself walking through the woods with a pair of binoculars and his notebook. Observing birds he can't see here on the lawn. Writing down all their names, memorizing all their songs.

But life is more than hobbies and personal desires. Life is

responsibility. Life is the yellowed skeleton leering in the corner of the office inside the clinic built by his father for an entire town.

"We need the income," Richard tells Trudy.

"We've been making it work all right this summer."

"Because Vera's been seeing a steady stream of patients."

"And why couldn't that become a permanent arrangement?"

Richard has thought the same thing countless times. The people of Dalton like Vera—more than that, they seem to have accepted her as his stand-in at the clinic. There might be a few old-school men who'd rather not have a woman asking them to turn their heads and cough, but there have been no requests for discharges, no irate phone calls from patients claiming to have been done any disservice.

And yet.

"She has her own life somewhere else," says Richard. "She wouldn't want to stick around here. And even if she did, I can't afford to pay her what she must make in Bangor."

"What if you fired Janine? She's barely ever there, anyway."

"I'd just feel so guilty . . . ."

"Oh, for Chrissake, Richard." Trudy's voice is steel, but her eyes are soft. "Don't you know what they say? You can't save anyone else on the airplane until you put on your own damn oxygen mask."

A little while later, she goes inside. He hears her opening a can of cat food, telling Mycroft to quit his yowling and practice a little patience. Then the phone rings, and he can tell by the way she answers that it's Bev on the other line. She pads on quiet feet deeper into the house, carrying the phone and her words away from him.

He watches the finches and sparrows dance around the flowers. There's still a surprising amount of color for this late in the season, bright splashes of pink and red and yellow.

In the forsythia bushes, there's a flutter of gray wings,

and then the telltale meow, followed by an impressive run of notes—high to soft, quick to slow, trills and crescendos and staccato bursts. You'd never hear that kind of song stuck inside an office, or even on a boat at sea. That song is reserved for solid earth—green and fertile, alive and breathing.

Richard has decisions to make. Fifty years old, so much wasted life behind and so many unknowns ahead.

For now, all he can do is settle into the porch chair. Watch the birds throw hymns to the sky.

Gathering

Mid-August, Trudy calls Vera at her parents' house and tells her she's invited to Bev Theroux's house for a barbecue. "I know it's last minute," she says, "but I'm guessing you've got some time in your schedule."

Vera glances across the living room, where her parents are sitting on the couch yelling at their latest movie—"It really was the one-armed man!" It's dim and airless in the house but bright outside, still plenty of green left on the trees, and the idea of being out in it, part of it, is like a sigh of relief.

"I'll be there," Vera tells Trudy. "Would it be all right if I invite Rose and the boys?"

"Already did. Bevy always makes way too much damn food at these things, so ask your folks, too."

But Vera's parents are content to stay home with their movies. "It's Sunday," they say. "This is what we do on Sundays."

The party at the house on Russell Street is in full swing when Vera arrives with a Tupperware of whoopie pies her mother happened to make the night before. Walking into the backyard, she's greeted by Bev, who somehow seems taller than when she came into the clinic a week ago for her annual physical (no complaints other than the usual hot flashes). Richard invites Vera to sit beside him on the deck as Trudy steps out of the house in a peach-colored dress, carrying an armful of paper plates. Marshall assures Vera that Annette is okay, just not up for a big gathering yet, then turns back to Bill, the two of them deep in conversation about what a hot summer it's been, how hard that can be on the crops. On the lawn, Rose and Nate are playing freeze tag with the kids—Sophie has gotten everyone but Brandon, who runs around the spruce trees. A boombox plays classic rock. The sun is bright but gentle, and the breeze smells of evergreens and charcoal.

A feeling of easy contentment stretches between everyone; Vera is already relaxed by the time Trudy hands her a can of beer. Possibly more relaxed than she's ever felt at a party. It's not like she never went to gatherings like this down in Bangor. There were barbecues, weddings, retirement celebrations . . . When she and Gavin lived together, they hosted wine-and-cheese nights with his married friends. But at most of those events, Vera often felt like she was putting on a show, trying to prove something intangible to all the people around her. Sometimes at those parties, after a few drinks, she would slip into her old accent with certain words like *borrow* or *tomorrow*. "You sound so Canadian," people would say, and Vera would try to correct them, remind them she was a County girl—to which they would shrug and laugh and ask if there was a difference.

Now, she sips her beer and listens to the chatter around her. The long 'o' sound in the same words she often got wrong when she was living away from here. The way Bill shouts out a spirited-yet-casual *Tabernak* when a hotdog slips off the grill and bounces across the deck. The gossip about neighbors with French last names, pronounced as un-Frenchly as possible. And against it all, the backdrop of trees, sky. How long since Vera has felt this at peace, this at home?

Too long. Maybe never.

Everyone eats around two picnic tables crammed together under the pines. Vera sits across from Nate and Rose, and she has to stop herself from laughing each time the two exchange a glance stolen right off the pages of those bodice-rippers Rose used to read—a confession drawn out after beers at Frenchie's the other night. How long has it been since Vera had a friend like Rose, where the conversation whips right along and the inside jokes, only a few months old, already feel as comfy as a worn pair of slippers?

Too long. Maybe never.

After everyone has finished their burgers and snappers and potato salad, and Sophie, Adam, and Brandon have run off toward the tire swing, a satisfied lull falls over the adults who remain at the tables. Marshall turns to Nate with a strange expression on his face.

"I have an announcement," he says.

And then he drops the news like a handful of grenades. The Frazier mill, no longer in the hands of the Fraziers. Their family home, on the market for some other family to find and make their own.

Bill, Trudy, and Richard ask all sorts of questions—what will happen to the millworkers; how long until the house on the hill is sold. Rose and Bev, sharp-eared and worry-eyed, pay close attention to the answers Marshall gives, but they don't contribute to the conversation. Neither does Nate, which Vera thinks is odd, until he gives her a nod that says he's known for a while. He shrugs as if to say *What can you do*, and Vera is reminded so much of her parents she almost laughs. With them, the gesture would look like their usual ambivalence, but with Nate, it feels more like resigned acceptance. For the first time since she's gotten to know him this summer, he appears almost content, a man who has learned the hard way when to fight the current and when to flow along with it.

Back at the house later, Vera sits in the window seat of her old room, gazing down at the yard as her parents plod over the lawn. Her mother's leg is nearly healed, bones melded back together, but the muscle has gone unused for months. Her father holds her upright, one arm wound through hers, the other braced against the small of her back. Occasionally their voices drift up into Vera's window, her mother swearing at her slow progress; her father assuring her they have nothing but time.

"No biggie," he says whenever she stumbles. "Just keep it going, Gretch."

They are stubborn, predictable, passive, far too dependent on carbohydrates. But they have been happily married forty years. They watch movies together on Sunday afternoons. They give each other dandelions and bacon cheeseburgers, and they say everything that needs saying in just a few words, or sometimes without words at all.

Vera is proud of the woman she has become without a partner. But watching her parents as they take a breather under the spruce trees, she feels that familiar ache in her chest, like a rock lodged under her sternum. When her father guides her mother into the hammock that hasn't been used in years, Vera is certain the thing will collapse to the ground. But the hammock holds. It bears the weight of her mother, and then her father, too, as he curls his body around hers. Their laughter floats up into Vera's window as they sway together beneath the trees, through sun and shade, light and shadow.

Gretchen and Jerry Curtis have never left Dalton, and up until recently, Vera thought that made them somehow deficient, or at the very least scared to see what else might exist in a world beyond their familiar town. But now, watching them laugh under the same trees they fell in love with back when they bought the house four decades ago, Vera sees something different in her parents' choice to never leave.

Her mother said it herself, earlier this summer. *Why go somewhere else when everything you need is right here?*

The next day, Vera and Rose are in the middle of their morning pre-opening routine when there's a knock at the front window of the clinic. Glancing up from the *Highlights* magazines,

Vera sees Richard standing outside, dressed in athletic pants and a shirt with a rip on the collar.

Rose lets him in, asking why he didn't use his key, and Richard says he left it at the house. "I wasn't planning on coming. But I was out on a walk and it just seemed like as good a time as any."

An infectious energy seems to roll off him along with the faint smell of perspiration and Selsun Blue. Vera noticed it yesterday at the barbecue, too—something lighter in his eyes, or maybe something brighter.

"Where's Janine?" he asks, looking around the room as if the mostly useless nurse will appear from behind the ficus tree.

"Late again. You want us to call her?"

"No, I'll call her later, tell her myself . . . That's part of what I need to talk to you two about."

"Are you shutting the place down, Dr. H?" asks Rose in a small voice.

"Honestly," Richard says, "if I had come in here yesterday morning, that's exactly what I would have told you. But with Marshall's news about the mill . . . Well, I couldn't live with myself if Dalton lost the mill and the clinic in one fell swoop. So hear me out."

He lays out his plan for the clinic, a plan he and Trudy mulled over well into the night. He wants to operate the clinic in an advisory capacity, use his time to focus on the administrative side of the clinic. He wants to firmly suggest Janine find a job better suited to her "laidback" personality so he can give Rose the raise she should have gotten a long time ago.

"And," says Richard, turning to Vera, "I want you to stay. You've done a great job this summer. Patients like you, even the old curmudgeons."

He and Rose stare at her, waiting for an answer. Vera stands in a patch of sun and squints out at the parking lot, surrounded by trees whose leaves are slowly fading into yellow. Above them, so much sky. Less than a half mile away, her parents are no doubt sitting out on the back porch sipping their coffee, talking about lawn-mowing and laundry. Tonight, they will convince Vera to eat some of the rib-eye her father bought on sale at Bergeron's. The three of them will talk about all the same things they've talked about all of Vera's life—but instead of feeling bored and confined, as she once did, Vera will feel comforted and grateful for the routine.

Maybe after her parents are asleep, she will go out alone, take a walk through the mostly-empty streets to revel in the quiet night, disrupted only by the groan of a log truck or the horn of a passing freight train. Maybe she'll pass the For Sale sign outside the Pelletiers' ranch on Howard Street and imagine her own furniture inside it, all the houseplants she could put in the picture windows. And even there, in the middle of town, she will be able to look up and see a thousand more stars than she could ever see in Bangor. And the sight will give her the sort of feeling she lost a long time ago in that distant city. The feeling that maybe this is it. Maybe this is home.

I t happens so fast.

One moment, Sophie is weaving a crown of grass under the oaks while Nate waters the begonias. Sun smiling down, birds singing everywhere. A feeling of peace in the air, rightness in the world.

Then Sophie's piercing shriek splits that world wide open.

Nate drops the hose and sprints across the yard toward her. She is twisted around, staring at a red welt on the back of her calf. Her eyes are starry with pain, lower lip clenched beneath her teeth. Falling onto his knees in front of her, Nate examines the wound, then he casts his eyes over the ground. Finally, he finds it—a tiny, curled-up comma of black and yellow, quivering in the grass.

"I didn't see him, Daddy," Sophie says in a shaky voice. "Is he going to be okay? Or is he gonna die now?"

Usually, Nate would be touched by her concern for the earth and its creatures. But right now, all he can think about is the poison coursing through her veins, already triggering whatever response happens inside a body allergic to that toxin.

The one time he saw it happen to Bridget, they were about ten years old, playing in the field outside at recess. Within seconds of the bee stinging her, she couldn't talk, and her breath would only come out in panicked gasps. Ms. McGreevy rushed her up to the school nurse, who worked some kind of magic. By the time they let Nate into the office to see her, Bridget was

316 · SHANNON BOWRING

sitting up on the cot, grinning, two popsicles in her hand. A blue one for her, and a green one for him.

"Does your throat feel funny, Soph?"

"Nothing feels funny. It just hurts where he got me."

"Can you breathe?"

"I'm okay." Her voice has lost its wobble, though she still stares at the bee with haunted guilt in her eyes.

But maybe he should give her an injection with one of those EpiPens, anyway. Maybe the poison is still working its way through her body, waiting to attack minutes or hours from now, just when he thinks it's safe again.

His heart has imploded; its pieces rattle against his rib cage. The sun is a hateful thing. He doesn't know what to do. He doesn't know what to do. He has no idea what to do.

Then Nate hears Bridget's voice as clear as if she were kneeling right beside him. *The clinic*, she says. *Take her to the clinic.*

Nate parks his truck across two spots. He slams off the ignition, bolts around to Sophie's side of the truck, gathering her in his arms even though she insists she can walk. He races to the entrance, shoving his way through the door—thank God no one else is in the waiting room—and up to the front desk, where Rose is talking on the phone to someone about insurance.

"Where's Vera?" he asks, breathless. "Sophie was stung by a bee—"

Before he can finish the sentence, Rose slams down the phone and opens the door of the office. "Bring her in here quick. Come on, Nate, move your ass. Sit her down in my chair right there."

"What are you doing?"

"Vera had to run an errand and Janine called out sick again, so you're stuck with me." Rose rifles through her purse, emerging with an EpiPen, then turns to face Sophie, who is spinning the swivel chair as fast as she can, giggling. "But actually, it looks like you don't need to worry."

"No, her mother was allergic. It could be some kind of delayed reaction. I really think Vera should take a look at her."

"If something bad was going to happen," says Rose, "it would've happened by now. Trust me. Brandon's allergic to strawberries. I been through this before."

Inside Nate, every nerve is painfully alive. Every shallow breath a torment. Rose's eyes lock onto his, and she gives him a subtle nod before turning back to smile at Sophie.

"Why don't you go out and take a look at the new Waldo books Vera bought?"

"Can I have a lollipop first?"

"For sure."

Sophie takes the candy from Rose and gives Nate a look that says *I told you so* before skipping away into the waiting room. Doesn't look back once.

The hurt intensifies, bundling in a tight wad of torture in the center of his chest. Is this how Dr. Haskell felt during his heart attack? It's like lightning keeps shocking him.

"Sit down, Nate."

"I can't—"

Rose coaxes him onto the chair. Her face is close to his, but it's blurry, as if he's looking at her through textured glass. Prickles of heat zap along his spine. He is suffocating, or maybe drowning, or maybe burning from the inside out . . .

She places her cool hands on either side of his neck. When she speaks, her voice is so low he has to strain to hear her. "Everything's okay," she says. "Nothing bad happened. Nothing bad is gonna happen. Just breathe."

He tries, but it's so damn hard.

"Again, Nate. Just keep breathing."

After what might be an hour, or a few minutes, the fist in his chest uncurls, and the pain begins to ease. With each inhale-exhale, Rose comes into sharper focus. Smooth skin, slightly tanned. Eyes the color of burnt honey. Tiny gold dragonfly on the chain of her necklace, in the hollow of her throat. Her hands are still pressed to his neck, and Nate can feel the thrum of his blood fluttering against her palms.

"I'm sorry, Ro," he says. "That hasn't happened to me since right after Bridget . . . well, not for a long time."

"Nothing to be sorry about."

How many times will this woman have to witness him fall apart?

"Hey."

He looks up to see Rose staring at him, her gaze soft and unwavering like she knows exactly what he's thinking. Like he was saying it all out loud just for her.

"Seriously, Nate," she says. "You have nothing to be sorry for."

He and Sophie don't speak on the ride home, though she lovingly pats his hand when he rests it on the gear shift. It's such an adult gesture, the kind of reassuring he should be doing for her.

He wants to apologize to her for the terror he constantly carries inside him, just beneath the surface of his skin. *I wasn't always like this*, he wants to say. But how could she ever believe him, when he has a hard time believing it himself?

As he drives past all the known places—forest, river, meadow—Nate's mind is a flicker of confused images and memories. There's Bridget, seventeen, leaning in to kiss him under the blinking red light of the radio tower. There's Rose, the intimate comfort of her palms against his neck. Bridget again, in her wedding gown on a parquet dance floor in her parents' yard, tossing a green-and-yellow bouquet. Rose in a white sundress swaying under manufactured rain. Bridget arched over a nearly-finished canvas, sunrise colors, hair a mess. Rose bent down to tell her boys they can each like different Power Rangers.

By the time he pulls into the driveway, Nate is bone-deep tired. But earlier today, before the world broke open, Sophie requested chicken fricassee for supper. The biscuits take so much effort and so much time to make—no use putting it off.

"Come on," he says as he goes to open the truck door. "Let's get you fed."

In the passenger seat, Sophie unclips her belt but stays where she is. Her hair is already falling out of the braid Rose wrapped it in while he was splashing his face with cold water in the clinic bathroom. "Wait," she says. "Is that how Mumma died? Did a bee sting her and make her sick?"

Someday she will need to hear the whole story. The entire ugly truth of it.

"No, Soph. Mumma had a kind of sickness that's hard to explain. I promise I'll tell you about it when you're older. When you're ready."

"I'm not ready now?"

"Not yet. I know you don't want to hear that, but you just have to trust me."

Sophie gives him that stare, that frown, and Nate is sure she's going to demand the truth. Every last, worst part of it. Then she nods. "Fine," she says. "But I want *extra* biscuits tonight."

It's the easiest deal he's ever made.

Later, after his mother picks up Sophie for a slumber party out at the house on Russell Street, Nate steps down off his porch to admire the patch of heliopsis Greg planted yesterday. So much brightness.

Then he heads into the house, which smells of clean laundry and trapped sunshine. For the first time in five years, Nate steps to the door of Bridget's studio on the second floor, pulling in a deep breath before pushing it open. Everything is just where she left it, easel in the middle of the room, purple-sky canvas half finished. Evening light fills the room, makes the walls and floor glow—this was her favorite time of day. The golden hour, everything prettier than usual.

Nate moves down the hall, to the bathroom, closed since the night Bridget died. Pausing longer this time, hand curled around the cool knob, he pushes this door open, too.

A fine layer of dust coats every porcelain surface, and the curtains have yellowed. Nate feels a pang of terror when he turns to look at the clawfoot tub, half-expecting to see the same scene that greeted him when he returned that June night five years ago. But it's just a tub, hollow and clean. Still a bit haunted, though. Still eerie. Maybe he will buy a different one, or install a tiled walk-in shower.

In his bedroom, Nate opens the closet and shuffles the hanging shirts, pushing everything aside until his fingers brush against the thick, satiny fabric. He pulls the jacket from the closet, tracing the familiar white stitching. *Dalton Police Department.* His name badge is still silver, only a little tarnished.

It's been so long. He has gained weight, lost weight, gained it again. He's beaten men bloody, buried the only woman he ever loved. He has become an entirely different person than the young rookie who used to wear this uniform.

Back turned away from the full-length mirror, he slips one arm, then the other, into the jacket. So far, feels all right. He zips the front, surprised and relieved at the ease with which it pulls shut. He straightens the collar once. Twice.

Then Nate turns to face the mirror, and when he sees his reflection wearing the jacket, his breath comes out in a stuttering kind of half-laugh, half-cry.

After all this time, it's still a perfect fit.

Rose has just closed the boys' bedroom door when the phone rings, and she hurries to yank the receiver off the wall, feeling a stab of fear in her throat. No one other than Tommy calls this late; he must be drunk again, or stoned, or both, and she has had enough, she's going to tell him she'll get a restraining order if she has to, he can't keep calling here, can't keep butting into this life she and the kids have built without him—

But it's Nate on the phone, apologizing before she can say anything. "I didn't realize the time," he says. "Hope I didn't wake Adam and Brandon."

Tugging the cord behind her, Rose steps out the front door and onto the cement slab. All around her, a cricket chorus. An almost-full moon.

"It's okay. Everything all right? How's Sophie?"

"She's fine. Just like you said she would be." Nate laughs, but he sounds embarrassed.

Rose closes her eyes, remembering how terrified he looked as he sat in her chair at the clinic, the warm race of his pulse against her palms. It's the same look that flashes on Brandon's face when his asthma takes over. The same look on Adam's face as he held out his brother's two broken teeth in the palm of his hand.

"Good," Rose tells Nate. "I'm real glad to hear that."

Silence falls between them, and she presses the phone close to her ear to hear his breath. There's something so comforting

322 · SHANNON BOWRING

about that sound, the even in-and-out. After a few moments, he clears his throat.

"So, listen, Ro. There's something I was hoping you could help me with."

She listens close, not wanting to miss a single word.

The next morning, Rose dresses in a pair of cutoff shorts and an old t-shirt. Chocolate-chip Eggos for breakfast, with real butter and real maple syrup—her tiny splurge to celebrate the raise Dr. Haskell promised her, and the fact that Vera is going to stay at the clinic. It's been a hectic week but a good one, calling patients and explaining the new arrangement.

After the boys are fed, Rose walks them over to Marian's trailer, handing the old hag the requested twenty bucks up front for the "spontaneous weekend work"—as if she has any plans other than clipping her toenails and eating frosting straight out of the can.

"When will you be back, Mumma?" asks Brandon, his breath all sugar-sweetness.

"This afternoon. Not long at all."

Adam gives her a long, hard hug. "Can we play Mouse Trap tonight, Mum?"

"For sure."

Rose pauses in front of Marian's door to turn back and look at them. Her boys. Dark hair like hers. Skin like toasted almonds from a summer spent in the sun. They've been getting along better since the teeth-pulling incident, but she worries it's just a matter of time before Adam loses his temper again and finds a new way to hurt Brandon. It's those eyes—his father's eyes. So much anger.

The drive out to Milton Landing doesn't take long. Rose cranks down the windows to let the breeze rip through her hair and sings along to a Don Henley song on the radio, one she forgot she liked.

At the farmhouse, Nate is waiting for her on the front porch. He's dressed the same as Rose, and they laugh, comparing outfits, before he invites her inside. The rooms are as light and alive as she remembers from when she and the boys were here a couple months ago, like all the people who ever lived here have never really left. A good kind of haunting.

"When do you have to pick up Sophie?" she asks as Nate leads her up the creaky stairs.

"Not till four. Hopefully that gives us enough time."

When they step into Sophie's room, Rose sees he has pushed the furniture into the center of the floor and covered it with tarps. Blue painters' tape edges the trim-work and windows; nearly every section of wall has already been primed. Several gallons of Sunflower Summer are cracked open, waiting.

"Started it after Ma picked up Sophie last night," says Nate, brushing his fingers against one wall to see if it's still wet.

Rose steps over to the final unprimed spot, a square of green between two windows that overlook the side yard, all those fields and hills rolling all the way to Mount Katahdin. "You want me to get this while you start on the painting?" she asks, already reaching for the primer-covered roller.

When Nate doesn't answer, she turns to see him staring at the green as if seeing a ghost, and she knows without asking it's something about Bridget. Or maybe he's seeing Bridget herself. And maybe that should make Rose feel jealous—in the old days, it would have—but now she just feels a grown-up, silent sort of understanding.

Without saying anything, she picks up the painters' tape and carefully blocks out the patch of original color. "There," she says, stepping back to make sure it's even. "Now we'll just paint around that."

Nate reaches out and takes her hand in his, sending those old shivers up and down her skin. He squeezes her fingers, and

Rose squeezes back. They stand there for what feels like a long time and no time at all, staring at the square of green, the same shade as the meadow outside. It just keeps rolling. It just goes on and on.

Later, while the yellow paint dries, they go for a walk across the yard, the field, through the woods, all the way down to the river. In the midafternoon light, birds sing and flutter from pine to spruce, spruce to fir.

They sit on the shore with their feet plunged in the cold water. Both of them smell like sweat and paint, and Rose has the urge to run into the current, let it wash her clean.

"I've been thinking," says Nate. "I might go talk to the Chief. Ask what it would take to get back on the force."

His voice is so much like the one she remembers from his rookie days that Rose feels as if she's fallen back through time. She might as well be twenty years old again, back in the cop shop brewing Nate a cup of coffee or fetching a bottle of Maalox for Chief Halstead. She doesn't miss that job. She was never meant to stay there long. Nate, though . . .

He used to come into the station lit up and smiling, talking about how he helped Helen McGreevy get back into her locked car, or how he'd been asked by Mr. Dozier to give a talk at the grade school about why he chose to be a policeman. "Why did you?" Rose asked that day, and Nate grinned as he told her it was the only thing he'd ever wanted to be. The only job he'd ever imagined for himself.

Now, on the riverbank, he turns to her with a look on his face like he's about to ask her how the sun formed itself in the sky. "Do you think that's a good idea?"

"I think," says Rose, "that it's probably the thing you were born to do. If you believe in that sorta thing."

"I think I'm still figuring out what I believe."

They fall quiet, watching the sunlight flash like diamonds

on the water. Hearing all the birds who don't ever seem to get tired of singing.

There are a lot of things Rose wants to talk about—the changes at the clinic, and Vera's invitation to go with her to look at the house for sale on Howard Street, and the Fraziers' decision to leave town. She wants to tell Nate how much she loved the barbecue at his parents' house last weekend, how at home she felt there, even though she's never actually had a home or a family like that before. She wants to confess she doesn't miss her mother, because her mother never chose her, even when Rose was younger than Sophie is now. She wants to ask if Nate and Sophie might want to go fishing before the summer ends— the boys want to learn, and she has no idea where to start. How to teach them.

But Rose feels like there will be time for all those words later. For now, she and Nate just sit together with their feet in the water, staring out toward the opposite shore, the line where the forest meets the river. Green running into blue.

She drives home with the radio off, nothing but the sound and smell of early fall to keep her company. She's tired, and her back aches from stretching in weird positions to paint along Sophie's baseboard. But for the first time in maybe forever, she feels wide awake. Nate drives his pickup right behind her, and whenever she glances in the rearview, he's looking back at her, smiling. It's not a dangerous road, but she feels safer knowing he's back there.

At the top of Depot Hill, Rose turns right, toward the trailer, while Nate puts on his left blinker, headed for his parents' house to pick up Sophie. They wave goodbye, Nate tossing in a few quick horn beeps, before going their separate ways. As she drives down Main Street, Rose wonders what Sophie will say and think when he reveals the surprise. All that new color.

When she turns into the dirt driveway between her trailer

326 - SHANNON BOWRING

and Marian's, Rose is hit with a wave of something like the hormonal dread she always gets a few days before her period. But, she thinks, unsettled, the timing isn't right for that.

Stepping out of the car, she turns first to Marian's place, where dingy towels flap on the clothesline. There's a feeling of deadness in the air, the absent noise of birds, crickets.

Then the door of Rose's trailer slaps open, and she looks over to see Adam sprinting toward her, Brandon right behind him. Adam has a starry shimmer in his eyes, but Brandon looks as worried as he does every time he wakes her in the middle of the night to tell her about his bad dreams.

"Mum, you won't believe it! You won't believe who's here!"

Just as Adam throws his skinny arms around her waist, and just as Brandon hides himself behind her legs, Rose sees him. First only a pair of steel-toed boots stepping down onto the cracked slab. The rest of him follows quick after that—faded black jeans. Gray shirt. Arms ropy with muscle. Slicked back dark hair. Cigarette dangling from the corner of a mouth she's kissed a thousand times. Eyes that squint at the sun as if daring it to come down out of the sky and fight him.

Tommy.

SOUTHBOUND

His last day in Dalton, Greg wakes early. Dresses in the dim light of his room. Steps into the dewy morning and stretches beneath the leaves before setting off on a jog down High Street, toward Main.

Feet on pavement, squares of light outside the Store 'N More, distant thrumming sound of a mill that won't belong to a familiar name much longer. As Greg runs around the town, he wonders what will happen here now without the Fraziers. How long will everything go on as always? The next time he returns, whenever that might be, will Dalton feel completely different?

Up and down all the streets he knows best. Delicious ache, delirious oblivion with each lungful of air. Outside the hardware store, a breather. His father's red truck is parked in the back, and the office lights are on. Greg knows exactly what he would find inside, the order forms and invoices, his father in the middle of it all. Making the math work, solving the riddle of numbers and bottom lines.

"Let me show you, son," he might say if Greg went into that office right now. "Let me teach you what I know."

They haven't shared more than polite conversation since the night Greg told his father he didn't want his life. Since the night Sarah lost the baby. Things have been too weird and too quiet at the house since then—even Aimee has kept her music low, has softened the way she stomps through every room.

Greg spares one more glance for the hardware store, then

he keeps running. Up, down, all around the town. Clouds this morning, but sometimes the sun comes peeking through.

At home, all his bags are packed. The car has clean oil and a full tank of gas; the Delorme sits on the passenger seat, a few pages earmarked for easy access. His mother has not-so-secretly hidden fifty bucks in his wallet.

"Are you sure you have everything you need?" she asks, her eyes darting around the kitchen. She'd probably hand him all her wooden spoons and potholders, just to be able to give him something.

"It's okay, Mom," says Greg, wrapping her in a hug, feeling guilty about how much taller than her he has become. "It's not like I'm going off into outer space. It's just the road. It's just a week, then I'll be back at school."

"But if you need anything . . . "

"I'll call."

His mother holds him a few long moments, and Greg lets himself sink into it, breathing in her familiar perfume of brown sugar and dish soap. She's been spending a lot of time with Sarah out on the Best property, coming home with a kind of weariness in her eyes he has never seen there before.

A few days after Sarah's miscarriage, Greg told his mother the same thing he'd told his father in the basement. He was grateful; he was sorry; he probably wouldn't return next summer to work in the store, and he definitely wouldn't spend the rest of his life running it. "How did your father take this?" his mother asked. It was her only question, and Greg didn't bother replying, because they both already knew the answer. She told him, sounding only a little bit angry, that his fall semester was already paid; they'd have to discuss different arrangements later on, after everything settled down.

Now, he gently breaks away from his mother's embrace and promises again that he'll call as soon as he gets to his first stop. "I'll miss you," he says, and he means it.

Just as he shoves the last of his bags into the backseat of the car, Aimee comes running out into the driveway in polar-bear slippers, a Nirvana shirt, and plaid boxer shorts. Hair wild from restless sleep. For the first time all summer, there's no eyeliner on her face, and she looks almost like a kid again.

"Thanks a lot, loser," she says, pointing to the kitchen windows, where their mother's shadowy form paces back and forth. "Now she's all weepy and shit."

"Maybe you two could go off to Prescott for a girls' day. Get perms, have your nails done. That'd cheer her up."

"Bite me."

Things have been mostly the same between them since he came out to her the night of the street dance. But there have been moments like this, too, where Greg feels like he could actually be friends with her, that they might build up the kind of sibling relationship he and Sarah have never managed.

"Did you stop by the store and talk to Dad?"

Greg looks away, up toward the tops of the oak trees. "We said goodbye last night. That's good enough for now."

He feels bad for leaving her to deal with their parents, and all the sadness left over from the loss of their sister's baby. But she's tough, and Greg has done all he can do in Dalton for one summer, maybe for one lifetime, and all he wants now is to get in the car and leave, head out toward places he has never seen.

"Take it easy on the schnapps," he says.

"Try to kiss someone cute before you turn twenty," she says. "You don't want to end up an old maid."

Trudy is waiting for him on her porch when Greg pulls into the driveway. She's dressed in capris and a shirt the color of spring lilacs—not the right clothes for weeding.

As soon as he gets out of the car, she's right next to him, hand on her hip. "You're late," she says. "You said you'd be here ten minutes ago."

"What's the rush? Do you have a date?"

"Maybe I do."

"I think it's nice that elderly folks can still have fun. Is Bev taking you to Bingo or bowling?"

It's the first time he's said out loud what they both know he knows, and for a second Greg is afraid he's messed everything up, stepped too far past an invisible line. But then Trudy laughs, her silver eyes flashing.

They walk through the garden, all the fading color. The air smells of sweet decay; the sunflowers are starting to droop, and Greg feels relieved he won't be here to see them collapse under their own weight onto the ground.

"So," says Trudy as they circle around to the long-gone peonies. "I didn't ask before, but I'm nosy and impatient, so I'm going to ask now—did you tell your parents all of it?"

"I figured telling them I didn't want to inherit the family business was enough for one go-around. No need to throw in, *Oh and hey, I'm bi*, on top of it." Greg watches a pair of monarchs flap their orange wings around the milkweed. "Not yet, anyway."

There are a lot of things Trudy could say. But she stays quiet. She watches the butterflies, too. She knows just as well as Greg that these monarchs will soon be migrating south. All the way from Maine to Mexico, where they will overwinter before laying eggs, creating a brand-new generation that will find its way back north.

Someday.

And then it's into the car, down Main Street, up the hill that leads out of town and onto Route 11. Patchwork of silver-gray clouds and pale-blue sky, glimpses of staggering yellow. Blossoms in the potato fields. Deciduous trees starting to pull their leaves into tight fists, turning brittle, losing green. Preparing for winter.

Past the mill—deep lung hit of spruce sap and pine resin—and through the scattering of derelict buildings that make up Milton Landing on this side of the Aroostook River.

No music today. No *Twilight Zone* narrators. Only the sound of the world spooling out behind and ahead.

At the scenic overlook for Katahdin, Greg pulls over. There's a dairy farm nearby, and the smell of manure drifts on the wind. Grabbing the Delorme, he steps out of the car and onto the soft shoulder. His neck already aches from the drive, but every nerve is buzzing, humming from the purr of tires on pavement.

Giant blue book in hand, Greg stares out toward the mountain, remembering the story of the young boy who was once lost there. How he survived by following streams and sleeping in abandoned hunting cabins. How he lived off the plants he found in the wild, pine nettles and edible mushrooms and berries warm from the sun. Or maybe Greg is making that part up, misremembering. A person could survive that way, though. If they had to. If they had nowhere else to go, or at least no clear idea how to get someplace else.

All around him, the North Maine Woods stretches out in infinite miles, broken up by fields and farmsteads, rivers and valleys. The only landscape he's ever known.

Greg opens the map to the page he's studied so carefully over the past few days. He already knows the route by heart, but he traces it again anyway, feeling the sun warm the back of his neck.

He will follow this road onto the highway, and from there take a dozen other major routes and backroads to get where he's going. A place where all sorts of new-to-him life thrives—bayberry, felwort, beach rose, jack pine. All of it flourishing for untold centuries there in those unknown places. All of it growing, waiting for him.

ACKNOWLEDGEMENTS

I am indebted to an exhaustive list of family, friends, teachers, booksellers, librarians, and fellow authors who have supported me both in the writing of this novel and throughout my life. Thank you to everyone who has loved me, fed me, put up with me, read my shitty first drafts, hosted me for book events, followed me on social media even if social media isn't your thing (it's not mine, either), encouraged me to keep writing through all the many rejections, and helped me celebrate every success, big or small.

An extra-special shoutout to my former roomies of Apartment 413: Britney, Sara, and the incomparable Rachel, my English major soulmate. I absolutely did *not* forget to acknowledge you lovely, badass ladies in the first book; I was just saving it for this one.

I am beyond grateful for Judith Weber and Nat Sobel, and for the team at Europa Editions, who paired me with my Dream Editor. Autumn Toennis, I'm looking at you—I will never be able to thank you enough for the devotion, hard work, and enthusiasm you have thrown behind me and this fictional town at the top of Maine. From one Murderino to another, I'm so glad we found each other. SSDGM.

1. In the wake of his wife's death, Nate Theroux has no choice but to navigate the world as a single father to Sophie. What does he have working in his favor, or against it, as he takes on this role? Are there ways he could be doing better for his young daughter?

2. How do Rose Douglas's experiences as a single parent differ from Nate's? What works for or against her as she tries to raise her two boys?

3. While the isolated, rural landscape of Aroostook County often places limits on the inhabitants of Dalton, Maine, several of the characters in this novel often turn to that same landscape, and to Nature in general, for solace. Can you think of some examples?

4. Many people from small towns leave for a while only to return and settle for good. Do you believe Greg Fortin will leave Dalton permanently? Or do you sense he will continue to be called back despite his conflicted feelings about the town and the people who live there? Do you think Vera Curtis has come home forever?

5. By the end of *Where the Forest Meets the River*, Trudy and Richard Haskell have begun to speak to each other more openly about Trudy's romantic relationship with Bev Theroux. Do you feel this understanding has brought Trudy and Richard closer? Do you think the same sort of honest communication could ever be possible between Bev and her husband, Bill?

6. Romance is subtle in Dalton, but it does exist. What are some examples of this? What do these understated intimacies reflect or reveal about the town itself?

7. Loyalty is a common trait among several of the characters in *Where the Forest Meets the River*. How does this theme appear throughout the novel? Do the characters suffer or benefit from their various loyalties to themselves, to each other, and to Dalton?